FORGED BY BLOOD

A FairyLoot Exclusive Edition of

FORGED BY BLOOD

EHIGBOR OKOSUN

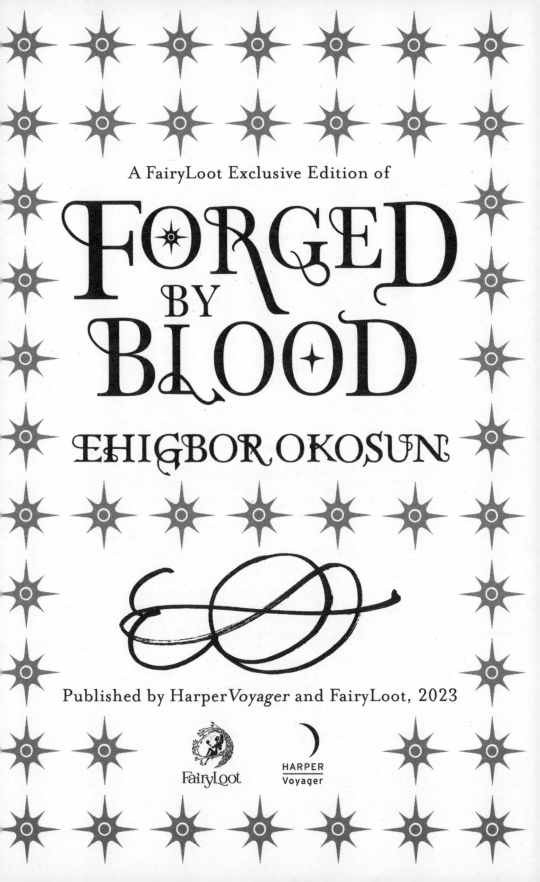

Published by HarperVoyager and FairyLoot, 2023

FairyLoot

HARPER
Voyager

Harper*Voyager*
An imprint of
HarperCollins*Publishers* Ltd
1 London Bridge Street
London SE1 9GF

www.harpercollins.co.uk

HarperCollins*Publishers*
Macken House
39/40 Mayor Street Upper
Dublin 1
D01 C9W8
Ireland

First published by HarperCollins*Publishers* 2023
1

A catalogue record for this book is available from the British Library

ISBN: 978-0-00-861589-5 (HB)
ISBN: 978-0-00-861590-1 (TPB)

Printed and bound in the UK using 100% renewable electricity
by CPI Group (UK) Ltd

To

The one who holds my life,

The one who taught me the meaning of a name,

The one who has my heart, always,

And my greatest gift

———————

CONTENTS

MAP   VIII

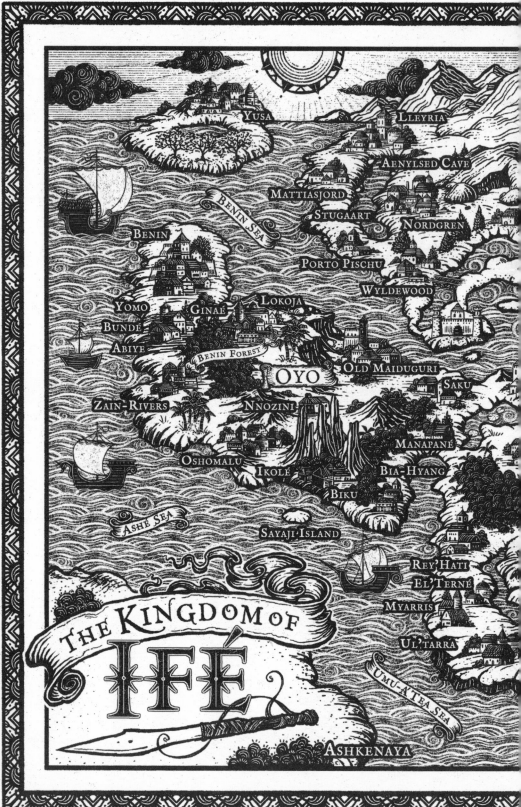

TRUST

"Please heal him," the woman says, begging Mummy with tear-filled eyes. "Please."

My mother grunts, but she takes the boy from the woman and sets him on our cot in the corner of the room.

This woman will get us killed, I know it.

But I waddle over, dragging the calabash behind me, its heavy wooden body leaning against my legs like a cow about to give birth. When I reach the edge of the cot, I open the neck and pour palm wine into the cracked bowl lying next to it. Mummy pulls the boy's eyelids up and peers at pale irises ringed with red cracks. Then she unbuttons his tunic and examines the network of bulging red veins spread across his pale skin.

"Dèmi?" she says.

"Okonkwo poisoning. It's been at least six hours. He won't last another," I say.

She nods. "Good. How long will the recovery be?"

"If he is healed now, then at most a day. But the healer will be exhausted for three."

She smiles, brushing a lock of my tightly coiled hair from my face, brown eyes shining with pride. Then she turns to the woman.

"Even if he's healed, your son might still pay a price in the future. Are you prepared?"

The woman's tearful face morphs so quickly into a mask of disgust that I fear I imagined her tears. She spits on the floor—*our* floor—before tossing a cloth bag on the ground. Several gold coins roll out, littering the mud like the kwasho bugs that crawl around in summertime. There is at least twenty lira, enough to feed us for two years, even with the extra trade taxes.

"Pure gold," she sneers. "More than you've ever seen in your miserable lives. That should be enough. Or do you need more?"

I bristle. "Gold will not stop the spirits—"

Mummy shoots me a glance and I swallow my words. She straightens her back. We only have the small kerosene lantern to light our hut, but her skin—brown like fresh kola nuts—glows golden in that light. Her braided hair is a crown adorning her heart-shaped face. For a moment, I see her again as she used to be, before she was cast out, a princess of Ifé.

"Healing is a balance. Life for life. Your boy ingested a lot of poison. I can only ask the spirits for mercy. What they do is up to them," she says, giving the woman a frosty look.

"You mean—you mean he might still die," the woman says, her creamy face growing paler.

"Mummy is the best healer in all Oyo," I say proudly. "She won't let him die."

The woman shrinks from my gaze, busying herself with loose threads on the waistline of her silk dress, arrogance driven away by fear. Turning back to Mummy, I hold out the cracked bowl without a word. I know what she would say, why she didn't bother responding: just because we don't understand others doesn't mean they deserve our ridicule or hatred.

Never mind that we're the only ones required to live by such a rule.

Mummy tilts the boy's head up and pours the palm wine into his mouth. He gurgles feebly but drinks it all. She lays him back down, and I fetch the palm oil and salt from the cupboard. There are only a few drops left in a jar of palm oil that was supposed to last six months. Too many healing rituals.

Harmattan season is upon us, and its dry, sandy winds drive children into the forests like a traveling musician draws crowds. The Aziza come during Harmattan, guiding hunters through the thick underbrush, flying from tree to tree. One child they choose will have a wish granted, so even with the prevalence of okonkwo bushes near Aziza tree houses, children flock to them all the same.

I would, too, if I didn't know better. Even the magic of the Aziza cannot call back the dead.

Mummy dips a finger in the oil and marks the boy's face. For softness, to ease his journey in the Spirit Realm. Then she dabs some salt on his tongue. To remind him of the taste of human life. I stretch a hand over his chest, but she shakes her head.

"You will wear out. I don't need half as much rest," I insist.

"It's too risky. My abilities are known, but yours—"

"What's happening over there?" the woman asks, voice rising to a shriek. "What are you saying?"

I realize now that Mummy and I have slipped into our native tongue, Yoruba, a relic of the past kingdom outlawed in public.

"She's preparing for the ritual," I say quickly in Ceorn, offering the woman an apologetic smile. "She wants to make sure everything goes well."

The woman narrows her eyes. "If anything happens to him, I'll make sure you rot in *meascan* prison, where you belong."

I draw in a breath, feeling as though I've been slapped.

You should be first to die, then, for letting your child fall ill in the first place.

I want to scream in her face. The woman spits again, and it takes everything I have to hold myself still. Meascan. Adalu. It's times like these, when these insults wash over me, that I drown in a well of anger. There are so many words for what we are, words sung over me like a lullaby of curses since my birth. The message is the same: We are not human. We are tainted. Tools to be used and discarded.

It never changes, this ugly dance. This woman no doubt came here for the winter festival—perhaps to meet a friend she hadn't seen in many moons, or even a lover. Wealthy Eingardians like her flock to Oyo like crows settling on a corpse. Celebrations here are cheaper; the people willing to bow when they see a light-skinned face; they are ready to worship, and Eingardians crave worship. When they run into trouble, they look to Mummy and me. They're willing to pay so dearly for illegal magical help, from curing boils to saving an infected leg. But after, when it's time for drinking and dancing, they remind us we will never sit at the same table—we are deadwood, cut down for the fire that warms their cold hearts and hateful faces, whittled into the benches they sit on. They beat us, insult us, and expect us to keep serving without complaint.

So Mummy and I make bitter leaf pastes for blemishes and pain, draw fever from hot skin, and exhaustion from weary bones. And when the soldiers come, purple-and-gold tunics flecked with traces of dried blood and iron swords like mirrors reflecting our terror, our patrons will be long gone, their needs met. It will be just Mummy and me then, trading coin for the privilege of survival, until the next rush.

Gathering the abandoned coins, I shove them at the woman. "Take it."

She backs away. "I've already paid. Don't go back on your word," she says, but her bottom lip quivers as she speaks, fearing we might do exactly that.

"Leave it, Dèmi. It's time," Mummy says.

I whirl around. "But she—"

"What have I taught you? Èrù jé ògá àjèjì. Ó si leso aláìmòkan èdá di ehànà."

Fear is a strange master. It makes monsters from the simplest of men. "But Mummy," I say, "she can't just—"

Mummy whispers, "You've heard it all before. *Let it go.*"

Shamed, I stand aside. I want to complain, to tell my mother that I, too, am afraid. The money is heavy in my hands, but I choke back a sob. This is the weight we must carry in order to live. The way the trades were going, we were due to run out of money at the end of the season. Our humanity means nothing if we are dead. As I spy the triumphant look on the woman's face, however, I wonder if my pride is too high a price to pay.

Mummy's attention is only for the sick boy before us, my tattered pride forgotten. She splays her fingers on the boy's chest and closes her eyes. "Blessed Olorun, Father of Spirits and Skies, please help your child find his way back home. Larada. Heal."

In a moment, her eyes turn from brown to amber, and white flame erupts from her fingers, consuming the boy. The woman cries out, but her voice sounds so far away. I watch as the fire eats the veins protruding from the boy's fair skin. Once the last sign of red is gone, the fire slims to smoke, dancing into the air until it disappears. With a loud gasp, the boy sits up, shaking like a leaf caught in the wind. His eyes are frenzied, as though he has woken from a bad dream.

Mummy strokes his back. "You're safe. Just lie back and rest."

He coughs weakly, leaning against her hand. "Did I die? I dreamt that I was elsewhere. A place where people's faces kept changing."

"You nearly did," I say, letting anger seep into my voice. "I don't know what you went into the forest for, but was it worth your life?"

The boy's gaze locks onto me, his eyes the blue of early dawn, sharp with flecks of gold sky woven through, and for a moment I am caught, watching the day bloom before me. He turns his head and I let go of the breath I didn't know I'd been holding. Here in Ikolé, many of us are the same, with skin like coconuts and honey, and eyes like burnt sugar. But because of the trades Mummy and I make in the market and the winter festival celebrations, I have seen a variety of colored eyes; green in the smiling merchants who come from the south, dark gray and deep blues in the cold-faced northern tourists. Mama Aladé, my mother's best friend, even has eyes that resemble the swirling purple-pink of twilight, but all that is nothing like the richness I find in this boy's face.

He shoves his hand in the pocket of his trousers and pulls it out again, offering me his closed fist. I take a step back, instantly on my guard before his fingers open to reveal a small blue flower with crumpled leaves and a patch of yellow in the center. I gasp, reaching for it before I can stop myself. Violets like these grow deep in the forest, in groves that only creatures like the Aziza and the tree spirits know of. They are rare treasures native to our Oyo region, not found in the frosty Eingardian northern mountains or the lush Berréan southern plains. Eingardian ladies covet them so much that the sale of this flower alone would feed us for five years. How did this boy get his hands on something so precious?

And then I remember he did so by risking his life.

I brush the soft petals with a finger, careful not to push too hard. The woman smacks my hand and moves in front of me, blocking him from view.

"Don't touch him, unless you want to die," she sneers.

Mummy pulls me to her side, taking my smarting hand in hers. "You didn't mind us touching him a moment ago, but now that the treatment is done, it is back to the old ways, isn't it?"

The woman stiffens, bright spots of color once again appearing on her cheeks. "I paid you. The work is done, so I'll leave with him now."

Mummy shakes her head. "You can't."

"Of course I—" the woman splutters.

"His body will be weak for a little while. Leave him here for a few hours and let him rest. When he has some strength you can take him then."

The woman's eyes widen with fear. "There's no need for that. He comes with me now. I have heard stories of your kind. I know what you do to children when their mothers' backs are turned. I—"

Whipping out the small knife hanging at her waist, Mummy slashes her palm, then offers her hand to the woman. "I make you a solemn promise that your son will not be harmed. May Olorun punish me for going back on my word." Then she clenches her fist and holds it over her heart. Blood drips onto the blue-and-white bodice of her dress, snaking onto the swirling patterns spread throughout.

I have never heard anyone make a blood oath, but the power in those words is enough to make me afraid. The woman's face is ashen, and she trembles before nodding her agreement. If I didn't know better, I would think her cognizant of the old ways, in awe of the oath that will become a death sentence for my mother if it is violated. She looks back at the boy. His eyes are closed, his chest rising and falling with an even cadence. Finally, she sniffs and says, "You will lose more than your life if anything happens to him. I can swear to that. I'll be back by eventide." She gathers up her skirts and sweeps out of our hut.

Mummy collapses onto a nearby chair, shoulders slumped, and for a moment I wonder if the woman exhausted her more than the healing. I rush to her, clasping her bleeding palm in mine. Calling upon the threads of magic humming through me, I pour some of that fire back onto Mummy's hand. The flesh throbs against my fingers as it knits itself back together, and when it is done, I press my cheek against her palm.

She smiles, but there are lines etched in the corners of her eyes and beads of sweat dripping onto her neck. Healing the boy has taken so much out of her, and the day has barely begun. Grabbing one of the carved bowls sitting on the table in the corner, I go to the pot hanging over the grate. When I pull off the lid, the smell of roasted pumpkin seeds and blanched greens rises into my nostrils and stirs my stomach, but I bite my lip and scrape diligently until I have enough egusi soup to fill the bowl. Soon the charred bottom of the pot is all that remains, a black hole jeering at the pangs straining my belly, but I set the soup in front of Mummy.

She pushes it toward me. "You must be hungry by now. Eat. I still have some work to do."

I free a block of pounded cassava from the plantain leaf it is wrapped in and push it into the soup. "You know I don't like my eba soaked. But you do. I'm still full from the yam porridge this morning, and you didn't have any."

"Dèmi . . ."

I brush by her, fetch the pouch full of dried bitter leaves from the cupboard, and pour some into the mortar on the table. She keeps trying to catch my eye, but I focus on knocking the pestle into that mortar, beating until I hear the sloshing sound of Mummy's fingers in the soup.

"I'll bring you some bread from Papa Adawu," she says between bites of food.

"Try and get goat meat too. We're running out."

She nods, licking her fingers like a cat washing itself, trying to catch every nook and cranny. Then she takes a swig of water and stands abruptly. "What would I do without my little helper?" she says, stroking my cheek.

I smile, showing off the gap in my front teeth, twin to hers. "You would be very lonely."

She picks up the basket in the corner and balances it on top of the wrapped caftan adorning her coily hair. Pieces of fabric hang out, like fruit dangling on a tree. Bold colors, in different shapes and sizes, all in preparation for the coming winter ceremonies. I pour the coins from the bag into the ogbene tied round her waist, squashing the folds of the cloth so the coins don't fall out. Then I draw back the thatched door to let her through. She smiles at me, sunlight glistening on her skin, both hands bracing the basket on her head. Her long fingers are worn with calluses and marks, but the basket sits on her head like a crown, and her chin, held high, separates her from the other women milling about, carrying their wares to the market.

"Look after the boy, my dear. I'll be back soon." She blows me a kiss, and then she is off, disappearing into the distance, like a shadow slipping into the night.

I watch until I no longer see that slender back, then secure the latch behind the door and carry the green paste from the mortar to the cot. The boy lies there, fair eyelashes kissing the skin underneath his eyes. I tug softly on his chin, trying to pull open his mouth. His eyes fly open, and I nearly drop the mortar in fright.

"I thought you were asleep."

He pushes with his elbows until he is sitting up. His mouth is drawn and his cheeks red when he speaks. "Sorry. I had to do that or else Edith would never leave."

"Edith?" I raise an eyebrow. In Oyo, it's disrespectful to call your parents by their given names. "You call your mother—"

"She's *not* my mother," he says insistently. "She's raised me since I was little, but she's not my mother."

I shove the mortar under his nose. "I'm only giving you extra medicine. See? So please just take it and go to sleep. We don't want trouble from your Edith."

He doesn't, though. Instead he holds out the violet. "My real mother is sick, but she likes these flowers. They only grow in this area though."

"So?"

"So I went to the forest to get them," he says sheepishly. "I thought . . . I thought she'd feel better if she saw these."

He is staring at me with those sea-colored eyes, but I look away, focusing instead on the small crumpled flower in his hand. "May I?"

He nods and I scoop it gently into my palm, ignoring the tingle that races up my fingers as they brush against his skin. I focus instead on the soft, silky feeling of the petals, and immediately the wrinkled petals smoothen, the violet spreading out in my palm like a flower in bloom. I shove the violet back into his hands, but it is too late.

He grabs my wrist, eyes wide and excited. "How did you do that?"

"Do what?" I snap, wrenching my wrist out of his hold.

To my surprise, he puts the flower down and claps his hands together in a pleading gesture. "I saw it. You have magic, too, don't you? I won't tell anyone, I swear, so will you show it to me? Please?"

I cross my arms. "I don't know what you're talking about. Even if I did, why would I do that? So you could set the kingdom guards on me like your Edith threatened to do to my mother?"

He sinks back against the wall, wilting. "I'm sorry. I don't mean to pry. I . . . I'm not like Edith. She's afraid of magic, but I'm not." He wrings his hands. "We don't have magic in Eingard anymore. All the magic users in our part of the kingdom were rounded up and killed a long time ago. We grow up hearing tales of how evil magic is. But I had an uncle who was different. My mother's brother. He used to show me all kinds of things and talk to me about magic."

"What happened to him?"

His skin goes pale—which is saying something—and he seems a small child hiding from the memory of a nightmare. I perch on the edge of the cot, my hand resting near his knee. He sniffles. "The king's guard took him away."

I shift closer now, pressing my back into the cool mud wall, feeling him trembling next to me. I remember the first time I saw someone taken away from our village. Those gold-and-purple uniforms, that serpentine insignia, the way Mummy seized up like a statue and hid me in her skirts. I can still hear that lone Oluso's screams as they tied him to their metal poles and carried him off . . .

I stare at the boy, and he stares back, sorrow heavy in his eyes. I sigh. "You *promise* not to tell anyone?"

He smiles. "I don't have anyone to tell."

I don't know what that means, yet Mummy's warnings fly into my head, remembrances that I wear like the cowry shell bangles that grace my wrists: Trusting another person is like swimming in a river. You can rest in the currents, but you must be prepared for the whorls that will come, and know there's a chance that, one day, you will crash against the rocks and drown in the raging waters.

This thought is powerful, and yet so are his eyes—so earnest—gazing at me.

I spread my arms wide. My magic against my skin. The musky, hot air in the room swirls about my fingertips, and within seconds there are glowing white spheres flying about the room. One glides to my fingertip and, touching it, I think of the violet, of flowers in full bloom littering the forest floor. The white spheres shift into flowering shapes, swimming about like lilies on the water.

He gasps, reaching for one, but the white flower floats away from him. "How?" he whispers.

"They're wind spirits. I asked them to join us for a little while."

I wave my hands in the air, picturing the sparkling brightness of the stars littering the night sky. All at once, the flowers shift into a shower of tiny lights, raining all around us. He jumps again, trying to catch one, but they slip through his fingers and zip around him. I watch with amusement. Before my magic first woke, I was like that, too, eager to touch the wind spirits that flitted about my mother. As though touching them would help me find the missing piece, the hidden path to my magic that lay in me all along. It is inevitable that this boy, too, feels the call, that his spirit desires to taste the magical world where it first drew breath, a world that has been sealed away from Aje like him. Seeing his beaming face awakes an ache in my chest, sorrow for the joys he will never experience, a silent mourning for the threads of his magic that were cut before he left the womb.

"How do you do all this?"

I shrug. "I don't know. I just think of them and ask them to come. Then I think of what shape I want them to arrive in."

"But where do they come from?" he asks excitedly. "How does the magic work?"

I raise an eyebrow. "They really didn't teach you anything up in the north, huh?"

He lowers his eyes. "As I said, we're told magic is evil, and unless we control people like you, you'll use it to murder us."

I fling myself to my feet and all at once the wind spirits fade. I am not sure if it's the heat or my anger that burns my skin when I speak again. "Is that what *you* think? That Oluso are murderers?"

The boy shakes his head vigorously. "No, it's just—"

I wave a hand and green fire bursts from my fingertips, coiling itself around his arms and legs like vines creeping along a wall. His eyes widen, but instead of the rage I expect, his expression is still that of sheer wonder. The curled lip I have grown accustomed to, the snarl people give when they find out what my mother is, is nowhere to be seen. The boy is grinning, showing off even, pearly teeth.

I feel a little quiver in my chest, but I ignore it. "I could kill you right now," I say menacingly.

"But you won't." I'm about to say something, but he pushes on. "If you wanted, you and your mother could have let me die, but you saved me. I know that, and I'm profoundly grateful. I wasn't trying to insult you, I swear. I just . . . I just wanted to let you know that I don't know anything about"—he waves a hand around the hut, indicating both my home and my magic—"anything. So can we start again? Please?"

The confidence in his voice irks me, but my anger is already fading. I wave my hand again and the vines dissolve. He holds out his palm, offering the common greeting among friends. "I'm Jonas, from the Maven Keep of Eingard. You?"

His name tickles my tongue as I try to push it out. Yo-nas. Definitely a Northerner. I hesitate a moment, then clap my palm to his, stroking the skin of his hand with my thumb. "I'm Dèmi. This is my village."

He smiles. "Dèmi, I like that name. Isn't it of the old language? What does it mean?"

I shrug, shifting my attention to the abandoned mortar sitting on the corner of the bed. Perhaps it's a good thing few people speak Yoruba now. The collapse of the old kingdom happened nine years ago, a year before I was born, but I hear the longing in my mother's voice every time she speaks. Mourning for the days when Ifé was strong and beautiful, for a time when the four regions lived together in relative harmony. But those days are long gone, and my name is a reminder of that. My name is a curse, and although I have pledged Jonas my friendship, this is one river I do not wish to wade in.

"I'm not sure," I say finally. "My mother taught me some Yoruba, but since there's a heavy penalty for speaking the old tongues . . ."

I drift off. Language is just one of the ways Alistair Sorenson, our new king, stripped us of our dignity. Being caught using any language other than Ceorn, the native language of Eingard, is deserving of public flogging and being sent to the mines.

Jonas flushes, the tips of his ears going pink. "I just thought it was cool. Your name, I mean. I've heard all the people in Oyo have interesting names. All the names have special meanings. My father chose my name. It was his father's. He doesn't know what it means, but he hopes I'll take after my grandfather."

"So it has meaning too."

He shrugs. "I guess."

"And do you?"

"Do I what?"

"Take after your grandfather?"

He smiles, but the light doesn't reach his eyes. "In some ways, but I would rather not. He wasn't a good person." He clears his throat. "So . . . you never answered my question from before. How does the magic work?"

I *had* answered his question with "I don't know." So I wasn't sure what he was getting at.

"What do you mean?"

"I mean why do some people have it but others don't? I asked that question once in school and got punished for it."

I lift an eyebrow. "They beat you in your Eingardian schools?"

He flushes again. "No. They inform our guardians and send us home for the day. Canings are . . . too public."

For Oyo-born like me, punishments mean slaps, kicks, and canings. If I were to talk back to Sister Aislinn, the Eingardian missionary who runs the village school, I would be flogged in front of my classmates. Or worse, if they decided my crime was big enough, I could be sent to the blood mines or a noble Eingardian house as an indentured worker. Mama Aladé's two eldest children were taken last year, for participating in a sit-down protest when the raids began. When we saw her son Tolu two moons ago, after a year in the mines, he had permanent scars and could not be out in the sun after being kept in the dark all the time. Mama Aladé's daughter, Wunmi, came back from one of the Eingardian keeps missing two of her fingers, most of her teeth, and sporting a swollen belly.

But I do not want to think of that now. To see Wunmi with her heavy eyes that drip tears all day long and the belly that pulses and dances under her fingers. I cannot think about what the mistress of her keep will do if Wunmi does not return the day after her child is born. Or of how the baby will squall, mouth like a tornado, shrieking and crying and shaking the earth to find what has been denied it, seeking shelter in an uncaring world. Instead, I think of the old stories, the tales I know like the folds in my skin. The beginning of everything.

I tell him.

"We all used to have it. Magic, I mean. Olorun blessed all of mankind with it, different kinds that were meant for us to use to help each other."

I spread my fingers, and the wind spirits return, weaving into shapes like threads building a tapestry. Soon there are fourteen people sitting shoulder to shoulder in a circle, arms raised to the fire in their midst—tiny ghostly figures.

"Our magic began as that. Gifts to each of the seven tribes, men and women. Some received the power to heal, others to call truth up to another's lips and so much more. Some could even change shape and form. Our ancestors called themselves the first Oluso. Spirit-born. They created the land of Ifé and spread out into various regions. Oyo to the west, Eingard to the north, Berréa to the south, and Goma to the east. There was peace for a time . . . and then things changed."

The ghostly figures morph into mist, and in their place are lumpy, misshapen heaps, with arms and legs sticking out like spines on a rose, and red—darker than any rose—streaming onto the cloth covering the cot. Jonas edges back a little.

"Some of the Oluso began to fight, to wage war on one another in a quest for power. But doing this broke the sacred covenant, and because of that they paid a price. After that, all the children born to them were hollow. Aje."

Jonas nods slowly. "Someone called me that last year. But I didn't know what it meant."

I look away from the piercing blue of his eyes, training my gaze instead on the image on the bed. It morphs again, forming small figures running about in a field. Children. They are laughing and singing, calling to one another, dancing. But one is hanging off to the side, away from the others, alone. It reminds me of the monthly village meetings on market day, and the way some of the adults stare at my mother when she speaks during them. Of those evenings when I come back after spending the day with the village children with bits of pawpaw stuck to my skin and purpling bruises the size of tomatoes. On those evenings, Mummy tells me of our history, of what it is to be Oluso, while scrubbing the sticky resin away, but my head is filled with images of the other children, their mouths wide like the mami wata that hides in rivers, their grasping hands dragging me into the sea of their hate.

"It means you are normal. Free to live your life without fear of being trapped and killed," I say through gritted teeth. "For breaking their vows, Oluso who killed or used their powers to harm the innocent paid a grievous price. They lost their powers very slowly, and with it, their minds. And the children born to them were born without magic. Once people saw what was happening, they changed their ways, for fear of becoming Aje too. That is what it is. To Oluso, Aje are broken people. People with no link to the Spirit Realm. You're born to wander the earth until your spirits return without tasting the joys of your natural powers. But to the rest of the kingdom, you are normal, human. There are more people like you, and less like me, so those of us with powers must be hunted down."

"Isn't it more than that?" Jonas asks, an edge in his voice. "Aren't there magic users who still use their powers against the weak? There was the attack on the regional governor last year, and the massacre ten years ago that started the war—"

"No!"

I shout the word before I can stop myself. My hands are shaking, and I quiver as though a cold draft has entered the room, but he does not notice. His face is a thunderous mask, his eyes hard and mouth set in a grim line. I clutch at the necklace around my neck, feeling the burn of cold iron until I brush against the ring hanging from it. All at once, the tension leaves me, like steam escaping a kettle. I savor the silky feeling of the ring and chant words in my head over and over again like a curse: *I am not my father. I was not born evil.*

Finally calm, I meet Jonas's gaze, holding my head high.

"Oluso cannot kill. Not without a price," I say again, speaking softly now. "Ten years ago . . . I don't know. I wasn't born yet. But I'm telling the truth. Losing the powers you have is like dying. I've heard stories—tales of Oluso who broke the sacred vow. There is a man in our village, Baba Seyi. He is the local madman. He can't even eat without help. Fifteen years ago, he started a fire in a rival merchant's house that killed a child. He's suffered for it ever since."

Jonas sighs, his expression softening. "I . . . I didn't mean to get so angry. It's just"—he pauses, dragging a hand through his wavy, golden hair—"my mother. She got hurt ten years ago. I was one. A magic attack."

I fold, suddenly ashamed. "I didn't know. I'm sorry."

There is raw pain in his eyes, and I have the sudden urge to hug him, to press him into my side and pour warmth into his slumped frame, the way Mummy does with me after every market day. Instead, I drop my hands from my necklace and curl them into fists at my side.

He shakes his head. "Don't worry about it. It was a long time ago."

I swallow, trying to hold in the sharp pain creeping up my throat, but soon hot tears blur my vision. It is in moments like this that I wonder whether the townspeople are right, whether I deserve every blow their children give me. Oluso are meant to use their powers for good, to help all of humanity. This is the great responsibility we must bear, the very reason we are born the way we are. When I hear stories like these, or see Baba Seyi in the streets, I find it hard to lift my head. Mummy always reminds me that we are people, too, and no single Oluso is responsible for the choices of another. But right now, before this boy, I feel so small. His words are a knife flaying me open.

Suddenly, I feel a burst of warmth as Jonas's arms encircle me. The smell of earth and lavender tickles my nose as he presses his neck against mine. "It's okay," he says, "I don't think it's your fault. Like I said, it was a long time ago."

My heart is thundering wildly in my chest, threatening to burst, and all I want to do is tear myself away and hide. Then he pats my back, stroking softly, and I go limp, leaning against him like a child clinging to its mother. My throat is tight, but when I finally catch my breath again, I whisper, "I'm sorry."

"For what? Being born?"

I pull away, swiping my sleeve across my nose. "I'll help, I promise. I'll ask my mother to heal yours."

His eyes widen. "Would you?" He furrows his brow and starts again, "No. You don't have to do that. It wouldn't work anyway. I wouldn't have any money to pay you. And my father . . . my father would never agree to it."

"Why not? It's for your mother."

"He doesn't trust magic users." He stops, choosing his next words carefully. "As in, one of . . . one of your kind hurt my mother, so he wouldn't believe that someone else would try to help her."

I nod. "That's exactly why we *have* to do this. We can change his mind. Don't worry about the money, I'm sure my mother will be okay with it. Let me ask her. Please."

He stares, his expression unreadable. When he speaks, his voice trembles. "You would do this? For me? Show me kindness even though we've just met . . . and I am . . . I am one of them?"

I am not sure if he's referring to being Eingardian or Aje, but either way I don't care. I smile, showing off the gap in my front teeth. "Yes, I'll help you."

He laughs, a soft, tinkling sound that fills the room, disbelief in his eyes. "Why?"

I grab one of his hands in mine and squeeze tight. "Because you're my friend."

BETRAYAL

"So what does your father do?" I ask, dragging the ring on my necklace back and forth.

It is almost eventide. For the last two hours, Jonas and I have been huddled in the dark, sitting shoulder to shoulder on the narrow cot where Mummy and I usually sleep, sharing pieces of our lives. So far, it's nice to have a friend, or at least a friend who chose me. Mama Aladé's youngest, Biola, and I play together from time to time, but her mother is mine's best friend, so we have to try and get along. I'm almost sure she hates me.

Jonas scrunches his mouth, grunting before answering, "He's a soldier. He doesn't really talk to me, so I'm not sure of what exactly he does, but that's the closest word that describes what he is."

I nod. "And your mother? What did she do before . . . before her accident?"

He smiles, eyes twinkling. "She was a singer. My father met her when he was out in Nordgren." Seeing the puzzled look on my face, he adds, "It's the northernmost city in Eingard. The seat of power. It's also where they have the big schools, you know, for combat, art studies, medicine."

I didn't know, but nod like I do.

"Every year," he continues, "the schools hold some kind of festival, and the students from them meet each other. My mother asked my father to dance and he fell for her then." He scrunches his mouth again. "At least, that's what my mother told me. My father doesn't seem the romantic type."

"My mother is a weaver. She makes everyday cloth and some for special occasions. Festivals," I say quickly, trying to divert his attention from whatever seems to be troubling him. "I'll ask her to show you when she gets back. They're beautiful."

I wave my fingers, picturing the winter festival fabric Mummy wove only a few nights before, and the wind spirits appear before us, glowing in the dark of the room. They mesh into a silken, twilight-colored cloth with streaks of periwinkle and orange twisting through it. "It's called a Song of Twilight. My mother names all her pieces. She says that different people have different styles that appeal to them, and that they are drawn to the names they like best."

He reaches out to stroke the cloth, pausing to look at me. "It won't disappear once I touch it, will it?"

I shake my head. "No. You can touch it. It's trying to touch the wind spirits themselves that is difficult if you have no magic. When they're in material form, they are just as real as you and me."

He strokes the cloth gently, as though soothing a wild animal. Then he sits back and asks, "And what about your father? What does he do?"

I drop my hand from the ring on my necklace and immediately the cloth vanishes. "I don't know," I lie, getting up. "I've never met him and my mother doesn't talk about him. It's just her and me." This last part, at least, is true. I want it to stay true. I want nothing to do with my father.

I busy myself with arranging the few things on the table. Two wooden bowls and some recently cleaned spoons are all the food-ware Mummy and I own, so there isn't much to arrange, but it buys me a few moments to think of what to say next. I can feel Jonas's eyes burning into me, so I don't dare look up. I don't want to see pity in those eyes, especially not now. "I don't know anything more about him, and no, I don't like talking about it, so don't ask me any-more," I say, attempting to balance some of the spoons perfectly across one of the bowls.

"I won't. I know more than most what it's like to have things you don't want to share. Trust me."

He clears his throat. "Still, if you ever feel like talking about it, I'm here. Or at least, I'll listen whenever—"

A knock interrupts his next words. I jerk. Mummy never knocks. She never has to. Oluso mothers form spirit bonds with their children upon birth that allow them to sense each other's presence. But those spirit bonds fade as the child grows, as mine began to two years before, and although I am listening, ears piqued, I cannot hear the familiar tingle of Mummy's magic. Then a series of whistles sounds out, two low trumpets and a trill, the call of a diduo, the gray bush shrike with its sharp beak and pebbled eyes. I rush to the door and unfasten the latch.

On those nights when she pulled sticky bits of pawpaw from my hair, Mummy would tell me of the diduo whose images were woven into the former green, white, and gold flags of Ifé. Being small did not stop them from impaling their prey on trees before flying the carcasses back to their young. No matter how big the problem, Ifé, too, would conquer it. No matter how much the Ajes hunted us, the Oluso would survive. As remnants of the royal family, outliving even the now extinct bird, the diduo's cry seemed only too fitting to be our signal.

Flinging the door open, I push into the doorway, then step back. Edith stands there, a self-assured smile on her face. With her are several guards, dying sunlight gleaming off their metal swords, gold-and-purple uniforms darkened by the fading light. She sweeps into the hut, knocking me aside as she rushes to the bed.

"Young master," she says, taking Jonas's hands in hers. "Young master, are you all right?"

I count the guards blocking the doorway. There are five, maybe more.

I don't dare breathe. It's been two months since the last raid. I thought we were safe.

After the last raid, Mummy warned me.

"Dèmi, if we're ever separated—"

"Why would we be separated?"

Mummy chuckled as she twisted locks of my hair together. "Listen, will you? If there is a raid, you need to run. Don't fight. Even if they take me—"

I pulled away so quickly that her fingers snagged in my hair, yanking at my roots. Tears stung my eyes as the pain seared me. "I won't run," I declared. "I'd rather die with you. I'll never leave you behind."

Mummy watched me, stone-faced. "You have to run. Hide. Go to the forest. Anything but magic."

"But Mum—"

She grabbed my shoulder, her eyes firm and resolute. "Survive. That's all you need to do. No magic. I'll find you. No matter where you are. Just live."

Live.

The word rings through my head as a guard approaches, shaking me out of the memory.

Taking a deep breath, I press myself flat against the wall, trying to make myself as small as possible. The window is my best hope, but I am nowhere close to it. If I am fortunate, nothing will happen. Edith will leave with Jonas and I'll wait for Mummy. But just in case, I imbue my legs with magic. I will run so fast they won't be able to see me.

"I'm fine, Edith. The cure worked well. Why did you come back with the guards? The woman promised not to hurt me," Jonas says.

Edith shakes her head vigorously. "I could not take that chance, young master. Sir Markham would have my head if you got hurt. Not to mention Lord Ala—"

"It's all right," Jonas says, shooting me a reassuring glance. He smiles at Edith. "I'm completely unharmed, old dear. Let's go home right now."

Silently, I thank Olorun. Jonas will convince Edith to leave, and they will take the guards away. Everything will be fine. Festivals are times of remembrance and peace. The guards don't arrest people during them . . .

Before he can take a step, however, Edith catches his arm. "I'm sorry, young master, but we can't leave. We need to arrest the woman and her brat."

He whirls around, defiant. "You promised them safety. You can't go back on your word."

Edith rises to her feet, towering over him. "I can and I will." Pointing at me, she yells to the guards, "Seize her!"

Now.

I close my eyes, reaching for the threads of my magic, pulling until I'm pulsing, then I throw my head back and scream. The shriek of an Aje child is unpleasing to the ear, but an Oluso's screams are enough to cause pain for Ajes, at least for a few seconds. When I open my eyes, Edith is on the floor, hands pressed to her ears, a ribbon of red slithering through her fingers. The guards stagger on their feet, holding their heads. Only Jonas stands upright, watching me with frightened eyes.

"I'm sorry!" I shout. Then I bolt through the door of our hut, brushing past the guards. If I keep a good pace, I can go by the market and warn Mummy before they can catch up to us. I sprint, dodging small children dancing around in a ring, weaving past several mud huts that loom like great shadows now that the sun has passed from the sky. Stones cut at my bare feet as I charge down the market path, and soon I feel a wet stickiness and jolts of pain as I push toward the well-lit square in the center of our village, but I ignore it all.

I know when I am getting closer, because a multitude of kerosene lamps appear on either sides of the path, and the smell of bolè hits my nostrils. My stomach rumbles in response to the spicy, delicious aroma of roasted plantains cooked with fish, but I clench my teeth and keep going. There are more kerosene lamps hanging from invisible wires, dancing in the night sky like the fireflies that come out after the rainy season, when everything is hot and sticky. There are several stalls now, wooden shelters with names etched into their roofs and colorful cloth hanging from their beams. There are scraps of green, brown, and gold cloth twined on some stalls, but most of them sport blue, white, and purple—colors of the season.

It is almost winter festival, and here in Ikolé, that means a week of eating and dancing, singing songs, and watching plays. The okosun will come, with his gourds and horns, and the whole village will gather around as he sings the history of the land of Ifé. When he is finished, the village will fete him. He will eat bolè and agidi, drink palm wine for free, and sleep in the nicest house in the village, because the village people understand the weight he carries—the pain of traveling from village to village and holding the entire history of our people alone, of continuing until his body breaks down and he passes the knowledge along to an apprentice. Then the Egbabonelimwin will perform, their bodies arrayed in cowry shells, coral beads, and bright cloth. They will wear elaborate masks, each one speaking of an ancestor or the creatures from the Spirit Realm. They will twist and turn, bending themselves into impossible positions, whipping through the air in the masquerade dance, telling the story of our ancestors while enjoying the freedom of dance.

Even now, many shops are already preparing, sporting dark-red and brown carved masks that the masquerade dancers will wear. The sweet smell of fresh palm wine is sailing through the air. Papa Adawu's boys are sitting by his stall, playing the drums, and people are dancing about, moving with abandon, as though the festival is already upon us. But the only beats I hear come from the thundering of my heart and the slap of my feet against the dirt. As much as I want to stop, to slip to the ground and rest, to suck on peppermint sweets like the other children do and enjoy the sweetness of the night air, I cannot. It does not matter that I earned the right to help the okosun this year by getting the highest marks at school. That he will not hear the song I wrote or have me there to polish the strings of his akpata and ring the agogo to help the dancers keep rhythm. Life will go on, whether or not Mummy and I are there to enjoy its fruits. Doubtless, Bayo, the head boy in our class, will be happy to polish the okosun's harp himself and ring the dancers' bell. The thought riles me, but I push it away.

Right now, all that matters is surviving.

I run faster, pushing as hard as I can. There, next to Mama Enaho's sweet shop, is my mother's stall. It is the only stall without adornments, consisting solely of a small table with a low roof affixed to it, and a squat wooden bench behind it.

"Mummy," I cry. "They've come. We need to go."

She looks up from counting coins into her ogbene. When she catches sight of me, she stands abruptly, grabbing my shoulders and looking me over. "Dèmi, what happened?" she asks, face creased with worry. "How could you run out here like this? Look at your feet."

I shake my head, hot tears coming now. Fear eats at my mind, making me tremble. "Mummy," I blubber, "there's no time for that. The guards are here—at our house. They came for us."

I hear it then, people shouting and screaming, thunderous footsteps getting closer and closer. I whip around. Guards pour in from every direction, swarming into the village square like bees descending on the wildflowers in rainy season. Papa Adawu's sons have stopped drumming and all around us people are frozen with fear, clutching their children or standing still, as though any movement will cause swift retribution from the guards.

"For me," my mother whispers, stepping in front of me.

Her voice comes alive in my mind. "I don't care what happens, Dèmi. Even if they take me, you need to run. Run as far and as a fast as you can."

I clutch her dress, crying out loud, "You can't leave me. I won't go anywhere without you."

The guards stop their advance as they surround us, standing like the carved statues in the shrines around our village, hands on the hilts of their swords, eyes pinned to us. Then a voice calls out and they part ways like waves splitting upon a rock, clearing a path in the middle. The captain of the guard, taller than the rest and distinguished by the giant horned helmet, walks out with Jonas and Edith in tow, coming closer until he is standing halfway between the rest of the guards and us.

"Are these the lawbreakers you mentioned? A woman and a small child? I hope you are not wasting my time," the captain says.

I gasp. The voice that sang out of that helmet is rich and high, undoubtedly a woman's. The captain grabs one of the horns of her helmet and yanks it off her head, revealing short black hair and a soft face. Her eyes are dark, like two hard pieces of flint, her nose straight but slightly off at the end as though broken multiple times. An ugly scar stretches from the corner of one eye across her nose and down to the edge of her mouth, but she is still beautiful, almost terrifyingly so.

Holding her helmet under her arm, she addresses Mummy. "I'm sorry, but an accusation has been made. I have to ask you to come with us."

Mummy lifts her head and drops her hands to her side. Her brow furrows and something unreadable passes in her eyes, then she squares her shoulders and faces the other woman, face calm, as though nothing has happened. "Can I ask what I am accused of?"

"Sorcery."

The word sets off a torrent of whispers. The villagers come alive from their frightened stupor if only to watch the ongoing scene with hungry eyes and mutter to one another. Right now they are vultures, waiting for fresh meat, and the thought sends a chill up my spine. There are so many here who Mummy has helped, parents with sick children, elders with irreparable injuries, women who struggled to give birth. We've taken care of the villagers for so long. Surely, one of them will speak up for us . . . right?

Someone does—but not who I expect. Jonas rushes to the captain. "It's not true. I was feeling ill so they let me stay in their hut for some time so I could rest. That was all. Edith is mistaken."

The captain lifts a dark eyebrow, and Edith immediately stumbles forward. "I have no reason to lie, Your Excellency," she says, wringing her hands. "It is as I reported. The woman is a magic user."

The captain sighs, then draws her sword out in a swift motion. The sword screeches as it rubs against its iron scabbard, hissing like a snake preparing to strike. She puts her sword to Edith's throat. "Start at the beginning. How do you know that this woman is a magic user?"

This is different from what I was expecting. Usually when the king's guard come for raids they do not ask questions—they strike swiftly, going straight to the hut of the person they are hunting and dragging them out, killing anyone who gets in their way. Why is this captain not ordering me and my mother tied up?

Gulping, Edith stammers out, "I . . . I am sorry, Your Excellency. You see the . . . the young master was hurt, and I . . . I panicked. I asked the local people if they knew anyone who could heal, and they led me to this woman." She swallows again. "I was witness to the woman using magic. She . . . she healed the young master. And the child helped her. She brought out potions and such."

I take a step forward, anger burning in my chest, wanting to scream at Edith. We are not so weak like their so-called herbalists that we need potions to heal, but her foolish lie incriminates me nonetheless. Mummy stops me with a hand and a single incline of the head. I don't need to read her mind to understand what she is telling me. Even now, I can hear her calm voice in my head, reminding me of the best places to hide in the forest.

"And did you pay them?" the captain says, pressing her blade closer to Edith's throat.

"I did," Edith says quickly, not daring to move.

The captain draws her sword away, slipping it back into its sheath. "Then what's the problem?" She leans closer to Edith, a disapproving scowl on her face. The other woman shrinks. "I don't see why you couldn't have gone on your merry way. You made a deal with them, and then you broke it by sending for us. Tell me, what is the punishment for someone who breaks their word in our kingdom, hmm? Shall I tell your master about this?"

Suddenly, she grabs Edith's neck, pressing her gauntleted hands against the other woman's fair skin. Mummy takes a step forward, but Jonas gets between the women first and yanks at the captain's arm. "Edith made a mistake. Please. Let's forget this ever happened."

The captain considers for a moment, then releases Edith. She falls to the ground, gasping and sobbing. Jonas throws his arms around her, making soothing noises. The captain turns toward us and smiles, revealing sharp, white teeth with pointed ends like a dog. She bows with a flourish. When she straightens, her dark eyes gleam and her lips remain curved.

My mother tightens her grip on my hand. "What happens now?" she asks calmly.

I know better, though, than to trust that serenity—I hear the edge in my mother's voice, the slight tremble to the commanding words she spoke. I have never heard fear in my mother's voice before now. And then I feel it, something hot and wet slithering down my legs, followed by a dripping that rings too loudly in my ears. The acrid smell seeps into my nose and makes me want to disappear. I thought I had shamed myself earlier today by crying in front of Jonas, but peeing in front of the king's guard brings a fresh stab of mortification deep in my belly.

"I'm sorry," I say automatically, clutching at my mother's hand. I haven't peed on myself since the nightmares of two years before, when my powers awoke. Some townspeople snicker, harsh laughter catching the cool breeze blowing around us.

"Shh." My mother takes off the extra cloth tied over the skirt of her dress and pulls it under my arms, wrapping until my soiled iro skirt is out of sight. She fastens a knot under my armpit, then wipes the fresh tears from my face. "What have I told you? There's no need to cry over small things like this. You're a big girl now."

She turns back to the captain, one hand on her hip. "Unless you are charging us, I am taking my daughter home. You have frightened my child enough for one day."

The captain merely waves a hand. The guards part once more. "We've determined that it's just a misunderstanding. You are free to go."

My mother looks back at her stall, where the money from the day's earnings is still sitting, lying haphazardly across the table. Then she pulls me forward and walks hurriedly past the captain. As we pass, I lock eyes with Jonas for a moment, then I look away, focusing instead on the dark of the muddy ground. I can't think about the promise I made to him now or if I'll ever see him again. Having escaped being captured by the king's guard is miracle enough for the day. Believing I could have a friend—an Eingardian Aje at that— was wishful thinking after all.

As we reach the edge of the square where the first line of guards is standing, I feel something ruffle behind us, shifting the wind currents. My mother moves immediately, shoving me away from her and pirouetting just in time to catch the knife thrown at us between her hands. One guard breaks ranks, charging at us, but my mother sidesteps as he brings his drawn blade down and hits his back with the pommel of the knife. Another grabs for me, but Mummy is there, knocking him out with a swift kick to the face.

"Very good," the captain says, her eyes glittering with amusement. She holds two more knives, each with a jagged blade like a bolt of lightning and an intricately carved silver handle. "I wanted to see just how good you were, but I knew I wouldn't get anything out of you at first. Not while you were too busy playing the average villager."

She tears the shoulder and arm brace off her right arm, then rolls up her sleeve. Her pale, muscular arm is decorated with a long, twisting scar, spread out like branches springing from a tree. She pokes the reddened, raw-looking flesh and winces in pain. Then she pulls her sleeve down again. "Remember this? I haven't been able to use this arm properly since." She grins. "Yetundé, you're as lovely as ever. Have you forgotten what your best friend looks like? I never forgot you."

My mother goes rigid, and now I understand the strange look she wore only a few minutes before. "Mari," she says, a small smile blooming on her face. "Good to see you are well."

Mari's grin grows even wider and it resembles the jackal mask hanging from the stall to the right of my mother's. It is one of the many faces of the Eloko, the night children who eat animal and human flesh and trade knowledge for blood debts.

"I would've been in much better shape had you not tried to kill me," Mari says, fingering the tip of the blades she is holding.

I look at Mummy. There is no way that my mother—the very person who reminds me every day of my responsibility as an Oluso, and how I am never to use my powers to hurt people—would try to kill anyone.

Mummy sighs. "You're still telling that story. You know better than anyone, Mar—if I wanted to kill you, you'd be dead. But here you are."

Mari nods, all humor gone from her face. "Here I am," she says in a singsong voice. "No thanks to you." She screams at the guards, "Get the girl," then she runs full-speed at Mummy. Mummy spreads her fingers and a long, wooden staff materializes. She holds it up in time to parry the blades coming at her, then turns the staff on its end and smacks Mari in the chest.

Two guards spring toward me, but I dance nimbly out of their reach. Another runs at me with his sword, but Mummy is there, knocking him back with her staff. "Run!" she yells.

"I'm not leaving you!"

Covering my fist with one hand, I reach for my magic. There had been a gale storm in our village two years ago, one that came out of nowhere and destroyed everything in its path, wrecking huts and market stalls, felling trees, and flinging lanterns away. As it pushed through the village, the storm grew, feeding like a starved animal, expanding with each twist it made. And then, as quickly as it had come, it stopped, fading into nothing. The villagers, for once, knelt and praised Olorun for their protection, because no one had been harmed. But they did not know my mother was their saving grace that day. The one who held me down and poured her magic into me until the restless threads of my burgeoning power became taut and wound themselves around my heart. I nearly destroyed our village just by tapping into my magic for the first time.

I am *more* than capable enough of blowing all these guards away.

Pain explodes in my chest as my mother slams her staff into me. I fall, landing hard on the floor.

"Don't." The word echoes in my mind. "Remember what I taught you." I catch sight of her wild, frenzied eyes before another blade comes down and a red patch grows beneath her right breast.

"Don't ever turn your back on an opponent. Weren't you the one who taught me that?" Mari says, crooning into my mother's ear before yanking the knife out.

Mummy's eyes roll back into her head, and I scream. The sound reverberates through me, cutting through my insides, forcing its way into the world like a child being born. Then my head is on fire and I slump forward, staggered by the surprise blow. Someone gives me a kick in the ribs, and Mari is there, standing above me, a hyena studying its disabled prey before striking the killing blow.

She flicks yellow globs out of her ears. "Beeswax. Your mother and I grew up . . . close. I always knew how to make her scream. She screamed so deliciously." She drags me up by the front of the wrapper my mother gave me, and peers into my face.

"I almost didn't recognize her, you know, because of you. My Yetu was always glowing, the prettiest girl in the room." She brushes a finger across my cheek. "But now her face looks tired and she seems so much smaller. I suppose that's what happens when you have a child. Shame, I never knew you were coming. Maybe if I had . . ."

She sighs, then wipes the bloody knife on my wrapper, staining it. "Another time." Jerking her head toward a guard, she says, "Take her. I need at least one to show for my efforts." She tosses me to the ground.

The guard reaches for me, but Jonas is there, shielding me with arms spread out. "You can't do this. She's just lost her mother," he says.

Mummy. I crawl to the crumpled heap a few feet away. Her eyes are closed, but her body is still warm. The blood has soaked through, blurring the patterns on her beautiful dress. I want to cry, but the tears are buried in my throat. I see it then, the slight twitch in her hand, and the way her chest moves ever so slightly. Uttering a cry of relief, I press my fingers against her wound. Green fire explodes from my fingertips, pouring into her body, trying to drag the broken pieces of flesh together.

Nothing happens. Something clutches at me, and I can hear someone gasping, but I ignore it all. Blood is running between my fingers and it will not stop. I bite my lip and try again, pouring in as much magic as I can muster, but her body is losing its warmth.

"Please don't go," I whisper.

I drag her head into my lap and rock. "Nènè mè, Ìyá," I say, calling her in both my father's language and hers. What does it matter that our languages are forbidden? My mother is being stolen from me. At the very least, they can let me call her Mother, let her hear those words as send-off as she is carried into the Spirit Realm.

Suddenly, she opens her eyes and grabs my hand. With a gasp, she whispers, "Dèmi, Dèmi, you must leave. Go. Now."

Then white flame springs from her fingers and consumes me, wrapping around my body until I feel like I will burst. All around me voices shout and people scream, but they all seem so far away.

Mummy's voice echoes in my ears.

You have to live, Dèmi. For both of us. My time has come. Yours is not yet here. Get far away, and live. Don't be afraid. I will always be with you.

I try to scream, to beg her to stay with me, but my voice is crushed inside my chest. Black ribbons lace my vision, and the soft glow of the moon slowly disappears from sight. Tired now, I surrender as I am pulled further and further into a blank, empty sea.

TRAITOR

When I come to, I am alone, buried in the dark. I suck in a breath, and the scent of roasted pumpkin seeds kisses my nostrils. There is light to my right side, so I crawl toward it, careful to avoid the iron stakes driven in the middle of my would-be coffin. The year my magic awoke, Mummy burned her hands and nearly killed herself fashioning an iron skeleton for our cot. Its purpose was to keep my magic from spilling out and harming the townspeople as I slept. Instead, it gave me nightmares. Every night I lay there, hearing the iron sing, skin aflame as my magic tried to wrestle its way out, powerless as a sacrifice on an altar.

I scramble out from underneath the cot, shuddering. I make myself a promise then—never again. I will never live so powerlessly, shackle myself, for people who wouldn't even care if I die tonight.

Around me, everything is wrong. Our earthen pots are broken, shattered pieces littering the floor. The kerosene lamp is lying on the ground, casting a shadow that resembles a frown on the wall. There are pieces of fabric strewn about, and the corner table stands on its side, two of its legs bent at odd angles. Our cupboards are empty, their doors hanging askew like ripened pawpaw bending the stalk of its tree before dropping to the ground and blasting open.

The memories of the day come rushing at me and I fall into the puddle of palm oil and salt decorating the ground, the reddish orange of the oil spreading through the salt like blood staining wool. Mummy.

It's too much. I slam my head to my knees and wrap my arms around myself, rocking and rocking, sobbing until my throat feels dry and my head is heavy. Mummy is gone. I am alone.

Live, my daughter. Mummy's voice again, refusing me even a moment of grief. After all, grief is the indulgence of the living.

Swiping at my tears, I pull myself up on shaking legs. Mummy sent me here with the last of her magic. I have to keep going. I don't have much time. Who knows when the guards will think to double back to our hut?

My head aches and my chest is tight, as though a snake is curled around my ribs, crushing my heart and lungs. Bracing against the wall, I spread my fingers over the spot where Mari kicked me and pour forth my magic. The pain of bones moving back into the right places is enough to make me scream, but I bite my lip until I draw blood. It is times like these that I am glad of what I am. A normal child would have died from these injuries, but Oluso, even the ones who cannot heal, have stronger bodies than most.

Still, with all the magic I have used today, I will be weak for the next few days. So even though the cut on my lip stings, I need to let it heal naturally. I must save my magic and use it to escape the village. Once I am past the first reach of the forest, I will trek for three days until I reach Benin, the giant port city several miles away. There, I can hide and find the friends Mummy often told me about, the friends she was going to introduce me to one day. I choke back a sob. There were still so many things we were supposed to do together. Meeting one of Mummy's old friends is exactly what tore her away from me.

Focus.

Mummy's voice again. I smile through my tears.

Staggering, I move about the hut, avoiding jagged pieces of clay and splintered wood. They did this. The king's guard came, destroyed the only home I had ever known, and took my mother to an early grave. For all their preaching about Oluso using their powers for evil, they used theirs to destroy the lives of a mother and her child. I shudder, remembering the glee on Mari's face as she pressed her knife into Mummy's breast. She will pay.

"*Olorun*," I whisper, "*if you can hear me, then grant me this. Let me be the one to avenge my mother.*"

Then the tears begin again, and I give in, letting the sobs wrack my body. I know what Mummy would say, even now I hear her voice in my mind: *Revenge is a poison, Dèmi. Drink it and you can destroy your enemies, but you will die long before you see them take their last breaths.*

I can't do what I am pledging to do. Even now, I can't disappoint Mummy. But what then? She trained me for all kinds of things, but never this. In all our scenarios, we survived *together*. Now I am being asked to survive without her, and I don't know how.

Nonsense, Dèmi. Get up. Start moving.

Mummy's voice again. Chiding. Urging.

"I'm going!" I scream at the air. "Just watch, I'll make it, and I'll come back. I'll avenge you."

Throwing off my stained wrapper, I lay out one of Mummy's, the only clean one, on the floor. Quickly, I gather up some of the fabric and select a few clothes from the reed basket in the corner, placing them carefully in the middle of the wrapper. I take only a few things: some dresses, an iro skirt, the jerkin and trousers—a hard-won gift from Mummy. She always said a woman could do everything a man could while wearing a dress and carrying twins. Nevertheless,

I loved the smooth feeling of the tough fabric and hated the way Bayo stared at my legs in public, so I pleaded until she fashioned me these trousers. I also take my ceremonial aso ebi—complete with a colorful gele that Mummy wrapped on my head before every festival. Pulling the ends of the wrapper, I tie it to the giant wooden stick that served as our fire poker.

As I hunt for a food bowl, I step on something hard and nearly lose my footing. Lying against the red of our mud floor is a long strip of blue fabric, twisted and cinched to form a purse. I pick up my mother's ogbene and nearly start crying again as I weigh it in my hands. She sent with me this. She must have slipped it into the wrapper she gave me. Had she known what would happen as she tied the knots of the cloth around my waist?

A niggling thought slips into my mind: my mother's rebuke when I threw the money back at Jonas's nanny only this afternoon. Had she known even then? No. Mummy always to seemed to know when things were happening, but she would not have left me like this. Not given me cold metal coins as comfort when all I wanted was her warmth and her smiling face looking over me as I woke every morning.

Stuffing the coins into my makeshift sack, I pull the bundle onto my back and make my way to the back cupboard. There, in the corner of the hut, the jar of palm wine is still standing. I pour some into the food bowl lying close to it, then place the filled bowl gently back down. I stand, then bend my knees, bowing low until my forehead touches the ground. I do this three times, then gather my bundle up again and go to the door. When I get to another village, far away from here, I will give my mother proper burial rites. I will send her a message in the Spirit Realm so she knows not to worry for me. For now, though, I can honor her sacrifice only by surviving. I will live, for both of us.

A loud scratching sound comes from the door. Leaping over broken pottery, I slide under the cot just as the door opens. Well-made boots move into the room, the intruder tracing my steps as though they had been watching me. Then just by the cot, the intruder stops and reaches down for a ring resting on top of a curled silver pile. I feel my neck, but I already know the truth. The pale hand picks up my father's ring, the last remembrance I have of my mother, and pockets it.

Rage fills me, and I barely keep myself from leaping out and confronting the thief. Whoever they are, I will find them and make them wish they never touched that ring. I won't let them take the last piece of my parents from me. But I need to be wise. Inching back, I roll closer to the edge of the cot and peek out, gasping before I can stop myself.

Jonas stands in the ruins of my home, eyes wide, a wrinkle creasing his brow. He drops to the ground in one swift motion, a cat preparing to trap a mouse. We lock eyes and he smiles, joy illuminating his icy blue eyes. There is another sound from the door, and he slaps his finger to his lips. "Shh."

I nod, not daring to make a sound as he gets up, stretching in a show of nonchalance.

"Find anything, young master?" a man asks.

"Not yet, Chief Darby. Still looking. Please leave me for a few moments."

"Young master, we are under express orders—"

"You killed the woman and her child. Edith is upset. I just want to look for the brooch I bought her and get a little peace and quiet. Is that too much to ask?"

"No, sir. I understand. We'll be outside."

There are footsteps, then a rustling as the door shuts once more.

"You can come out now," Jonas whispers.

I scramble out from underneath the cot and he rushes to me. But I shove him, eyes narrowed. "How come you talk to the guards that way?"

He flushes, hand brushing the fair hair at the nape of his neck. "My father's a soldier. He's head of a keep, remember? They know him, so they don't mess with me."

"Then why didn't they listen to you at the market? Why couldn't they leave us alone? Why couldn't you make them stop?"

He envelops me in his arms, stroking my hair. "I'm sorry. I am so sorry. This should never have happened."

That's what he has to say? That my mother should never have been *murdered*? I want to hit him, to curse him for allowing Edith into my home, but I remember him standing between me and a guard, pleading that my mother had done nothing wrong, and I sink into his arms, sighing. Something warm crawls onto my neck, accompanied by a few sniffles. He's crying. We stay like that for a few moments, holding each other, mourning together. I am not sure if I am the comforter or the one being comforted, but having him here, not being alone, makes my heart lighter.

When he pulls away, he looks me over. "Are you hurt?"

"I fixed it."

He nods, letting go abruptly. "So what do we do now?"

"*We* don't do anything. I'm sorry, I know I made you a promise before, but I can't keep it. My mother is dead. I need to leave the village."

"I'll help you."

I shake my head vigorously. "You can't. I need to go alone."

He gestures with his chin toward the door. "How are you going to get past them?" He takes my hand. "Let me help. I can look out while you escape."

I hold out my hand. "Or you can give me my ring and pretend I was never here. Don't get involved."

He clutches the ring to his breast. "Why do I get the feeling that you'll disappear the moment I give you this?"

"I won't," I snap.

"You will. Let me help. The guards listen to me at least."

There is another rustle at the door, and a voice shouts, "Young master, your entourage has informed us that you need to leave in the next hour. Please come out by then."

"See? I've already bought us an hour." Jonas crows, "I can do more. Maybe help you get supplies."

I make my decision then. "Okay. You can help. So, what's the brilliant plan? How are you getting me out of here?"

He grins, hoisting my makeshift sack onto his shoulder. "Already ahead of you." Climbing onto the cot, he pushes softly at the wooden door of our window and pops his head out. He lowers the sack carefully to the ground, then beckons me closer and bends over. "Get on my back and push off. That way you'll be able to control your fall. I'll be right behind you."

I wriggle out of the small window, slipping softly to the ground. He launches out after me, legs first, holding on to the edge of the window and then easing himself to the ground. Outside, the clouds have gathered in the night sky, smothering the moon with their gray mist. We creep along the side of the hut, peering at the guards who are standing by the front door, then scurry toward the back corner of the low stone wall surrounding my home. Once we are over the wall, we crouch and catch our breaths.

"Where to now? I was carried here, so I don't really remember how to get to the forest," Jonas says.

"There is someone I need to visit first. This way."

"What? No, we need to—"

But I'm already moving, and I hear him following behind me.

We run, keeping off the main path, crossing into the grassy backyards of the huts on my side of the village. When we reach another low stone wall, we climb over it and I dart over to the raised wooden slab at the back of the hut before us. I knock four times, wait a beat, then knock three more times. The back door of the hut opens, and Mama Aladé peers out, her golden skin almost gray in the night air.

"Dèmi," she gasps, enveloping me in her arms. "We thought they killed you too. What happened?"

"I am fine, Auntie. Mummy protected me."

"Oh, what do we do now? We need to find a place to hide you, but the elders in this village have sold out, curse them. They all—" She stops, looking at Jonas as though a ghost has materialized in front of her.

I press her arm. "It's okay, Auntie. He's my friend. He helped me get away."

She narrows her eyes, then waves a hand at Jonas, beckoning. "Come." He steps forward and she places a hand to his forehead. Her eyes glow briefly, then she nods, satisfied. Oluso like Mama Aladé have Cloren blood. They project into the future, but since the future is unpredictable, their visions can change over time. They see what could be, not what is, but any knowledge is crucial at the moment.

Yet she speaks to Jonas first, surprising both of us: "You have a difficult road ahead of you, young one. It will be riddled with pain, but still you must keep faith, do you understand?"

Jonas stares at her, and something passes between them that I cannot see, but after a moment he nods.

"Do you have any words for me, Mama?" I ask.

She smiles and massages my hand, pulling each of the fingers gently. "No, sweet girl. I spoke words over you the day you were born, and that is enough. I cannot do any more than that."

I'm disappointed—I had hoped for some guidance. It's why I had come here in the first place. I'm about to say so when the door behind her swings open and Biola is there, her beautiful face twisted in a scowl. She glances from her mother to me and Jonas, and says, "There are people looking for you, Mama. Soldiers at the door with some elders."

Mama Aladé frowns. "They are here too soon."

Biola turns back to me, appraising me with those intense violet eyes, slim nose wrinkled as though in distaste. Somewhere inside me, I have always been envious of her. With her long, slim fingers and light skin that makes my too-dark skin and short, bony fingers seem uglier in comparison. Her face is pointed where mine is round, and although we have the same high cheekbones, she has a slim nose to carry it off, while mine is stubby and round at the end. From the time we were children, all the villagers seemed to love her and despise me. Lighter skin is always more fashionable and seen as more beautiful. Hair that cascades down your back rather than curls tightly on your head more lovely. Worse, since our mothers were best friends, we were always together, the wrinkled acorn and the oak tree, constantly being compared. Mummy said it wasn't always this way, that before Alistair Sorenson seized power, beauty came in different forms. But Mummy is gone.

I resist the urge to hide behind Jonas even now because I know I must look a mess. I also know there's nothing stopping her from selling us out to save herself and her mother. Biola opens her mouth, then sighs and closes it. She unwraps the bulging apron tied around her waist and hands it to me. "There is food enough for three days in there. Six eggs, fresh bread I made this morning, dried stock fish, and some chicken legs. Don't eat it all at once."

She turns back to her mother. "I told them you were weeding something out in the garden. They will be waiting too long by now. We need to go."

Mama Aladé squeezes my hand. "Will you still be here when I get back?" I look down at my feet, and she lets go. "Be well, Dèmi. Come back and see us once you have a chance. You are family. You are always welcome here."

She hurries inside. Biola grabs my hand and squeezes it too, a stern look on her face. "Good luck, little coco yam," she says, using her nickname for me. "You are stronger than all of us. I know it." She nods at Jonas, then follows after her mother, locking the door behind her.

I stand still for a second, looking at my trembling fingers. Was Biola actually just nice to me?

Jonas taps my shoulder. "What now?"

I tie my food stash more securely and stuff it into my makeshift sack. I had come for direction, a blessing, comfort—anything Mama Aladé could spare. Instead I got supplies and some reassurance. Coming here wasn't a waste after all.

I look at Jonas. "Now we go to the forest. Pay attention because you'll have to find your way back."

He nods and we're off. We run another mile until we reach the outskirts of the village, the dirt road with thick bushes growing on either side of it. Just beyond that is the forest, trees looming before us like mountains, large and forbidding in the night. In that tangled darkness is my safe haven, so no matter how much my legs are shaking, I will keep moving forward.

We are only a few feet down the road when we hear the footsteps, the thundering clatter like a herd of stampeding animals. Jonas jerks his head toward a bush and I scramble inside the thicket, its thin branches scratching me. He stands a little bit away, peering out as lanterns spring up on the horizon, their flame eating away at the comforting darkness. A soldier yells, "I see him!"

"Captain Mari," Jonas calls, waving.

I swallow. Why does she of all people have to be here? Why couldn't it be a few guards?

The soldiers stop just a few feet away, spread out on all sides like a peacock's feathers, and the captain jogs over to Jonas. She takes off her helmet and draws her sword. My heart seizes with fear, reliving the nightmare of a few hours before. To my surprise, though, she kneels, head bowed, offering the blade to Jonas.

He stiffens, but he puts his hand on her bent shoulder. "You may rise."

"Thank you, my liege."

I freeze.

Liege?

Mari sheathes her sword. "No sign of the girl. I suspect it is as you suggested and she is dead. It seems a waste to kill her child rather than allow her to be taken into custody, but then again, Yetundé was not known for making the wisest of choices."

He clears his throat, and she chuckles. "Yes, excuse me, my liege. Just the facts then. We have scouts looking out just in case the girl was spirited away somewhere, but right now, that is doubtful. I'll leave soldiers here for the next few days to monitor things. Don't worry, if she appears, we'll smoke her out."

"And what then?"

Mari grins, tongue darting out to the scar at the corner of her mouth. "Then she's mine as promised."

"I never promised such a thing!" Jonas shouts.

Mari purses her lips. "Now, now, my liege. Let's not get testy. After all, this promise goes beyond even you."

I rock back on my heels as though I've been struck. *Promise?* Who is Jonas, exactly, and why is he—

"How is Edith?" Jonas asks, stalking past Mari. She follows at a leisurely pace, moving farther from my hiding spot. "Why did you frighten her like that?"

She smiles, pointed teeth showing. "Just a little masquerade on my part, my liege. Edith did hers in helping us set the trap and telling us of where Yetundé and her child would be. I heard that you also did your best. You befriended the girl and put her at ease so our soldiers could do their job effectively. Commendable of you."

My ears are ringing, Mari's words echoing over and over like a bad dream. My hands are clammy and I can't breathe. So that was it then. Jonas pretended to be my friend, and Edith informed on us. But how? Jonas's illness was very real. Did they risk his life just to get at us? That didn't make any sense. And how did they know about the diduo signal? I can't think. I need to get away.

They have me surrounded. Jonas knows where I am—he *brought* me here, and it's only a matter of time before he gives me up. I need to run. I must get to the forest first. Once I am there, I will be safe. There are so many places to hide, so many secret things in Ikolé Forest. They will not find me.

I edge back. Too late, I hear a twig crack beneath me. Mari pivots instantly, black eyes trained on me like a hunting dog's, wild with hunger.

"Hello, dearest," she snarls. Then she's on me in a flash, sword flying overhead.

I scramble back. Her sword crashes into the bush. I dive for the forest.

"Wait!" Jonas shouts, but I don't stop.

Someone whistles, and two guards jog out of the forest mouth, swords drawn, spirits of death coming to claim their prize.

I freeze. Behind me, Mari calls out in her singsong voice. "That's right. Nowhere to run, dearest. You're mine now."

I look between her and the guards. She's right. I'm caught.

"Don't hurt her," Jonas pleads. And I hate him all the more.

I should have ripped my father's ring from his hands and run when I had the chance. I feel so foolish.

"We're supposed to capture magic users, not execute them," he finishes weakly.

"Excuse me if I don't agree, my liege. This child is the daughter of one of the most dangerous magic users in our kingdom. It is our duty to extinguish her."

Without further delay Mari flies at me again, slashing with her sword. I drop my sack, close my eyes, and everything slows as I call the wind spirits.

I can feel the blade as it cuts through the air, speeding toward me, her arm as it swings away from her body.

Shield, I think, imagining myself in a small ball, like the cocoons the butterflies hide in. I open my eyes.

The blade slams into the air before me, suspended in mid-strike. Mari tries to pull her weapon back, but I am faster.

"Sword!" I scream. A torrent of wind bathes my fingers and a sword of white fire grows in my hand. Mari's sword clatters to the ground, and in that moment I strike, rushing forward and thrusting my blade into her stomach. She gasps, desperately trying to suck in air, staring with bulging, accusing eyes. Then she seizes in a tremor and falls back.

I didn't expect to have my revenge so soon.

I let go as she falls, and my windblade dissipates. The world comes into focus once more, and Jonas gapes at me, face pale. But he has no right to judge—he betrayed me first. The soldiers be-hind him stand shocked, then they stir like a nest of disturbed lo-custs, shouting and charging. I scoop my sack up and run, heading straight for the two guards that emerged from the forest. One drops his sword and dives at me, but I dance past him. The other rushes me, sword thrusting out, and I twist away from him too. But as I spin past, his blade catches my side and I scream. He collapses, drop-ping his sword and slamming his hands to his ears.

I clutch at the wound, pressing as the sticky wetness of my blood seeps through my dress. Mummy taught me about the taste of iron, of how the Eingardian king harnessed it as a weapon to eradicate all Oluso. She even gave me an iron necklace to help me build up a tolerance to it. The ring Jonas has now. For years, the constant pain of wearing the necklace reminded me of the weight I bore, of the great responsibility I had as an Oluso to use my powers well. The pain became so normal that I never felt it anymore. But now I have done what I should not—I have used my magic to harm another—and the brush of the guard's sword is enough to make all that tolerance fade away until it feels like I am burning alive. I can-not focus. I need to get away, now.

Summoning the last bits of my magic, I pour it into my legs and keep going, running until I hit the tangle of the forest. It is dark, and the only light I have is snatches of moonlight between trees, but I keep going, pushing until my lungs feel like they will burst. I cut my feet on rocks and stones littering the forest floor, yet I still do not stop. Tree branches catch my clothing and tear at my hair, but I keep my eyes trained forward. I am tired, my limbs numb and heavy when I finally stumble over a root and go down hard.

I roll until I slam into the base of a tree. My head feels so heavy now, but I ease myself up, hugging my sack to me. My feet hurt, my wound hurts, and in the haze of darkness, I see something spread over it, branching out in thick veins. Then I smell the soft, rosy scent and see the pink flower hanging from the spiny-looking bush just near my feet. *Okonkwo poisoning.* How funny is it the words I uttered just earlier today have come back to haunt me?

I close my eyes, pressing my back into the knobby, scratchy tree trunk. I am too spent to even heal myself, and I don't know what to do next.

"Mummy, help me," I call out weakly, but the forest is silent, save for the twitters of birds hanging overhead.

I let my head slump. Nothing matters anymore. I have failed. I could not save Mummy or myself, and I could not keep my promise. I hurt Mari—maybe even killed her—with my magic, and even if I make it out of here alive, I will pay for that act for the rest of my life. I open my eyes, but everything is blurry now, the world swimming out of focus.

"I'm sorry," I whisper to the night air. "I'm so sorry."

Then I see them: glittering lights, sparkling beacons in the darkness that shine like stars in the night sky. They dance closer and closer and I can vaguely make out giant wings, greater than any butterfly's. My head is pounding now, and it hurts my eyes to look, so I take a breath and let the darkness claim me. As I drift away, one thought echoes in my mind—the Aziza are here.

BROKEN

Nine years later . . .

"Dèmi. Dèmi!"

Nana frowns at me, her smooth forehead crinkled in worry, half-moon eyes asking a question.

"I'm okay. I have a headache. You know, the usual."

I spoon the last bit of rice porridge into my mouth and shove up from the table. Without a word, I take the baby clinging to Nana's hip and bounce her. She gurgles, waving tiny fists at me. I kiss her forehead and hand her back to her mother. It's funny how children turn out, like stamps pressed out in rubber seals, faithful representations of those who bore us, but malleable, too, changeable in more ways than our forebears would like. Haru is only six months old, but she has the same eyes as her mother, the slim nose and straight black hair that fans her round face. Nana has longer hair that drifts down to her waist like a waterfall, and a pointed chin, but Haru resembles her just the same. Seeing them every day reminds me of my mother, as though it is not enough that every time I see my reflection in my washbasin, I see her face staring back at me.

But my skin was always darker than my mother's, whereas Haru has the same golden-brown skin that Nana does. Where Nana's eyes are brown, almost black, just like mine, Haru's eyes are mismatched—one brown, one green, just like her father. As I learned soon after my mother died, my dark eyes were not the only gift my father left me. Because while my face resembles my mother's, the difference is the hardness in it, the taut way I hold my mouth that hasn't truly smiled in nine years. There is more of my father in me than I once realized, and now that I know who he truly was, I understand how I survived all those years ago—why I deserve to be alone.

"Dèmi." Nana calls my name again, dragging me away from my ugly family secrets. "You act strange around the start of Harmattan season, but this year seems worse. Is it your name day?"

I stroke Haru's head, arranging her soft wisps of hair and smile. "It's really a headache. I haven't had time to sleep much this past week. My name day isn't for another two days."

She sucks her teeth. "Baba needs to stop pushing you so hard."

I shrug. "He wants me to get stronger. Where's Will?"

She rolls her eyes. "Out getting wood for the fire."

"How long has he been doing that?"

"He left at Rabbit Hour."

I shake my head. The town bells rang seven times as I started eating, marking Crow Hour. Rabbit Hour, when dew is fresh, and the sun swims into the arms of a waking sky, is long past. "I'll get him. I assume he's at Baba's."

Without waiting for a reply, I grab my leather belt pouch and ogbene from their wooden pegs and fasten both to my waist. The belt goes under my ogbene so I can hide the hunting knife I carry with me at all times. I have never cut someone with it, but pulling out the curved blade is enough to scare would-be thieves and attackers away from me. Better yet, it proves to the market-square guards that I am merely human, because what magic user would willingly burn themselves with iron? As such, they accept me. Since no one, excepting Will and Nana, really knows me here, I have passed the last nine years in Benin undisturbed. Except for the nightmares that ensnare me at night.

There is no escaping those.

"I'll be back after first watch. Before it gets too hot."

Nana readjusts Haru on her hip. "Mmm," she mumbles, not quite sure she believes anything I've said this morning. "Be careful."

"I will. I'll send Will home, then go to the market. Don't open the shop without him, please. You know what happened last time."

She bats her eyelashes at me. "All I know is you were there to scare off a foolish guard who couldn't take no for an answer." She sighs. "If I didn't have Haru, I would have broken his wrist myself, but I don't want to expose my child to violence. Not this early."

"We took a risk, Nana. He could have—"

"So we should have let him harass us, and keep trying to put his fingers where they didn't belong? I taught you better than that, Dèmi." She studies me, one eyebrow raised, and shame pools in my belly. I think of the guards at the gates and the way their hands glide over me, as though they are feeling around in darkness.

"He brought the magistrate, Nana. Tried to have us arrested for attacking him."

"We had witnesses who vouched for us."

"So did he. The magistrate ruled on our side because his wife loves the shop."

She grins, eyes flashing with triumph. "Lucky for us she wants new winter fabrics then."

I smile, the tightness in my chest falling away like a scab from an old wound, and head to the small corridor that leads to the back door of the house. The entire house is made of wood, rich oak pieces unlike the reddish mud that made up the hut my mother and I once lived in. Besides the dining room, the kitchen, and the small rooms upstairs that Will, Nana, Haru, and I sleep in, there are two large rooms at the front of the house that serve as the shop. One for stocking new wares, and the main room for selling art pieces. Nana and Will are crafters. Will makes musical instruments, and Nana glass pieces and jewelry. Most recently they started selling colorful pieces of fabric in the shop as well, but they tell the customers that the pieces are imported every time someone asks after them. I am grateful for that. Life is simpler that way.

As I reach the back door, Nana squeezes my shoulder. I turn to find her staring with glowing amber eyes. "You will be given a choice today. Go with what is in your heart."

Her eyes fade to dark brown once more, and she sighs again. "I'm sorry, I can't tell you more. The vision was hazy. I could only hear voices."

"That's enough. Thank you. Really." I kiss Haru on the cheek and flash Nana another smile. "I'll be out and back before you know it." Then I fling myself through the door, not looking back, in case she senses my discomfort. These days I don't take anything for granted, not even a few words of warning. Not after what happened nine years ago.

Even now, while Haru is so young, Nana does not want her child to see violence. But children like us are born under the shroud of violence. The magic that sings through our veins and weaves its strings tightly around our hearts is the very reason violence seems to find us. My mother thought she could escape it if she put me in a cocoon, raising me with only little bits of knowledge about what I am.

But I know better now.

Bracing against the chill air, I ease into a run, heading down the grassy path in the field behind the house. There are still bits of green back here, bright spots in the patchwork of dun the field has become. There are birds flying, smudges of black splashed across the grayish-blue sky. In a few minutes, the air might turn brown, the sky obscured by the dust storm that will roll in, so I savor the view. Benin doesn't get as many Harmattan storms as Ikolé did, partly because it sits next to a giant sea, but the dust storms here are followed by days of thundering rain, which makes everything muddy.

I soon come upon the slanted cabin in the distance, a sliver of blue smoke dancing into the air from its chimney. Sprinting the last few steps, I throw the front door open. Three men sit on the floor, watching three large snails crawl across it, shouting as one snail begins to pull ahead. They look up as I come in, sheepish grins passing across their faces.

The youngest, with curly brown hair, tawny skin, and twinkling hazel eyes, leaps to his feet, hands stuck awkwardly in the pockets of his trousers. Colin. He's only two years older than me. Nineteen. Not a man really, still on the edge of being one, with broad shoulders and a deep voice that declare him one, but the softness in his face betraying him.

"It's not what you think," he says. "Baba wanted to extract some snail juice for his latest experiment, and we tried to help, but then . . ."

I cross my arms. He lowers his head in mock sincerity, peeking at me from beneath long eyelashes.

The eldest, a man with skin as dark as mine and white hair dotting his head and chin, nods. "Good of you to join us." Without another word, he motions to a large clay pot behind me, and it rises into the air, speeding toward my head.

I turn quickly, slamming my fist into it. As the pieces rain down, I twist my fingers, and they swim into the air again, refashioning themselves into the pot. Grinning, I face Baba Sylvanus. He strokes his chin. "A bit slow to respond, but otherwise good."

"*Slow?* I—" I start. I stop, wincing in pain. The knuckles of my right hand are covered with blood. Uttering a curse, I flex my fingers. White fire springs up and consumes them, then it disappears along with the blood.

"Slow," Colin adds, twirling the end of his curled braid with his fingers. I shoot him a glare.

"Slow," Baba confirms. "You misjudged the amount of force you needed and wasted magic to heal yourself. Colin, remind Dèmi of our lesson for the week?"

Colin clears his throat. "Strong opponents strike without sparing a moment. It's better to take a hit and land the killing blow than miss your chance altogether."

I drop to my knees and bend my head over my clasped arms. "Thank you for your guidance, Baba."

"Rise. Yetundé taught you well. You have her control, and Osezele's strength. It makes me proud. They were my best students."

I tense at the mention of my father's name, but I wait, hoping Baba will say more. After a moment, he sighs. "But you're not here to hear an old man reminisce about the past." He waves a hand toward the man still hunched over the snails. "Collect this rascal before he derails my work for the day."

Will grins at me, mismatched eyes dancing in amusement. I grab his ear and his grin disappears. "Nana has to open the shop soon. Where's the firewood you collected?"

"Wait, wait. I did go out for firewood, but . . . could you please stop pulling?"

I release him, and he rubs his reddened ear, brighter than his pale, coppery skin. He tucks his offended ear behind a dirty blond lock and rises to his feet. "Fine, let's go. I'm lucky she didn't send you out later. I don't know what you might have done to me for being out for two hours instead of one."

I smile now, making sure to bare my teeth. "Don't feed my imagination, Will. I can spend all day coming up with punishments for you."

Colin grins, tossing an arm around both of us. "Willard, *you're* supposed to be the parent. How come your ward always has to come fetch you?"

I shrug him off. "Hurry before I drag you," I say to Will before stalking out. Nine years and the word "parent" still makes me uncomfortable.

Colin tries to catch my eye, but I look away. When I turn back a moment later, he's gone.

Will waves at Baba and follows me out.

As we walk, I marvel at how tall Will is. In Ikolé, many of the men were over six feet. But from what I've seen, the tallest Eingardians hover just under six. Will, with his wide face and large hands, stands three inches over six, and when I walk next to him with my five-foot-four-inch frame, I feel impossibly small. Then again, he is only half-Eingardian—though he passes for full in every season but summer. His height undoubtedly came from the unnamed Oyo woman who gave him up.

"How is Haru this morning?"

I shrug. "How should I know? You should check on your child first thing in the morning instead of gallivanting about."

He ruffles my hair, careful as he threads his fingers through my thick, coily mane. "Sometimes when I gallivant about, my children come to check on me, and that's always nice."

"That's not the same thing and you know it," I say dryly.

"Why not?"

"Haru is actually your child. I'm just your ward."

The skin between his bushy brows puckers. "I wish you'd stop thinking like that. When Nana and I found you, you became our child. I wish you'd accept that."

I bite my lip to keep a stinging remark from coming out. He and Nana have taken care of me and treated me like I was their own for nine years. I don't know why that makes me so angry right now. I'm saved from having to say anything when Colin appears beside us, materializing out of thin air. Startled, I smack him on the shoulder as he laughs.

"You should've seen your face," he gasps out. "I would've thought you would be used to me by now."

"You're right—I should be used to you being an ass." I speed up my pace. "If someone sees you, we'll all spend the next few days under quarantine while the guards track you down."

"I'd just teleport myself to my father's place and hide out for a few days."

"Then you'll have put us all in danger and the guards might never leave. Must be nice to be able to run away all the time."

He shoots me a wounded look. "Would you prefer the guards catch and kill me?"

I don't answer. He knows better than to ask that question. Will clears his throat as we reach our house. "What will you two be up to today?" he asks, voice seemingly nonchalant.

I lift an eyebrow. "I'm going to help Amara in the market today, like I always do."

Colin grins. "I'm going to help Dèmi, like I always do."

Will nods slowly, eyeing both of us. "Have fun. Dèmi, you have training tonight, so don't stay out too late." He winks and I roll my eyes. "Whatever you think is happening here," I say, pointing between me and Colin, "it's not, so stop imagining things."

Colin smacks his palm over his heart as though I've wounded him. "But I thought—"

"And you keep thinking that."

I walk away then, ignoring them as they call after me. Taking the path directly in front of our shop, I keep going until I reach the top of the hill. From here, I can see the rusted red gates and the long white wall down below. Four guards stand on either side of the open gates, checking people as they walk in. I sigh and head toward them. Since Benin is a port city, and a great place to find transportation to other parts of the kingdom, all kinds of people come here. No one looks twice when they see fair-skinned Will holding Nana's hand as they enter the main market or when I walk in behind them. When I go in alone, however, it's a different story.

I start onto the main road. All the houses in Benin are arranged on the outside, and seven roads lead straight into the heart of the city, like spokes on a wheel. Beyond the red gates is the main market, with shops built on wooden platforms that hang above the water on stilts. Past the shops is the dock and the wide Benué Sea, where fishermen catch fish at all hours of the day, hauling well-knit nets above canoes and riding the unpredictable waves. Eingardian ships, big wooden longboats, come in at all hours of the day, delivering leather, minerals, and other wares that would spoil if they were sent down through the forests, because Eingard is at least a week's journey from Oyo. Goma ships come in, too, sleek junkets with blue sails that signal their arrival, bearing fresh fruit and vegetables that are sometimes salted or dried. Since Berréa sits to the south of Benin, the merchants there travel up with their goods, reed baskets and wooden flutes and fine silks that are beautiful and smooth.

It is said that Alistair Sorenson won the war eighteen years ago by taking over Benin. Since the city is the very heart of Ifé and the center of trade, conquering it was the key to controlling the king-dom. When the royal family realized that their people would starve if imports from Benin could not come in, they gave themselves up to Alistair Sorenson in a truce. They expected to usher him in as the new ruler peacefully—instead there was bloodshed.

Of course there was.

I shudder as I come up to the gates, remembering one of the rumors I first heard upon coming to Benin: that the red paint for the gates was made with the blood of the royal family—*my* family. I shake myself. Can't think about that; not today. I need to find Amara. There will be time enough to grieve once my name day comes.

A guard stops me, light glinting off the serpentine insignia deco-rating the hilt of his sword. He looks me up and down, his face pale and sunken like the rice porridge I ate this morning, his eyes lin-gering too long on my chest and hips. He licks his lips, his tongue abnormally red, as though he has been drinking blood. I groan inwardly as he leans closer, revealing stained, yellow teeth. The man is obviously a koko user, the red of the small flower staining his mouth while the effects of its poison over time have rotted his teeth. A small piece of koko can give you impossible dreams and make you feel as though you are flying. I wouldn't know. Seeing how the drug can cut a person's life in half, I make it a point to stay away from it and those who abuse it.

Unfortunately I don't have that luxury at the moment.

I tap my left shoulder with my right hand twice in the common Oyo greeting, and offer a blessing for the day, hoping to distract him. "Midé's Day shines upon you. May your day swell with hope."

"Your clothes are looking a little bulky. Let's check them," he says, in lieu of the answering phase. He goes straight ahead and slithers his hands over me, patting extra long when he comes to my breasts.

I curl my hands into fists. The way he is going, he will be dead in a few years anyway, if not a few weeks. The smell of decay is heavy on his hot breath. I turn my head. Anything to be away from him. The guard to his left catches my eye then. He is young, with brown skin like the rare iroko trees that grew in Ikolé, Oyo-born. His lips are drawn, and the muscles in his neck taut like a bowstring as he watches the first guard "search" me. When his eyes meet mine, I see a trace of fiery anger, but as the first guard squats to rub his hands down my leg, he looks away.

I rock back, the sudden shift knocking the first guard off balance, and he stumbles in the dirt. He glares, but another woman walks up then, pink-shell skin like the touch-and-die flowers that litter our backyard. The first guard coughs and swats me forward. "You can go. Dress lightly next time. We wouldn't want to accidentally hurt you because it looks like you might have a weapon, would we?"

He bows to the woman and waves a hand. "Right this way, my lady." She stares at both of us before passing through the gate.

I charge toward the market gates. But before I get through, the second guard thrusts out a purple-and-gold cloak, blocking my path. "May hope light your way," he says, finishing the greeting from earlier. "There's a storm today." His voice is heavy, but his eyes are dark, ghostly mirrors that hold nothing.

When I don't respond, he shakes the cloak again. "There'll be rain."

Hooking my fingers into the side of my ogbene, I trace the edge of my knife, letting the iron bite into my skin as I say, "I was born in the rain. Didn't have a cloak then. Don't need one now."

"I'm sorry," he blurts as I march past. "I should have stopped him from touching you. I—I don't have power, not really."

I pause, swallowing the lump in my throat. "What is that uniform if not power?"

He bristles, opening his mouth to no doubt tell me how wrong I am. Then there's a shout behind us. The first guard towers over an elderly Oyo-born woman. "Dewan," he shouts to my guard, "arrest this one. She bit me! And she won't submit to a search."

Dewan lowers his head, the fight gone from his eyes.

"Go on," I crow. "Don't forget to apologize to her too."

Then I march through the market gates, eyes forward. Behind me, Dewan pleads, "Sir, I'll do the search. Please go get some ointment for your hand."

In the last several years, more non-Eingardians have joined the king's army, as it's the easiest way out of poverty. But too many times, when the Eingardian guards persist in searching the ridge of my back and the spaces between my breasts for imaginary weapons, the other guards look on with open mouths and bulging eyes like ghosts searching for a living vessel, wanting something, but not daring to breathe. Then there are those whose lips stay parted, saliva dripping, with eyes that roam over me as though they, too, are partaking in a feast.

They're all horrible in my mind. At least the Eingardians don't pretend to hide who they are.

I press my finger hard against the tip of my blade until pain swells, savoring the glow that fills me as the skin pulls itself back together again. Since my mother died and the townspeople I'd lived with all my life just watched, I stopped expecting anything, even of fellow Oyo-born. Purple-and-gold uniforms taint skin like the blood rushing through my veins marks me. I don't need them. There is more power in my little finger than they have in their entire bodies. I am stronger than they'll ever be. Then I remember what Baba told me, the truth of where that strength was born, and the glow fades.

Coming to the main walkway, I take a sharp right, weaving through people until I find the stall covered on all sides except the front by a thick, well-woven blanket. There is a reed basket on the table attached to the stall, and colorful skeins of wool gathered inside it, but no one standing behind the bench.

"Amara," I call, checking the side of the stall. Maybe she is carrying something for a customer. I sit on the bench behind the table. Still, it would not be like my careful best friend to leave her stall unattended. Resting my head in my hands, I half close my eyes, concentrating. If she were still alive, Mummy would be proud to know that I've developed greater control of my magic, that I can use it in public now without Ajes being able to see its effects, just like she could. Pain stabs at my heart at the memory of her, and I have to start the process again; emptying my mind, reaching for my magic. On the worn bench, I glean faint traces of blue, threads lingering about like an aroma. Leaping up, I follow them, wandering unseeing through the market.

As I pass by, merchants yell from colorful canopies.

"Akara for sale, twenty kobo!"

"Agege bread, two for thirty kobo!"

A woman darts in front of me, carrying a yellow cream in a wooden bowl. She peers at me, nodding to herself. "Jeje cream, made fresh this morning. Two weeks' worth. You can become as fair as me, or even fairer." She holds out a hand. "Five hundred kobo."

I stare, taking in her lank black hair and dawn-colored skin, the smug, knowing expression on her face. There is one drawback to living in this city. In Ikolé, we were far away from all the latest happenings in the kingdom. "Fashion" was an empty word. Benin merchants pride themselves in creating trends that will influence even Eingard, but often what that means is trying to please the Eingardian lords who live in the region. So this year, there are heat pressers for those of us with coily hair who want to achieve the straight locks of Eingardian women; creams designed to lighten the skin to a soft gold, no doubt what she wants to sell me.

Stifling my swelling anger, I spit out, "Sister, are you trying to poison me?"

She stiffens, annoyance flashing across her face. Then all too quickly she smiles. "I'm sorry. I don't understand what you said. Can you repeat that in Ceorn, please?"

I smile. I don't know what possessed me to ask the question in Yoruba, but her reaction confirms my suspicions all the same. "Where are you from? Ibadan? Akure?" I ask in Yoruba again.

She hisses. "I was trying to help you, but if you want to remain ugly, stay that way. Get away from here, you olodo. I don't have time for you." She stalks off, muttering under her breath.

I hear it now, the deep tones in her voice, the pounding rhythm of her words that resembles the way Oyo people, my people, speak. Now that all of Ifé is under Eingardian control, there are many who grow up without learning their native tongue, children who have the gift of their heritage stolen from them before they can speak. And there are others—many who listened to Alistair Sorenson when he offered to build a new world, when he promised that all of Ifé would be born anew if we would let go of the ways of our ancestors and conform to his ways. One language for all. One way of being. For that reason, my skin is an offense, my hair even worse.

I turn to go, then stop and smile. The woman could speak Yoruba after all, the curses she uttered at me as she left prove as much. I scan the platform again, looking for the blue threads that led me here in the first place, and I spot them, Amara hanging on to a trader's thick arm. As I run toward her, the trader pulls his arm from her grasp, throwing her back. When she grabs at the whip in his hand, he plunges his hand into her thick brown hair and yanks.

She screams and waves her arms wildly, like a baby bird trying to fly. He flings her to the ground.

"Stop!" I cry, throwing myself between them. "What are you doing?"

The trader advances, face and neck an angry purple. "You want to attack me too?" he barks.

I can barely understand his words. His Ceorn is so thick that I shake my head furiously, palms up like I'm trying to calm an angry dog.

"Whatever my friend has done, I'm sorry. We mean no trouble."

Pulling Amara up, I whisper sharply, "What happened?"

He points his whip at Amara. "Take her away from here. If I see you here again, I will call the guards."

"Why *don't* we call them? Why don't we call them so they can see how you're treating those children?" Amara screams, pushing away from me.

I wrap my arms around her torso, holding back her struggling form. "Stop," I say in her ear. "Start explaining. What's going on?"

When Amara gets angry, she is fire, burning everything in her path. Her small body pulses with energy, and her tawny skin takes on a darker tint as blood rushes to her face. She twists around, blinking big brown eyes as though registering my presence for the first time. "He is an okri dealer. He has two children leashed up in cages like animals. Why are you stopping me?"

I slacken my hold on her. Turning to the trader, I lower my voice and ask, "Sir, may I see your wares?"

He smacks the air with his whip, giving a small smile when Amara jumps. "For what reason?"

"I'd like to buy—"

"Can you afford what I am selling?" He jerks his chin toward

Amara, at the burn scar visible on her ankle. "Did you buy or 'liberate' this one? I'm a merchant. I only deal with serious people."

I loosen the ogbene at my waist and shake it out. Gold coins fall into my hand like rain spilling from the clouds. "Five lira. Is that enough for you to consider me serious?"

He eyes the coins, licking his lips before nodding. "You can come in." When Amara follows, he shakes his head. "Not her. And walk in front of me. I don't want any trouble." He steals a look around before beckoning me to a tent a few paces away.

Amara flares, but I shake my head. "Stay here. I mean it." She shoots me a challenging look but obeys, mouth turned down in a determined sulk.

The tent is big, about the size of three stalls, and it is dark inside, save for a small kerosene lamp in the corner. There are rust-colored cushions spread out over the floor, a makeshift theater for the main attraction that lies beyond. In front of those cushions is a metal cage. The air is hot and thick with incense, the scent of frankincense and myrrh smothering everything. Yet it isn't enough to hide the sharp smell coming from the cage, and I know without a doubt that that smell is urine.

I creep closer, stepping on the cushions as I go. The trader clucks in annoyance, dusting off a cushion, but all I see is the cage. In it are two children, small and white-haired, with reddened eyes and freckled skin. They huddle next to each other on a woven mat, the threadbare rags on their bodies barely hiding the sharpness of their limbs. The boy looks no older than six, but his ribs are jutting out and his shorts are stained. As I press closer, ignoring the burn of the iron bars against my skin, the girl, who looks about ten, wraps her arms around him and holds him close, shielding him from the horror of my eyes. Chains bind their ankles, and the skin around those chains is heavily scarred, burned and marked like Amara's.

Without a word, I push my wrist through the bars and hold it up, concentrating until the glowing green mark on my left wrist is visible. The girl gasps, sitting up in excitement. The trader yells from behind me, "What are you making noise for? Stand up so she can see you."

Like a marionette, the girl hobbles closer to the bars, stopping right in front of me and turning every which way. When she turns her back, I see red welts in the pale skin, and a glowing purple mark between her shoulder blades. The mark is twin to the one on my wrist and on Amara's neck, a crescent with a flower in full bloom between its arches—the mark of an Oluso.

"Where are you from?" I ask her, speaking softly. Anger burns inside me, and my voice trembles with the effort of holding it in. Tears are brimming in the corners of my eyes, but I will them away. These children do not need my tears. They need my eyes wide open. They need me to see them and do something.

The trader's breath comes hot and fast on my neck. "I don't need you to be asking them questions, girlie. Decide if you want one and pay up. The boy is still young. He'll be a good entertainer in the future. He's not much right now, so I'll let you have him for a bargain. Five lira."

"And the girl?" I clench my fists, pushing out the words with difficulty.

He shrugs. "The girl can freeze over fire. She's my main source of income. I'd need something like a hundred lira before I'd consider parting with her."

"How much for a show?"

He narrows his eyes. "I thought you were looking to buy. If you ain't, get out. You can pay five hundred kobo like the other mugs to watch them during the festival in two days."

Once, at the New Moon Festival a few years before, I saw children like these for the first time. Okri. Forsaken. Standing in cages, chains binding their ankles. Merchants standing in front of them and shouting:

Come and see the shapeshifting boy, only one lira!

This girl can make water appear out of nowhere, only five hundred kobo!

Will pulled me away from the display, but too late I saw that those children had eyes like mine, the eyes of an Oluso. Only, theirs were hollow and tired, empty as they watched people throw money at the merchant's feet.

Five hundred kobo. A month's wages to watch tortured children perform and buy treatments for coveted lighter skin. I see the expectation in the trader's watchful eyes. He can gain almost a year's wages for a little boy who is no more than baggage to him, and no one will pay almost twenty years' worth of money for an Oluso girl he can keep using until she dies. I wonder, too, how these children ended up like this, why their caretakers missed out on a chance to sell them to the regional lords. After all, everyone knows that fair-skinned Oluso who can be beaten into submission are better entertainers for their lords' guests. Selling a child does not matter as long as they have the curse of magic.

"So what will it be? Will you take the boy or not? I have other customers coming today, important ones—you won't get a second chance." The trader sniffs.

I look at the girl still standing there, staring at me through the bars of her prison, and the little boy who is quivering, eyes wide like a rabbit running from a fox.

"I'll take them both. In exchange, I won't kill you."

The trader rears up, startled. "What?" He flicks his whip. "Don't mess with me. If you're not going to buy, get out. I have to prepare my wares for serious customers."

That's when I lose it. Leaning forward, I jab his side with my elbow, then when he steps off balance, I sweep my leg around and kick him in the back, knocking him to the floor. He crashes onto a few wooden boxes stacked next to the cage and makes a feeble, gurgling sound.

"Where is the key?" I ask the girl.

She blinks as though waking from a nightmare. "I don't know where he keeps it."

The trader is still on the floor, puffing like a balloon as he breathes. More than anything, I want to take his whip and beat him, to give him a taste of what he has done to these children. Instead, I bite the inside of my cheek so hard that blood seeps into my mouth, then I pull the threads of my magic, pouring it into my hands. I grab two of the cage bars, and my fingers smart as though they are holding a pan that's been sitting on coals. I have been exposed to too much iron today and I might not be able to walk later, but I need my strength now. I pull at the cage bars, forcing them apart like the wire strings on the instruments Will makes. Sweat clouds my brow, and my stomach feels heavy, but I keep yanking until there is a sizeable space between those bars.

Breathing hard, I beckon to the girl. "Bring your brother. Let's go."

The little boy, his thumb stuck in his mouth, looks at his sister. She puts an arm around him. "Where are you taking us? If you're going to sell us, too, leave us here. Master Shep might be angry all the time, but at least he feeds us. We get more food on festival days."

My heart is heavy, and my eyes begin to smart again. I sniff and shake my head. "I won't be selling you. I don't know who did this to you, but I'm not like them. You're coming to live with me. I know good people who can take care of you. Promise."

The girl says nothing, just studies me with serious eyes, then after a moment she tugs the little boy's hand. "Rollo, we are going now, okay?"

He nods mutely and I reach for the boy. The girl steps in front of him, shaking her head. "I can carry him."

I stare at her too-thin frame and the chain still hanging from her leg. There is no way she will get far carrying him, not like this. But I nod and beckon her to the mouth of the tent. "My friend will help us. Let me get her."

"Amara," I whisper loudly, looking around. She pops up next to the tent opening so quickly that I stagger back.

"Couldn't wait for you. Knew it would turn out like this. What's our plan?" she asks.

"We have a minute, two at the most. I knocked him out, but he'll be up again soon. We need to get them to Will's. But they still have their chains on."

"How do we get them through the gates?"

I pause a moment, scanning our surroundings. The tent is toward the back of the market, close to one of the small docks that lead to the sea. There are not many people around. If we're fortunate, no one will remember us being around here once the trader comes to and inevitably goes looking for the children.

"Fetch our cloaks from the stall. We can bundle them up and hide out for a while, then carry them with the rest of your wares when we're leaving. The guards are always too tired for late-night searches. They'll be busy taking bets for the festival challenges."

Amara scowls, her brown hair fanning her wrinkled forehead, making her look much older than her fourteen years. "What if that olodo finds out where my stall is and starts searching there? That won't work."

There are at least a thousand shops in the Benin market, and because businesses grow rapidly, oftentimes shops move spaces. It would be difficult for a stranger to find his way around. Still, if he had help from the guards and they put out Amara's description, there's no telling what might happen. With these children's distinct features, we might not be able to smuggle them through the open market without someone taking note of their paper-white skin and white hair. I look out to the swirling blue-black of the sea. After losing my mother, I often wished that sea would open up and swallow me whole, drown my miseries in its hidden depths. But today it is a welcome sight, an oasis in the midst of a desert.

"Do you still talk to Gideon?"

Amara arches an eyebrow, but the faint pink in her cheeks betrays her. "Maybe."

"Find him. We'll hide the children on his boat for the day, then take them through with his cargo when he goes into town tonight. He has one or two things set aside for Will anyway."

She nods. "Where can I meet you?"

I jerk my head toward the small canoe tied at the end of the dock. "I'll take them a little ways away. He won't think to look there."

"But you can't swim. With the storm coming in, you risk dying if you go out there. What if something happens before Gideon and I can find you?"

Next to me, the little girl shifts, her arms going protectively around her brother once more. Her eyes are wary, but there is something else in them too—a fierceness born of necessity, the will to survive. I think of Mummy's words, one of the many sayings she gave me when I complained about the way the other village children treated me: *Keep your eyes forward and your chin up. They cannot take anything from you that you do not give them.*

The world took my mother's life and was trying to take these children's, but I wasn't going to let that happen. Not to them, and not to anyone.

No more.

"If you're not willing to risk me to save these children, back out now. I'm going out there, whether you like it or not. You of all people should understand."

Amara purses her lips in a grim line, then nods. She lifts her left ankle and rotates it, the scar decorating it twisting like rubber being stretched and cut. Then she runs in the direction of the larger dock, moving awkwardly like an acrobat trying to balance on a ball, long limbs flailing about. I will need to sit with her later, to help heal the pain all the running will do to her ankle, but right now, I have a bigger task at hand.

"I can't promise I'll succeed in getting you free, but I will die trying. Will you come with me?" I ask the girl.

She laces bony, grubby fingers in mine, and I lead them to the canoe.

TROUBLE

We have only just entered the canoe when the trader calls after us, "Stop! Thief!"

I dart a quick look around. No one in sight. Good. I shove my fist through the middle finger and thumb of my left hand and close those fingers around my wrist. Ceorn for "wishing you horse dung for every meal."

Then, plunging the oars into the raging waves, I push away from the dock, rowing as fast as I can. We are nowhere near the main causeway where most of the ships are docked doing business, but I don't want to take any chances. There might be a lone fisherman working nearby who will hear the trader's cries and come after us.

I'll paddle for a few minutes, then turn us around and find another dock. The trader will think we're still out on the sea, and I will be able to meet Amara. All is not lost. I stare ahead, focusing on the gray sky and the vast, spreading sea that feels like the end of the world. Soon, the trader's cries fade into air and mist.

"Otìtò, Rollo. Don't cry," the girl pleads, stroking her brother's hair. "We'll be in a new place soon. Somewhere warm with sweet food, just like home."

Something she says gives me pause, but I don't have time to

process her words because just then I see the ship. It's twice as big as the biggest ship I have ever seen, with twenty circular windows in its wooden side and a long, misshapen masthead. It is still a ways off, about a league, but from here I see Alistair Sorenson's serpentine insignia cast in purple and gold on the cream-colored sails.

I stop rowing. Figures scurry about the top level of the ship. With the spyglasses anchored all along the prow, it's only a matter of time before they see us. We must find another way. I look back. The dock is a misted-over flatness that seems too far away. I can't risk taking the children back there, but going any farther out puts them at the risk of being caught. The ship is getting closer, closing in with impossible speed, but I can't move, plagued by indecision.

"Auntie, what's happening?" the girl asks.

I force a smile. "Can you do me a favor? Can you wrap yourself and your brother in the tarp down there?"

To my surprise, her eyes fill with tears. "You're going to drown us, aren't you? Like our cousin tried to. And when we wouldn't drown, he sold us."

She sobs, clutching her hand to her lips as I stare openmouthed. Rollo, unnerved now, joins in, wailing loudly. Flustered, I drop the oars and hug them to me. "I'm not going to drown you. I promise. I'm just trying to keep you safe. You see that ship over there?" The girl peeks out from under my arm. "It's a bad ship." I continue, "I don't want the people there to catch you and send you back to that trader."

I pull back so they can see my face. "I will *never* do anything to hurt you."

The girl stops crying, scrutinizing me. "Promise?" she mumbles, sniffling.

"If I lie, may Olorun strike me down."

"Who is that?"

I stiffen. Is it possible that this child knows nothing about her magical heritage? My mother regaled me with tales of Olorun and the Oluso from the moment I was born. Somehow, I expected the same for this child. Then again, her cousin sold her and her younger brother into slavery. I doubt that he would have wanted to arm her with the true knowledge of what she is.

"Someone important," I say quickly. "The one who gives us our magic."

The girl brightens. "You mean Y'l-shad. Papa told us about her, before he left. He said she gave us our powers to protect ourselves." Her words spill out like a fountain, airy and full of hope. "I call on Y'l-shad whenever I'm scared. The day our cousin tried to drown us, she saved us."

"How?"

Lightning cracks across the sky, a streak of white in the rising darkness, illuminating the monstrous ship. Half a league now. We need to move.

Rollo burrows into me, but the girl laces her fingers together and closes her eyes. When she speaks, her voice is calm, even. "I speak to the water, and she hears me."

She plunges a hand in the waves and within seconds colorful bubbles spring up, floating in the air around us.

"Water spirits," I whisper, holding my breath in awe.

She strokes the water's surface again and the bubbles fly back at it, falling with loud thuds as though the water itself has become solid ground. Splotches of white grow on the waves, spreading like a blight, transforming everything in its path until there is a small island of ice around us. Puffing with the effort, the girl offers me a weary smile. I have only ever seen magic like this once before. If we survive this ordeal, I am sure this girl will be a fine new student for Will.

If we survive.

Because the ship is now upon us.

I consider the slab of ice we're marooned on and the sea breeze blowing heavily around us—and that gives me an idea. "What is your name?" I ask the girl.

"Amina."

"Amina, I need you to hold on to your brother really tightly. Can you do that? You don't have to cover yourselves with the tarp, but it will help. Things are going to become very cold really quickly."

"Are we going in the water?"

"No. We're going to hide right here."

There are shouts now, echoes sounding from the ship. The figurehead that was once far away has transformed from a misshapen lump into a crowned woman, her breasts bared, her long, carved hair flowing in the wind. Someone onboard is waving at us.

Stepping out of the canoe, I test my bare feet against the icy ground. Ice cuts into my flesh, producing fresh stabs of pain, but I ignore my shaking legs and try to find my footing. Once secure, I grab Amina's hand and pull her and Rollo out. They are bundled, white heads barely visible above the muddy tarp.

Holding them close, I stretch one hand out and catch the sea breeze. I have never attempted what I'm trying now, and performing this magic will take all the strength I have left, but I hope it will buy Amara enough time to reach us. As the wind washes over my fingers, I fan them about, mimicking the motion of the spinning top Haru often plays with. All at once, cool air rises all around us, dancing toward the sky. Gray ribbons of water and air begin to form, rolling themselves out around us, unfurling until the ship becomes a blurred shadow and the air is thick with fog. Satisfied, I run at the canoe and shove, slipping with the force of motion. The canoe groans as it slides across the ice shelf, then tumbles into the water upside down, bobbing away. Let the ship boarders think they've drowned us. This should be enough.

Breathing hard, I sit and press my legs against the ice. Cold water seeps through my leather jerkin, mixing with my sweat, making me hot and freezing all at once. My cloth trousers are soaked, and my feet numb. I rub my fingers together and pray Amara finds us soon. Even if she lost sight of my sign traces, surely the giant ball of fog sitting amidst the sea will give her a clue.

"Now what do we do?" Amina asks, popping her head fully out of the tarp.

I pull her and Rollo close, trying to warm them. "We wait. My friend will find us soon and you'll get to go home with me."

Someone, though, has other plans.

I see a spark, a crack of lightning exploding in the fog, then a black ball comes flying, passing over us and landing on the edge of the ice shelf with a loud crash. Amina screams, and I have only seconds to push her and Rollo back when the ice splits, plunging me into the freezing waters below. The cold stabs at my skin, shocking me into stillness, and as pain washes over me, I try desperately to remember Will's instructions.

Don't panic. Hands together. Imagine dancing through the water.

Dancing through the water. I cling to the words as I gather my strength—then slam my hands together and push against the water, cutting through until I reach the surface. I barely have time to gasp in air when a wave comes through and knocks me under again.

This time, though, I can't think. I open my mouth and the water rushes in, choking me. Everything is dark. I flail my arms and legs—anything to get away, but I am smothered. Then my fingers brush against something solid. Ice. Mustering what's left of my strength,

I kick toward it, using my magic to propel me higher. I shoot out of the water, flopping onto the ice shelf, coughing as the seawater claws its way out of my throat.

So much for dancing through the water.

My lungs are burning, and my arms are limp, but I crawl to the edge of the slab, calling about. "Amina! Rollo!" The rest of the ice shelf lingers only a few feet away from me, but the children are nowhere to be seen.

"No, no, no," I cry, struggling to my feet. "Amina! Rollo!" I turn around, searching frantically, but the tarp is gone.

Someone touches my shoulder, and I scream. Wet fingers slip over my mouth, and I throw myself backward, determined to fight my attacker. But as I struggle, the pressure behind me disappears, and someone pulls me forward. I stare into Colin's sparking, angry eyes.

"Hold on," he barks. Then he yanks me to him and squeezes tight. In a moment, I'm shaking, catching snatches of the wind on my salty skin as we hurtle through the air. My eyes are wide open, but lights and sound elude me, passing through me as though I am glass. The sensation seems to go on forever, then suddenly I am lying on a hard floor, warmth bathing my skin from the fire, Will and Nana's concerned faces overhead.

"What happened?" I croak.

Will places a hand against my forehead and I shudder. "Amara spoke to us and Colin went to get you. How could you do all that on your own?" He utters the words in a soft voice, and that breathy, clipped tone is all I need to know how angry he really is.

"I'm sorry. There wasn't time . . . I wasn't thinking."

"Right. You were just *doing*, believing you could handle things on your own and ignoring the consequences. You and Yetundé. Cut from the same cloth."

Nana puts a hand on his shoulder. "Now isn't the time. We have other things to tend to. You can talk to her tonight."

I desperately want to know what Will was about to say, but suddenly I remember more important things. Gasping, I struggle into a sitting position. "The children! There were two kids with me, Rollo and Amina. They're out on the water, in a canoe . . . or on ice . . . or swimming—"

"Colin rescued them *first*," Will says sternly, telling me all I need to know about what he thinks of my priorities. "They're in the spare bedroom, getting some rest. You'll need to look at them. The burn marks are really bad," he says a bit more gently—but not much.

He takes Haru from Nana. "I'll close up. Can you take it from here? I"—he looks at me, and I can't tell if it's disgust, disappointment, or both—"can't stay another moment."

He leaves, Haru's happy gurgles tinkling as they go. Shame stirs in my heart, and I wish I were invisible. "I didn't mean to upset him," I say quietly. "I didn't mean for this to happen."

Nana smiles. "I know. But it did. And you know how he is. He's angry that he could have lost you. We all could. Your mother treated him like her own brother, you know. She was the one who cared for him when his mother died. He wouldn't forgive himself if he let anything happen to you."

"There were children in danger. I had to act."

"I know. But maybe you didn't need to act so fast?"

She's being kind, but I can hear she's upset too. Yet I know she'll understand when I say, "I had to, Nana. I couldn't wait another minute. You would've done the same if you were there."

Sighing, she offers me a hand, pulling me to my feet. Blood rushes to my head and I stumble when I try to take a step. She puts an arm around my shoulder and holds me still. "Take a minute. You've been through a lot."

Pain blooms from my side, shocking me into a cry. Cursing, Nana drags my knife out from under my soaked ogbene. She throws it carelessly aside, but it flies in a straight arc and embeds itself in the wall neatly.

Rubbing the stinging area, I scoff. "You still have it. I had to practice to throw that well, and you do it without even thinking."

She grins. "Twenty-three years of practice ought to count for something."

"Are you telling me you started throwing knives at age four?"

"You've met my father. What do you think? Enough knife talk—let's check out your wound."

I lean on her as we make our way into the dining room.

A few hours later, we are sitting down to a dinner of okra soup with goat meat and fufu. I eat heartily, ignoring the intense looks Colin keeps shooting my way. This is my favorite meal, partly because I love okra soup and goat meat the best, and mostly because it reminds me of early days with my mother, when we would take turns pounding coco yam until it became fufu. The food we cooked together always tasted the sweetest—especially when we didn't have that much—and nothing has been able to match that since. For some reason, though, today's food is the most delicious meal I can remember having in years.

Amina sits licking her fingers, staring at me over an empty bowl. I raise an eyebrow and she looks toward the pot of soup in the middle of the table. I nudge one of the wrapped mounds of fufu toward her and spoon out another bowl of soup. She smiles like I've given her a present, which I suppose I did, and attacks the food. Soon after, Rollo, too, his plate empty, gives me the same wondering look. When I finish giving him more, I turn to Will.

"Can we keep them here for a while? They can't go out anyway."

He nods gravely. "I already planned to. Not here, but close by.

They could stay with Baba Sylvanus. The guards don't visit his house on a regular basis."

Benin is too large for the guards to conduct raids the way they did in Ikolé, so our guard visits are limited to twice a year when they come for taxes, and of course, because we have the shop, the random guard will come to buy wares for a loved one. Baba has not paid taxes in the eight years I have been here. For reasons I have never understood, the guards fear him. Perhaps it is his reputation as the local madman, or because he has the habit of staring at people, of looking as though he can see through your very soul. Perhaps both of those reasons amount to the same thing. Either way, this serves our purposes well, and whenever we want to hide something, we put it in Baba's house.

Amina abruptly stops eating and looks from me to Will. "Are you sending us away?" she asks, voice trembling.

Amara ruffles her hair. "No, little one. We have an uncle who lives up the road. He will look after you. It's safer for you both to stay with him."

"I want stay here," Rollo mumbles, the first words I've heard him speak all day. "Why no stay here?" He starts to cry, and Nana, sitting to his left, picks him up and rocks him.

Amina stands, wringing her hands. "Can't we just stay here? Papa sent us away, too, to live at our cousin's house while he went to the mines. He promised he would be back, but he never came, and then our cousin gave us to Master Shep."

"Where is your mother?" Amara asks.

"She died after Rollo was born. The king's guard came to our village. Papa took Rollo and me and ran. She was too sick to come, and the guards wouldn't let her see Auntie Sola."

"Auntie Sola?"

"Mama's friend. She used to help whenever we got sick, or when someone got injured. She would pray to Y'l-shad and heal the person."

Something sparks my memory, a word that Amina used when she was comforting Rollo earlier. *Otìtò*. "Obokhian," I say to Amina, welcoming her in my father's language.

She smiles so widely at me that her gaunt cheeks puff up before erupting in a flood of Esan. I hold a hand up. "Slow down, the others can't understand you."

"But you can," she says, switching to Ceorn now and dancing in her chair. "You can! Are you Ishan too?"

I give her a weak smile. "Half. My father was the Ishan one. My mother was Oyo."

She gasps, her eyes wide. "Wow, so you're like me too. My mother was Hausa. My father was Ishan." She wrinkles her nose. "The other children in Jos laughed at us for that. They made fun of my skin and said it was because I was a half-breed."

Anger leaps up in my chest, a familiar knot growing there. "Forget all that. It's ignorant talk. Ishan people are Oyo, too, no matter how fair-skinned they are."

She nods matter-of-factly. "I know. Papa's skin got dark in the sun too, just like any Oyo person. But Mama said my skin and Rollo's was just different. That Y'l-shad made us ash for her own reasons. I wonder what her reasons were though. We're even lighter than Northerners."

"We can discuss all that tomorrow, okay?" Nana says, readjusting a now-sleeping Rollo in her arms. "For now, finish your food, and we'll wash up for bed." Amina looks worried, but Nana reassures her, "You're staying here tonight."

Amina yawns, as though the words are a sleeping spell. "I am tired."

Before following Nana to the door, she runs over to me, pressing her body to mine. "Ùruèsé," she whispers in Esan. Thank you.

If only she knew who my father was; how much of a disgrace he is to the Ishan people; that he is to blame in part for the way all of Ifé has changed, she would not be thanking me.

"Colin, Amara, I assume you're staying? We need to talk," Will says simply before following after his wife, carrying a sleeping Haru.

"It's nice to know I'm not the one in trouble this time," Colin says, twisting his mouth.

"Hey, it's not her fault. We had a plan. It wasn't supposed to go wrong," Amara says quickly, looking between us.

"Your plan included Dèmi almost drowning?" He faces Amara, but his eyes are fixed on me. "You could have asked for my help, you know. I know this time of year makes you feel low, but going out to sea alone makes you seem like you have a death wish."

I bristle, fingers flexed, back up, ready to spit angry words when several raps sound at the door. We freeze, glancing at one another, then finally with a shrug, Amara gets up and goes to the door. "I'll check. It's probably Baba Sylvanus."

She presses her face against the door, then looks back at us, fear in her eyes. "The guards are here."

BETTING

Colin pulls Amara away from the small glass fixture in the middle of the wooden door. "Hide," he whispers. "Tell Will and Nana what's going on. I'll buy some time."

"How did they find us so quickly?" I ask. "No one saw us come from that trader's tent, I checked."

Colin shakes his head. "We don't have time to theorize now. Go."

Another round of raps against the door, and that is all the prompting I need. Grabbing Amara by the arm, I pull her into the parlor and up the stairs toward the bedrooms. As we cross the landing, Will and Nana emerge from the middle room, where Amina and Rollo are sleeping.

Will takes one look at my face and narrows his eyes. "What is it?"

"They're here."

I don't even have to explain who "they" are. Will bounds down the stairs two at a time, Nana following in his wake. Amara runs into the room directly in front of us, a spare room with a few things in it marking it as mine, but I hesitate to follow her.

"Come on," she whispers. "Maybe they've come for something else. We'll just make things worse by being out in the open."

I shake my head, a feeling of dread growing in my belly. Something is wrong. I can't hide and leave Will, Nana, and Colin to face all this alone. If the guards are here because of me and they hurt them, I will never be able to live with it. I can't lose my family again, not like this.

"You go," I whisper to Amara. "I have an idea." Then I am off, throwing myself over the railing and catching the cold, damp air with my magic to buffer my descent. After many years of practice and training with Nana, Will, and Baba, I am softer than a cat when I leap, and I need that softness now. Creeping up to the closed door between the parlor and the dining room, I press my ear to it.

There is a scraping sound, like metal being sharpened on a whetstone, and after it passes I hear Will's gruff voice asking, "And to what do we owe the pleasure of your visit, Lord Ekwensi?"

A man responds, but the words are hard to hear at first, and I strain just a bit closer.

". . . I was curious. I asked around if anyone knew such a girl and was led here by a young lady, a jeje cream seller. She says she's seen the girl with you."

My mind flashes to the woman in the market, her ugly smirk mocking me even now. I feel a small swell of satisfaction from having resisted buying her cream. With the venom she was spewing, it probably would have poisoned me.

Will's voice gets quieter, so faint I can hardly hear it. "What if I said your informant was mistaken? What would you say to that?"

"I would have to verify that was the case, and if it is not—"

"You'll set your rabid dogs to kill everyday citizens?"

I throw the door open. That quiet, menacing tone of Will's is enough excuse for the guards to attack him. Several pairs of eyes fall on me, but I train my gaze on the tall, dark-skinned man with the peppered full beard standing in front of Will. "Leave them. Your issue is with me."

The man shifts in my direction, and the slight movement of his muscular frame reminds me of a lion, steady and deliberate in its movements, poised to strike while looking calm. Will takes a step toward me, and three guards step up from behind the strange man, swords drawn. The man Will called Lord Ekwensi merely glances at them and they draw back, sheathing their swords.

"My apologies. Regional lords are not meant to move without guards these days. Room for too many surprises. This year alone, two regional lords have died. In truth, the first was old and his falling from the parapets of his castle keep was due to his failing eyesight." The man grins as though he's telling a joke. "The king is paranoid, and my young friends here have been bathed and schooled in that paranoia since they were pups. Please excuse them."

I stiffen. I have never heard one of Sorenson's dogs, especially a regional lord, utter criticism of the king, let alone apologize to someone like me. Regional lords preside over several towns and are lesser in power only to the provincial lords who rule whole regions and Alistair Sorenson himself. Like a lion hunting its prey, this man could be baiting me, luring me into a false sense of security, so I don't let down my guard even as I smile and say, "There is nothing to excuse. They are merely doing their jobs. I'm sure the king, as well, has his reasons for mistrusting his own people."

The man smiles as though amused. "It seems you don't share my opinion. What a pity." He settles into one of the dining-room chairs and pours himself some tea, completely at ease. Colin steps closer to me, half shielding me from view.

"I'm not sure what you mean," I say cautiously.

Swirling the contents of the cup, he leans back. "To me, the king is nothing more than a suspicious man who thinks murdering those he fears will prolong his weak grasp on the kingdom. He's worse than a self-centered child. He wants to rule all of Ifé? Fine.

But he lost the heart of the people the moment he ordered the royal family murdered, and nothing—not even my position in his government—will change my opinion on that."

"Why do you serve him then?" Nana asks, her face an unreadable mask.

The man sips his tea, letting out a low, appreciative hum. "Ginger in wintertime. Always a delight." Setting down his cup, he leans toward me. "Why will a wild dog rescued from frost and hunger beg for scraps at the table with a full belly?"

"Because it is ungrateful?" Colin says, moving to obstruct the man's view of me entirely.

The man flicks his eyes to Colin, then shifts his gaze to me as I step forward. "What do you think?"

The words are called out of me, and I speak before I even know what I will answer. "It knows hunger, and fear. It prepares for the day when the food will run out or its masters will turn on him. It trusts no one."

The man smiles again, this one wider than the first, and his brown eyes gleam with excitement. "I knew you would understand." He offers his hand to me. "Lord Tobias Ekwensi. I am regional lord over the Ikwara and Ogun areas, and a recent admirer of yours. I saw you from the ship earlier today."

His words flow like honey to my ears, and I find myself moving to clasp his hand, but Colin's fingers on my shoulder bring me to my senses. "I don't know what you speak of, my lord," I say in a flat voice, shifting my gaze to the ground in a show of deference.

To my surprise, his tone grows solemn and he nods gravely. "Yes, I understand you don't want to call attention to your adventure at sea today. After all, it's dangerous to be people like us right now."

I jerk up. "Us?"

He turns to Will. "I assure you I mean no harm. No word spoken here will be reported by my guards, nor will anything we agree to ever be recorded. You have my solemn promise." Will does not respond, the hardness in his eyes speaking for him.

Lord Ekwensi stands. "I respect your reluctance to believe me," he says, removing his thick black gloves. "When your enemy comes to your door, you have no choice but to be on guard. I want to make things clear. I am no enemy."

He stretches out his right hand. The long, bony fingers and raw fingertips are not what hold my attention, however. It is the faint orange glow emanating from his skin, a crescent moon with a flower blooming in its midst.

I stare in disbelief. I look to the others and they all wear the same expression, eyes wide in surprise, faces still with shock. I blink but the mark is still there, unmistakable like the carved tattoos rich families in Ikolé give their bastards. Those families were afraid of their children marrying the offspring of their hidden shame. For some reason I cannot explain, I am afraid of what this mark means. Lord Ekwensi is one of us. Family. But how did he become a regional lord to a king determined to wipe all Oluso out of existence?

As though he can hear my thoughts, Lord Ekwensi says, "I joined Sorenson's army to save my younger sister during the war. His army attacked our village and the officers promised that our families would come to no harm if we helped them. My sister still died and I've been paying for the choice since. I believed I could save more of our people if I joined his army, keep them from being butchered. That didn't exactly work out." He pours himself another cup of tea, a slight trembling in his fingers. When he speaks again, the tremor is gone. "As you can see, I have made a place for myself, and I want to use my position to help free our people from the tyrannical madness of our king."

"How have you hidden this for so long? Surely there are onyoshi who would have exposed you by now, my lord," Will asks. I have the urge to laugh, but the absurdity of the current situation makes it difficult. For all his hatred of the Oluso, Alistair Sorenson employs onyoshi, broken Oluso who have lost their powers but still retain the ability to see the marks of other Oluso. Despite his insistence that Yoruba is now a dirty language, he uses our word for "thief" to name these traitors who earn their living by helping him hunt down other Oluso.

I hate and fear them. But Lord Ekwensi seems to have no reservations about the onyoshi. "No need for formalities. Call me Tobi, or Ekwensi. As for all that . . . there's no need for me to hide. At least from them. Look closer." He flexes his fingers. His Oluso mark deepens from orange to an angry crimson, then the lines fade, and a soft red glow bathes his hand. His fingers shrink and curl, deteriorating before our very eyes as though they are being eaten by flame. Suddenly, his face seizes with pain and he cries out, and that is when I realize what is happening.

"You're one of them," I whisper. "Onyoshi." Colin pulls me to him, as though his touch can temper the horror already filling my insides.

One of the guards comes forward with a gourd. He opens it, pouring a blood-orange liquid onto Lord Ekwensi's hand. Ekwensi massages his fingers, rubbing the liquid into his skin. "It is just as you say," he says, chuckling. "I have been called that, amongst other things."

Out of the corner of my eye, I see Will take a step closer to Lord Ekwensi, but Nana puts a restraining hand on his arm and shakes her head. "Tell us why you are here," she says, still wearing that impassive look. "It's not just because you think you saw Dèmi in the harbor. You need something. What is it?"

"Nana, you can't seriously trust—" Will starts. She holds up a hand.

"I asked a question of you," she says to Ekwensi. "Please answer it."

Ekwensi accedes to her logic with a nod. "Of course. I came here for two reasons. First, I *did* see this young woman from the ship and decided that I needed her help. Second, I had a deal with a trader in these parts for two children. I met with my liaison today and he informed me that the children had been stolen. So I came here."

My heart sinks. Rollo and Amina. I promised them safety and a new life, but instead I sealed their fates. Now they will die, along with everyone I love. I want to rage, to call up a windstorm that will blow this man and his guards out of our lives, but I stand stiff. It was my foolishness that caused this in the first place, the wild impulses Baba always warned me to control. Nine years ago, my willingness to involve myself with a stranger got my mother killed, and now the same thing is happening again. A dark thought swims into my mind. Unless . . . unless I can sacrifice my life, and take this man and his guards with me. I swallow. Am I even capable of such a thing?

"What do you need Dèmi's help for?" Nana asks, the words jolting me out of my somber reverie.

"A secret mission, only slightly dangerous."

"No," Will says.

Surprisingly, Ekwensi laughs. "Please wait until I say what I came here to say, yes?" He asks politely, but there is steel there, and it's clear he's been regional lord long enough to not be told no too often. Will swallows and nods. "Thank you." Ekwensi turns back to Nana. "I need her to retrieve something, and if she is able to complete the task, I will thank you all and leave you alone. If she cannot, then I'm afraid I'll have to inform my business partner, the original purchaser of those children, and tell him I ran into a problem. I am always willing to make bargains. He, on the other hand, is brother to the king and not very forgiving."

"Are you threatening us?" Colin hisses, his hands curling into fists. I am frozen with fear, digesting the fact that the king's brother was the buyer the merchant spoke of. Then anger stirs up inside me again. Did that merchant ever intend to sell Rollo to me? He was probably going to pocket my money and leave me with nothing.

I almost laugh at the ridiculousness of feeling outraged at nearly being double-crossed by the man I stole from.

At the same time, Nana shoots Colin a look and he backs down. She pulls out one of her daggers, tracing her fingers along its tip. "Sorry for the interruption. Colin is young. Please explain. In detail."

Nana has a way of speaking that calls the truth out of other people. My mother once told me that certain Oluso were granted the power of truth. Their words encouraged people to reveal their darkest desires and hidden shame. They could ask a person to do something and the person would comply, but only if that act was what the person truly wanted. Their power lay in revealing men's hearts rather than control. Nana does not possess this power, but having the ability to see future possibilities gives her the confidence to act as though she does. And if Lord Ekwensi is what he says he is—what our eyes say he is—he would know of such powers . . . and perhaps not know if Nana had them.

"Certainly. It's simple: I have no desire to harm the children you are harboring, or any of you. I need something I'm certain this young woman is capable of getting for me. As I said, I suggest we enter into a deal. I will forget about this little incident, and promise you future protection, and in return, Dèmi will help me."

The sound of my name on his lips sends a chill up my spine, but his words echo in my mind. If I retrieve what this man wants, can he really guarantee that my family will be safe? I look to the guards standing at the door. They are silent, faces blank like statues carved in stone. The three of them are strikingly different; one with tawny skin and light brown hair, another with a pinkish face and blond wisps tucked behind his ears, the last with brown skin and nappy, coily hair. Oddly, however, they look the same. There is something beyond the gold-and-purple uniforms they wear, perhaps the way they all stand at attention, hands resting on their sword hilts. Or the emptiness in their expressions, the strange way in which they look through the room as though unseeing.

"Why do you want her help specifically? Why not ask someone else? Surely, there must be someone who can retrieve whatever it is you want. You're a regional lord," Colin says, his forehead crinkled.

"The answer to that is also simple," Ekwensi says. "I am a poor judge of character and an even poorer believer in men. I only trust what my eyes can see. You understand that, with my history, this is only natural. I don't make decisions lightly, but when I make them, I find it hard to be dissuaded." He pulls something out of his coat, a long, thin cone with a glass attached at the end and golden filigree decorating it—a spyglass. "I made a decision after seeing your friend through this. While our ship was bearing upon her and she was stranded, she displayed great control of her magic and used it to create a massive fog. The control she expressed in that dire situation led me to believe that she's the right person for this job. I've met many of our kind over the years, and not many have control of their abilities the way our young Dèmi here does."

His words are silky, slipping into my mind as easily as thread weaving into cloth. A warm rush of pride fills my breast, rising like the festival balloons the city artisans make for the small children. Then I see Will's troubled expression and the balloon in my chest bursts, fear and mistrust consuming the falling pieces.

"You're blackmailing us," I say in a muted voice. "Help you or risk being outed to the king's brother. That's the only simple thing about all this." Ekwensi just stands there, and his silence is all the confirmation I need. "There's one thing I'd like to understand, though," I continue. "What exactly is it that you want so badly but can't get yourself?"

"I can help you," Colin interjects. "Surely if you were watching before, you know what magic I have. I could go in her stead. It doesn't *have* to be her."

"Thank you, but I am uninterested in your offer. If mere teleportation was all that was needed, I could hire someone . . . less likely to attract attention."

Colin's jaw hardens, but he looks away, a shadow in his gaze.

"Colin is right. Why me? What can I do that he can't?"

Ekwensi sighs, and the sound is heavy, a tree giving out under the strain of a storm, groaning as it catapults to its death. He walks over to me and Colin, circling until he's at my side.

"When I first saw you," he starts, tracing a finger along, but not quite touching, my face, "I saw that wild look in your eyes, the one you have on now." I flinch, and he grins, dropping his hands. "The look of a dog who refuses to run with a pack, someone who knows what it's like to be betrayed. I thought you were observant, wise, adaptable. I thought that we were similar in that regard, but it seems I was wrong."

"You look at me and see a *dog*?" I protest, but he ignores me.

"There is a provincial election in two weeks, at the end of the winter festival. The king will appoint one of his regional lords to take charge of all of Oyo, or at least, what's left of it. I want to win that right. Right now, as a regional lord, I only have power over my jurisdiction and I have to report to some of the other lords every month. If you recall, there have been no raids in the Ogun area this year. I convinced the king that the people in my area would help his agenda if he let me, someone who looks like most of them, have a position of power. That way, they would not feel that their heritage was being taken from them. I did this to save what few Oluso I could. *If* I win the king's approval in the next few weeks, and he grants me leadership of Oyo, I can help save what is left of our people, and give all Oyo a voice in the royal council at Eingard."

I consider quickly. There is a rumor that there were no raids in the Ogun area this year, but I dismissed it as misinformation at best or a ploy to entrap unsuspecting Oluso at worst. It is true, as well, that right now the people of Oyo have no voice in the Eingardian council. It wasn't always that way, though.

When my grandmother was in power eighteen years before, there was a council of twelve. The council was tasked with guiding the decisions of the ruler of Ifé, and sometimes overriding those decisions if need be. Three people were selected from the four regions to make twelve.

I hear Mummy's voice in my head now, recounting those days. "It was wonderful, Dèmi. Our ancestors believed that Olorun desired balance, so the council was created. Of the twelve, there had to be an elder, someone who had seen and tasted all of life, and a young one, someone new to the throes of it. One person had to see without eyes, understand without ears, and speak without a voice. Half the council were women and half men. One member had many children, and another none."

"But if one person couldn't talk, how would that be fair? How could they say anything?" I asked her then.

She'd smiled a knowing smile. "The ruler of Ifé has the responsibility to treat all peoples justly. Olorun gave them that position for a reason. Many move through the world without need for sight. There are languages for those who cannot hear. Our ruler was to respect all the council members, and listen to them equally. That was the point of the council, to be mirrors so that our queen would always make the right decisions and leave none unforgotten."

"And did she? Always?"

The memory fades as someone brushes against my fingers. I look into Colin's concerned eyes. "Are you all right?"

"Thinking," I say quickly. I turn my attention back to Lord Ekwensi. What he wants is ambitious—perhaps impossible—but in a way, he is right. Since Alistair Sorenson became king, the royal council has been perverted. Ten men and two women from wealthy families, all Sorenson's allies, and all Eingardians—save one, and that member not Oyo—are the new council now.

"And will you?" I ask Lord Ekwensi. "Will you really be a voice for all of us?"

He nods solemnly. "I told you, I don't trust others. I do what I can when I can. I want to do more. I want to help our people, and maybe by doing this, I help someone from Goma as well win a position in the council, and maybe a Berréan who isn't so obviously in Sorenson's pocket."

Colin's hand tightens on my shoulder, but I am looking at Nana, at the slight turn of her mouth, the only break in her impenetrable mask. I know what she is thinking. She moved from southern Goma to marry Will nine years ago, and four years after that, the provincial lords limited border access to certain people they considered problematic. Being one half of a mixed marriage branded Nana a problem. There are times now, when I see her holding Haru with a faraway look in her eyes, that I know she is wondering whether her child will ever meet her grandparents. I think of the words she gave me earlier today, that I would have to make a choice. At first I thought that choice was to save Rollo and Amina, but now I know the truth. My choice is here.

I have to help Lord Ekwensi.

Not only to protect everyone in this room and those hidden upstairs but also to give Haru back the rest of her family. I won't have her heritage stolen from her the way mine was taken from me. And while Lord Ekwensi can't promise that he can make such changes, a world without him on the council has no chance at all.

"What do I need to get for you?" I ask, the words tumbling out in a rush. With this simple thing, I can rewrite history. I can make my mother proud and protect the people dearest to me.

"Wait—no. When did we agree to this? At least let me—" Colin protests.

"It's not what but whom," Ekwensi interrupts, smiling, even white teeth stark against his dark mustache and beard. "The king's nephew will be arriving at Benin Palace tomorrow. He is to tour the area before going south to Ikolé and Abeokuta. I want you to get hold of him and bring him to me. Once he's in my possession, I will return him to the king unharmed. The king, naturally, will reward my help with the provincial position."

"You want her to *kidnap* someone?" Will says, his face going red.

"This just sounds impossible *and* illegal," Colin adds. "Do you think you can fool us into doing something that will get us killed?"

I ignore them, focusing on Lord Ekwensi. There is a hidden passion there, in the way his eyes are drinking me in as though I will disappear, and the attention is enough to make my stomach knot up. Before I even understand why, I say, "I'll do it. Tell me what I need to know."

His smile widens all the more, even as Colin yells at me, "Dèmi, you can't do this!" My friend grabs my shoulders. "Think for a second what you're agreeing to. You know we can't give our word lightly. What if this is a trap?"

I shake him off. I'm not doing this lightly—I haven't done anything lightly for the last nine years.

"If this is a trap, then I deserve to die for being so stupid." I look past him to Nana. "You told me I had to make a choice today. This is it. I'm saying yes." I flip back to Lord Ekwensi. "You promise that you'll really do the things you say?"

He offers me his hand. "I give you my word. As long as you hold up your end of the bargain, I'll leave you and your family and the children alone. As for the council, I can't guarantee I can change everyone's mind—especially the king's—but I *will* always be an advocate for our people. And," he says with a wry smile, "if I betray you, you can always hunt me down and kill me. Even right now, my guards and I are less powerful than all of you in this room. You hold the power."

I nod, not quite believing his self-disparagement, knowing that his assurance doesn't really matter. We're backed into a corner and we must act. I turn to Will. He is silent, mouth pressed in a grim line, pure anguish on his face. I know, too, that he has considered things like I have, and that he saw the hope in Nana's face. Finally, he nods and says, "I don't know, Abidèmi, but it's your choice to make."

I stiffen. Will is angry, or he would not have used that name. Yet once the word came off his lips, it was all the fire I needed to offer my hand and shake Lord Ekwensi's outstretched one.

Abidèmi. The meaning is cruel, but definite: A girl born without a father. The name my mother gave to sever my destiny from my father's.

If I'm being truthful, my father is the real reason I have to go through all this. My father not only gave Alistair Sorenson an excuse to start the war but guaranteed his victory. The Oluso, once hailed as Olorun's messengers on Earth, are slaves beholden to every Aje whim because of my father's cruelty. I will not give up Will, the only father I've ever known, and the people I love because of my father's mistakes. If there's even the smallest chance that Tobias Ekwensi can lessen the suffering he caused, I will honor this deal.

And, if not . . .

Well, he already offered an answer to that.

Lord Ekwensi bows over my hand, brushing his lips over my fingers. The expression is so Eingardian that I jerk away, drawing my stinging fingers to the safety of my chest.

"Excellent," he says, chuckling.

But as the word echoes in the room, and crawls into me, I try to squash the still, small voice whispering that I may have made a giant mistake. It's too late to turn back though.

TREASON

"I'm going with you," Colin says. He's perched on the window seat like a bird of prey, his hulking frame swallowing the rays of the late afternoon sun.

I ignore him, focusing on the things spread out on my cot. Cloth sack, medicine packet, winter cloak, my hunting knife, and the letter Ekwensi gave me last night. Satisfied, I pack them neatly into the leather satchel Nana gifted me for my name day two years before.

"Let me help you. We can't just trust Lord Ekwensi. What if things don't go according to plan?"

I laugh. "Of course I can't trust him." But I keep packing.

I stop, though, fingers on my hunting knife, letting the iciness of the metal cut into my skin. Even though I don't trust Ekwensi fully, the plan is relatively simple and there's no reason to take this along if things unfold as planned. Benin Palace is on the outer edge of the city, away from the main market. All I have to do is present Ekwensi's letter to one of the palace guards, then take my place as a maid for the winter festival opening celebration the palace is hosting. Once I'm inside, it shouldn't be too difficult to spike the prince's food with the kanuwort in my satchel and let the bitter medicine take its toll. A sleeping prince will be easy to gather into a sack and smuggle out before the guards even know he is gone, and no one will notice a lowly Oyo-born maid wheeling soiled cloth out of the palace gates—not when there are thousands of us running our fingers ragged, trying to prepare for the festival in time. No need for violence or bloodshed, no need for my knife.

Still, I slip it into the satchel.

Two arms wrap around my waist and Colin's breath tickles the skin behind my ear. "Dèmi, just let me help you. Let *someone* help you for once. You don't have to do this alone."

I stiffen, and in an instant his warmth leaves my back. He tosses himself on the bed in nonchalance but the fierce look in his eyes is anything but, daring me to challenge him. "It's been years and *I* still don't have your complete trust, but you want to waste it on a stranger who is blackmailing us?"

I shake my head. "It's not that. It's—" I stop, trying to find a word to express the conflicting emotions warring in me.

All I can think of is my father, of everything I know about him, and of the kids sleeping just one room down from us, exhausted and hollowed from years of suffering. My father took away those children's futures by killing for Alistair Sorenson, but I can give it back to them.

"I don't trust Ekwensi," I repeat. "I trust that he wants to be appointed so badly that he's willing to leave his fate in my hands. I'm sure he has some kind of backup plan in case I fail, but I saw the hunger in his eyes. He wants to rule Oyo. He is willing to gamble for that."

"Yeah, but he's using *you* as the stakes."

"But we get a share of the prize should he win. I think that's worth it."

"How do you know he won't be just as bad as Alistair Sorenson?"

"He could be. But Will confirmed what he said about Ogun. It's been an Oluso safe haven for months. I don't think Lord Ekwensi would risk the king's wrath just to win my trust, do you?"

Colin scowls at me, pressing his rigid back to the wall and crossing his arms. I crawl onto the bed, stroking his cheek as I sit. "I do trust you, Col. More than you know."

His expression softens, and he reaches for my hand. I let him twine my fingers with his. "I just want to do what's best for those children," I say, "and for Will and Nana, and everyone. Can you understand?"

He sighs. "I know you're more than capable of dealing with this on your own. I just want to help a little bit, give you options."

"How can you help me?"

He rolls his eyes. "I can teleport, remember? I'm an entry and escape plan wrapped in an attractive package."

"You've never been to Benin Palace," I say. Colin's magic allows him to teleport to places he has previously visited, and to Oluso whose signs he has been exposed to.

He shrugs. "I'll find your sign. Think about it: this way, there won't be a letter linking you to the palace and things go much faster. If Ekwensi was going to betray us, we can circumvent him. It's foolproof."

I chew my bottom lip thoughtfully. "True. And if the prince proves a little troublesome or heavier than expected, you can help there too." As Oluso, we have greater physical strength and stamina than Ajes, but having Colin there to deal with the extra weight is ideal. I'll admit, too, that this is a much better plan than Ekwensi's.

I nod. "Okay, I like that. But if we aren't delivering Ekwensi's letter and meeting the planned escort, how will I know where to go in the palace?"

For a moment, I think I see panic on Colin's face, then his lips spread into a sly smile. "I know people there. There was that girl last summer's eve, the one with the dreads. You remember her."

I pull my hand from his abruptly. "Spare me the details of your conquests. But if you're certain she'll be at the palace this evening, let's get going. If Ekwensi is to be believed, the prince arrives at the palace at the end of Gull Hour."

He takes my arm, looking sheepish now. "I didn't see her again after that, I swear. I don't have feelings for her. I never have."

He moves closer, amber eyes asking a question, lips parted slightly. I'm tempted to spring up and dance away like I have so many times before, but this time something stirs in me—anger at the mention of that girl from last summer, if I'm being honest with myself—and I grab the collar of his shirt and pull him to me. I press my lips against his in a gossamer kiss. His whole body comes alive, arms snaking around my waist. I kiss him again, lingering this time, running my finger up his ear, and playing with the ornate silver cuff there, stroking the dark spiral tattoos creeping up his neck.

He deepens the kiss, licking my lip before slipping his tongue into my mouth, tasting me. I sink against him the way I have seen other girls do over the years. His heart pounds against my fingers, the heat erupting from our mouths making me flushed and dizzy. He tugs me down onto the bed, but when I push him lightly, he pulls back, hazy eyes drinking me in.

"Too fast?"

"Hmm," I mumble, stroking his chin. "Wrong time." The ache in my chest, the emptiness there, tells a different story. But I can't tell him that.

He catches my hand, pressing a kiss against my palm. "After all this, could we . . . could we try?" he asks. His eyes are earnest, so full of longing, so I respond the way I know best—by running away.

Leaning in, I kiss his cheek, then stand abruptly, disentangling myself. "I'll tell Will you're coming. You should get ready to convince your girlfriend to let us in."

"She's not my—"

I laugh, and he smiles, still breathing hard as I make my escape, no doubt hopeful we'll do this again. I hurry along the hall, praying he didn't notice that my heart sat like a stone in my chest while his trembled at my fingertips. I don't believe in love or, at least, I don't believe I am capable of the kind Colin wants. He dreams of becoming Oluso mates like Will and Nana, and I don't have the heart to tell him I already know he isn't mine.

It's not something I've told anyone. I know, though, that every Oluso born has a spirit mate, another Oluso who bonds with them on a deeper level. When I first heard of this I was horrified, angry that the choice of my future mate—if I decided to take one—was already made for me. Will and Nana explained that it was different, that Olorun bonded two spirits that would resonate with each other. There is no choosing what your mate will be like—their skin color, gender, background. And in this, there is true beauty. Being from Eingard didn't stop Will from finding and falling for Nana, even though most Eingardians—despite also shunning him for having Oyo blood—would look down on his choice. Will is passionate and brash while Nana is fierce and intuitive, but the love they have for each other is in their every movement—the joy when their eyes meet, the way they glide together when they walk. As mates, they also share a mental bond, one that allows them to communicate without words and share experiences with the other person through their eyes. Growing up with them meant never knowing when Will was listening in to my conversations with Nana, and vice versa, but it was something I envied all the same.

I once wished I would one day meet my mate. Then I learned about my father, of how my mother was drawn to him because he was her mate. I stopped making wishes that day.

I'm still not sure if I want a mate. But I know if I am supposed to feel special around them—to *know* that they are my person—then I am certain of one thing.

Colin isn't the one.

I knock lightly on Will and Nana's door, and it creaks open. I find them sitting on the edge of their bed, an empty chair directly in front of them as if they expected me. I take my place in the chair and cross my arms, hugging myself.

"Colin wants to come along. It'll give me another option. He can get me in and out."

Nana speaks first. "Good," she says nodding. "I was going to suggest that. Or ask you to take Will along."

Will, like Colin, has Madsen blood. He can perform the same teleportation magic, and he has a better grasp of magic and greater stamina. Still, I refuse. Colin knows what he's getting into. He volunteered to go along. If Will comes instead and anything happens to him, I won't be able to live with myself.

"I'm not so sure," Will says. "Colin has been stable of late, but he could always—"

"He won't," I interrupt. "His magic *is* under control."

Teleportation magic requires complete attention to avoid accidents. The more people being teleported, the more magic and focus required. The risk of severing a limb or accidentally killing a loved one is too high. Colin's magical control is great. But in the last year he's had flare-ups, moments where his magic is unpredictable. Last summer, he materialized bleeding, toenails and trousers missing. Since then we've been afraid. His toenails grew back though.

"Colin and I will be perfectly fine," I continue, feeling protective of my best friend. Colin has worked so hard. Hearing this doubt, especially from his mentor, would crush him. "It's a simple job," I repeat.

"I'm not so sure about that," Nana says, worry creasing her

brow. "I've been a little uneasy since Lord Ekwensi left yesterday. I don't know if it's just nerves or a sign, but I had a dream last night. I saw you walking alone on a long road. There was a shadow behind you, matching your every step, but when I looked closer I couldn't see its face." She takes my hands. "Dèmi, you have to be careful. I know you don't like it when we say this, but you are our family. You're the child Will and I were fortunate to have sent to us. Don't forget that."

There are soft tears in her eyes, and that more than anything else makes me afraid. I expect an emotional display like this more from Will, but Nana showing me this side of herself is something else altogether. I squeeze her hands. "I'll be okay, I promise."

Will looks as though he wants to say something else, but he sighs and asks, "Do you have everything?"

I take my satchel out of the hidden pocket at the bottom of my long iro skirt. My tar-colored blouse and skirt will help me blend into the darkness once the palace evening festivities are in full swing.

He nods approval and pulls out a bracelet. It's beautiful, with glistening cowry shells like the other bracelets adorning my wrists. There is a single shell with a blue tint, and I know before I touch it that ice coats the surface.

"It will take too long to track your sign if you run into trouble. If you're in danger, smash this bead. I will come to you immediately."

I rub my fingers against the smooth shells. "This must have taken a lot of energy to make."

Which is when I finally notice the dark circles beneath his eyes, the slackness in his cheeks. He must have stayed up all last night to make this. Infusing physical materials with magic requires the crafter to put a bit of themselves into the item, especially if the magic is supposed to last a while. This bracelet is worth a day of Will's life.

Will smiles, spilling dirty-blond hair onto his forehead. "Haven't made something that delicate in a while, so it was good practice if nothing else. You'll sleep better wearing it. Nightmares don't last forever."

I slip the bracelet onto my wrist. "Thank you," I say, spreading my arms wide. Will and Nana exchange a look, then they are on their feet, embracing me.

"If I had known making you jewelry would get you to accept hugs, I would have done it a long time ago," Will says as I pull away, smiling fondly. "Come back to us safely."

"I'll try."

A few hours later, I am on the road with Colin walking toward the edge of the city as the sun slips from the sky. As the hot ground becomes cold and dry, and the last bits of orange-pink light are swallowed up by darkness, the palace comes into sight. Its white walls shine eerily in the darkness, and the gold figures etched onto them look like shadows. The golden lion statues on each side of the gates seem larger than usual, their eyes glistening in the moonlight, their mouths wide and jeering. I half expect them to come alive and swallow the guards beside them. There are lanterns shining beyond those gates, swinging to and fro in the wind, lighting the way for palace guests who are either wealthy or well-connected enough to be invited to the opening ceremony for the winter festival.

We keep walking past the main gates, hanging along the wall until we are at the side of the palace. We slip into one of the thick side hedges and watch. Once I am certain no one is about, I turn to Colin. "Where to, comrade?"

"Zara is waiting by the back well."

"And you're sure she'll help? Didn't you break her heart?"

"I never break their hearts," he says with a grin. "If anything, I just leave them wanting more." I roll my eyes, and he goes on. "Once we're through, she'll take us to the servants' passage in the main hall. The prince's rooms are one floor up from there."

"Okay. I'll go straight to the kitchen and work from there. If someone spots me out or anything goes wrong, I want you to leave. Get out and warn Will."

Colin narrows his eyes. "I thought we discussed this. I'm not leaving you behind."

"*You* discussed it. I said no such thing." I grab his arms and close my eyes. "Let's go."

He hisses but does not push any further. Within seconds, there is a light fluttering in my stomach, and I brace myself as my limbs begin to tingle. A breeze brushes the back of my neck, and I barely tighten my fingers on Colin's arms before we are moving, gliding through the air. We hit the ground moments later, and I lie there, grateful for the solid, heavy feeling of the earth beneath me. Those twinkling lanterns are dancing before my eyes, and it takes a minute before I can reconcile the patches in my vision with the colorful cloth festooning the courtyard trees.

A figure darts out from behind a round stone well, catching Colin by the waist, and he topples to the ground, tangled with it. I jerk up, ready to help, but Colin has already flipped his assailant over and has their hands imprisoned beneath his. The figure gives a soft, tinkling laugh and I move closer. It's a girl with long, dreaded hair spread out beneath her and skin so dark it looks blue. Her glowing eyes make her look otherworldly, as beautiful as an Aziza queen.

"I knew you would come back," she whispers in a deep, silky voice. "People don't leave me. I leave them."

Colin flashes a quick glance at me before pulling the girl to her feet. "We can talk later, Zara," he says. "Can you take us where we're supposed to go?"

Zara appraises me with a quick look. Then she smirks. "Business first. I'll take you to the kitchens. We can shack"—she pauses, licking her lips—"I mean catch up after. Dinner is starting. If we don't hurry, you won't get paid. Coin's good tonight. One lira to every servant who does a good job."

Colin whistles. "I can see why you stay on here."

She shrugs. "The head cook is nice to us because she knows she can't make the kind of magic we do in the kitchen. All she knows is how to make Eingardian meals. Thin soups, bread, you know. The officials these days want stew or periwinkle soup or yam pottage. She doesn't know the difference between a coco yam and an overgrown potato."

She says this all to Colin, barely sparing a glance for me, which is fine—the less she remembers of me, the better. She picks up a wooden bucket and beckons us to follow her. Colin reaches to take the bucket from her, but she smacks his hand—playfully, nauseatingly—away. We cross the courtyard at a brisk pace. There are several buildings, all made from stone and varying in size. We head through a rusted door into the largest one. We walk quickly along a corridor passing several people as we go. There are young women like me, dressed similarly in dark skirts and blouses, running up and down the corridor with different items. There are plenty of men, too, decked out in white shirts paired with black vests, dark trousers, and boots.

Zara bumps her hip against another girl balancing a tray with porcelain cups on it. The girl sways slightly, then flings out a hand to catch a falling cup without taking her eyes off Zara's face. "What is it? I don't have time to play with you. The prince wants to dine in his room alone tonight. He's feeling ill. Madam is pulling me from the main room to serve him," she whispers.

Zara twists her plump lips into a pout. "Sorry, Nne. Just testing you. Anyway, Nneka, I need a favor. These two are new. The girl has a thing for royalty and she's dying for a look at the prince. Why don't you pawn him off on her?"

I shoot Colin a look. Since when did I have a professed obsession with royalty? He tugs at his shirt collar and looks away.

"The boy is useful for *many* things," Zara continues with a lascivious smile. "I can find something for him to do if you don't have anything."

Nneka glances at us briefly, then nods. "I'll take both of them actually. The prince's tray is about to be sent up, so it's perfect timing. Madam also wants extra firewood delivered upstairs."

Zara runs her finger against Colin's cheek. "I'll see you later tonight?" Before he can answer, she moves closer to me. "A little advice? Don't overstep. Even if the prince does taste you, his councilors will make sure anything that comes out of it dies. His father hates half-castes."

She flounces away, hips swinging from side to side, confident as a queen having instructed her servant. My cheeks are burning, and my heart hurts, but I try to forget the insult I just received. Even in the days of the old kingdom, there were women who would sleep with lords and generals in hopes of having a child and becoming Seconds, powerful concubines who were well provided for but never publicly acknowledged. Now, with Eingardians holding most of the power, more children whose parents hail from different regions— called half-castes by blood purists—are being born. The only thing worse than a half-caste in Alistair Sorenson's kingdom are Oluso, and not by much. At least, in his eyes, a half-caste's appearance can be explained away, but an Oluso's tainted blood will manifest itself in magic sooner or later.

Colin bristles. "She has the tongue of a serpent. I forgot about that."

Nneka raises an eyebrow. "I don't have time for whatever drama you think you're part of. This isn't a masquerade or time to satisfy some fantasy. If you're here to work, follow me." I mean to protest but realize it doesn't matter. If I do as Nneka says, we should be able to finish this quickly and quietly.

She walks into the room on the right and we follow suit. The room is large, with several grates built into the wall. Several women kneel over basins filled with water, washing plates. Others hover around the long, wooden table in the middle of the room. The table is filled with food, the smell of roasting duck smothering the air.

A red-faced, gray-haired woman wearing a large apron hustles over. "Nneka, what's this? The prince will have been waiting ages by now. You were supposed to pull the tea things and go upstairs immediately."

Nneka drops in a curtsy, and her voice raises several octaves in pitch as she addresses the woman. "I'm sorry, Madam. I have the tea ready to go, but you were feeling exhausted, so I went and got some extra help. This girl will go up with the prince's food, and the boy will help stock more firewood."

The woman barely glances at us. She fans the air in front of her face. "Thank you, Nneka. You're always so diligent. I think I'll have a sit now. Too much standing is bad for my back."

"Of course, Madam. Please rest. Leave the work to us."

Nneka sets her tray down and pulls me to the table. She places a bowl of garden egg stew on the tray, then adds some eba, a skewer full of roasted suya, and another plate filled with golden-crusted coconut cake. The smell of the roasted, peppered meat on the skewer makes my stomach tumble, and I nearly pinch myself when she adds a small bowl full of chin-chin, the crunchy breadlike balls Mummy used to make me as a snack.

She hands me the tray, staring me in the eyes. "Upstairs, third door on the left. Six guards at the door. You can't miss it."

I turn to go and she catches my sleeve. "If anything is gone from this tray, I will know." She waves at Colin. "You, come this way."

Cold air brushes my cheeks as I leave the stifling warmth of the kitchen and make my way down the corridor. I follow the stairs I find at the end and make my way onto the next floor. The second floor is beautiful, with lavish scenes painted on the walls and a red carpet winding down the corridor. On the landing, I look around before pouring the kanuwort into the stew and stirring it with my finger. When I reach the prince's room, I lower my head and curtsy, holding the tray out in front. One of the guards waves a hand and another opens the door for me. Just like that I pass in, keeping my head low. Like with Zara ignoring me, the fewer people who remember me, the better.

A man asks, "What is it?"

A large bed laden with several pillows takes up most of the space in the room. There is a wooden screen in the corner to the left of it. To the right, there is an alcove with curtains shrouding it leading out to a balcony, and next to that alcove, a young man sits at a desk, his back to me. The light emanating from the small candle by his arm makes his long, fair hair look like wrought gold. It casts a shadow against the wall, and I watch his shadowy fingers dance about, scribbling something. Then the hands stop, and the muscular back tenses up.

"What is it?" the young man asks again, turning slightly.

"My lord . . . my prince . . . I-I have your dinner," I stammer out. Inwardly, I curse myself. What did people call the prince these days? I have no servant etiquette or preparatory knowledge to speak of. Downstairs, I briefly considered asking Nneka, but I didn't want her asking too many questions in return.

The chair scrapes back, and the prince stands, but I keep the tray in front of me and stare at the ground. Soft hands brush against mine as he takes the tray. "Thank you. You may go," he says, retreating to the desk. His voice is familiar, deep, but soft like a breezy wind washing over me. Where have I heard it before?

I cough as he sets the food down and starts writing again. "My prince, I have been instructed to stay with you. The palace maids are busy attending to the rest of the preparations for the ceremony, and the head cook doesn't want you to wait for anything."

"There is no need for that. I'll go down to the kitchen if I want anything. I want some peace and quiet, so please leave."

I stare blankly. What kind of prince offers to serve himself? Alistair Sorenson is notorious for refusing to mix with those he considers lowly born. Perhaps his nephew is no different. I inch closer, catching a glimpse of small rows of loopy handwriting, no more than seven words to a line. Is he writing poetry?

Suddenly, the prince turns, catching my wrist with one hand, the other hand spread flat against the paper, concealing it. The candlelight flickers. His eyes are dark in the faded light, his face unsmiling. "It's a capital offense to spy on personal communications, especially royal missives. If you don't want to get in trouble, leave. Do you understand?"

"Yes, my—" I stop as the candlelight flares brightly once again and his icy blue eyes come into focus. I know these eyes. Nine years could not erase them from my mind, and now, seeing them once again, I feel a familiar twisting in my chest. The instant joy that leaps up inside me gives way to smoldering anger, and before I can stop myself, I spit out, "It's also a capital offense to commit murder, but here we are."

He stands so abruptly that I almost lose my balance. His grip tight on my wrist, he eyes me suspiciously. "If you intend to kill me, you should have struck. There are six guards outside. All I have to do is call out. You'll be dead in seconds."

He's much taller than I remember, taller even than Will, and his shoulders have broadened with time. The once-slim body that occupied my mother's cot is now lithe and muscular. I lift my chin, glaring up at him. "Call them then, because there's no way you're leaving this room in one piece."

To my surprise, he shoves me away, stalking to the curtains. His brow furrowed, he looks at me with anguished eyes. "Please, whoever you are, leave. I've no desire to get you killed. I understand that you may have grievances with my uncle, but I am not him. You're young. You've a whole life to live. Don't ruin it by coming after me. Go. I won't mention this to anyone. Leave as quickly as you can."

The sliver of excitement that grew in me dies as I realize he has no idea who I am. For nine years, I have thought about Jonas, wondered who he really was and how exactly he got involved in destroying my life. I often wondered if he thought about me at all, or cared if that little girl he knew died. I have my answer now.

I shake my head. "You expect me to fall for that? The moment I walk out of here you'll set the guards to hunt me. I trusted you once, I won't do it again."

"Again?"

I spy it then, a small ring hanging from the cord around his neck—my father's ring.

"You were always so good at taking others' things."

I run at him, evading his arms and striking him in the stomach with a quick jab. He doubles over, gasping, and I slam my elbow into his back, knocking him to the floor. Grunting, he scrambles to his knees, but I am faster. Drawing my knife from my hidden pocket, I straddle him and press it to his neck.

"Who are you? What do you want?" he asks, breathing hard.

With one swift motion, I slip the knife under the cord dangling from his neck and cut it, sending the ring into my waiting palm. "I'm the rightful owner of this ring."

His eyes widen, and his face pales. "Dèmi?"

He breathes my name, and my heart explodes. The sound of my name on his lips makes me want to smile, to rejoice that he remembers me, even after all this time. I squash those confusing feelings. Instead I press my hand against his cheek and hiss, "You don't deserve to say that name," then bring up the hilt of my knife and slam it against the back of his head. He slumps onto the floor.

Fingers trembling, I put my ear to his chest, listening until I hear the pounding drum of his heart, then I curse myself for the flood of relief that springs up in me. The rage that drove me to strike him is extinguished almost as soon as it came. Blood is spilling out behind his head, so I cradle him in my arms and press my fingers against the wound, pouring my magic into it. Within seconds, the bleeding stops. Shifting out from under him, I take a pillow from the bed and put it under his head. I won't give Jonas the satisfaction of dying an easy death, not after what he did to me and Mummy.

Quickly, I scan the room, considering my options. Colin is to meet me in a half hour, the allotted time it would take the kanuwort to work, and there is no way of telling him things have gone wrong. Jonas will wake up soon, and then the situation will be out of my control. If he calls out, I'll have to fight the guards, and the whole plan will go to ashes and smoke. I need to get him out of here on my own.

Pulling the cloth sack from my skirt, I lay it out beside him. The sack is a few inches short, but he will fit if I bunch up his knees. I stretch my hand and green fire springs out, curling like vines growing on a wall, securing his arms and legs. He stirs, moving sluggishly, blinking as he tries to bring the world into focus.

When he meets my eyes again, I am standing over him, finger to my lips. "Be absolutely quiet. I don't intend to kill you just now, but you might force my hand by calling out. I'd certainly have to kill your guards, and I'm sure you're 'noble' enough to not want that either. Do you understand?"

"What do you want with me?" he asks in a muted voice.

I kneel until my face is close to his. "There are lot of things I'm thinking about right now, so until I decide what to do, I suggest you stay silent."

His eyes are soft, pleading as he says, "Dèmi, I didn't mean for what happened to your mother to happen. I never—"

I clench my fist and the vines tighten around him. His face grows flushed as he struggles to breathe. "Don't call my name," I growl. "And don't talk about my mother. You don't have that right."

"What the hell are you doing?"

I fling myself around, and Jonas sucks in air as the vines slacken their hold. Colin stands a few feet away, face tense with horror. He seizes my arm. "Dèmi, this isn't the plan. We're to capture him, not torture him. What happened?"

"Why are you here so early?"

"That's not important. What's going on?"

"Drastic measures. He didn't eat the food. It's a good thing you came. We need to get out of here. Now."

A loud knock comes at the door, followed by a guard's voice. "My liege, may I enter? Lord Kairen is here. He wishes to know how you're doing."

Colin and I share a quick glance, then he swipes the cloth sack from the floor. "Let's go. Leave him."

I shake my head. "I'm not leaving here without him. If we go now, we *all* go."

Colin wipes his palms against his shirt. "I need a moment. Can't concentrate."

"I thought you had that under control."

"I'm trying," he snarls. "Not all of us have stellar focus. One moment."

The knock comes again. "My liege? Are you all right?"

Colin reaches for my hand. "Forget it, let me take you. Can't do three people right now."

I step away, mind working quickly, my attention on Jonas. "You said you didn't want me hurt. Prove it. Ask the guard to go away. If you want to get out of this alive and you don't want anyone killed, help me," I whisper softly. I wave a hand and the binds that restrain him melt into the air.

He stares, those eyes considering me as though I have transformed into something inhuman. For a moment, he says nothing as the pounding on the door increases. The guard calls again: "My liege, if you can hear us, please respond or we will be forced to enter without your leave."

"Dèmi, leave him. Please. Forget the mission," Colin begs.

I should leave with Colin right now, give up on this foolish gamble and hide with everyone I love. But then we'd be running forever. I'm tired of running.

"Will you do it or not?" I hiss, yanking Jonas by the collar.

His mouth settles into a grim smile. "I could, for a promise."

"You're not exactly in a position to negotiate."

"I'm in a little bit of a position, I'd think. So I won't do it unless you promise."

Barely holding my anger, I snarl, "What do you want?"

His smile gives way to a solemn look. "Don't abandon me. No matter what happens to me from this moment, you must be there. Even if I get killed, be my witness, from beginning to end."

My lips are dry, and my chest hurts as though I've just received a blow. This promise is too intimate, like vows soldiers sworn to each other take before entering the battlefield. "Why?"

"Do you agree or not?"

"No. She doesn't. We're going," Colin says, hand firm on my wrist. "Dèmi, let go of him."

The guard shouts, "My liege, we're coming in."

Shoving both men off, I slash my left palm. Jonas sits up, pressing my bleeding palm to his heart. His eyes are full of wonder, and something else—relief. Then as the door swings open, he edges closer, erasing the gap between us. His lips are on mine, his free hand tangled in my hair and my bleeding hand concealed between our writhing bodies.

There are several polite coughs, then a quiet "Excuse me, my liege, I did not know you were . . . occupied."

Jonas pulls away and I try to breathe through the hot air brushing my neck and face. The streaks of blood on his soft, white tunic have left a patched stain right above his heart, a gruesome badge marking the promise we made.

He faces the intruder. "Do I need your permission for things like this—" He stops, half-lidded dreamy expression fading to tight attention in an instant.

Another voice swims into the room. One I'd hoped to never hear again. "Well, well, well. Your uncle and I *were* getting worried. I sent you my prettiest guard, hoped you would take a liking to him. But it seems you've finally chosen a lover after all."

Mari.

Please don't recognize me. Walk away, I silently beg.

She steps closer, but Jonas is faster, jumping to his feet, blocking me from view. "I'd like some privacy, Mari. Must you disrupt this too?" His tone smacks of genuine annoyance, but that doesn't stop the fear strangling my heart. We've played this game before.

Her footsteps cease. "Apologies, my liege. I was *merely* curious." As she turns to go, I dart a quick glance, catching a glimpse of a flowing, lavender silk dress and the ornate hilts of the two jagged daggers fastened to her hips.

Did Jonas actually help me?

The thought dies as Mari whips around, palming both hilts. "My liege, you must be quicker." She shifts, grinning at me. "Hello, darling. Grown up now, are we?"

Everything happens at once. Colin leaps out from behind the screen, knife raised, and collides with Mari, blade to blade, setting off a shower of sparks. I roll back to my feet, summoning the vines in time to catch Jonas as he runs to Mari's side, then I call the wind spirits, forming a wind wall at the doorway as a man runs up.

"Your Highness," he shouts, but his words seem far away, drowned in a torrent of wind.

"I see you've learned some new tricks," Mari huffs, punctuating each word with stabs at Colin.

Forming my windblade, I twist to block the dagger she thrusts inches from Colin's stomach.

"I see you're still alive," I spit defiantly.

Suddenly she drops low, knocking me to the floor with a sweeping kick. Colin tumbles past her, momentum propelling him forward.

"Dèmi!" he screams, but in that second he's distracted, she slams her elbow into his neck, driving him into the wooden screen. I scramble as she bears down on me again, punching me in the belly.

"Mari, stop!" Jonas yells. "We have use for them." The vines shake violently as my magic flares out of control, flinging him against his desk. He lands on top, knocking over the candelabra and a flurry of papers.

She grins. "Still feeling soft, my liege?"

I bring my windblade up, and she catches it in one hand, face burning red as the magic tears into her skin. The shock of her touch on my blade, like fingers prying into my very soul, shakes me. I lose control, windblade dissolving, and she backhands me. I collapse, cheek smarting, blood and dust filling my mouth.

"You need to learn the appropriate time for force and mercy. This is mercy," she finishes.

Colin rises to his knees. "You call this kindness?" he spits, wiping the blood from his mouth. Mari glances at him, smile widening as though she's been handed a gift.

I shift my fingers and the lantern behind her rises into the air.

She cackles, "Two for one today. It's as they say—you find what you're seeking in the most unusual of places."

The lantern flies at her. She turns to block it, both arms up, and I spring, kicking her in the knee as Colin slams into her back. As she topples forward, I spin out of the way, catching Colin by the arm.

"Can you—"

"Hold on tight," he finishes, not needing to hear my request.

I hold Jonas's arm and the vines unravel as he sucks in air. Colin completes the circle, taking his other arm as Mari growls, lunging at us. Lightness grows in my stomach, and my vision gets hazy as Colin's magic swirls, pulling us through the very fabric of the world into another place. As we disappear, I close my eyes, ignoring the questions I see in Colin's. I focus instead on killing the thought swimming in my mind—the sensations that didn't go away even after Mari attacked—the memory of the way my heart raced when Jonas had me in his arms. Lights and sound dance through me, and I lose all sense of myself, but that constant thought keeps me anchored, reminding me that when Jonas kissed me, my body reacted before I could think—and I kissed him back.

BARGAINING

I groan as I tumble onto rocks littering the forest floor. There is a throbbing ache in my left knee and the fresh cuts on my arms and face sting in the chilly night wind. Cursing, I wobble onto shaky legs, sore all over. A wall of trees stands before me, thick trunks blocking out the moon's pale light, branches long and tangled like a fisherman's net, waiting to trap unsuspecting creatures.

"Colin?" I shout, panic seizing me.

"Here," he coughs.

He stands gingerly, using the tree he landed next to for support. "Limbs intact. You?"

I rush to him, throwing my arms around him. "That's not funny." I turn, wincing at the sharp pain in my belly. "Where's Jonas?"

"Up here," Jonas calls. I squint overhead and spot him, legs splayed awkwardly on either side of a thick branch, arms secured by my magic vines. He blows a leaf out of his long, blond hair. "Would love to get down. I don't think this branch is sturdy."

"Or you're heavy, and the poor branch is trying its best," Colin says, glaring as though he could burn Jonas alive with his gaze.

I wave a hand, and the vines shift, depositing Jonas softly on the ground.

"I wish you'd dropped him," Colin says. "He needs a good beating. Seems no one taught him to ask before kissing someone."

I flush and change the subject. "How did you get us out of there?"

He fingers his ear cuff, a telltale sign of nervousness. "I just thought of what would happen, you know, if she'd won. I thought of what she'd do to you and my mind cleared up."

I swallow. I don't want to think about that. Had that fight gone on longer, we'd be dead. Colin and I have battle training and magic, but Mari is a killer—something we can never be. Unless we wish to die painfully.

Pushing the thoughts aside, I stretch on my toes, planting a kiss on his cheek. "Thanks, Col," I whisper, stroking my finger along the winged pattern on his earlobe, making the dangling, curved blade at the end of the cuff dance. He kisses my open palm, giving me a little lick. I start to pull back, too aware of Jonas's intense stare, then I stop. Why should it matter what he thinks?

Jonas grunts. "Sorry to interrupt, but the horns are out."

I listen, taking in my surroundings for the first time. He's right. The air rings with loud wails, a rallying cry from the horns at every guard tower in Benin. The message is clear—the hunt is on. We are the intended prey.

"If you want to make it far, we leave now. Mari will no doubt lead the chase," Jonas says. He ricochets to his feet, rolling onto his back and using the momentum to catapult himself up.

Startled, I jump. How can the rumored useless prince move like this?

Colin leans forward, hand on his dagger.

"My father believes a good king must be a good soldier," Jonas says in answer to our unasked questions. "I've had to learn all kinds of things." He saunters past me, stopping at the base of a particularly large tree. "Whenever you're ready, my lady." He smiles. "I assume you have a plan. Or do we wait for Mari to find us?"

I cover my surprise with malice. "You don't give orders here. I do." My magic flares, the vines tightening their grip on his wrists. "Now, answer carefully. Why aren't you afraid?" I snarl.

He shrugs, still wearing that infuriating smile. "Because I trust you?"

I narrow my eyes. Colin takes a menacing step. The horns grow louder, their song gleeful and triumphant, smothering the very atmosphere.

"Is that the wrong answer?" Jonas asks, seemingly nonchalant.

"This is a trap isn't it? You knew we'd be there tonight," Colin starts. "Lord—"

I clap a hand over his mouth. "Shut up. We don't know that. That would be too much for a few Oluso, don't you think?"

"But he's too calm," Colin argues. "Why isn't he frightened? The prince is a wastrel and a disappointment, right? Why does he know your name?"

Jonas pipes up. "I'm right here, you know? The disappointment? Could you at least be nice in front of me?" He pouts, but his light tone belies his expression.

I grit my teeth. "I'll explain later. Get us to the meeting point."

Suddenly, light springs from the window of the house in the field behind us, turning the giant seven-pointed leaves surrounding it into shadowed, grasping hands. If we wait too long, someone will spot us.

"Colin," I say, sudden alarm making my voice tremble.

He rubs his neck. "I can't."

"What do you mean?"

"It means lover boy has us in a corner. I don't have the energy to take us any farther. Not now."

I seize his arm. "This is no time to joke. You said you were pre-pared for this."

"I *was!*" he shouts, yanking his arm away. "I blew my energy getting us in and out of the palace." Blue flame fills his eyes, magic radiating off him in waves. "I failed you," he says, mouth twisting. "I've failed you."

In addition to control, Oluso magic requires stamina, which varies widely from person to person. I could always recover faster than Mummy, no matter how much magic I used. Despite training with Will and Baba for years, Colin's stamina is apparently lack-ing. He has no more strength to channel any magic. Which means the magic erupting from him now is his very soul—raw, unfiltered, dangerous.

Lowering my voice to a soft steel, I hold out a hand, imploring, "I understand. Calm down. Please."

Jonas takes a step toward me, shoulders tensed as though pre-paring to attack. "Back away from him," he commands.

I ignore him. "Colin," I say gently. "You're scaring me."

He flinches, face contorting as though he's just realized where he is. The flames snuff out, and he clutches at his throat, gasping. "I'm sorry, I didn't mean—" he starts.

I touch his shoulder lightly. "It's okay."

The horns blare again, and now I hear barking and whining. The dogs are hungry for blood. We have to run.

"Track the meeting sign," I say. "We need to find a new path to our destination. I'll let Will know where we are."

Whatever just happened, whatever Colin is going through, we'll face it together—later. Right now, we need to survive. Since Lord Ekwensi exposed us to his sign, Colin should be able to track it even with what little magic he has left while I store up my magic for our journey.

Closing my eyes, I imagine a bird, the kind that Nana often feeds in her garden, its speckled brown-and-white forehead and long, thin beak. When I open my eyes, the bird is in hand, only the faint glow around it marking it as one of my wind spirits.

"Let Will know we're all right. The journey will take longer than expected. Tell him all that happened," I instruct the bird in Yoruba. There's no way I'm letting my guard down with Jonas around. Even if I die on this mission, I won't drag Will and Nana down with me.

When I release the bird, Jonas straightens, but there's something off about his demeanor. His body is tense, his gaze watchful. When he speaks, all traces of humor are gone. "What now?"

"Now, if you want to stay alive, keep your head down and go where I tell you to."

I turn to Colin. "What's our course?"

Colin eyes Jonas warily, responding in a low whisper, "We're two weeks' journey away from Old Maiduguri by foot if we go the usual route. But if we cut through Benin Forest, and bypass Akahia, we can get to Lokoja in the next two days. If we rest there for a bit, I'll be strong enough to bring us closer. I just need a day or two, then I can get us to Bauchi from there. We can walk to Old Maiduguri in a day."

"We can do this in a week then?"

"Fastest way I can measure out."

I nod. "Lead the way."

He jerks his chin toward Jonas. "He'll slow us down."

"I can keep up so long as my hands are free," Jonas retorts.

Colin smirks, a hint of levity back in his expression. "Nice try."

Jonas shrugs. "We would get wherever you wanted faster if I could run, but it's up to you two. Sooner or later, Mari will be here. I just don't want to see you torn apart."

I flick a finger toward him, and his bonds unravel. Then in a flash, the vine curls itself around his right hand and wraps its other end around my left. I give him my cheekiest smile. "This is a bond of pure magic. It anchors you to me. The bond will do whatever it must to ensure that you are never far from me, even if it means your death. We're crossing the forest, and I don't intend to lag behind, so I suggest you fit yourself to my pace. Run. If you fall, I *will* drag you."

To my discomfort, he smiles back. "We made a promise, remember? You have to be with me wherever I go. I won't be escaping."

I stiffen, the remembrance of the promise stirring up fear and excitement. Even now, in the midst of danger, my body is singing, aching for Jonas. I steel my jaw. I need to get myself under control. I won't be fooled by this pretty-faced serpent. No doubt the oath is corrupting my emotions.

"Shut up and start moving," I say harshly. Then, turning on my heel, I run for the trees.

BETWEEN

As we pass into the forest, the slivers of moonlight die away, and darkness swallows us up. I send out a wind spirit, and we follow its pale light into the darkness like moths drawn to a flame. I can barely see the thin, orange wisps of magic swimming in the air, the thread Colin made to track Lord Ekwensi's Oluso sign. And after a short while, I can't tell which direction we're going. We slow to a walk. Benin Forest is silent, steeped in deep slumber, and it is this, more than anything, that raises the hairs at the back of my neck.

Soon, we hear low thuds, a soft beat like a gangan drum drawing its listeners into tales of joy and sorrow. Slivers of moonlight break through the trees, cutting into us like several pairs of eyes. A loud hoot comes, and Colin jumps before spotting the glowing yellow eyes of an owl peering at us from a nearby tree. The bushes nearby rustle in the wind, and the air hums and buzzes with the flutters of insects scaling trees. The earth dances, spreading around my toes. I clutch Jonas's shoulder for support. The forest is alive.

Jonas presses close. "What's happening?"

"I'm not sure."

Mummy used to tell me that the forests of Ifé were a different world altogether, a part of the Spirit Realm attached to our world, but not wholly connected to it. As a girl, I would follow her into Ikolé Forest and watch as she hunted around for kwasho bugs and elu. To me, it was magic enough that we could tap the kwashos' back with a small stone and they would open their shells and spill out gold dust. The elu leaves stained our fingers indigo before we could grind them up and dry them to make the indigo dye the traders craved. It was obvious, to those who had eyes that could see, that the forest was special, that the trees had a way of singing, and the rusty earth beneath our feet shifted ever so slightly as we pressed into it. Magic was there, in the richly colored flowers and the long, ridged backs of palm trees and winding sycamores. In the tinkling sound of small brooks scattered around, and the chirps of birds picking at seeds on the ground.

This, though . . . this feels different.

A whisper catches my ear, and I whip around. Jonas tightens his grip on my shoulder. I shake him off.

"What is it?" he asks.

Another whisper. A laugh rings out.

"Did you hear that?"

He widens his stance, alert. "I heard it that time."

"We need to get moving. Could be an Eloko. It's nighttime," Colin says, breaking into a sprint.

Grabbing Jonas's hand, I run after Colin's quickly disappearing frame. The Eloko love to play tricks on unsuspecting travelers, and I have no desire to be caught up in one of their night dreams. There were hunters last year who went missing for a fortnight. When they finally reappeared—with swollen eyes and wrinkled skin, their bodies aged considerably—they revealed they had stumbled upon Eloko territory and made a deal with it. They asked for riches and power, enough to experience over a lifetime. They lay on the forest floor for weeks, shrouded from discovery, living out their wildest dreams whilst their bodies were drained of life. I can't think of anything I want so badly as to give a portion of my life for it, but even if I could, I do not want to play Eloko games.

We run blindly, shoving through bushes and scraping past trees, but the whispers and laughs follow us, and in a few minutes, we are standing again by the giant yew tree with the owl watching us silently from above.

"Dèmi," Colin says, his voice tight.

"I don't know. I need to think. Hold on."

Mummy's voice brushes my ears: *Dèmi, the forests are a gift. They remind us of what we came from. Many fear the forests, because they do not understand them, but you have nothing to fear. The same kind of magic that flows through you birthed the forests. If you are ever in trouble, ask the forest for help.*

I take a deep breath, calming myself as much as possible. Then, folding my palms out, I call out, "Ìyá, help me."

A voice answers, deep and rumbling, wrapping around me like a warm coat. "What ails you, my child?"

I look around. There is no one to be seen. Swallowing, I push back my growing fear and continue. "Ìyá, we come seeking shelter and safe passage, but we cannot find our way."

"My child, this is your home. Your path will always be clear here. Just open your eyes."

An array of twinkling green lights appears in the darkness, swarming around us like bees. We huddle together, Jonas and Colin on each side of me. The lights grow, spreading into thick wisps of smoke, and the sound of drumbeats arises once more, but now with the pounding there is singing, rich voices humming a wordless song. I open my mouth and sing, following along in this tune I cannot name, echoing sounds I never knew I had.

Then the singing stops, and the smoke begins to clear. The twinkling lights fade until there are four left. One brushes against my out-stretched palm before gliding over to the yew tree from earlier. There it transforms, growing into thick shadow, the leaves on the ground below kicking up in the wind surrounding it. The shadow moves into the circle of moonlight now cutting straight through the trees, and I see her. Orange-brown coily hair, with a pointed face, and thick, curved, branchlike hands. Several white marks stretch diagonally across her brown face in an orderly pattern, and small white dots line her eyes. She smiles and her marble eyes glow in the moonlight.

"Omoyé, you are welcome here."

I move automatically, offering a ceremonial bow: knee bent, hands clasped. "Thank you, Auntie. I come in peace."

She makes no sound as she walks, but the ground rumbles as she moves toward me, roots snaking up in places where her long, webbed feet touch. As she touches my shoulder and pulls me up, I spy a small red flower peeking between her toes, but when I blink and look again, it's gone.

"What is that?" Colin mutters.

I stiffen, clutching at the woodlike fingers on my shoulder. "I am sorry, Auntie. He has never seen a tree spirit before. Please forgive his ignorance."

She throws her head back and laughs, loud barks like the shrieks of a hyena. Colin, to his credit, looks sheepish.

"I am Yawara, but you may call me Auntie Ya," the spirit says when the echoes of her laughter die.

She waves and the three remaining lights transform. One is a small girl with a fully marked face, long, fanning ears like an ele-phant, and glowing yellow eyes. The next two are clearly a pair—a man with dreaded hair and curved blue marks on his dark cheeks matching a woman with golden feathers adorning her flaxen hair and the same marks carved into her bronze skin.

But it is what lies beyond them that holds my attention. Gone are the twisting trees, the rocky ground, and the thick, heavy dark of night. I stand in a clearing with soft grass kissing my feet and periwinkle flowers littered about, heads dancing in the breeze like a ball bobbing on water. The trees seem thicker and taller than before, with colorful bushes that sprout from their bodies. Tufts of gold, red, and green twist up their trunks shining eerily in the sea of blue light the moon drowns everything in. In the valley below, water spirits in their true forms glide on the surface of a river, weaving gossamer webs. Wind spirits dangle about above their heads like stars in the sky, sparkling with light for all to see. And at the crest of the valley, there are bigger trees, giants that meld together at their tops in odd shapes, with yellow light pouring through round, windowed openings and leaves shrouding angled protrusions—Aziza tree houses.

It's the most marvelous thing I've ever seen.

Auntie Ya thrusts her arms wide. "Welcome, young ones, to Benin Forest."

"It's beautiful," Jonas whispers. If I didn't know better, I would accept the reverence in his voice as just that, but after what happened nine years ago, I can't stop ugly words from tumbling out.

"So beautiful you want to conquer it?" I ask, smirking. "The forest spirits are stronger and craftier than you think. You can't kill them as easily as you slaughter our kind."

His head snaps back and I think I glimpse sadness in his eyes. But in a blink it's gone. He offers me a sharp smile. "They say conquest is the truest form of worship."

I glower. "You dare to say that here? You really want to die."

"I deserve that." His smile softens into something resembling reverence. "But I have no interest in conquest. This is my first time seeing something like this, is all."

I hate his soft, reasonable response. I hate that I want to apologize. I hate that I nearly responded, *Me too*, as though we could ever have anything in common.

Auntie Ya glides over to him. "The forests are a halfway point between the Spirit Realm and the physical. We do not intentionally hide its gifts, but you must understand: many of the forest spirits are peaceful and have no wish to war with humankind. The Oluso were once our mediators, those who protected our lands, and bridged the gap between us and humankind." She sighs heavily. "But the Oluso are too fragmented to continue that work now. So, we share what we can. We leave our fruits available for those who wander into our territory. We don't begrudge the hunter their prey, the wine tapper their drink, or the woodcutter a share of our bounty. Every now and then, we help travelers on their way through our lands. But we keep ourselves hidden to all except those Ìyá deems worthy."

"Ìyá?" Jonas asks.

"Mother," Colin says. "It means 'mother,' right, Dèmi?"

Auntie Ya shoots me a questioning glance.

"Ìyá is the mother spirit who watches over the forests," I explain, then I bow once more to Auntie Ya. "Forgive them, they were never taught the ancestral ways."

The forest spirits are ancient, older even than Oluso. As Oluso, we can channel different spirits according to our bloodlines, but we must always be careful of the forest spirits—respectful—especially since we're passing through their lands. Though the elemental spirits—wind, water, light, darkness—are covenant-bound to protect the souls Olorun sent into the physical realm, the forest spirits are charged with balance. They move freely between realms and have no qualms about dragging someone they deem ill-fitted to life into the shadowy depths of the Spirit Realm.

To my surprise, Auntie Ya laughs again, that unsettling sound making my stomach tighten. "*He* knows more than you think." She points to the bond between Jonas and me. "After all, he was wise enough to pair himself with you."

She can't be serious.

I hide my disrespectful thoughts with an amused smile, concealing the mix of horror and pleasure at her suggestion.

Colin snorts. "There's nothing between them," he says. "We're just trying to keep track of him."

The flaxen-haired tree spirit cocks her head. "It doesn't look that way to me," she says in a tinkling voice. She squeezes the male tree spirit's arm. "Don't you think so, Obi? That's what we said when our families were asking about our pairing. Look at us now." The male spirit nods, the stern look on his face briefly altered by the soft look he gives the flaxen-haired spirit.

Colin takes my hand in his. "Actually, Dèmi and I are promised."

I feel a flicker of annoyance, but he's not lying. Two years before, Colin and I talked about becoming mates if we couldn't find another person we could trust the way we trusted each other. It was a toothless vow between friends. I haven't told him I'd rather be alone. Still, I know Colin is only trying to satisfy the spirits' curiosity.

I pinch his elbow—hard. "We're working things out. We're not ready to be bonded," I say, quickly. I steal a glance at Jonas, but his brow is creased, eyes focused beyond. I follow his gaze, but there is nothing save trees and darkness at the edge of the clearing.

Auntie Ya smiles, bemused. "Ìyá opened the passageway for you, so there must be something you need. Might I ask why you are journeying through our lands?"

"We're on our way to Lokoja, and we didn't want to take the merchants' road," I answer. We need to keep things simple. Keep from saying anything that will offend. Human squabbles are little more than entertainment for forest spirits, but conflict is the perfect excuse for them to pass judgment. They might find it hard to understand why I kidnapped Jonas, even if his uncle would destroy their children—the forests they've protected all this time—if he were to learn of their existence.

Colin furrows his brow at the half-lie. Jonas grins when I shoot him a meaningful look.

Keep your mouth shut, I will him silently.

"I see. Is that all you wish to tell me? You have no need of anything else?"

"We need nothing else," Colin says, offering me a slight nod.

I know I'll have to explain later, but it's times like this I'm thankful he's here. For all his foolery, Colin knows me better than anyone else.

Auntie Ya claps. "In that case, it's a good thing I brought Chi Chi." She beckons to the young tree spirit, and the girl bounds forward, her ears flapping excitedly. "This is Ogechi. Chi Chi for short. She is one of our best seekers. She will help you find exactly where you need to go, and she's useful when you encounter wild beasts."

Chi Chi sidles up and sniffs me before Auntie Ya pulls her back. "Abidèmi is your elder. Greet her first." I flinch, wondering how she learned my name, when Chi Chi lets out a series of whistles and twitters.

"Chi Chi is better at speaking Ologiri than anything else. She does understand Yoruba and Ceorn, but she is young and to her bird speech is the most interesting thing right now. She and her parents, Adé and Obi, have volunteered to guide you through Benin Forest."

Obi offers a small nod, then starts off, marching toward the river below. Adé shakes her head, the feathers in her hair ruffling with the movement. "As opposed to our daughter, my mate isn't much interested in *any* speech. Come. There are a few things we must share." She twines her arm around Jonas's free one. "You are unattached still, yes?" He reddens and she smiles pointedly, flicking her gaze to me before turning her attention back to him. "Don't worry. We'll soon change that."

She tugs him forward, but I pull back with my bound hand, jerking him to a stop. "I don't mean to offend, Auntie, but we're in a hurry. We need to get to Lokoja as soon as possible. We don't mean to intrude. We just want to find the way and leave."

She cocks an eyebrow. "I thought you knew."

"Knew what?"

"Ìyá called you here. We can only show you the way you must go. We can't interfere."

"So," Colin starts, "what you're saying is we can't leave?"

Her feathers fan out as she answers, and I'm reminded of a peacock, proud and imposing. "When it is time, you will be sent on your way."

"When?" I ask, trying to keep panic from my voice. Time passes differently in the Spirit Realm. We need to meet Ekwensi as soon as possible. Any delay might create unforeseen consequences. I can't afford to fail this mission—not when the fate of the Oyo Oluso is resting on me.

But if the tree spirits don't help us, and we end up back in the forest, there's every chance the guards will capture us.

A sharp tingle races up my arm as Auntie Ya touches me. "Do you mistrust us, Abidèmi?"

"No, not at all," I say, shaking my head vigorously.

Chi Chi tugs at the hem of my skirt and slips her hand into mine, smiling at me with those golden, pupilless eyes as though she understands. It is that, more than anything, that makes me calm down. "We will do things as you wish."

There are children younger than Chi Chi who will be taken from their mothers this year, children like Amina and Rollo. All because of the gifts they were born with, and the tainted blood that flows through their veins. Even if Auntie Ya can understand, accept the truth of what we are doing in this forest, I can't take the risk.

Auntie Ya considers me as though she sees my very soul, and I hold my breath, trying to ignore the shame coiling in my belly. Finally, she nods. "Let's go on then. There are a few waiting to greet you." Chi Chi erupts into more whistles and runs to the end of the clearing, leaping up and gliding into the air like a bird catching the wind. Adé latches onto Colin as well and walks on, with Jonas on the other side. I hang back with Auntie Ya, walking quickly enough to keep the bond between Jonas's hand and mine from growing taut.

"Before I forget," Auntie Ya says quietly, "the Aziza wanted me to pass along a message."

"What is it?" I ask, words tumbling and breathless.

"It is time, dear child, to pay your debt. Life for life and blood for blood."

"But it's not yet my eighteenth—" I stop short. In the hassle of the last few days, I'd forgotten. Eighteen years before, on this day, the moon and Mama Aladé were my mother's only witnesses as she clutched the earth with her bare hands, holding a wad of dried bitter leaf in her teeth as her hips rocked up and down, a ferry struggling to bring her child through the sea of her womb into the world. But the eighteen years aren't what matter, not really.

No, what Auntie Ya is reminding me of happened nine years ago, while I lay in the darkness calling for my mother, poison slowly draining me of life—the day I called out and the Aziza found me. Since then my name days have been marked with sadness, the remembrance of my mother's blood seeping into the ground while mine was being cleansed from the sting of death.

I swallow as I realize what this means. What Adé meant when she said I was brought here for a reason.

Today, I am eighteen, and it is my turn to die.

TRIAL

Auntie Ya squeezes my hand, and it is an oddly soft sensation, like flower petals brushing against my fingers. "Don't despair. Ìyá takes care of her own, and the Aziza are fair in their dealings. Whatever the reason they summoned you, I am certain all will be well."

"How can it be, though?" How can it be when I'm walking to my death?

"You shall see. This is how it should be. How it needs to be."

She nudges me forward with that lack of an answer, and I give her a sick smile as we walk on. My mind is a jumbled mess, worry spreading through me like the toxic blooms the mami wata shoot out when they feel threatened. It is said the Aziza do not forgive those who cannot honor their debts, and the price for reneging on a magical contract such as the one I made with them nine years ago is a special horror of its own. Just two days ago, I was fearless in front of Lord Ekwensi, gambling my life on this journey as though it were not already spoken for. As I trudge on, I remind myself of why I am here with each step. If I succeed, one day, Haru will get to see her grandparents; Amina and Rollo will grow up to have children of their own; Oluso like me won't have to make magical bargains to stay alive while running from the kingdom forces seeking to destroy us. A bubble of hope rises in my heart. Perhaps I can convince the Aziza to spare me for a few days, at least to get Jonas safely to Ekwensi.

The dark cloud that hovers over me is not enough to obscure the wonders all around, though. The sky is wider than before, blue-and-purple ribbons of light tangling with the clouds. The moon bathes us in her silvery glow, and wind spirits shimmer above us, pouring invisible curtains of light over everything. The rocks on the path gleam with color, greens and blues winking at us like gemstones. The flowers fan out their petals as we pass by, coming alive in the light like flames roaring into being.

I am so caught up in the beauty that I don't notice we have stopped until I smack into something. Jonas is blocking my way, mouth wide, eyes fixed on the river. I look out onto the water and see what has frozen him in place. The river is longer than I first thought, dancing its way across the valley as far as I can see, but it is what is in the river that has Jonas's—and my—attention. The water spirits play in it, their long, silvery tails gleaming as they splash water at each other, the bony ridges on their backs twisting like wooden puppets on display at festival shows. A baby water spirit with short tufts of hair and white-pink skin tries to scoop water in tiny, webbed hands while her mother uses her hair tendrils to hold her in place.

"Omioja. Those are the true forms of the water spirits," I say.

"They're beautiful."

"This is what your uncle fears, what he would destroy."

"I know." His shoulders droop. "But I am not my uncle. I can appreciate beauty when I see it."

"It's not just beauty, though. It's *life*. Even if this was ugly in our eyes, it still shouldn't be wiped away." I twist my mouth into a sneer. "And you can drop the act. We both know what the truth is."

He looks like he has more to say, but Auntie Ya and the others are watching, eyes gleaming with curiosity and excitement. Colin seems morose, his mouth pressed in a thin line. Jonas sighs and turns back around, pointing at the water spirit closest to the edge. "What is that on their backs? And why does she have legs?"

Auntie Ya laughs. "He. Don't let Oladele hear you say that. He is particularly sensitive about his unbraided hair . . . oh. Too late."

Oladele turns, his long, curly hair fanning in the wind, his slitted nose lifted toward us. He stalks over, webbed feet slapping the ground, and places a hand against Jonas's chest. Jonas flies backward, the bond between us pulling me to him. We land a few feet away against something squishy, tangled with each other.

Colin darts over and helps me up. Jonas jumps to his feet, but his slight wince tells me he is feeling as winded as I am. I point to the giant bubble floating over the spot where we fell. "Without that, we might have broken several bones."

"Thank you," he says, rubbing his neck.

"Don't thank me. Thank him," I say, jerking my chin toward Oladele. "Water spirits can command water magic in ways we can't even dream of. I wouldn't have been able to react in time, even if I did have water magic."

Jonas flushes, then bows his head to Oladele. "I'm sorry. I didn't mean to call you wrongly."

Oladele crosses his arms, the fins on the backs of them jutting out like sharp blades. Auntie Ya touches his shoulder, and he grimaces before running at the river and diving in. He emerges a moment later, slamming his tail in our direction and sending a spray of water at us before swimming away.

Jonas nods in wonder. "Their feet become tails in water. I suppose the back ridges must be for swimming too." He sighs, brushing water droplets from his clothes. "But I don't think he accepted my apology. He seemed angry when he left."

"Omioja hair is an extremely powerful weapon. It can extend as they will it to and is tougher than the strongest iron." I nod toward the mother sitting at the edge of the river with the ends of her crown braids wrapped tightly around her baby's waist, dangling her over the water. "Female omioja are the leaders of every tribe, and they braid the hair of only those they deem worthy, those who have proven they can control their powers. It's a rite of passage that every omioja wants to achieve. A coming-of-age for males especially. Without being declared worthy, they cannot be trusted to go into battle or to mate."

"So, he's not angry about being called a girl but rather that I reminded him that he was unworthy."

"Exactly."

I don't know why I'm explaining anything to him. Perhaps there's a part of me—a tiny, minuscule part—that wants to see him sorry. Have him apologize. But what would that really change? If he needs to see the beauty and diversity of our magic to consider us worthy of existing, what happens when we are imperfect? Blemished?

Jonas laughs, the sound angry and harsh. "I guess it's my nature. I seem to cause misunderstandings wherever I go." He mumbles something else under his breath, and upon hearing the whispered words, I whip around, catching him by the collar. "What did you say?"

Before he can answer, a piercing scream erupts into the air, and I let go of him, dazed. The sound is like glass shattering, sharp enough to make me want to cover my ears and get far away. Water splashes onto my ankles. I look over to see the omioja baby enveloped by black tentacles, being dragged down the river by something with a protruding, jagged fin. The baby's face is scrunched, her little body jerking around. The mother swims after the kidnapper, bouncing atop the waves like a skipping stone. Her long, green hair is spread into thick tendrils, straining to reach her baby.

"Mami wata!" Auntie Ya screams. She waves at Adé. "Quick, stop it!" Adé swipes at the air and a long, wooden javelin materializes in her hand. She leans back and throws it. It flies, sailing past the swimming mother with unnatural speed, landing in the waves a few feet in front of the mami wata.

"You missed," Colin cries. But Auntie Ya shakes her head. Adé curls up her fist and strikes the ground. The earth rumbles, a wave of energy knocking us off our feet and traveling down the river, spraying water everywhere.

A massive tree springs up from where the javelin was thrown, branches stretching out like multiple arms, blocking the rest of the river. As the mami wata's fin edges closer, the branches shoot out like spears, stabbing at the water below. There's a fearsome, hoarse shriek. The black tentacles drag the baby omioja underwater and dark purple liquid spreads out into the water at the base of the tree. The mother omioja dives into those murky waters, then emerges moments later, red welts coating her pale skin.

"Naya!" she screams, looking frantically about. "Naya! Where are you?"

"This is bad. The mami wata will possess the child if we don't move quickly, but we can't get through its poison," Adé says.

"Why not?" Jonas asks.

"Mami wata poison destroys the flesh and induces blindness. That's why the mother can't find her baby. She can't see. Plus, we're forest spirits. The water is not our domain. We cannot interfere with it without informing the elder water spirits. Even the magic we just performed was taking a risk."

Reaching down, I rip off the bottom half of my skirt and start tearing at the arms of my blouse. "What are you doing?" Colin asks, his eyes wild. "Didn't you hear what she said? Poison? Blindness? And you can't swim."

"I can heal myself, remember? I'll be fine from the poison. And I don't need to swim. I just need to sink."

"You mean drown?"

"I'll use the river floor to hide and poke at the mami wata's injury."

Jonas tugs at the bond between our wrists then. "And I can pull her out once she gets down there."

I narrow my eyes, suddenly second-guessing this plan. Maybe it would be better to use Jonas as bait and entice the mami wata to come upstream than to trust Jonas with my life again.

Auntie Ya hums her approval. "That's a good idea."

"It's a terrible idea!" Colin says.

The forest spirit ignores him, however. "We have to hurry. The mami wata won't fight while it's focused on possessing the baby. See if you can distract it."

Colin grabs my shoulder as I stand. "Let *me* help you. I can pull you out."

I shake him off. "There's no time to reset the binding magic. The bond is meant to last several days."

"How do you know you can trust him?" he says, glaring at Jonas.

"I don't. But there's a baby's life at stake, and I don't have time to waste. Do you?"

"This is why you almost died for Amina and Rollo. You try to save everyone, all the time."

I squeeze his hand softly. "Isn't that why you like me?"

"One of many reasons." He sighs, resigned. "Come back to me," Colin says, then he kisses my forehead. "Promise?"

I shoot him a tight grin. "If I die, who else would keep you out of trouble?" He laughs, a little twinkle back in his eyes.

"That's why we need to bond together," he calls after me as I take off running, Jonas keeping step beside me.

We skid to a stop at the riverbank, and I snatch up any stones I can find, stuffing them hastily in my pockets. Jonas looks on, his expression grim. If I didn't know better, I would think he was worried about me.

"The cord will extend enough for me to get deeper, so all you have to do is wait until I give you a signal," I say.

"How will I know when you're ready?"

"The cord will tighten around your wrist when it's time. If you don't pull me up, you may lose a hand. Or you might end up bound to my corpse for the next week, and I doubt you would want that."

The last bit is a small lie, or at least, an uncertainty. When Oluso die, bits of our magic linger like ghosts, invisible traces that weave into the atmosphere, threads to remind the world we were. Over time, those traces attach to other living things, manifesting in different ways: a blond lock of hair on a dark-haired baby, a patch of field that is fertile year-round. Oluso who know they will die often imbue an object with a part of themselves and give it to a loved one. I have often thought of imbuing something for Will and Nana, but because of the pain I felt when my mother died, I am afraid to leave anything behind. If I could erase their memories of me with my last breath, I would, rather than give them a token to cry over. If I can see this mission through and change the fate of the Oyo Oluso, it is enough. As long as I can do that, the world does not need to remember me.

Then again, I'm not sure Jonas doesn't want me dead, considering what he did nine years ago. But he's out of luck—if he kills me here, the forest spirits will devour him.

Yet Jonas tugs at the cord between our wrists and nods gravely. "We made a promise, remember? I don't want you dead. I'll be waiting for your signal." His gaze is earnest, eyes shining with determination, and I swallow before turning away.

If Jonas turned out to be a silvertongue, I would hardly be surprised. His lies almost sound like truth. Almost.

Jumping into the water, I clench my teeth as I wait for the icy cold to overwhelm me, but to my surprise the water is hot. Soon, I am waist deep, skin brushing against the first dregs of poison, and I fold under the sudden weight, as though the river has become a swamp. I stir my fingers in the water, pouring in magic until the waves around me twist and eddy, forcing the poison away. Then I swallow a breath of air, try to remind myself that I am not afraid, and plunge in.

Rolling upside down, I use magic to push away from the surface. The river is not too deep, and being Oluso, I can breathe a little longer underwater than Ajes can. The water is dark, but there are glowing shells along the bottom of the river, and I stumble along the path they create. In a moment, I spot a severed tentacle lying a few feet away from me, a long piece of wood anchoring it to the ground. I edge closer, trailing the tentacle's length, and catch sight of the mami wata. I have heard tales all my life of this fearsome creature, but seeing it up close makes the Ikolé village children's tales seem like pleasant daydreams. It is tall—or long, depending on where you're seeing it—with black tentacles growing from its head, and a bony, sunken feminine face. Its mouth is wide, with sharp, spear-like teeth, and its tail is covered with scars and short spikes. Dark bubbles, like black pearls, float up to the surface from a gash in its side. Strangely, the mami wata has slender arms resembling a human's, and right now those arms are wrapped tight around Naya, pressing her to its breast.

As I watch, the mami wata's chest opens, ribs splaying out on each side of Naya, and the baby takes on a translucent glow. I try to move forward, but the water rushes against me, dragging me back. Bracing against a pillar of jagged rocks jutting up from the riverbed, I push lightly off and fan my arms furiously, trying to mimic the motions Will demonstrated when he tried to teach me how to swim. I get a little closer before I start to sink back, but I can hear music now, a soft tinkling of shells and a swell of voices ringing in my ears—the mami wata's spell. All of a sudden, I feel heavy and my eyes start to droop. Then my feet brush something sharp and the burst of pain is enough to bring me to my senses.

Sidestepping the broken shell pieces on the riverbed, I dig my feet into the mulchy soil as firmly as I can and splay my fingers, drawing a spear of white fire with my magic. I throw it at the mami wata, aiming for its bleeding side, but just as quickly it turns toward me, one tentacle lashing out and taking the blow. Naya opens her eyes and wriggles, her body losing its translucent glow, and the mami wata cocks its head at me, teeth bared, tentacles swirling around like arrows poised to strike.

My lungs are burning, but I try again, throwing another spear at the mami wata before choking back a mouthful of murky water. The spear stabs into another tentacle, and the mami wata shrieks, the wail deafening in the rush of water filling my ears. It drops Naya, and as she glides onto the river floor, it charges me, kicking up a spray of bubbles and poison. I spin helplessly, trying to catch my bearings, and glimpse a shadow gliding along the river floor scooping Naya up in its arms. I don't have time to wonder at that when the mami wata's tentacles slam into me. I crash into the riverbed, lungs burning, gasping for air. The mami wata slithers closer, dead eyes trained on me. Then the cord around my wrist shakes. An arm closes around my waist and pulls me toward the surface.

As I hit the open air, I swallow deeply, welcoming the rush of air into my mouth before collapsing in a fit of coughs and sputters. I try to lift my head, but it feels too heavy and I slump against my rescuer's shoulder instead.

"I told you already, I don't want you dead," Jonas says. "Can you open your eyes?"

"They burn. I'm burning," I gasp out.

He presses a hand against my face and I sink into the coolness of his touch. "Hold on, help is coming."

I clutch at his hand, ignoring the stabs of pain that make my fingers tremble. "Naya—did they get her out?"

"Move. I will take charge here." A woman speaks, tone clipped and rapid.

Jonas eases me onto the ground, and I feel strangely bereft, reaching out a hand before I can stop myself. "Wait."

He squeezes my hand. "I'm here. You'll be all right in a moment. Just—"

"Abidèmi, lie still. That's an order."

I freeze. I know that voice. Two hands press onto me, one above my chest and the other on my belly. My skin grows cold, then all at once warmth envelops me, and the pain is gone. I open my eyes and meet white-gold ones. The Aziza queen is as beautiful as nine years before, her dusky skin, high cheekbones and full lips giving her the appearance of a young woman. The otherworldly gleam in her eyes marks her as something more.

I scramble into a bow, head to the ground. "Ayaba," I say, "thank you for your blessing."

"Rise."

I obey, keeping my face turned down in a show of respect. She grabs my chin and draws it up, though, looking hard at me. She is resplendent in a gown of burnished gold. Her braided, silvery hair peeks out from her kofia, the long circular cap that frames her face like a halo. Her muscled neck is adorned with a halter necklace ringed with cowry shells and animal bones. Her wings flare from her back, a glint of moonlight highlighting the patchwork of veins in the gossamer.

"I trust you heard that I sent for you."

"Yes, my queen. I was on my way, but there was trouble, a—"

She raises a hand. "Taken care of." She steps back. A large bubble floats above the river, swirls of murky gray and milky water sloshing around inside it, like an oversized version of a child's marble. Inside, the mami wata thrashes, tentacles slapping against the bubble's walls, turning frantically as though at any moment it might find a way to escape its prison. Oladele sits underneath it like a shadow, his dark skin velvet blue in the moonlight, shaking like a tree in a windstorm. Naya bounces happily against his chest until Auntie Ya leads the mother omioja over, and the mother scoops her baby up. Oladele does not speak even as the mother omioja cries, thanking him profusely.

The Aziza queen turns back to me. "Thanks to your distraction, he was able to save the child and restrain the mami wata. Now we just have to see if he survives the rest of the trial."

"Trial?"

"It takes a lot of energy to keep a spirit such as the mami wata caged for hours. The elder spirits have decided to use this opportunity to test Oladele's readiness."

I bristle at that. "But my queen, he was in the water—surely exposure to the poison will have weakened him."

She lifts her chin, expression full of amusement and disdain. "And what better way to prove his strength? We do not fight battles only when we are in the peak of health, but whenever there is a cause we must take up. I thought you of all people would understand that, Abidèmi."

I bow again. "Forgive me, Ayaba. I spoke out of turn."

She gives a curt nod. "Come. We have much to discuss." She beckons to Jonas, who stands behind me with his head bowed. "You too, you are welcome here."

"Thank you, Olá re." I lift an eyebrow at hearing Jonas use the Yoruba word for "majesty" but say nothing.

She glides away, stopping short as she passes Oladele. She brushes her fingers against his head so quickly that I almost believe I imagined it, but immediately Oladele settles into stillness, and the muscles in his neck and face relax. The Aziza queen leaves without a backward glance, wings catching the wind like paper dancing on air while I take Jonas's hand and get to my feet.

"'Olá re'?" I ask, staring.

"We are required to choose a historical topic at school, so we can be better citizens. Most warrior initiates choose the history of weapons, or a course on governance if they're interested in politics. I chose Yoruba."

I snatch my hand from his. I regret the action almost instantly when he tenses in return, but my anger is too great, leaping like flames devouring wood.

"Why?" I demand. "You have no need for a dead language."

"Yoruba is beautiful. Perhaps it should be revived."

I sneer. "Just because you heard a few Yoruba words from an Eingardian scholar doesn't mean you know the language. You know nothing."

It's not fair. I have to hold on to the scraps of Yoruba I have, practice it with Baba Sylvanus painstakingly so I don't forget. So I don't lose the power to dream in my own tongue. But he just decides on a whim to take that—my remaining birthright—from me too.

He sighs. "Earlier, when I asked about Ìyá, it wasn't because I couldn't understand the word. I just didn't know why you used it. There's a lot I still don't know, but I have a good teacher." He smiles, but his eyes are heavy and sad. "Part of being a prince means I receive special dispensation. I asked to hire my own private tutor, and I went and found an old Oyo scholar, a remnant of the former court, to teach me. No one knows I'm studying Yoruba, or it would get my teacher killed. Everyone thinks he's my combat practice dummy."

I slump, anger leeching out like pus from an oozing wound. I didn't expect that he would risk anything to learn our language. "Again: Why? Why would you risk getting caught just to learn a few words?"

He runs a hand through his hair, tucking an errant side braid back in place. "Because it's more than a few words. It's a new set of eyes. A prince should understand the minds of his people, should he not? How can I understand things if I don't learn a language at least half the kingdom speaks, even if they do so in secret? And . . . I had another personal reason. Something I wanted to know."

I lift my head at this. "What's that?"

He smiles, eyes sparkling with genuine warmth. "A secret."

Trying to ignore the way my heart tightens at his answer, I turn and stalk toward the tree house that the Aziza queen flew into, moving as briskly as I can without running. He falls into step with me, so close I never feel the tug of our binding on my wrist.

"Thank you for saving me back there," I begrudgingly grind out. "I took in too much poison, so I couldn't give the signal in time. I didn't think you'd pull me up."

"I figured after a while that you needed help. Glad I could be there to lend a hand."

I stop, whirling toward him so suddenly that the now shortened link between our wrists vibrates with the force of my movement. "This doesn't mean I trust you. But . . . can we make some kind of truce?"

"Truce?" he repeats.

I choose my next words carefully, watching him closely all the while. "I don't want to fight in front of the Aziza. I don't want them asking questions. And it takes too much of my energy to wonder if you're going to try something and betray me. For now, we're stuck with each other, so let's just deal with it."

I offer a hand. "Deal?"

"We already had a deal. And even if we didn't—and even if you don't believe me—I'd never do anything to hurt you." He clasps my hand in his. "I have no idea where we're going, but I have no intention of betraying you. Please trust that at least."

I nod and pull my hand from his, but his fingers linger on mine a moment longer before he releases me and I curse myself for how much I miss them. We walk in silence and soon we reach the rope stairs hanging from the base of the Aziza tree house and start climbing. The cord wrapped around our wrists forces us to climb side by side. As we climb, fingers and skin brushing, bodies in rhythm, I keep my gaze focused upward and try to ignore the little voice in my mind that whispers that I have already betrayed myself.

BOND

When we reach the platform attached to the base of the Aziza tree house, I stop and try to organize my clothes as best as I can. There are not many who get the chance to appear before the Aziza, and I want to show myself as respectable in their eyes.

Except my skirt is damaged beyond repair, its frayed ends resting inches above my knees, and my blouse is in a sorrier state, the torn fabric hugging my navel like a cracked split formed during an earthquake. I brush my fingers against my hair, feel the damp, tightly scrunched curls, and sigh. Detangling my hair will be a nightmare now, even if I use magic. I need to buy some coconut oil and a bone comb as soon as we reach Lokoja if I don't want to struggle with my hair for the next week. I think of the flat black iron tongs that are so popular in the Benin Market this year—the secret of the Eingardian women's flattened tresses. When the merchants first set them out in their shops, they called out as I passed by, promising that I would never have to spend hours coaxing my hair into a style again, and for a moment I considered it. I wanted springing curls that didn't tighten up in the rain or blow out of control on windy days. I wanted to forget the memory of roasted pumpkin seeds and palm oil, the scents that clung to my mother's skin and reminded me of the days she would sit me down and braid my hair while I squirmed away from her. And just for once, I wanted to hold that iron and press it against my skin and hair without waiting for the pain that would bloom afterward, making my hands shake and my hair turn dry and brittle, reminding me that I was Oluso.

I shudder now, horrified at the thought. No outward glamour is worth the price of my soul. Tangled hair or not, I will not sacrifice the blood humming in my veins nor the magic threads that form the underpinnings of my heart. I am Oluso, for better or worse. I hold my head up, shoulders back and straight like Mummy would have had me do, and walk through the tree-house door. Whether the Aziza will find me presentable, I cannot say, but I will not hide my face in shame.

The inner room is wider than the tree house's face suggested, big enough to fit the main downstairs rooms in the Benin house I share with Will and Nana. Giant lanterns hang from the ceiling, pouring yellow light over the folded, shimmering wings that hang like half cocoons on the hundred or so Aziza seated on the floor facing a small bower. The Aziza queen perches there on a wooden throne, with branches jutting from the top like overgrown thorns and gnarled knots of wood forming the armrests. Magic is thick in the air, falling over me like rain when it first begins to pour, kissing my skin and making me feel as though I could fly. There is laughter, and a roar of noise as voices echo one another, then someone looks over at us, taps the Aziza next to them, and the room stills into silence, a sea of white-gold eyes trained on us.

Colin springs up from the far wall and stumbles through the network of Aziza, rushing to me and pulling me into a hug. "I was worried," he whispers against my hair.

"I'm okay." I inch away even though I want nothing more than to lean into him, too, aware of all those eyes watching us.

"She'll fall over if you lean on her like that," Jonas says, smirking.

Colin glares at him, then pulls me closer. "I wanted to go in after you, but they"—he nods toward Obi and Adé, who are standing in the corner of the room—"made me come here. The queen had requested my presence, and I wasn't to interfere." His eyes are burning with anger, but there is something else lurking in those coppery depths—fear.

Ayaba speaks, her voice thundering through the room. "I asked for you, and I asked that you not interfere. Do you question my judgment?" She leans forward, mouth curved slightly, but her expression is somber.

"Forgive him, Ayaba," I say quickly, pinching Colin's arm when he opens his mouth to protest. "He spoke unwisely."

Colin has always had a wild streak, a marked disregard for authority. When we met seven years before, he was a runaway sinking his hands into Will's pockets. Then when we started studying magic together, it was enchanting, intoxicating even, to watch him flout Baba Sylvanus's warnings and struggle to control his magic in his own way. He breathed defiance effortlessly, like steam bubbling up inside a pot, ready to spill out into the world, while I hung back and watched, afraid to make the slightest mistake. I envied the confidence he exuded like a perfume, and now I wish I could wear that scent. I need bravado and more to face what I know Ayaba will ask of me.

Colin frowns, brow puckering. "I can speak for myself."

Chastened, I stroke his palm with my thumb. "I'm sorry," I whisper. "Habit."

Ayaba waves a hand, and the Aziza move apart, clearing a path to the middle. "Come."

Colin's hand tightens on my arm, but I step away and move forward. As I pass, the Aziza surge forward like a wave, closing me in until I am marooned in their midst. I catch a glimpse of their faces, youthful and sleek like the queen's, some as dark or darker than mine, others ruddy, golden and sun-kissed, a patchwork of colors like the ones that bloomed across my mother's fabrics, but with the same unearthly tiger eyes. They stand, watching me, feasting on my fear.

"Abidèmi, you owe a life debt, and I called you here to pay it."

Jonas inches closer to me when I nod.

Colin steps up as well. "What do you mean—"

The queen snaps to him. "Silence. I am not communing with you. A life debt is between the debtor and the creditor alone." She stands abruptly, dress dancing as she moves, and throws back her head. "Aziza, gbo mi!" Hear me.

As her voice shakes the room, the Aziza lift their hands and let their wings flare. "A gbo o," they answer. We hear you.

"Abidèmi, the child we claimed several moons ago, has returned to us to pay her debt. Life for life and blood for blood. You are my witnesses."

The Aziza echo her cry. "Life for life and blood for blood. We witness you."

The Aziza queen plucks a particularly sharp, curved bone from her necklace and holds it out to me. "Omoyé." My child, she calls, smiling at me, a warm gaze that a mother reserves for her child alone. As though the instrument of my destruction is not dangling from her fingertips.

Colin shouts, "Whatever debt she owes, can't she repay it another way?"

Jonas joins in, his voice hard. "Why save her at the river if you're just going to kill her like this?"

I think the same thing. But it is not up to us to know the ways of the Aziza. True to this, Ayaba does not answer. Even though I don't want to, I dare not refuse. Swallowing, I walk toward her, every step heavier than the last. My mind races frantically as I consider what

I could say, how to buy myself more time, but I am a log set adrift on the sea, carried away without room for recourse. There is a rustle of movement behind me, but just as quickly as it began, it dies down, and I don't look back—I dare not take my eyes off Ayaba. In a few steps, I am in front of the queen, taking the bone blade from her hands. The blade is smooth and surprisingly fragile in my hands.

"Abidèmi, you understand, don't you? The Aziza cannot create life the way Olorun does. When we saved you as a child, we bore the burden of death you carried. In the nine years since you left us, no new life has been given us, no Aziza has been born alive."

"*What?*" I exclaim, shock chilling my skin. I didn't know. It is said that when Olorun fashioned humankind, the Aziza were born, too, to care for the spirits passing into the physical realm. When a child is brought into the world, Aje or Oluso, the Aziza are there unseen, watching over its life, welcoming its spirit as it takes its first breath in the world. And when death comes smiling upon weary souls, they guide the spirits on their journey home, singing them into the next world. They are also Ìyá's hands and feet, keeping the balance between the water, wind, and forest spirits, helping creatures in need. The Aziza live for centuries, but they form families and communities just as we do. For all their magic, they are not immune to the ails we face. Violence, illness, and death visit them too, in their turn.

Nine years ago, before they left me at the edge of Benin Forest, I spent a few weeks with the Aziza, the equivalent of several months in the Human Realm, recovering from the wounds the Eingardian soldiers inflicted and the poison fever that nearly stole my life. There were a few Aziza with heavy bellies, glowing with the expectation of new life. The queen was one of them.

"Your baby?" I ask.

"Gone. She did not live more than an hour."

"Kiara," I say softly, remembering the name the queen shared with me while tucking me into a makeshift cot to sleep. I scrape my fingernails against my palm. "And the other children?"

"Buried with her in Ikolé Forest. She isn't alone with five others to keep her company."

The Aziza are not to interfere with life and death. In saving me, they wove new threads into the pattern that was to be my life. Now that I know the true cost of my survival, the fire in my heart burns brighter than before. With the borrowed time I have left, I must honor the sacrifice the Aziza made and prevent more Oluso from dying.

I lick my dry lips. "So if you kill me, all this will end. You will have children again."

"You don't know that," Colin interrupts. "You don't even—"

"Colin," I say, baring my teeth.

"But Dèmi—"

I snap. "Not. Another. Word."

He holds my gaze, eyes filled with fear and anguish, but I don't back down, glaring until he looks away. From the corner of my eye, I catch Jonas also watching, a slight tremor in his jaw. I turn away, annoyed at the gleeful thrill that passes through me when I see that hint of fear on his face. No doubt he's figured out that if I die here, he might never be able to leave the Spirit Realm. But there are bigger matters at hand.

Turning to Ayaba, I clutch the blade to my chest, pressing the tip against my heart. "I accept. You saved my life, so it is yours. I promised that then." Then I offer the blade back to her. "But I need to ask one thing—a few days to complete a task. I know I ask for too much, but Ayaba, this could mean so much good for my people if I am able to finish what I started." I end with a deep bow. "I am at your mercy."

Ayaba grabs my shoulders, her fingers tight on my arms. "Is that what you think? That we seek your life?" Her eyes are anguished, white gold softened to a molten silver. Yet what else could they want? What else makes sense? I'm confused, and when I don't respond, she steps back, her face settling into a controlled mask. But her tone is bitter, her words clipped and coming fast. "I thought by now that you would have grown to trust us, to see us as your family, but it seems I was mistaken. Do you think I would have given up my baby in exchange for a mere human life?"

"But I owe a blood debt," I say, confused. "I cost you your child, and others. It is only just—"

"You speak of *justice*?" she says, her commanding voice smothering my objections. Her eyes glow as she rises to full height, dangerous and exacting. "What do you know of justice? I offered you my life blood, prolonging your life in exchange for the child I carried for five long years. I chose you as family, taught you of our ways, and yet you return here parroting such foolishness. Are humankind so forgetful? You believe Aziza are murderous ghouls like those you call your brethren?"

I shake my head, pleading. "I don't. I just thought—" I shut my mouth, trying to think of why it's so hard to believe in Ayaba, in anyone. Weights and scales, promises and blood debts I can understand. But kindness? Unasked kindness? I'm not sure I deserve it.

"You didn't believe in us," Ayaba says, settling back on her throne. Her beautiful face is sunken, worn by the perils of life.

I flush, neck hot with shame and embarrassment. "Forgive me, Ayaba. I didn't mean to be so ungrateful." I touch the hem of her robes, a complete surrender. "It is I who have failed you. The Aziza are my family. Earlier, I was merely expressing that I trust you with my life. That I'm yours to command. I chose my words poorly."

My eyes sting with unshed tears, and my heart aches with sorrow and regret. I didn't know—even after all this time, somehow, I couldn't admit to myself that the day Mummy died was the day I stopped believing in love. Stopped believing I could give or receive it, that I was worthy of it at all. Because if I was, as Mummy said, born to be loved, why would I be hunted in the streets like a bush rat? Why would I live my daily life hoping that everyone would just let me be?

And now I have offended one of the only beings who has ever shown me kindness.

Ayaba sighs, then kneels, gathering me to her. "It is not surprising you are like this. You were born accompanying death, after all. A moon with a smothered sun."

I search her eyes, looking for a hint as to what she might mean, but she merely tilts her head. "A story for another time. Come. Let us move past this."

The Aziza, seeing more of the spirit and physical realm than any other beings, speak in ways that are difficult to understand. They rate words as purposeful as actions, promises and prophesies that must be kept to the last. Their words are not chosen lightly and can mean many things, but they do not understand, because of their limited interactions with the rhythms of human life save birth and death, that their words can be confusing, and their actions even more so.

Ayaba runs her fingers down the length of my arm, stopping as she reaches the blade I'm holding. "This belonged to Anasazi, an elephant matriarch who shepherded her herd to Sapèlè from Jos during the last war your kind engaged in. Eight human days, she trekked." As she speaks, streaks the color of molten flame appear on the blade, carving out images: an elephant rearing up, proud and majestic; a woman hugging two children, her eyes crying tears of blood. And in the background, fire, shadows—chaos.

"Soldiers set fires to the forests for their own amusement. A great many were lost," Ayaba continues. "Anasazi trekked for days without rest, food or water. And when she arrived, after seeing her herd placed safely in our territory, she went out into the fields and died alone. I sung her away myself."

I stroke the blade, tracing the ridges the images have formed in the otherwise smooth body. Elephants are sacred creatures in Oyo, and as such are the other symbol woven onto our now-abandoned green-and-gold flag. It is said that they helped the Oluso when mankind was first born, teaching them the ways of the forests and the seas, showing them how to care for their young. When elephants die, their bodies turn to stone and ash, enriching the earth. There are rumors, however, that elephants sometimes leave a piece of themselves behind, a gift to those they consider worthy of carrying on their legacies.

This knife, then, confirms those legends.

"I ask of you, take this blade as a pledge, a promise that you will defend our people when the time comes."

I look up at this.

"What is coming, Ayaba?"

"The winds shift, and the hearts of humankind burn with hunger. A time will come when you, Abidèmi, must raise your blade to help my people. Your people. When I saved your life, I sensed your mother's presence around you. I knew from that what was to come. Anasazi left that bone for a heart that would fight past the raging tides of war and chaos for its people—yours. I saved your life knowing it would require sacrifice. I ask you, then, to honor that sacrifice in this way: Do you pledge to defend our family with all that you are? To spill your blood for ours, and leave this life behind if need be?"

"You want her to kill for you? Because if that's what you want, you're asking the wrong person. Dèmi's no killer," Colin shouts. He strains against the guards holding javelins crossed against his neck. Jonas is similarly detained, but he is calm as though unafraid.

"I do not ask that. All of Ifé groans in pain. The kingdom drinks from a cup mired in death and blood. Abidèmi is a single soul in many. She, like so many others, has her part to play. I merely ask that as she walks on her path, she remembers the Aziza as family, and pledges to treat them as such. We Aziza do not form family bonds with just anybody. Each Aziza here is willing to fight to the last to protect one another. We are not fickle and wayward like your kind, nor do we joy in unnecessary bloodshed."

"Really? If you're all so peaceful, why are we restrained?"

"Because you are impetuous, and I do it for *your* protection." The queen lifts an eyebrow, and immediately the guards step away from Jonas and Colin. "I did not expect you to understand, as your ways are different from ours. Each has their own traditions, even the sons of men. We do not interfere with yours, but you seemed poised to interfere with ours. But now you're unfettered, so you can stand there—silently." She dismisses him with a flick of her head and smiles at me, warmth returned to her face.

"Abidèmi, will you make this pledge? Will you walk with us?"

Her question crashes over me. This wasn't Amara asking for me to walk with her after market. This wasn't even Ekwensi asking me to kidnap Jonas. This was something deeper—not a task but a commitment. A commitment of blood and soul that I hadn't felt since my mother died.

Or . . . had I?

All of this courses through me in an instant, and in that moment I clasp the blade to my breast and bow. "Ayaba, the day you pulled me from the forest, the Aziza became my family. I am honored to be recognized as such. I will make this pledge."

She smiles, and the air grows light, the tension in the room chased away like an unwelcome memory. The Aziza around begin to talk again, laughing and whispering as though nothing has passed. Someone in the corner starts singing, and soon, someone else accompanies the singer with drums. A few Aziza dance in a small circle of space near the back of the room, wings fluttering as their bodies writhe and brush against one another.

Their joviality makes me feel as if what I did wasn't momentous—something that changed the very core of my being. But then it dawns on me: to the Aziza, where family is everything, to become part of that family is as natural as singing and chatting and whatever else occupies their time. To them, I had agreed to breathe air and drink water, and it delights me how powerful such casual acceptance could be.

Colin reaches me first, slapping an arm against my shoulder. "Next time don't go making deals using your life as a bargaining chip. I really thought she would kill you. I'm glad she didn't, though," he says, holding his gaze with mine until I flush just a bit. Then, because Colin is Colin, he looks around the room. "So this is what an Aziza tree house looks like on the inside. It's actually nice. I imagined something scarier. Cocoons hanging from the ceiling, spider webs everywhere."

I laugh, shaking my head. Jonas slips quietly next to me. "Were you . . . did you nearly die from your injuries that night?" he asks. I don't have to think about which night he means.

His brows furrow together when I don't answer. "Why? Couldn't you have healed yourself?"

"Magic isn't an unending spring. Use too much, and you might die. I used plenty that day, and I was injured. Oh, and I ran into a thicket of okonkwo bushes. Ironic, right?" I try to keep the anger from my voice as I answer, but I fail, the words tumbling out like blows. The embers of goodwill that sparked in me at the river have cooled to ash, tempered by the news of what the Aziza did to save my life.

Seven lives; my mother's and six Aziza lost because I trusted the wrong person. No—these are Jonas's transgressions and his alone.

Colin narrows his eyes. "Is he talking about what I think he's talking about?" He looks between us, focusing on me. "How does he know about what happened to you in Ikolé?"

I wince. Colin knows what happened nine years ago—or at least half of it. After years of him pestering me about why I never celebrated my name day, I told him the guards killed my mother on a raid. I never mentioned Jonas. I don't know why I kept it secret—probably because Jonas's betrayal seemed too much to share, a personal wound I wanted to lick on my own. Will, Nana, and Baba Sylvanus alone knew the truth of it all. I did not know then whether I could trust Colin with the web of pain and sadness, the questions and uncertainties intertwined with the horror of those memories. Now, though, the choice is out of my hands, and I hate knowing what my own anguish will cause my friend.

"Col—I can explain," I blurt.

"It was my fault the king's guard came to Dèmi's village," Jonas says resolutely.

Colin seethes, the words rattling in the air around us, then he strikes, a hand on Jonas's neck. "You did *what*?"

A frisson of energy passes through the air, jerking the boys apart, sending them flying like stones during a hurricane. The magic bond yanks me along, slamming me into Jonas.

Then just as quickly, we land, drifting to the ground like feathers.

Ayaba towers over us. "If this isn't a lawful challenge, I won't have it here. There is a place and time for all this."

My cheeks go hot, and I sputter out, "This isn't a challenge, Ayaba. They are just being silly."

Colin and Jonas both glare at me when I say that, but I let them. Better than getting into a fight in Ayaba's court. Especially a fight about me.

Because a challenge between the Aziza occurs only when there are two equally matched suitors who desire to marry another Aziza. They compete in different ways, from tests of wisdom to wrestling, all in effort to display their strengths for their intended to see. The Aziza in question may choose the victor or the loser, according to their own standard of worth, and when the decision is made, there is no more question on the issue. The suitors must accept the decision or risk being exiled.

I am *definitely* not looking to marry either of these two.

The queen nods gravely, then takes my hand, pulling me into a hug. The action is so startling that I stand stiff, unsure of how to respond, and all too quickly, it is over.

"You should call me Nene, now that you have accepted me as your mother."

I wince. As queen, Ayaba is the mother of all Aziza. By accepting her as family, she *has* become my mother. But I can't even think of Nana, who has taken care of me for nine years as my mother. My mother is dead. I don't want another.

"Thank you, Nene," I say stiffly. I haven't spoken that endearment since I cried it over my mother's body.

She leans in and whispers, "If I were you, I would refuse any challenge from these two. One will bring you sadness and despair; the other, death."

"I have no interest in either of them—"

Ayaba unravels me with a knowing look. Avoiding her gaze, I glance at the two in question. Jonas looks at the floor, fingers playing absentmindedly with his collar while Colin glares at him, hands in fists. The queen squeezes my shoulder. "It may be as you say. But if you must choose one, choose wisely." Then she leaves, and the words wash over me—*sadness and despair; death*—raising a chill in my spine.

TENDING

I don't have time to reflect on Ayaba's words for very long, because Adé appears at my elbow. "You set off at first light. Chi Chi will guide you. There are Eloko on the other side of this forest. Winter is their hunting season."

"Thank you." There are bound to be guards now, too, searching for signs of their prince, yet another obstacle to overcome. I smile gratefully at Adé, hoping the slight tremor in my hands doesn't give me away. "I'm more concerned with those two than any Eloko."

Adé looks at the boys and smiles. Colin's eyebrows are drawn together, his expression settled in a scowl as he talks hurriedly at Jonas. For his part, Jonas seems exhausted, his shoulders slumped and mouth pressed in a thin line, but there is defiance in the unflinching way he meets Colin's assault.

"I was like that not long ago. Another spirit made eyes at Obi when we first got together." Adé grins, eyes gleaming with excitement. "Let's just say she doesn't visit this region anymore, even for holidays."

"I thought forest spirits were nonviolent."

She winks. "Of course. But my mother always said I seemed more human than most. And I didn't do anything bad. Just allowed her to fall into a trap of her own making. Imagine! Setting a trap for *me*." She cackles, and when her high-pitched giggles finally rattle to a stop, she says, "I was fortunate. Obi knew what he wanted. He chose me. How will you choose?"

I shake my head violently. "I already told Ayaba: there is no choice. I'm not made for others. That's not what they're fighting about."

"No? Excuse my impertinence then. I'll take you to your sleeping chambers. You don't want to be late to the sending ceremony."

"Sending ceremony?"

Her expression becomes grave, almost wistful. "For the mami wata. Fetch your friends. You'll see it in the morning."

I don't need any more prompting. Colin's hands are once again on Jonas's collar. Marching up to them, I yank their sleeves. "I won't have you fighting." Colin starts to protest, but I hiss at him, "If you can't control yourself, have the sense to remember where we are. The queen will not hesitate to exile you for fighting, and once she does you'll be at the mercy of the forest. The Eloko are particularly agitated during this time of year, and I won't be there to protect you."

He wrenches his arm from my grasp. "I don't need you to protect me."

"Good. Because I have a mission to complete. I don't have time to hold your hand."

He sneers, the ugliness of it making my stomach clench. "No. You have *his* hand to hold. That's why you trust him more than me. He's the reason your mother is dead, but you make promises with him and treat me, who came here *just for you*, like nothing."

I draw back as though I've been slapped. I want to punch him, hit that beautiful, always-laughing face that is now full of disappointment and anguish. I want to smash my fist into the wall and scream, *It's not like that. Why can't you see?*

But I don't. I don't have any excuses. I am the fool who trusted Jonas, still tangled up in him even now. The fool who feels cherished, truly loved, when Colin smiles at me, his heart in his eyes.

So I seethe, making my voice cutting and deadly. "If that's how you feel, go home. I'll finish this mission on my own."

His face crumples but I leave before I hear what he says next. My heart is pounding, and blood rushes against my ears. The room is hot, and I wend my way through it blindly until I am out on the balcony again, soaking in cool air and looking out at a fading moon.

"He didn't mean that, you know. He lashed out because he's angry. He is hurting and confused, like you."

"What do you know about hurt?" I snap, the anger spilling out now. In my haste, I had forgotten the bond that linked Jonas and me, and an echo of the promise we made in the palace lingers in my ears. *Wherever I go, you must be there.*

Jonas's back is to me, his gaze trained on the ground, studying it intently. "I have caused enough of it and received enough of it to know."

"I don't need advice from *you*," I sneer. "We may have a truce, but that doesn't make us friends. One day, I'll make you answer for your crimes."

He shrugs, unfazed. "We're companions then, at least for a short time."

I put my hands on my head, resisting the urge to claw at my scalp until the pain stops the rush of thoughts swirling in my mind. Because behind my anger is shame and fear, companions that have dogged me since my mother died, stalking me like oversized playful puppies, barking laughter as their claws rip me apart.

"He's not going to leave," Jonas continues. "I would say you should trust me, but we both know there's no way you'll do that. So trust *him*. After all, he's come with you this far, hasn't he?"

I suck in a breath. "He's come this far because he wants to prove himself to me."

There's a pause, then Jonas asks, "Has he?"

I sag against the wall. "There's nothing to prove. I know what he's like. He always says things that he regrets." I close my eyes, the cool breeze kissing away the heat on my skin. "Colin has been my friend for years, and here I am like a fool, worried he'll turn his back on me."

"If you know it's foolish, why do you worry?" His voice is closer than before.

I open my eyes. He is leaning next to me, smiling. "You know why."

The smile melts off his face instantly. "Dèmi, I—"

Adé, Obi, and Colin spill out of the tree house and into the night air. Colin makes a point of ignoring Jonas, drawing me toward the railing. "I'm sorry. I didn't mean it. Any of it. I know what this mission means. I chose to come along. I'm not taking it back."

I cross my arms. "Are you going to threaten me again the next time we fight? If you are, my offer still stands. You can leave." I hate that my words come out as a squeak, unsteady and afraid in my own ears.

"I'm not going anywhere. I chose you."

I suddenly want to kiss him.

He curls his mouth in a half-smile. "I can't teleport home now anyway, and I don't want to be in the forest with the Eloko alone. Not without you to watch my back."

I smile in spite of myself. "You mean without me to save you, right?"

He grins widely now. "Just because you saved me from those gwylfins last year doesn't mean I can't take care of myself."

"Those were baby gwylfins. And you ran from them. You know they get excited when people run. They thought you were playing."

Obi bursts into a low chuckle, and I relax, the tension in the air withering away. He coughs apologetically, and mutters, "Sorry. Chi Chi's best friend is a young gwylfin. I imagined you running from Ogié. The vision was highly entertaining."

Colin groans, and I shrug. Adé hooks her arm in his. "Come now, you can be upset later. Maybe if there's time in the morning, we'll introduce you to Ogié's family before you leave."

He grimaces. "Please don't."

She laughs and pinches his cheek. "We'll see." She pulls him toward the railing. There is a rope and wood bridge leading to the next tree. She opens the small gate by it and steps out onto the bridge. The wind blows a breeze through and the bridge shakes, but she stands unfazed. "You'll be sleeping over here. Follow me."

Colin edges back, and I know what he's thinking. Having magic that hurls him through the air doesn't faze him, but being a few feet off the ground has always made him nervous. I push past him, glad for his interruption, as it means I won't have to finish my discussion with Jonas. I skim my fingers against the rope railing, not stopping until I reach the next platform. Jonas steps up after me, and a trembling Colin after him, heaving an audible sigh of relief as he crosses onto the platform.

Adé leads us into the other tree house, similar to the first with lanterns hanging at different lengths and roots stretched out across the floor. There are several Aziza in there, most of them children, with small, developing wings and white-gold eyes, but all around the same height. Some are running around, throwing flecks of speckled dust at one another, letting out shrieks of laughter. A few are sitting with older Aziza, getting their wings cleaned for the night. As we pass by, the children stop playing, drinking us in with their curious eyes instead. A small girl who stood talking animatedly to an older male Aziza while he brushed her hair ducks behind him when we reach the end of the room. Adé opens a door and ushers us hurriedly into a long corridor, but I see the look on the girl's dark face, the mix of wonder and fear that transforms it, as though we are monsters born of her childish nightmares.

"Most of the children have not been exposed to humans," Adé says, shrugging.

"Why? They aren't too small. I don't think there was a single one under ten," I answer. "Shouldn't they have seen a birth by now?"

Once an Aziza reaches the age of twenty, they begin their life's work of keeping balance, aiding dying souls to the Spirit Realm and coaxing new ones into life. Many, however, witness a human birth as early as age five, so they can cultivate respect for the beauty of life in all creatures.

"Ayaba thought it best for them to remain here. With the lack of new life in this community, many are afraid. There are other concerns."

I lift my head at this. "Concerns?"

"The king's guard are burning down large portions of the forests. In turn, the elder Aziza decided to limit outings into the physical realm. Even more reason for the children to stay here."

"Burning down the forests?" Jonas mutters, surprise heavy in his voice. "Why?"

"That's what we should be asking you," Colin says.

Jonas's neck turns an ugly shade of red, but he says nothing. Adé opens a door several rooms down. There are hammocks spread out in a pattern resembling a spider's web, some hanging from the ceiling, others strung across the wooden beams that reach from ceiling to floor. Beneath the web of hammocks, there are bundles of cloth rolled out on the floor, and a long, embroidered pillow lies along them.

Adé points to the cloth on the floor. "You'll stay here for the night. I know humans are particular about their sleeping arrangements, but this is the best we could do on short notice."

It takes me a moment to understand what she's hinting at. Feeling hot, I tug at my collar. "Sharing won't be too bad, I think. But are there more pillows at least? Without that, things would get . . . messy."

Obi floats up to an overhead hammock, and tosses a small pillow down. He nods. "Chi Chi likes to have her own pillow too." Then he walks out, pulling the smirking Adé along before she can put in another word.

Colin scoops up the extra pillow and tosses it to me. "You and His Royal Highness can sleep on either end. I'll play peacekeeper in the middle." And with that, he flounces onto our makeshift bedding, head resting at the end of the long pillow. When Jonas and I do not move, he raises an eyebrow. "Come on. You heard them. We have to be up early, so we should sleep now."

Sighing, I toss the pillow to the ground. "Keep still this time. I don't want to wake up with your foot next to my face."

He snorts. "That was one time."

"I'd rather not get between you two," Jonas snaps, voice thick with annoyance. "I'd like to sleep alone. Can't you lengthen the bond?"

I touch our bond and it tightens, drawing him to me. "Unfortunately for you," I say menacingly, "it doesn't get that much longer. But that means I can keep you right next to me where I can watch you."

He leans in until we are nose to nose. "I wouldn't mind that at all. I just hope *you* don't regret it."

Colin catapults between us, slamming a hand against Jonas's chest, knocking him to the ground. "As I said, I'll be in the middle. You can sleep there for all I care."

Jonas raises both hands in surrender. "Apologies. No complaints here." Then he points to the hammocks above us. "Why are they all so small?"

Grateful for the distraction, I crane my neck. He's right. The hammocks are fairly small, as though made for young children, some even smaller, infant-sized. I notice something else too. The ceiling is not quite a ceiling but a series of connected wooden beams, not fully enclosed. Beyond it, the night sky is wide open, the twilight blue of it bearing down on us, the stars twinkling heavily, brighter than before. I feel a prickle go up my arms. I thought this room familiar when we first stepped in: I have seen this all before. In person, and in my mind—during the nights when the unrelenting nightmares force me to relive the day my mother died. I lay on this very floor nine years ago, recovering from my injuries in bouts of fitful sleep, my mother's body becoming dust and ash while Aziza mothers tended to their young ones right above my head.

"It's a nursery."

He nods. "Isn't it dangerous to put babies up so high?"

"They have wings. This is how they learn to use them."

"But what happens . . . what would happen if one fell? If something was wrong with their wings or they didn't know how to use them?"

Hugging the pillow to my chest, I kneel, trying to hold back the sudden wave of pain blooming in my heart. "That wouldn't happen. For the first month of an Aziza child's life, until they can properly use their wings, their mothers sleep here, waiting, so if their children fall, they are there to catch them."

He looks up again, eyes shining with what I think might be tears. "That's beautiful."

I remember that nine years ago, he spoke of his ill mother. I wonder now if what he said was true or just part of a carefully planned plot to gain my confidence. The question is there on the tip of my tongue, straining its wings as it tries to fly from me and out into the world. But Colin speaks first, and the moment is lost.

"I thought it might be nice to be Aziza and live here. It's a lovely place. But I couldn't survive a childhood like that. Falling to my death while sleeping does not sound appealing."

Laying my pillow down, I press into the floor and wrap myself securely in a separate bolt of cloth, leaving my hand out so the bond lies across Colin's chest. I feel it shake a moment later as Jonas draws himself onto the other end of our makeshift bedding. Within moments, Colin is snoring, and I lie there, looking up at those hammocks, little boats sailing across the blue of the night sky, wondering what it would be like to have my child up there, if I could ever close my eyes knowing that they might crash down like a meteor falling to Earth. I think, too, of Mummy, of how she died with her eyes wide open, so she could see me get away. Colin's snore peters into a quiet whistling noise, and I know by then that he is long gone, lost in sleep.

Jonas's voice steals into the quiet air, loud enough for me to hear, but not so loud that Colin stirs. "I didn't lie. My mother is ill. She's dying."

"My mother is dead. Because of you."

"I know."

"You don't know anything," I spit. "I should've killed you. Instead of surviving alone, I should've killed you."

He takes a ragged breath, his voice harsh and somber when he speaks again. "I'm sorry. More than you will ever know."

The tears come now, the ache in me so much I fear I will break into pieces. "I don't believe you."

"I know that too."

Tears become sobs, but I choke them back, afraid of waking Colin. "I don't want your apologies. I want my mother back."

"I want that too. More than anything."

I spring at this, catapulting over Colin, and press my blade into Jonas's neck. "Lie one more time. I dare you," I growl, trembling with the force of my fury.

Gone is the self-assured veneer he wears like a cloak. The face in front of me is twisted with pain, sorrow evident in those deep-set eyes. He places his hands around my blade, pushing it farther against his neck. "I promise you," he rasps. "I'll help you. Whatever this is, I'll go along. I owe you that much."

Blood runs down his pale neck, dripping onto my fingers. I bare my teeth, horror and surprise making my words unsteady. "You feel *guilt*? Now?" I scoff. "You lived comfortably thinking my mother and I were dead. I could kill you right now."

His voice is trembling as he says, one more time, "I know."

The anguish in his voice sounds real, but I am not sure if it is born of truth or fear. And I don't care. I ease off onto my feet, slipping my knife back into my belt. He lies there, clutching his neck, and I let him. The wound isn't deep enough to kill. He deserves a scar at the very least, but I doubt it will even do that much.

Colin sits up, holding his arms out for me, and I collapse. I don't even ask how much he heard. Instead, I fold into his embrace and hold on tight as he strokes my hair. I shut my eyes, and let the questions sink into the back of my mind, waiting until sleep comes on the wings of silence, ferrying me into a world where I let go and fall.

TIME

When I wake, the sky is a swirl of pink and blue, the early rays of sunrise bathing us with its golden glow. My skin is warm, the ache in my limbs dissipated. I stretch out, enjoying the curve of my arms and the pull in my muscled legs. Next to me, Colin stirs, shifting his arm so it lies across Jonas's waist, but he does not wake. Jonas, for his part, has a hand pressed to his mouth and his body curled inward, like a tortoise wriggling into its shell. His cheeks are wet as though he's been crying, and his neck is strained at an awkward angle, on it a fresh, puckering scar.

Creeping softly, I draw my knife across a finger, mixing the dried blood from Jonas's cut with mine. I tap my bleeding finger against my tongue, and the world melts away as fog fills the air around me.

Rising to my feet, I call out into the expanse. "I'm here." My voice echoes back at me in a mocking cry.

The shadowed figure beyond morphs into Ekwensi's imposing frame. "Not early, and not late. Right on time," he says, chuckling. Maybe it's a consequence of projecting into the Spirit Realm, but he seems bigger than before, his shoulders blocking out the pale moonlight illuminating the fog. His eyes are marbled white, pupilless and mesmerizing.

"You knew I'd call?" I ask, trying to sound confident, uncowed.

"I didn't." He steps closer, stopping when I flinch. "But lone wolves like you and me often starve. I knew you wouldn't follow instructions. It was only a matter of time before you requested my help."

"The king's guard know the prince is missing. There was a woman—"

He nods. "Captain Mari. Dark-haired beauty. She's strong—second only to Captain Iyanna—the King's hunting dog. She loves to chase."

"And if she catches us?"

"She won't. You're faster. And I can always send a friend to help."

"Then tell me what's next. What happens after you get the prince?"

"I told you: he's ransomed. I 'save' him. We win—power, freedom."

"Vengeance?" I ask. "What if the king retaliates? What then?"

He smiles, and I feel like a schoolgirl again, basking in my teacher's praise. "You were absolutely the right choice. Wise, thoughtful." He waves a hand and a long bench appears. "Come, sit with me a while."

I perch on the edge of the bench. He crosses his legs and leans back. "There's a legend of an Oluso, Iron Blood Osezele."

I still at my father's name. Ekwensi continues, taking no notice. "I'm sure you've heard of him. Maybe in childhood songs, threats parents give to their children." He turns to me now. "Do you know of him?"

"I know he slaughtered fifty thousand Oluso at once eighteen years ago," I mutter, fingering the ring on my necklace. "He destroyed the capital and won the war for Eingard in one blow."

Ekwensi bellows, laughing so hard he shakes. I look around, despite knowing that no one can hear us. This is after all, an audience in my mind, a space in the Spirit Realm for me and Ekwensi alone.

"Is murder that funny?" I snap.

He wipes a tear from his eyes. "Excuse me. I just—I can't believe they're still telling people that."

I frown. "But he did do that. I know it."

Ekwensi leans closer. "My dear, the truth is a many-faced thing. The sky cries, rages, shines, devours, and hides herself. Is she not still the sky?"

I bristle, annoyed at being found wanting. "What are you getting at?"

"Did they teach you in that school of yours how many Oluso lived in the capital then?"

"I don't know," I admit begrudgingly. Baba only told me what my father did. He never explained why.

"Over four hundred thousand. And what do you think happened to all of them?"

"They died?"

He spreads his hands wide, an okosun weaving tales for a spellbound audience. "They survived, every single one."

"How?"

He springs to his feet. "After you deliver, I'll tell you. Three days then?"

"I need a week. We're almost to Lokoja."

"Five days. That's the best I can do." He steps back, fading into the gray. "I've a friend in Lokoja. Pay him a visit. He'll help."

"Who's your friend?" I call after his retreating back.

"He'll find you." His voice echoes through the fog, then I'm sitting on the Aziza nursery floor again, Colin and Jonas still asleep behind me. I realize then that Ekwensi never answered my question.

Adé bursts in, Obi and Chi Chi close behind.

"Ceremony time," Obi says. He pats Chi Chi's shoulder, and she squawks, jolting the boys awake. Colin sits up, searching the room in confusion, letting out a string of High Berréan curses before he sees the tree spirits.

Obi slips his hands over Chi Chi's ears. "Morning to you too," he says before escorting his daughter from the room.

Adé laughs. "'Child born from a mother's dung.' I've never heard that one before. Creative. I like it." Colin lowers his head sheepishly. She hands me a bundle of clothes. "There's a washbasin in the next room. Change before you come down. They're imbued with magic, so they're more resilient than what you're all wearing. I'll do your hair during the ceremony. Everyone is waiting by the river."

I pull a gown from the top of the pile. It is not a gown, exactly, but a long piece made mostly of leather. It has short arm cuffs, a round neckline, an extra piece of leather sewed onto the blouse area, and it ends in a stiff skirt that falls a little under my knees. There are two pairs of trousers, and short-sleeved shirts with leather vests in the pile as well. I pass those to Jonas and Colin, then Adé hands me a pair of woven, thatched boots. They are just my size, with a colorfully painted body, and drawings of masks sketched onto the surface. The masks remind me of the ones from Ikolé, the masks we used to make to celebrate the festivals.

"Ayaba made these boots herself. For your name day."

I smile, running my fingers over the soft leather.

"This too."

She hands me a clay mask with a long, slanted nose, curved eyes, and the twisted horns of an antelope. The mask is tawny, with flecks of white, like antelope skin, and sits securely on my face, leaving only my mouth uncovered, as though it were made for me.

"Ayaba says this will serve its purpose in good time, so carry it well."

I place it gently on top of my satchel. "Thank her for me."

She nods and leaves the room.

I turn to Jonas, looking everywhere but his eyes. The scar on his neck is a flowering smile. Somehow, after that conversation about my father, I feel like a complete hypocrite. I finger my necklace, reminding myself my father's sins are not my own. Then I mumble, "I'll go first. Stand outside the door."

I carry my clothes and shoes into the next room, not stopping even as Colin calls after me. I need peace, if only for a few moments. I add a little magic to the bond, breathing a sigh of relief as it passes through my clothes. The bath is hot but comfortable, the feeling of warm water caressing my skin and seeping into my bones almost too good to give up. Still, I bathe quickly, stopping only to rub a cream that smells of flowers and cocoa onto my wrinkled skin before shrugging my new clothes on.

Jonas goes in after me while I stand in the corridor, blocking the sliver of a view the slightly open door offers. I rub my fingers against the bond wrapped around my wrist, surprised at how comfortable it feels, like an accessory worn for pleasure. Shuddering, I study the root networks on the wall, marveling at the entwined maze spread out before me while Colin sits watching me.

"You look—" he starts.

"Better than anyone you've bedded?"

He kisses my hand, soft and sweet, like a petal fluttering in the wind. "You look like the woman I love."

This time, I don't avoid the question in his eyes. I twine my arms around his neck and lose myself in him. When Jonas slips out of the washroom, I push against the impulse to pull away from Colin, giving him one last breathy kiss instead. Then I sweep past Jonas, my answer clear—there's no forgiveness. He's nothing more than an obstacle in my way, and in five days, I'll be rid of him.

Soon, we are all ready, and we race down—Colin a little slower as we cross the rope bridge and descend from the ladder. There are Aziza, omioja, and tree and wind spirits gathered at the river, and in their midst, Oladele still sits, rigid as a statue, the bubble containing the mami wata floating above his head. Adé pulls me to the front. Ayaba gives me a tiny nod of acknowledgment before touching Oladele's shoulder. He stands on unsteady legs and makes his way into the crowd, collapsing into the arms of a few omioja. They buoy him up, stroking his skin, and someone presses a pawpaw into his hands. He bites into the fruit's orange flesh as Ayaba lifts her hands.

"Béèyànòkú, ìse ò tán."

"When there is life, there is hope," I whisper to Jonas and Colin, who stand beside me.

"Our sister became this fearsome thing you see before you because she lost her hope. My children, we know what it is to be there. A mother who loses her child in dire circumstances can become mami wata. We don't know what our sister's story is. Perhaps her child was stolen by humans." Ayaba pauses, her eyes flashing to me. "Or it died in a tragic accident. We do not know. We know only this: our sister is not too far gone to hear our voices. She lives, even in this wretched state. We must call her back."

Drums sound out, and someone starts singing, catching the rhythm of the drum. I don't know the words, but my lips move on their own, words flowing out all the same as others pick up the chorus. A few Aziza separate from the crowd and dance on the shores of the river, arms whirling about, hips shaking in unabashed delight. The mami wata thrashes as the drums grow louder, and the voices raise to match the crescendo of sound. Then drum and song cease and all is still. The bubble bursts, spilling into the water below. The dancers wade into the river and carry an omioja out. She is small, with short red hair, and gray, translucent skin that looks dull and tired.

Ayaba takes her hand. "What happened?"

The omioja coughs weakly. "I am from the northern seas. I was born in Asmarra River, to the clan there, but I followed my mate into the Stutgaart clan near Nordgren. The fishermen there—" She breaks, gasping for air. Another Aziza runs up with a bowl of water, and Ayaba presses it to the omioja's cracked lips. The omioja drinks it hungrily, then starts again. "They came in big boats with heavy nets. My baby—" She dissolves into tears. "They caught my baby."

Ayaba strokes her hair tenderly, holding her close as she sobs. "Your mate?"

The omioja shakes her head. "I don't know," she hiccups. "I was out alone with Luna. Then the boats came, and she got stuck. I tried everything to cut her free, but I couldn't. I can . . . I can still hear her screaming." She claws at her face, slicing it open. "I couldn't protect her. She called for me, but I couldn't protect her."

"Then the darkness came, and swallowed you up until you were no more," Ayaba says, pulling gently at the omioja's fingers. "What is your name?"

The omioja's eyes are red with pain, tears mingling with the bloody streaks spilling from the cuts on her face, coloring her gray skin like war paint.

"I don't know anymore."

"You do," Ayaba says. "What is your name?" She is quiet, but there is a strength in her voice, power.

"I don't—"

"Your name."

"It's . . . it's Eofa."

I let out a breath, tension seeping out like steam escaping an earthen pot.

"Eofa," Ayaba says, "I know the pain of having a child ripped from your arms, of seeing the life you sheltered and ushered into this world die out in mere moments." Her voice is warm now, her words a blanket blocking the chill in the early morning air. Eofa leans into her, clutching at Ayaba's skirts like a child seeking refuge in her mother's arms. But Ayaba stands back, leaving Eofa hunched in on herself, alone.

Voice firm once more, Ayaba says, "Although I know the pain in your heart, I cannot take your life in my hands. You know our laws. By opening your heart to darkness, you have broken them. You must live a life of exile, never knowing any comfort or home. None of our kind will raise a hand against you or plot to take your life, but you will live with the curse of the evil you have wrought all your days. Unless," she says, looking around, "one of your own will speak for you."

Eofa keels over, as though the words have struck a mortal blow. She glances from face to face, chasing after the shadow of a smile, the promise of redemption. Many step back. Adé catches my arm and pulls me away as Eofa scrambles onto her hands and knees, eyes frantic with terror and pain. I look at Adé, pleading, but she shakes her head. Then a green-haired woman steps out of the crowd, a baby in her arms—the mother who dove after the mami wata. The child is asleep, the purple mark spread across a pale cheek the only sign of the terror she endured.

"I will speak for her."

Eofa trembles, looking up at the woman. The woman stares ahead, unseeing, but she shifts her sleeping baby and reaches out a hand. Eofa latches onto that hand, clinging for dear life.

Ayaba speaks. "Adaline, are you sure? This woman would have taken your child from you. She has taken your sight already."

Eofa shakes her head, crying. "I didn't mean to. I couldn't stop. All I wanted was to get Luna back. I never meant to hurt anyone."

Adaline sits beside her. "I know. I thank Ìyá that Naya is safe. You'll be all right."

Eofa sniffs. "You have the right to demand my life. Why do you speak for me?"

Adaline smiles and pulls Eofa's hand to Naya's forehead. "Because I know the cries of a mother searching for her child. Eofa, I give you back your life. I will care for you in my home until you're well enough to go to yours. Start over. If Ìyá sees fit to bless you with more children, watch over them carefully. May Ìyá guide you on your way."

Naya stirs, and her tiny lips pucker in a wail. Adaline coos at her, patting her stomach until wails become happy gurgles. Adaline rises to her feet, pulling Eofa along with her. A male omioja with braided, silvery hair joins them and takes Naya. Tucking Adaline's hand in the crook of his other arm, he leads them away, Eofa trailing after them, eyes haunted and loving.

Ayaba looks at the crowd and asks, "Is this enough for you?"

The omioja nod their assent. Ayaba pauses, scouring the crowd until she locks eyes with one in particular, a gray and inky-haired woman braiding Oladele's hair. The woman bears an ugly scar, a sickle-shaped burn that stretches beyond the corner of her mouth like an unfinished smile. As she meets Ayaba's gaze, her eyes flash black, the bloom of color swallowing up the whites of her eyes. I blink, and the woman's eyes are brown once more. She is smiling, nodding as she sinks her fingers against Oladele's scalp, weaving with attention, as though the whole world is before her, and she weaves history, of past, present, and future, into those locks.

I touch my fingers to my mouth, tracing the corner of skin by my lips. Adé's voice is a tsenu fly creeping into my ear, tickling me uncomfortably as it searches for a place to nest. "Xiaoqing lost a child in her youth. Fishermen out whale hunting caught her son on their spears. She turned and ravaged the Daiying Sea for days before she was caught and purified. The scar is from then."

I fold my fingers against my blouse, shame and wonder swelling inside me. How would Adé not know what I was thinking when I stared at Xiaoqing so openly?

Adé shrugs and plucks at one of her feathers. "It was a long time ago, a hundred years now, perhaps? Ayaba pleaded with the omioja elders on Xiaoqing's behalf. That was what made the people feel she was fit to be queen. Xiaoqing is the omioja elder now."

"What are you trying to say?" I ask bluntly. "Because I don't understand any of it."

"What is difficult to understand?"

"What if—what if Eofa succeeded and killed Adaline's baby? Would anyone speak for her then?"

Adé considers a moment. "Someone would. Perhaps not Adaline. But maybe her kin."

"You're asking them to save someone who murdered their loved one."

Adé sighs. "In our world, there must be balance. Eofa's exile is not enough to pay for Naya's life. This way, Eofa is at Adaline's mercy. Adaline holds the power to decide."

"But she still saved her."

"To the omioja, it is better to gather with joy and weep in grief together. Eofa must now watch the child she would have smothered grow. You think she won't remember that every day of her life?"

I struggle with the words, trying to fashion pretty bows, but they still come out as spikes, barbed darts dripping with poison.

"Second chances are luxuries. In our world, people don't change, and you can't give or take second chances like presents."

Adé pats my shoulder. "You're Aziza now. You're part of this world as well. And this one gives second chances."

When I don't respond, she sighs. "A second chance might be the line between a path full of joy or forever darkness. Be safe on your journey. May Ìyá guide you on your way."

Colin sidles over next to me. "Are we ready to go?" Jonas stirs from the solitary spot where he's been standing a few feet away. I wonder if he heard anything I discussed with Adé.

Colin taps my shoulder. "Hello?"

"Yes. I was just asking her about something," I say, trying to step around him. There is a sense of urgency coiling up in my belly, birthing a tingle in my fingers. Adé lingers by Ayaba, and even though they are only a few steps from me, they suddenly feel far away. I push past Colin, but after a moment, I can no longer move. I start to panic, but Adé is still grinning, fingers waving, and I relax. Ayaba is watching me, her beautiful face solemn and joyful all at once, her mouth unmoving, but her words echoing in my mind.

Be safe, omoyé. May Ìyá guide you on your way. And remember, choose wisely.

There are Aziza, tree spirits, wind spirits, and omioja milling about, but they go still like characters in the tableaux Baba Sylvanus loves to paint, and the world blurs, colors folding up into a sheet of darkness, wrapping me until I no longer see my own hands.

"Wait!" I scream the word over and over in my head, but no one answers. Then the air bites my skin and bright light stings my eyes. I fall on my hands and knees like a marionette whose strings have been severed. Blinking, I stumble to my feet. Jonas is beside me, rubbing his eyes. Colin is already prowling around, taking in our surroundings. We are at the edge of a rocky shelf with low grasslands beyond, and the faint etchings of a city at the end of them. Behind us, the forest sits, leaves and flowers fluttering innocently as though they hold no secrets.

"Where are we?" Jonas asks.

"I don't know."

These are the first words we've exchanged since last night, the first time I've intimated that I don't have all the answers. But I don't care. All I know is that we're no longer among the Aziza, and the peace that stole into my heart—something I hadn't felt in a long time—is now gone.

Ekwensi's echoes drown out Ayaba's words in my head. Five days to make a journey that should take seven. We need to move.

A screech calls our attention to the tree in front of us. Chi Chi is perched in the boughs, hawk eyes trained on us, the stripes on her brown legs and arms matching the intricate marks on her face. She jumps, and her gown catches the wind, billowing out under her arms. She floats down in front of us like a feather kissing the ground.

"Lokoja. You're half a day from it. I will call my friends. They will take you." It's the first time she's spoken words we can understand, and her voice is quiet but deep, the sound of water dancing in an earthen pot.

She points to a path that is rocky and dirt-packed, a sliver of road that unfurls like a tongue down the side of a small mountain. "Follow me. If we hurry, you'll get there fast."

"You want us to go up there?" Colin asks, gulping.

She smiles, and her ears flap out as she does. "How else can you fly?"

BURNING

We trudge up the rocky path, pressing as near to the mountain wall as we can, as though the brush of stone against our fingers will be enough to ground us and make us forget the wall of sky and air that hems us in on the other side. In truth, there is enough room to walk abreast in the middle of the path, but only Chi Chi glides along there while the rest of us move slowly behind her. As a tree spirit, I doubt she fears falling to her death. I doubt even more that she would understand why *we* do. Below, golden-brown fields with patches of green stretch out like a moth-eaten blanket, and two lionesses run forward in twin lines, chasing an antelope whose brace of horns wave jauntily as it tries to get away. Long, bent trees sit scattered like weary spectators in a marketplace, waiting for the inevitable carnage.

"Explain to me again why we can't just walk through the lowlands to get to Lokoja. I would rather walk for half a day than go through this," Colin mutters behind me. He has one hand braced against my shoulder as though I can shield him from whatever lies ahead. All I can think is how, if he falls, I'm going to fall with him.

I don't disagree about going the long way, though.

Still, this job for Ekwensi has gone on long enough. "The sooner we get through this," I say, "the better. The longer we're on the road, the bigger the risk of getting caught."

He snorts. Loud screeches come from the mountaintop, raining on us like arrows falling from the sky. Jonas grinds to a halt, and I push my fingers against the mountain wall to keep from careening into his back. Colin digs his fingers deeper against my shoulder, and I look back in annoyance; sheepishly he eases up but doesn't let go. Chi Chi throws her head back and gives an answering screech, and my heart drops into my belly. As I wait with bated breath, I watch below as the antelope loses his battle. One of the lionesses leaps and catches him in the side while the other goes for his neck. Those glorious horns come down, cracking against the earth, and after a small wriggle, the antelope stops moving. I shudder.

Another screech comes, and Chi Chi's face blooms into a smile. She doesn't even look at the scene below. "They're excited to see us. Hurry."

"*Who's* excited to see us?" Colin asks, but Chi Chi doesn't answer. Rather, she picks up speed, and although I am wondering the same thing and my legs are trembling, I tap Jonas's back, pull my satchel straps in, and follow. I remember the mask Ayaba gave me, and think on things yet again. The mask was ornate, too fragile to be used as a weapon. So why did she give it to me? Did I make the right choice in taking Lord Ekwensi's gamble, or am I just another antelope walking into the path of slaughter, caught between death and despair?

We reach the mountain shelf, and the thoughts fly from my mind like pebbles scattering down the rock path. There are three creatures perched there, spread out like lizards basking in the morning sun. One cocks its head as we come into view and peers at us through slitted eyes. Colin takes a step back, insistent fingers pulling me along as Chi Chi bounces up to the creature looking at us and screeches at it. It lifts its muscular neck and slams it down like a whip, aiming at her, but before I can scream, she grabs onto its neck and throws herself over and onto its head. The creature blows air through its piggish snout while she strokes the two small horns peeking out behind pointed ears.

Chi Chi laughs, and waves to us. "Meet Ogié. She's shy, so greet her first."

I watch in awe as Ogié clambers up, stretching her stocky, muscular form, and opening blood red eyes. She is seven feet tall at least—a full size gwylfin—and her tail hovers in the air behind her, dancing like a snake poised to strike. While Colin and I hesitate, Jonas steps up, bowing his head slightly. "My lady." He says the words as though he were greeting a fellow courtier, and the stiffness in my limbs evaporates, a gasp resembling a laugh escaping my lips instead.

Peeling Colin's fingers off my arm, I square my shoulders and walk past Jonas. "That's not how you greet a gwylfin. This is." Stretching my hands out to Ogié, I wait. Ogié bends and sniffs me, then her paw comes up, and she rubs one claw against my face. Her touch is icy, a drink of cold water on a wintry day, burning my face and throat, yet she doesn't scratch me, so I don't move. She trails her finger down, then pulls away and snorts.

Chi Chi giggles. "She likes you."

My skin tingles where Ogié touched it, and the worry that filled me moments before is gone, replaced by a lightness that makes me feel like I could be snatched up by the wind at any moment.

I nod to Jonas. "Your turn. Gwylfins sense emotion through touch. They don't attack unless they feel threatened. You have to open yourself to their curiosity."

Jonas reaches out, and Ogié completes the ritual, this time nuzzling her snout against his fingers. He laughs. "It tickles."

Colin grunts. "Don't tell me you believe that nonsense Baba taught us. It's just their way of disarming us. These things have never been nice to me, even when I offered them my hands. Those babies chased me for over a mile last time."

Ogié leans back on jaunty legs and screeches, showing off rows of sharp teeth. Colin jumps back. "See? What is she roaring for?"

Chi Chi strokes Ogié's horns. "She's laughing. She says no need to smell you. The scent of your fear carries, even up here."

I clap a hand to my mouth, stifling the bubble of laughter threatening to escape. Jonas's eyes twinkle with amusement. Colin glares at us, arms crossed. When Ogié slinks her head toward him, he jumps away, and she screeches again, flashing her teeth in his face. Chi Chi grins. "Now she thinks it's funny to tease him."

"Tell her I don't find it funny," Colin says, stalking away. He catches sight of the other gwylfins, both larger than Ogié, lying with their eyes closed. He hurries in the opposite direction, going back to the edge of the mountain shelf.

I squeeze his hand. His hands are waxen and cold, like a candle whose flame has been extinguished. He glances at me, then looks away, but not before I see the widened pupils and drawn mouth. Shame pricks at my belly, and I massage those fingers, trying to reassure him. "I know being up here is a nightmare for you, and this mission hasn't been easy, but . . . thank you."

He shrugs. "I said I'd go with you. You didn't make me come."

"I know. But I want you to know that this means a lot to me."

He squeezes my fingers back, rubbing the inside of my palm with his thumb. "You don't have to thank me. I'd do anything for you in a heartbeat."

I swallow, suddenly aware of the dryness in my throat and the blistering kiss of the sun on my skin. I smile back and croak out, "I know. Thank you for being my friend."

He drops my hand. "I don't want to be thanked for that."

"I—"

"No. I'm sorry," he says. "It's just . . . I'm here to help, I am. We can figure out the other stuff later."

The other stuff. He makes it sound so easy, like deciding what I want for supper.

Sighing, I turn away, catching a flash of movement from the corner of my eye. Jonas brushes at his vest, suddenly absorbed in studying his jerkin.

"It's rude to eavesdrop," I say, and the tips of his ears prickle pink.

Colin presses his fingers against my back. "Come on. Let's get going already. The sooner we get off this mountain, the better."

He waves at Chi Chi, who sits on the ground, squawking happily to Ogié. "Can we leave for Lokoja now? I'm hungry, and I don't want your friend to suffer through my irritation."

The mention of food makes my stomach grumble, and I lick my lips. I think back to the spread I carried into Jonas's rooms only yesterday and wish I had thought to bring some of it along. Somehow, the cold yam porridge and meat pie I scarfed down before heading out to the palace yesterday has sustained me till now, but no more.

Chi Chi pouts. "No more playtime?" When I shake my head, she erupts in a series of snorts, and Ogié trumpets back to her.

"We play next time," she says, rubbing her head against Ogié's snout.

Ogié stumbles over to the other gwylfins and taps them with her tail. The first, bearing a single horn in the middle of its forehead and a ridged, black belly, rises to its feet, and unfurls large gray wings. The second and largest opens a lazy, red eye only after Ogié pokes it with her tail several times. Then it springs to its feet and growls at Ogié. Ogié lowers her head, and jabs at its side, and it snorts and curls its tail with hers.

Chi Chi points at the gwylfin with the single horn. "Osemalu, Ogié's twin brother. And Auntie Anozié, their mother."

Anozié is at least twice my height, larger than both her children. She presses her nose to my face, and I stand still, not daring to breathe as she curls her long neck around mine. She exhales a cloud of hot air onto my face, then whips her head back, screeching.

Chi Chi nods. "Auntie asked to carry you. Do you accept?"

Curling my trembling fingers into fists, I lift my head high. "I accept."

Anozié's head shoots out, darting toward me. I barely have time to move before she clamps her teeth down on the bond linking me and Jonas. The bond glows red, like a piece of metal thrust into a furnace, then fizzles into bits of green flame, evaporating into the air. I stare dumbfounded. The binding magic was one of the most advanced things I learned under Will and Baba. The amount of magic required to keep the bond in place, let alone break it, is immense. I knew gwylfins possessed magic, but until now I did not know how much.

Panic sets in as I realize that Jonas is now free. "Wait—" I start, but Anozié rears her head like a whip again and slams into me, robbing me of breath. I hear shouts as I slump forward, pain radiating from my stomach, then I am in the air. I flail, trying to catch snatches of wind, to keep from falling, but a ribbon of gray swims across my vision and I crash into something hard. I hang on, wrapping my arms around glittering scales and tucking my legs in. When my vision comes back, I am sprawled across Anozié's back, fingers resting on the bony protrusions that mark the start of her wings. We glide through the air, cutting through clouds with frightening speed. The sun claws at my face and back, but I dig my boots into Anozié's side and press my face down as the wind cuts at me, making it hard for me to keep my eyes open. We fly in a straight line, roaring toward the sun, then suddenly she stops, and my heart drops as she slams her wings closed over me and we fall, racing toward the earth.

My throat is so dry and the wind so harsh in my ears that I can barely hear the screams wracking my body. I fight to keep my fingers pressed to Anozié's back, and just when I fear I will lose my grip, she turns upright and we coast to a stop on the mountain shelf. Bile rises up in my throat, and my stomach churns with anger, but I manage to sit upright. Colin and Jonas are gone, along with Ogié and Osemalu.

Chi Chi claps her hands like a child witnessing a magic trick. "You were so good. I fell off my first time riding with Ogié, but you stayed on the whole time."

"Where are the others?" I croak.

"They'll come back soon." She wrinkles her nose. "The dark-haired one put up a fight." I tilt to one side, trying to catch my bearings enough to slip to the ground, but she shakes her head. "I wouldn't do that if I were you. You don't want to have to remount."

I rock forward, collapsing against Anozié's back. Cool air blows above my sweaty cheek, and when I blink my eyes open, Anozié's tail is inches from my face, the end spread like a fan, waving furiously. The ground thunders as Osemalu crashes onto the rock, screeching as he tries to balance on bent legs. He rears up and shakes, nearly tossing Colin to the ground, but Colin hangs on, squeezing his legs harder against Osemalu's torso. I am surprised that he looks merely annoyed, considering what we just went through.

Ogié touches down softly on my other side with Jonas in tow, hopping a little ways before coming to a stop. Jonas is flushed and grinning, rubbing Ogié's back tenderly as she struts like a peacock on display. I watch them for a moment. For now, Jonas cannot escape, unless he wants to risk being stuck in the middle of nowhere, trapped on a mountain with gwylfins, and worse, no food or water. But once we get to Lokoja it will be a different story.

I groan in frustration. I need to re-bond us when we get down there, and I can waste only so much magic.

Sulking a bit, Chi Chi kicks at the ground. "I wish I could stay and play some more, but I have to go home now. I want to see Lokoja, too, but Mama will box my ears if she found out I went into a human city without asking." She twists her mouth and looks at me. "Will you send something back for me? My cousin Marina got a bag of human sweets last year for her name day, but I've never gotten something like that."

I smile. "I'll send you some tom toms, and akara too. That way you get sweets and human food. I'm sure your cousin hasn't had human food."

I remember hanging on to my mother's waist as she walked in the Ikolé market, begging for the black-and-white-striped peppermint sweets that stuck to my fingers, and the savory fried buns that made my tongue dance. The memory makes my eyes sting and I sniff, wishing like I have every day for the last nine years to see my mother's face again.

Chi Chi beams with excitement. "Thank you, Auntie." She drops in a curtsy, ears flapping. "Don't forget, okay?"

"I won't."

Anozié arches her back, and I dig my fingers into the hollow of her shoulders, prepared this time. She wobbles around, then takes a few running steps. One, two, three, and we are off, soaring into the sky. I bend my body to hers, and when we dip below the clouds, I watch the grasslands below. There is a bloat of hippos, clustered together in a pool of water like stepping-stones. Giraffes pluck leaves from treetops, and baby antelopes dart around like chicks, flexing their long legs as they go. As the stone walls of Lokoja swell into sight, we dip lower, nearly kissing the ground, so close I could touch the flowers swanning about there.

We touch down moments later, and as I stumble onto shaky legs, a pangolin scurries past, pulling its coppery, scaled back into the hollow of a tree. Ogié and Osemalu land right after, and Osemalu tips, dumping Colin unceremoniously onto the ground. Jonas leaps off Ogié and stretches a hand out to Colin, but Colin ignores him, flinging himself up and cursing loudly in High Berréan.

"Didn't enjoy the ride?" I ask breathlessly.

He lifts an eyebrow. "Would you enjoy a ride on a creature who keeps trying to throw you off?"

I grin. "Maybe you're heavy."

He smirks. "You would know, since you can't beat me in our wrestling matches anymore."

Jonas makes a noise and puts his hand to his mouth as though he is trying not to smile, and heat blossoms in my cheeks. I punch Colin in the shoulder, hard enough to make him wince. "I can still destroy you, and you know it," I mutter.

"You're always welcome to try," he says with a look in his eyes that crushes my insides. Before I can respond, Anozié leaps onto the city wall. Ogié and Osemalu follow suit. She screeches, the sound echoing like claps of thunder, and there is a torrent of answering screams from beyond the wall.

"Demons!" a man screams.

"Wait, they don't attack unless provoked," screams another.

"Kill them!"

"This isn't good," Jonas says. Soldiers in purple and gold spill out of the turret a few yards above us, the glint of sun on their chain armor and swords sending out blinding sparks of light. I duck against the stone wall, terrified. All the gwylfins have done is help us, and now they will pay for their kindness.

Stretching my fingers out, I call upon my magic, waiting as it rises up in me like a wave. Just then, though, Anozié's tail slams into the wall in front of us, knocking loose some stones. She rears her head back and screeches again, and I hear a word clearly in my mind. *Go.*

I stand another moment, uncertain until the voice comes again. *Go.* And I understand what our three new friends are doing. Grabbing Jonas and Colin by the arms, I yell, "Move. They've got this."

Then I take off running, dodging fallen stones and fighting the urge to turn around as the guards shout a charge and footsteps pound along the wall like rain. I don't know where I'm going, but within minutes I am staring at the main gate, a towering wooden door flanked by two side gates that are now hanging open. I push through one and run along the deserted main road until I come to a patch of colorful buildings pressed next to each other like candies in a tin. A mass of people are outside, facing away from us, toward the city walls. I slow into a walk, nearly tumbling when Jonas slams into me. The person in front of me elbows me back, and I mumble a quick apology before making my way into a corner, one hand on Jonas's arm. Colin finds us a moment later.

"What's the plan?"

"I don't know. They gave us a distraction to get into the city, and I just knew we needed to move fast."

He grins. "Nice to know they're not so bad, even if they like messing with me." He stops, scanning the street. "Now what?"

"Now I need to make sure the gwylfins are okay."

The crowd erupts into a cheer, and I hop, trying to get a better view. Before I can protest, Jonas catches me by the waist and hefts me up. Anozié whips her tail, sending a few guards flying. They wriggle in the air like worms, and Ogié and Osemalu catch them in their paws, flying circles before swooping down and dumping them on the ground—none too gently, but not enough to seriously hurt them. Anozié spreads her wings wide, and some guards start running, scrambling toward the turrets on either side of the wall. She wraps her wings around her body, and the remaining guards rush in, swords lifted high. She slaps her wings open again and pushes off, the force of it sending swords into the sky like fireworks exploding. The guards are thrown back, falling on one another like dominoes. Anozié circles them, then turns, flying away from the city. Ogié and Osemalu join her, and within moments, they are gone, shadows evaporating under the glare of the sun.

The crowd is buzzing, people chattering and laughing excitedly. Jonas's arms begin to shake beneath me, and I push against them, dropping to my feet. "Thanks."

He pulls his hands from my waist abruptly. "Of course."

Colin thrusts a paper in my face. There is a sketch of Jonas, drawn by someone who obviously knows his features well, and an offer of a thousand lira, a lifetime's reward, for his safe return. Along the bottom, by Alistair Sorenson's stamp, are boldly printed words: "Five hundred extra for the perpetrators' heads."

I swallow, trembling as I read the words again. "Where did you get this?"

Colin points at a wooden board littered with identical notices a few yards away. As the crowd disperses, one slips off and falls to the floor. I thrust a finger at Jonas's chest. "I knew there was no way I could trust you. You left some kind of message, didn't you?"

He shakes his head, his face ashen. "I didn't do anything. How could I? *You* kidnapped *me*, remember?"

"You've been gone a day. How else would they have these out so quickly?"

Colin points to the inscription in the corner. "Two days. We left Benin on Yemé's Day. It's Tifè's Day now."

I run my fingers through my hair. Time in the Spirit Realm moves differently. We've wasted too much time. Ekwensi's five days have whittled down to three.

Jonas snatches the paper. "Elodie," he says with a sigh. "I sat for one of her portraits last year. My uncle must have gotten a hold of the picture and had copies made overnight."

I spit at the ground, angry that the next words on my tongue were stupid questions about a simple name instead of the death sentence I have just received. Colin smirks as he says, "This Elodie must know you well. She has your face down. Every detail."

Slamming a hand against Jonas's chest, I pin him to the alley wall. "We need to change your appearance. Don't think you can get away just because your uncle has people looking out for you. You won't escape without a fight."

He peers into my eyes as though he can see into my very soul. I lean away, and he nods then, pressing his lips together. "I don't doubt it. So, let's get a disguise for me, shall we?" He scrapes up a handful of dirt, spitting on it before smearing his face with his hands. He rubs the dirt in, smudging his cheeks and massaging it into his hair until blond gives way to a dirty wheat. Dragging a hand across his mouth, he stands and wipes his hands on his trousers.

"Will this do?"

Colin snickers, and I swallow again. Even with dirt decorating his face, those eyes still shine with a beauty that makes my skin itch. I nod. "That's fine, for now."

Someone taps my shoulder, and I whip around, fists clenched. A tall man with dark hair, and hair scattered along his sun-kissed face, glowers at me. "Where have you been? I've been looking all over for you," he asks, a hand on my arm.

I rear back, ready to strike, when he lowers his voice. "Tobias sent me. Come." I relax. Ekwensi kept his word after all.

A guard strolls up then. "What's happening here?" he yells. I lower my head, hoping he won't look too closely at my face. Colin steps up, his hand on Jonas's shoulder, very calmly moving around the blond to get between him and the guard.

"It's nothing, Selwyn. I just came out to fetch Sanaa's cousin. She has no magic. She's here for the body," the stranger says.

The guard rubs a hand against his cheek, his soft face like akara dough before it is fried. He looks young, his gray eyes wary and lip quivering as he watches us, but he brandishes his sword. "Who are the other two?"

Ekwensi's friend lies smoothly. "Apprentices. Captain's been wondering why new blades are taking so long. I called in help." He nods at Jonas and Colin. "Isn't that right, boys?"

Jonas speaks up first. "Yes, sir." Colin nods his assent.

The guard hurriedly tries to sheath his sword, missing the scabbard at first and nearly dropping it. He recovers quickly and fans his hand against his face, his neck and ears red. "Go on then, Etera. Wouldn't do to keep standing about in this blasted heat. Don't know how you bush people live with it."

I tense, and Etera's hand tightens on my arm. He clucks at the guard. "Wouldn't go around calling people that. I know our parts aren't nice and chilled like your precious Eingard, but we've been more than hospitable, don't you think?"

The guard sniffs, then pulls a compact from his pocket, taking out a small, red flower—koko. He pushes it between his teeth and chews, dripping saliva as he does. "Captain won't wait any longer for this week's weapons now that you have help." He licks his lips and puffs out his chest. His pupils are wider now, and he smiles lop-sidedly, the youth in his face melting into a mask of madness. "See you at the execution," he huffs, a breath between each word.

I have heard koko produces a fire in the belly that burns the in-sides, destroying the internal organs over time. I wonder how this guard who just complained of heat can take that fire into himself so willingly. Then Etera turns me around in one jerk, shielding my face with his body. He gestures at Jonas and Colin, and they fall into step with us. We walk past a few buildings, then turn into a narrow alleyway with patches of ivy clinging to its blue walls. He points toward a door at the end of the alley.

"Why—"

He puts a finger to his lips, looking around. I nod and follow him, ducking into the low doorway and stepping into darkness.

TRADING

I blink, waiting for my eyes to adjust to the dark stillness of the room. The air is hot and close, sweat crawling in between my breasts and sticking to the underside of my armpits. There is a soft hiss, and I jump as clammy fingers brush my outstretched hand. A sweet and musty stench, like sugar left burning in a pot, chokes the air, and when I huff and breathe through my mouth, something grainy and soft dances on my tongue. I spit as the bitter taste of ash and soot fills my mouth, and I stumble a few steps. Everything in me is screaming, begging to be let out. And suddenly, I am young again, waiting for Mummy to fetch me from the village school, hoping she will find me in the pit the other children have thrown me in.

"*We're going to bury you alive,*" they sing, high voices bandying the words about.

Then there is a quick spark, a match singing flame into being, and the bright orange of a kerosene lamp pulls Etera into the light again. He thrusts the lamp in my face, and I take it, steeling my shaking hands. Those childhood ghosts melt away like smoke running from flame.

———

"What did he tell you?" I ask. My voice sounds cracked, and my throat feels drier than before, but the words come out flat and even.

"He?" Colin asks. "You mean—"

I pinch his arm, and he yelps, the question dying on his lips. Jonas looks between us.

Etera moves around the room, lighting candles that sit on the thin, wooden ledges affixed to the corners of the walls. Now there is a table in full view, a large pair of metal tongs lying on it. A broken plate sits next to the tongs, its jagged edges catching the light. A thick apron hangs off a lone chair, and next to it a giant black pit hugs the wall, bulging out like a bag of sweets hidden in a child's too-small pocket—a simple forge, a living to many of Ifé's inhabitants.

But to me and my kind, a grave.

It is said that when Olorun wove the physical realm and set Ìyá to watch over the forests, he left Ogun, the iron spirit, in charge of the skeins that broke the earth, the mineral wefts that curled in the darkness of caves and ran like molten blood on swamp floors. When the first Oluso set about building Ifé, they relied on their silver-fingered brothers and sisters, the Oluso whose iron blood could call up minerals from the earth and carve them into shapes with a simple touch. Then war broke out, and the iron-bloods—deemed to be the most dangerous—were the first to be destroyed. The magic they once held became poison that ate the lifeblood of their brothers and sisters, a curse of remembrance.

I fan myself, as if those quick bursts of motion can calm my mind and drown out the heated air smothering my lungs. "You're an alagbede," I accuse. Why would Ekwensi work with an ironmaster?

He picks up the tongs, caressing the pincered edges. "I have a message for you. But I want to trade."

Alagbede. The word used to carry the honor of uniqueness, the prestige of being a blacksmith, a rare commodity to be sought out by whole villages. But since Alistair Sorenson learnt the hidden arts of metalwork from a lone iron-blood and used that knowledge to conquer Ifé, ironmasters have popped up everywhere. Enslaved people from Oyo, Goma, and Berréa mine the very mineral used as a sword against their people. And Ajes from all over the kingdom, afraid of the power the Oluso might wield, strike us down before we even begin to be.

What was it that Mummy liked to say? *The weeds choke out the flowers of the field so that they might survive, not thinking that once all the petals fall, the bees will cease to come. With the bees away, no new seeds will come, and without new life, the weeds must either eat themselves or die.*

I once believed those words were so sad, that if only the weeds would grow along with the flowers, there would be enough room for everyone. But I know better now. No weed helps a flower along when it can feed on the nutrients in its roots.

I hook my fingers in my belt, hand on my knife hilt. "Trade?"

"I give you the message. You protect my betrothed."

"And if I refuse?"

He drops the tongs, a look of sheer panic enveloping him. "I'm not asking much. It's a fair trade. Please."

"How can we trust you?" Colin asks, coming to my side.

"He said you were kindhearted. That you'd help," Etera begs.

I sigh. "We don't have much time. What do you need?"

His face transforms, sun-kissed skin giving way to dark brown, brown eyes shifting into marbled, fathomless white. Ekwensi.

"Contract honored," he intones. A purple Oluso mark glows faintly on his forehead.

"Ogun's blood," I curse, recoiling. "Skin-walking? This is what you meant by connecting me with your friend?"

Basaari, Oluso with the power of shadow, can take over people's bodies, but only with consent. Still, the practice is frowned upon as the contract often kills the host. Etera is an Aje. The odds that he'll die are even more certain.

Colin rubs his ears. "I can't hear," he says. Jonas wears a similarly puzzled look.

"Part of the contract," Ekwensi says. "They can't see me either. Right now, you're talking to our friend, but all they hear is blood rushing in their ears."

"You're onyoshi. Touching the Spirit Realm, I understand. But how are you doing this?"

Ekwensi tuts. "That, my friend, is the wrong question."

"What's the right one?"

Colin shakes me gently, fear gathering his brows. "Dèmi? What's happening?"

"Release them," I insist. Because of his magic, Colin has always feared that one day he'll lose his senses, wake up missing an eye or an ear. No doubt this is a nightmare.

"Help our friend here, and I'll grant you one more day."

Then Ekwensi's face is gone, Etera's back in its place. He runs his hands through his thick, dark hair, continuing as though he didn't temporarily lose control of his body. "My betrothed is to be executed. Save her. In exchange, I'll get you a boat to Old Maiduguri."

Colin massages his ears. "Thank Olorun, I heard that."

Jonas blows out a breath. "Me too."

"When's the execution?" I ask.

"Lizard Hour today."

I whistle. The city bells rang once for Bear Hour as we stood in the streets. Lizard Hour is in two cycles. "We'd better get moving then."

"We're helping him? After the stunt he just pulled?" Colin asks. "My ears are still ringing."

"Got any food?" I ask Etera. "You can fill us in while we eat."

Food rituals are sacred. When Oyo-born sit at a table, we enter a temporary bond of trust. We have to eat the food Etera offers, whether of fine quality or poor taste. Even if it is a paltry meal of akamu, we are to eat heartily to show our gratitude and, in doing so, honor Etera for caring for us. I lick my lips, recalling the taste of the corn porridge Mummy used to make and the heavy sweetness of the honey she poured on top when I complained of the sharp taste. Paltry or not, I would eat akamu if it were placed in front of me.

Etera opens the door to the next room. The smell of curried mince and beans tickles my nostrils. On a table there is a plate of half-moon pies and a steaming pot of ewa oloyin.

"You were expecting us," Jonas declares. When I frown, he shrugs. "That's more than enough food for one person."

I'm surprised he considers the food enough. The spread I served him at the palace alone could have easily fed four people.

Colin polishes off half a meat pie by the time I take a seat. When I squint at him, he protests, "We spent a whole night in the Spirit Realm—two days without food. Excuse me if I'm starving."

Etera drums his fingers nervously against the wooden tabletop. "Sanaa is at the Mu'ari Keep in the center of the town. There are tunnels underneath."

"You intend for us to break in?"

He shakes his head. "The tunnels are for after. Getting in is the easy part."

"Keeps are well staffed," Jonas says. "There'll be more guards since the recent attacks."

Etera nods. "There are. But I work for the keep dungeon. I can take in apprentices."

"But dungeons are restricted," Jonas counters. "The only person who can bring—"

He stops, but I snap "What?" annoyed that he's involving himself in this. He seems to have forgotten we're enemies.

Etera scrapes his fingers against his cheeks, clawing so hard I fear he'll draw blood. "The executioner can bring apprentices. I am Sanaa's executioner."

BOUND

"Remind me again why we agreed to this," Colin grumbles, wrinkling his nose at the putrid smell coming from the tunnel entrance.

I shove him forward. "Because it's foolish to take the kingdom's missing prince to a keep where he could escape. Or worse, get us killed."

"I could wear a disguise," Jonas offers. "Hide in Etera's cart. I promised to help."

I roll my eyes. "Then stay with Colin and don't bother running. I may hesitate to damage that pretty face, but Colin on the other hand . . ."

Colin grins wolfishly, throwing an arm around Jonas's shoulder. "We didn't promise to deliver him unscarred, just in one piece."

Etera rounds the corner, thrusting a thick, leather apron and a burnished faceplate at me. "It's silver," he says, when I flinch away from the faceplate. "Burned it so the guards can't tell the difference."

"Thank you," I say, accepting the faceplate begrudgingly. After a lifetime fearing iron, the thought of wearing any metal scares me.

"I told the captain I need help to burn the older bodies," he adds. "No one will stop us."

"There are dead bodies in there?" I ask, horror making my stomach churn.

"Not too late to swap," Colin says. "I'd take the dead over jumping into a bottomless pit," he continues, grimacing at the gaping hole by his feet.

Etera wrings his hands. "We can't change the plan. The guards would notice," he says. "The tunnel isn't deep. I've been in it many times."

"He doesn't mean it," I say, patting his shoulder. "No one would mistake him for a small woman anyway."

"That's the other messy bit." Colin sniffs. "This decoy business. Why do you have to swap with his fiancée? I'd much rather fight than leave you to escape the keep alone."

"You might get your wish if we don't hurry," I say as the city bells sound out three times. Then, pressing a kiss to his cheek, I whisper, "I'll be back. Promise."

He squeezes my hand and nods toward Jonas. "I won't lose him."

"You'd better not."

Slipping on the faceplate, I trot after Etera, pushing a wooden cart laden with gleaming iron blades. We walk hurriedly to a gated archway, stopping only to nod at the guards standing on either side. Then we wend our way through what feels like a maze, stone walls upon stone, with no distinguishing features until we come to a bolted iron door. I'm already regretting leaving Colin behind when Etera gives the door three quick raps.

A female guard with knotted twists opens the door, glancing about before ushering us in to a dark, eerily quiet corridor. "She's with the others. Leave the gate open and your cart here. My replacement will arrive soon."

"Thank you, Nnandi," Etera whispers.

"My brother and I have a home because you apprenticed me," she mutters, then she speeds on without a backward glance.

I half run, trying to match her pace, chasing the circle of light her torch casts in the pitch-blackness. When she slows and lifts her torch, I'm breathing hard, hot and sweaty under the faceplate. The light eats away at the shadows, revealing a mass of people huddled together like baby tortoises newly born, frightened eyes taking in the world around them.

Someone calls out, "It's Nnandi," and the mass undulates as the prisoners let out sighs of relief. Some edge back, shielding their eyes, no doubt used to the dark. The air is ripe with the stench of unwashed bodies and human waste. I step closer, stomach twisting with horror, bile clawing up my throat. "What is this place?" I whisper, pulling off the faceplate.

A boy rushes to the bars separating us. He is young, with coiled hair and copper skin. "Treat today?"

Nnandi pulls out fried buns wrapped with cloth and slips them between the bars. "I got akara this time. Share with your mother," she whispers.

Etera grips the bars. "Where's Sanaa?"

"Sleeping," a woman answers, scowling at us. "We all were."

"No need to yell at him, Cree," another says. "I'll wake her." She gently shakes a woman still curled on the ground, sucking her thumb like a child.

"What"—I lick my cracked lips—"are they in here for?"

But even before Nnandi answers, I know. Their Oluso marks give off light in the devouring darkness, faint like the dying embers of fireflies caught in a windstorm. Fury rises in me like a wave, and my heart slams against my chest. What more must we suffer for being born?

Etera fumbles with a ring of keys, shoving one into the door lock. "Sanaa, we're going," he says, working the door open. I step forward as I realize what this means. The prisoners stir, but to my surprise, they inch away from the open door.

Cree rocks forward on chained knees, the spiral tattoos on her face shifting as she comes into the light. I swallow. Those tattoos mark Cree as Angma, lightbringer Oluso, the human equivalent of an explosive.

"You're leaving us," she accuses.

The woman who woke Sanaa shushes her. "Sanaa's being executed."

"And we're being sold as asewós," Cree spits. "What's the difference?"

The difference is waking to an existence no better than a wild animal's, living chained to a bed for a patron's entertainment. Asewós with Oluso blood lie in the corners of public houses, holding themselves together as their bodies are stolen over and over. They watch as Aje-born asewós go home when they please, pray their patrons grow bored of their thin, weary faces, hope for death until the moon sings itself to sleep and the sun chases the waning moon into another day. All for the crime of tainted blood.

The difference, after all, is the mercy of a quick if brutal death rather than the slow, mind-breaking life as an asewó. I can't let this happen. Not to them—not to anyone I have the power to save.

"Elu's right," a man says, looking at the first woman. "I don't want to try another escape. I want to live."

"We will live," Elu says. "They'll sell us before the storm comes. I've seen it."

"If it wasn't for your visions, we wouldn't be here in the first place!" Cree yells. "You just had to warn the Ajes, didn't you?"

Sanaa hangs back, looking between the two women. Etera rushes in and gathers her up, pulling her off the ground in a hug that makes the beads in her braided hair clink.

I speak, scarcely recognizing the thunder that strikes me as my own voice: "We take them all."

Etera whirls on me, fear in his eyes. "We can't. There are too many."

"At least take the child," Cree pleads, nudging the boy from earlier forward. "Elu, you won't let your son die here, will you?"

"We take them all," I repeat. "We'll find a way."

Etera's face peels back to reveal Ekwensi's stony one. The Oluso around clutch their heads, groaning. "I asked for only one," Ekwensi says. "Take the girl and go."

"I won't!" I snap. "I'm not leaving anyone."

"Foolish, foolish girl. *Think*." He waves a hand to the abyss surrounding us. "How will you make it out of here?"

"I'll find a way."

He sighs, long and deep, like a parent enduring the trials of a wayward child. "And what happens next? You think they'll let you escape? They'll hunt you down before the day ends. They'll scour the city for every single Oluso. More will die because of your foolishness."

"They'll die if we leave them," I roar. "I won't leave a single one."

"Have it your way," he whispers. Then he disappears, and Etera faces me once again. He steps back, and I realize now that I'm breathing hard, fists flexed as though poised to strike.

I drop my hands and take a steadying breath. "We're all going, together," I declare.

"Yes, you are," Mari whispers in my ear.

I whip around just in time to meet her waiting fist. I slam into the ground, blood obscuring my already hazy vision. Then a second blow drives into my back and I go down hard. This time, when I fall into a dreamless sleep, her laughter chases me.

TWISTED

I wake on fire, screaming against the thick cloth wadded in my mouth. When I try to move, the iron binding on my wrists and ankles sears my skin, stabbing until I stop straining. My magic claws at me, trying to tear its way out. I drop my cheek against the rough wooden floor, spent.

The moon is high, oval, and clear, pouring blue light over coco yam leaves, their elephant ears flapping jauntily in the wind. We're in a field, the forbidding city walls looming behind us, a sea of lanterns borne by stalwart guards illuminating the raised stage I'm lying on.

"I was worried you'd miss this, but you woke just in time," Mari croons, kneeling by me. She yanks my head up and clucks, dabbing at my face with a cloth. "We almost ruined this beautiful face."

She flops on the edge of the platform and sweeps an arm around. "There. Now you have a better view."

Elu hangs from an iron beam on the next platform, arms bound above her head. Her black hair hangs back, exposing tattoos twin to Cree's on the entire left side of her face. Her eyes are swollen red lumps. Her legs are lashed to the edge of the beam, and just below her is a pool of golden, bubbling liquid—molten iron.

I scream against the gag and the cloth slips a little farther into my mouth, choking me. Mari rips the cloth out and pats my back as I sputter, gasping for air. "That was unpleasant, wasn't it? Breathe deep now," she says.

"Let her go," I beg, voice hoarse and crackling. "She didn't do anything. It was me. I snuck in there."

"I know." Mari nods. "Don't be too upset. This was happening regardless. Our king doesn't like it when his governors sell property without his permission." She smiles, revealing sharp teeth. "I get to have you though. I already asked."

I spit at her and she grabs my hair, slamming my face into the wood. Pain splits my head and I wheeze, trying to see past the colored specks dotting my vision.

"Now, now—I won't have you behaving like a bush animal," she says. "My Yetu was a lady." She rolls me upright, stroking my hair. "Now, be good for Mummy."

"You're not my mother," I grit out. "You *killed* my mother."

"She killed herself." Mari shrugs. "If Yetu hadn't betrayed me, I could have been your mother too." Before I can parse that out, she stands and shouts, "Bring the rest!"

The guards pour into the courtyard, pushing the imprisoned Oluso in front of the platform. Etera skulks in last, his wrists shackled. I try to catch his eye as he passes, but he keeps his head lowered. The message is clear—I'm on my own. Ekwensi did warn me.

I scan the courtyard, but I don't see Colin's sign anywhere near. He has to know that something went wrong since I haven't shown up at our meeting point. With any luck, he's getting help. I groan, remembering Jonas. What if that's how Mari found me? What if Colin's not all right?

The city bells spring to life, shrieking out a chorus that is angry and discordant. When the eleventh shriek pierces the air, marking the beginning of Snake Hour, Mari moves to the center of the plat-form.

"Elu Oyera," Mari shouts, "you are accused of sorcery. We will now administer the test of humanity. If—" She stops, exhaling. "Let's skip the formalities. They're so tedious. Drop her in."

I had forgotten that, as Oluso, our very bodies could be used against us. In the absence of onyoshi, the Eingardians extract our screams as proof that we deserve to die. Since Oluso screams are strong enough to bring an Aje to their knees, one scream is all the guards need to justify Elu's murder.

Mari settles into the gilded chair in the middle of the platform as the guards on each side of Elu lower her into the molten iron. Cree clutches the little boy to her chest as he wails, concealing his mother from sight. Etera keeps his gaze fixed on Sanaa, whose eyes are bulging with horror and fear.

"Stop!" I yell. "Please. Don't—"

Mari stuffs the gag back in my mouth. "Quiet. This is the best part."

Elu's eyes fly open as her skin makes contact with the iron. For the briefest of moments, her eyes meet mine—clear and determined—and I *know*. I know then that despite the iron devouring her whole, somehow, she could unseal her magic here and end it all. Nothing and no one would survive. Then she slumps, eyes rolling back in her head. She opens her mouth but nothing comes out.

Mari frowns. "We didn't cut out her tongue, did we?"

I thrash wildly, trying to edge up. I have to stop this madness.

Elu's legs jerk and there's a popping noise as her arms jut at impossible angles. Still she makes no sound.

Mari taps the arm of the chair impatiently. "Burn her," she says finally. "That will get her going."

Elu's son wails louder and Cree hunches over, trying to cover his ears. I push against the iron, tensing as the pain intensifies, making it hard to breathe. My magic wrestles inside me, and my heart swells as though it might burst.

Then I catch a flash of blue on my wrist—Will's bead.

The guards splash Elu with a brown liquid, so they don't see me as I rock back and swing my arms overhead. The guards put a torch to Elu's skin. I slam my wrists against the floor, swallowing my scream as bone gives way and pain shatters me. My bracelet slips off, lying in a pool of powdered blue dust.

Nothing happens.

Elu burns in the distance.

I sob, tasting salt and ash. My head is aching, my wrist singing in pain, but I close my eyes and wish like I did as a child in Mummy's arms.

Please, I beg Olorun wordlessly, *if you care for us at all, if you ever cared, do something.*

The world explodes in a haze of blue flames.

Colin bursts onto the platform, blue flame clinging to him like second skin, knife pressed to Jonas's heart. "Let them go or I'll kill him."

Mari tenses, rising to her feet. "Do so and I'll destroy your family."

What does *that* mean? But Colin just sneers. "You don't seem to understand. Let them go."

The guards move in, swords at the ready, but Mari raises a hand. "Release them."

"Captain—" a guard starts, but she flicks a dagger and it catches him in the throat. The guard thuds to the floor, blood pooling beneath him.

"I'll only repeat it once," she commands the others. "Release them." The guards begin unfastening the shackles of the Oluso.

Colin nods toward me. "Give me the key."

Mari steps forward, but he shakes his head. "Slide it over."

She pulls a key out of her vest, then tosses it to the floor. It lands a few feet too far and I know it's a trap . . .

Then everything happens at once.

Colin dives for the key, shoving Jonas at me, and Mari charges him, swiping at the air as he rolls away from her blade.

Jonas lands on top of me and I grunt as fresh pain stabs into my wrist. He takes the gag from my mouth. "You're in a sorry state," he says, attempting a smile, but his quivering lip gives away his fear.

With a yell, I slam my head into his, then scramble on top of him as he falls back, pressing my shackle chain against his throat. "You warned Mari, didn't you?"

He claws at the chain, gasping out, "Not me. I swear! Guard from earlier. Selwyn." His face is swelling an ugly shade of purple as he sputters, trying to breathe, but all I can hear are the ragged breaths cutting through my body, the silence as Elu writhes over that molten iron. My head is pounding, colored spots mixing with the sweat and blood clouding my eyes, but Elu's bloodless face will not leave my sight.

"Dèmi, please," he whispers, and I snap out of the memory, wrenching away from him. He inhales, and I sob, "Then where were you two? Why didn't you come sooner? If you had . . ."

"I'm sorry," he says, touching a hand to my cheek. Immediately my pain dissolves into a lightness. My shackles rattle and squeak, as though being pulled apart by an invisible hand. Colin rolls away from Mari and tosses the key over, then continues fighting my mother's murderer. The key lands by my foot.

I stomp on it just as Jonas reaches for it. "Free me, and I'll let go of my revenge," I offer, desperation turning my voice high and reedy. "You and I will be done. You'll owe me nothing."

He nudges me back, knocking me off balance. "I owe you too much," he says as he starts unlocking my shackles.

"You—" I start.

Just then Colin lands to our left, catapulting to his feet as Mari impales the spot where he'd just lain. The guards thunder onto the platform, surrounding us, and Mari huffs, "Return the prince and I won't serve your head to your father."

This is the second time Mari has said something that I can't quite parse, but before I can question it, Nana materializes behind her, slamming the flat of her dagger into Mari's back and sending her sprawling into a few guards. "Don't talk to my children that way."

Will appears next to a guard, knocking the man to the floor with his staff. "I knew this excursion was a bad idea," he says.

Colin grins, his focus still wholly on Mari. "Took you long enough."

Will moves until they're back-to-back, keeping the guards at bay. "I assume this one is the prince? Should he be so close to our Dèmi?"

I lift my undamaged hand, sending a blast of wind at the guards cornering the newly unshackled Oluso. They fly several feet in the air and scatter into the field like chaff. Several slam into Elu's platform.

"I'm more afraid *she* might kill *me*," Jonas mutters, rubbing his neck. I promise myself I'll apologize later. I owe him for the key, if nothing else.

Mari somersaults, grabbing a fallen guard's sword and swinging at Nana. Nana sidesteps, then grabs the other woman's hand, using the force of her momentum to twist her arm.

"Do you have enough for a jump?" Will asks Colin, parrying the blow of an overzealous guard.

I shake my throbbing head at the weakened Oluso in the center of the courtyard. "We can't leave them."

"How many?"

"Nineteen."

Will whistles. "I need two, three jumps. Colin can you—"

"He's not stable," I mutter, remembering the way Colin's magic flared in the forest, the glazed look in his eyes.

Colin stiffens. "I made it here. I can take a few."

Mari breaks free of Nana's hold and lunges for the younger woman's waist, but Nana flits out of reach. Beyond, Etera slams two guards together. Cree waves a torch in front of her, as though warding off evil spirits.

I drag myself to standing, swatting Jonas away as he tries to help. Biting into my cheek, I pour green fire over my broken wrist, keening as the bones fuse back together.

"I need time," Will says.

"How many guards?" I ask. My mind is racing, but a plan is forming, murky outlines taking on color and depth.

"Many," Colin says.

"Be specific."

"I don't exactly have time to count," he grinds out as he beats back three more guards.

"At least a hundred," Jonas says.

"Follow me!" I shout.

Taking Jonas's hand, I leap from the platform and bolt for the other Oluso, dragging him along. Colin and Will run after us, and Nana slips between Mari's legs, sliding to the ground. The guards pursue, dogs chasing after fleeing rabbits. One turns from the other Oluso, bearing down on me, but I catch the wind, propelling myself upward and kicking him squarely in the chest.

More guards flood in, torches held in front of them like swords, forming a half circle around me. One with a metal brace on his arm draws his sword and calls out, "Do not be afraid, brothers. It may have caught Roland and Farso by surprise, but we have the upper hand now. Keep some distance from it, and wait for my signal."

Anger brims in my belly as I realize that the *it* the commander speaks of is me. If they want to consider me an animal and hunt me like one, then I will show them how a cornered animal fights. Crouching, I bare my teeth and growl. Two stagger back. Leaping forward, I send another blast of wind at the guard nearest me, and he lands a few feet away, his torch catching on the coco yam leaves. The fire blazes at once, licking through the leaves like a hungry demon, then as the leaf surrenders, crumpling to the ground, the fire snatches at the next stalk.

I reach the other Oluso, creating a staff of white fire in time to parry the next sword driving down at Cree. Etera slaps the flat of his blade against the helmet of the guard yanking Sanaa's braids.

"We've nowhere to go," a man cries. "You should have left us in the keep. Now we'll all die."

I don't bother reminding him that he would have died at the keep, too, especially as reinforcements capture my attention, pouring into the field, swords reflecting the blaze of fire jumping from stalk to stalk like an unruly child. We edge back, huddling together as Mari skids to a stop. "Nowhere to run," she says.

I smile. "Didn't plan on it," I say before slamming my staff into the ground. The coco yam leaves sway as a torrent of wind swirls and eddies around me, lashing out at everything nearby. Then I twirl my staff above my head, imagining a marble big enough to fit a hundred people, and the wind weaves around us, howling as it forms a neat, spherical wall. The guards shriek as the wind catches the flames in the field, fanning their hunger until sparks and ash fill the air.

Mari crouches, digging her knives into the ground, desperately trying to keep from being blown away.

"Go!" I shout to Will.

But he's already linking arms with the new Oluso, forming a circle of eight. I blink and they're gone. Nana, Colin, and Jonas huddle with the others, sheltering against the wind.

The flames roar higher and the heat slaps against my face. I dig my staff into the ground, trying to hold on as I sag under the weight of magic leaving my body. My wind bubble falters, speed ratcheting down, and Mari lunges forward, pushing through.

Will reappears, linking arms with another circle of eight. Voices shout as more guards push closer to my wind bubble, arms shielding their faces, a wall of phantoms in the haze of chaff and fire consuming everything.

Colin covers my hands with his. "Hold on," he cries, and he erupts into blue flame, pouring some of his lifeblood into me.

"Don't—" I scream, and my wind bubble disintegrates.

Mari leaps forward, bringing her blade down toward Colin's shoulder, but Ekwensi throws himself in front of Colin, taking the blow. With the blade protruding from his chest, he pulls Mari in and cracks his head against hers, knocking her to the ground. Then he grins at me, croaking, "I've done my part. See you at the meeting point."

Ekwensi disappears, leaving a bleeding Etera in his place. Sanaa screams in anguish, rushing over to her lover's side.

Before I can help, a commander with a horned helmet arrives, yelling, "Stay back! Archers to the front!"

A group strides out, bows in their arms. I turn to run then, pulling Sanaa to her feet, but she refuses to move.

"You'll die here!" I shout.

"I won't die alone," she mutters, hugging Etera's body.

"Come on!" Colin shouts, tugging my hand.

"I won't leave her," I say, pulling Sanaa at the waist. "Let's go."

The commander's voice rings out like an okosun at a masquerade, singing a song of death. "Ready, aim, fire."

There is a whizzing sound, and the wind prickles at my back as arrows fly down in front of us.

Uttering a string of curses, Colin tosses Sanaa over his shoulder and takes off running. I rush after them.

Will reappears, gathering the stragglers—Nana, Cree, Jonas, and two others. I jerk right, pushing faster as the commander's voice comes again, a harsh scream now. "Fire!"

An arrow lands near my foot, and I ricochet, landing flat on my back, ankle twisted beneath me. I scream, trying to get up, and the commander's voice trumpets again.

"No!" Colin shouts.

Arrows sing toward us, raining like meteors racing to Earth. Then they stop, perched in midair like bees waiting for a flower's petals to open. I struggle to my feet, breathing hard, and a hand is there, pulling me up.

"I told you I wouldn't leave without you," Jonas says. He puts an arm under my armpit. "Can you walk?"

"How?" I ask.

"One foot in front of the other."

"That's not—"

My mind is empty, my mouth dry, and the fear in my belly still taut, cutting into me. Sweat sticks to my skin, and the fire has nearly caught up to us now. The arrows suspended in midair clatter to the ground like sticks tossed by children at a market fair. Then the commander's voice comes again, a screech at this point.

"Fire!"

Jonas stretches out a hand, and this time I see the silvery blue sparks that pass from his fingers. The new wave of arrows still and fall into the flames below, sending out sparks as their iron tips meld with flame. I suck in air and close my eyes, as though when I open them again the world will make sense once more.

"I meant to tell you," he says. "I didn't want you to find out like this."

So much for trust.

There is pain in his voice, and something else—a chilling fear I know all too well. The fear I carried as a child in Ikolé, wondering what would happen if people around me discovered what I really was. The fear I bore in Benin, because I knew, still know, what discovery would mean, for Will, and Nana, and everyone I care about. The fear that is the birthright of every Oluso, of what the world may do to them when they stretch their hands out to receive the gifts of their blood.

I know then what Jonas is. "You're an iron-blood."

Just like my father.

TRUTH

"Yes."

I sag against Jonas's arms, trying to will myself to speak, but my mind is in fog, the thundering of my heartbeat filling my ears.

"I'll explain, I promise," Jonas says, dragging me forward. "But we need to go."

A roar erupts, followed by the word "Charge!" But it seems so far away, an echo in the din enveloping me.

Jonas shakes me. "Dèmi, stay with me."

Maybe it is the softness in the way he says my name, or the desperation of that last word, but I snap to, pulling myself upright. My ankle sags beneath me, so I crouch, bringing Jonas along with me. "Support my back. This is going to hurt," I say before digging my fingers into my ankle. Green fire bathes my foot and I clench my teeth as the bones meld and shift into place. He pulls me up, and I rotate my foot before pressing down on it. The guards are closer now, unwilling to leave their prey even amidst the flames.

The archers stop, nocking more arrows, and I tug at Jonas's hand. He curls his fingers through mine and we take off, not stopping even as the remaining stalks slap against us and the fire runs beside us, devouring everything in its path. Smoke clouds the sky and drags air from my lungs, but I press on, holding on to those fingers as though they are a tether keeping me from being consumed. Jonas trips once, falling forward suddenly as a few arrows find their way to us, but we keep going, following strips of midnight sky.

Soon we are out of the field, huddled on a hill at the edge of a gorge. Will is standing in a puddle of water, breathing hard. Nana is holding him up, chanting in Goma-dori. It's been a while since I heard her local dialect, but I get the gist of the words well enough.

Meld heart and mind, consume water and earth, give life to darkness, and spirit a small death. On this bond, grant me an equal exchange. Power for blood, and life for this bond.

As we look on, Nana takes on a golden glow, and the light leaps from her to Will, swirling around his skin.

"Is it enough?" she asks.

"Not enough to reach Benin. Buys some time, though," he answers through gritted teeth.

"What's happening?" Cree asks, clutching Elu's son. "Can you take us or not?"

"Amplification," I huff. "He'll get us out of here. Don't worry."

As mates, Will and Nana can amplify the other's magic. What I don't tell Cree is that this amplification magic will render Nana ill and unable to fight. And if it fails, if the magic is not enough, we *will* die here.

Torches swim nearer to us, the guards breaking from the high wall of coco yam plants like scorpions readying to sting. The man to Cree's right, the same one who wanted to stay in the prison, rushes at Will, grabbing his arm.

"Get us out of here," he yells. "Back to the city. We'll hide there for a few days."

Cree tugs him away. "It's not safe, Haroun. The Harmattan storm will destroy the city. Remember, Elu said—"

"I don't care what your sister said. She's dead. I don't want to die," he yells, tearing at his wheat brown hair. "I never wanted to leave. It's her fault I'm in this mess."

Cree slaps him in the chest. "You would've died if not for her, you worthless excuse for a husband."

"A little longer," Will mutters. "Just a little more time."

Turning to me, Cree says, "Promise me you'll take care of the boy?"

Elu's son clings to her, burying his face in her tattered dress. "Auntie, don't leave me," he sobs.

A few guards charge us, but Colin takes them on, parrying their blows with his blade and elbowing one in the face when they try to jump on his back. More run uphill and I edge back.

"Will," I say, but he's already moving, gathering Elu's son to him, linking the other hand with Nana's. Haroun grabs onto the boy's hand and links arms with Sanaa and another woman as Colin runs back to me and Jonas. Only Cree stands unmoving.

"Auntie," the boy cries, "come with us."

I reach for Cree, but she steps away, eyes fixed on the parade of guards rushing toward us. Will shuts his eyes and his magic swirls, covering the linked Oluso in blue and golden light.

"Elu always cared too much," Cree says, lifting her arms. The tattoos on her face begin to shift and dance. "She was always taking care of everyone else. It's my turn."

I seize her arm, pleading, but she shakes me off. "I'll buy all the time we need. Just promise me you'll come back for Elu's bones when it's safe."

She twists her palms up as though in prayer. Her tattoos run down her face, crawling like shadows over her skin. As they move downward, golden tears flow from her eyes and her skin glows brighter and brighter.

Angma-Oluso are as rare as iron-bloods. They shine so bright at birth that their mothers go blind, and their magic must be tightly sealed to prevent harming others by accident. Even Elu gave up, kept her magic in even while she was tortured because unleashing it would not only destroy the entire brigade of guards but kill us all.

"Please," I beg Cree. "You'll die."

"Someone has to keep Elu company in the beyond," she whispers. "They may kill me, but at least I get to choose my death."

Colin pulls me to him as Cree rises into the air, her tattoos drifting downward like broken shackles, her aura so bright now that I can barely see. Down the hill, the guards scream and cower, attempting to shield their eyes from Cree's magic.

"Go now," Will shouts, then disappears with Nana and the others.

Colin grips Jonas's hand and mine, but I am transfixed, watching Cree ascend higher and higher. Then speeding shadows break the sanctity of that light, arrows flying haphazardly into the sky. The archers must be struggling to see. Why in Olorun's name are they shooting?

"Stop!" I yell, waving my arms. "Don't shoot!"

Colin recaptures my hand as an arrow impales Cree's arm. "They made their choice," he spits. Just then Cree's golden glow morphs into a deadly sunset and she throws her head back and keens. I lose all sense of myself as Colin's magic envelops me, pulling me safely away, except a single image, one that I know will haunt me as long as I live—Cree's terrible beauty as her body becomes flame itself and erupts into a cloud of fire, consuming the entire field and hills.

TREKKING

When my vision clears, we are lying in dirt at the side of a road. The night air is chilly, the wind howling and blowing puffs of sand in our faces.

"They didn't have to do that," I scream, pounding the ground with my fists. "Why? Why? She only wanted to blind them. She didn't mean to kill anyone."

I want to weep, scream, because Cree is dead, because I know those guards are dead, but I can't do anything now. I have to keep moving. But I can't seem to do it.

"What if she meant to? Does that change anything?" Colin says, jumping to his feet. "They killed themselves by attacking her. Cree can't be blamed."

"Oluso don't murder. We fight back," I insist, but the words sound hollow even in my own ears.

"Cree was fighting back. They created the danger she was in, and her magic reacted to the soldiers' actions."

"Hundreds of them are dead, Col."

"*Tens of thousands* of us have died, Dèmi." He rounds on me, his eyes sparking. "This is what war looks like. This is what survival looks like. Sometimes we don't get to save everyone. We don't get to be righteous. We get our hands dirty. We claw and scrape and do whatever we can to keep going."

"We can't become the monsters they think we are," I counter softly.

Colin sighs, exasperated. "Ajes believe what they want regardless of what we do." He steels his jaw, and suddenly he feels different, remote and domineering. "I'd rather be a living monster than a dead martyr. Those soldiers got what they deserved."

It's a brutal assessment, and one I'm not sure I agree with, but then I hear a moan and I can't think about the dead when the living need me. Jonas is on his side, hand clutched to his chest, shaking. "I thought teleporting would be more comfortable than traveling in a bag. Guess I was wrong," he says, attempting a grin. He winces, and coughs, red staining his pale lips. He draws his hand away, and now I see the dull head of an arrow poking through his chest.

"You're hurt," I say dumbly, pulling his fingers out of the way.

"So I am," Jonas says, his voice seeming distant even though he's right next to me.

"No!" I yell, feeling him fading. I reach out to him, but Colin takes my hand. Gently he says, "You can heal him later. We have to get off the open road."

"But—"

He shakes his head violently. "If we're discovered by a road patrol or ambushed by something out of those trees"—he points to the wall of iroko trees behind me—"we'll be risking more than his life." As if he heard my earlier thoughts, he says, "We can't do anything if we're dead."

Shifting Jonas up in my arms, I gesture to Colin. "Fine. Take his feet, come on. We need to get him somewhere warm."

"I . . ." Colin grimaces. "I don't think I can help." He's breathing too hard. The jump took too much out of him. But as concerned as I am, he's simply tired. Jonas . . .

I don't want to think about how bad Jonas is.

"Please. Just a little ways," I ask.

"Can't we just help him walk? His feet aren't broken."

I glare at him, and finally he comes over, wresting Jonas's arms from my grasp. "You take his feet. You see better in the dark. I don't want to drop him by accident."

Tucking Jonas's feet by my waist, I trudge down the small hillside into the forest below, inching carefully as we come under the shadow of the trees. My arms are burning by the time we can no longer see the road, and I guide Colin to a large, slanting rock slab, placing Jonas carefully in front of it.

"This will buffer against the worst of the wind." I press my fingers into Jonas's neck. "He's cold. We need to start a fire. Go see if you can find a few twigs. We trampled some on the way here."

As tired as he is, he gives me a mischievous grin. "It's really attractive when you give orders, you know. Makes me want to eat you up."

When I scowl at him, he backs away. "Sorry. I'm trying to ease things. You seem stressed." Is *that* how I seem? I let my eyes say that, though, and he sighs. "I'll get the twigs. You should stop worrying. He'll be fine."

He walks off, and I can't help but notice how slow he's moving. He's pushing himself, and he's doing it not just for me, but for Jonas. His timing is terrible in terms of his joking, but that's who Colin is—he wants to help but doesn't know how. I know he's thinking, too, of what we just witnessed—of Cree and Elu, and the price of being born one of us. I promise myself that when he comes back, I'll make sure he rests, hold his hand, and tell him how much he means to me. But right now, I need to focus on Jonas.

I dig through the contents of my bag until my fingers reach the blankets Will gave us. Pulling them out, I wrap one around Jonas's waist. He wheezes as I touch his chest and opens his eyes. "Where are we?"

"Somewhere safe."

"We hope," Colin says, depositing a pretty sizable amount of wood in varying sizes. "I'm going to get one more load before I start the fire. Don't want it dying out." He stomps off, and I marvel at how he has the energy before turning my attention back to Jonas.

I feel for the arrow tip protruding from his chest and use my other hand to grip the arrow body at his back. "We'll get this out soon. Colin is getting kindling for a fire."

He grabs my hand and shakes his head. "No."

"No?"

He pulls my hand down to his trousers, and I pull away instinctively. "Pocket," he mutters. "In my pocket."

Kneeling to keep from putting my weight on his body, I reach into his pocket and touch something slippery. A moment later, I hold up a glossy, dark stone for him to inspect. "Is this it?"

He nods with effort and points to a chunk of the rock he's lying against. "Here. You can make a fire by striking the rocks together. It's faster."

I waste no time in gathering a few leaves and putting together a cone of twigs around the pile. I then rip off a piece of my skirt, pulling it apart to create a nest of fuzz. I can see Jonas shivering, but I know it's crucial to get this right the first time, so I make sure there's enough wood to catch the flames when I finally light the leaves. Satisfied, I lean forward and strike the rocks against each other. They give off sparks the third time, and a drop of flame falls onto the piece of my skirt. I bend and blow on it, the way Baba taught us, until the flame grows bigger, eating the twigs and leaves shoved under it.

In the light of the fire, I see the intricate patterns woven into the mottled rock Jonas is leaning against. His pale skin looks even more colorless against that bright landscape. Reaching around his back, I clasp the arrow once more. "This will hurt, but I need you to stay still. I don't want to risk leaving a piece of this inside you, so please . . ." I break off, lips trembling now.

He squeezes my hand, and I squeeze back before bracing one hand against his shoulder and tugging at the arrow in his chest. He gasps and cries out as I drag the arrow out, screaming all the while. Blood spurts from the open wound, and I toss the arrow aside, slamming my hands against his chest. Closing my eyes, I pour as much magic as I can muster into the wound. I used a lot fighting the guards, and more healing my ankle and wrist, so I only hope there's enough to heal Jonas. There's no other choice, though—if not now, there will be no later for him. He can't die without answering my questions.

Green fire spreads from my fingers, covering my hands, and pain explodes in my head. I open my eyes, catching the stricken look on Jonas's face, but when I try to move my fingers, they don't respond. His blue lips take on color, and he pushes against me, trying to peel my fingers away from his chest.

"Stop!" he screams. "No more." He tears at my fingers as pain swells in my chest. Finally, he gasps, as though breathing for the first time as my eyes roll back into my head. There's a crash, and my ears are ringing from a torrent of what sounds like frantic yells. Then loud thuds like angry hoofbeats punching at the dirt complete the cacophony. I twitch uncontrollably as the magic overwhelming my senses cuts frantically through me, desperate for a means of escape.

Then strong, familiar arms tighten around me and drag me back, tossing me to the ground.

I lie there, staring at the trembling limbs of the trees ahead, their branches blocking out the night sky. Colin peers over me, talking to me, moving my arms, but I cannot feel his touch. My mind is swimming with terror, but my body refuses to obey. I want to scream, but my throat will not open, until finally my toes and fingers start tingling, and I realize that the screeching in my ears is the sound of my own cry.

Colin sits me up, and I drag him to me, kissing him full on the mouth, needing to feel anything but terror and pain and the remembrance of being trapped in my mind, unable to move my limbs. He returns the kiss, gentle enough that I want to linger there forever, but I tear myself away and take a breath of air, enjoying the feeling of the wind on my skin and the air tickling my nostrils. I run my tongue over my lips and start laughing.

Hands clenched into fists, Colin barks at Jonas, "What did you do to her?"

"Colin. Don't," I say quickly, getting between them. I kneel to Jonas again. "Are you all right?"

He smiles wearily, but his voice is still harsh and breathy. "I'm fine."

"But she's not!" Colin says.

"It's not his fault," I say, turning to him. "Colin, it's okay. I know you're tired and concerned, but I'm okay."

He frowns, but eventually nods. "You're sure?" There's so much concern in his face I think we might both cry. Yet, because of that, I already feel better. I nod, a smile on my face.

"I got some more wood," he says, pointing at the pile he had dropped in his rush to get to me. The crash I heard, I realize. "I'll get some more. Don't do anything that will make me worry while I'm gone. Please."

I nod. "Thank you."

I watch him walk into the darkness, waving him on every time he stops to look back at me, and then I turn to Jonas. He purses his lips, tears welling up in his eyes.

"I tried . . . I tried to stop you . . ."

"I know." I reach for his hand, but he pulls back. "Can I touch you?" I ask finally.

"Aren't you afraid?"

"That I might die? No. If you wanted to kill me, you could have already."

He watches me, still keeping his hands away. "I don't know what might happen."

"But I do. As I said, it's not your fault." I take his hand, massaging the fingers. "I should have known. Mummy talked about this, but I didn't remember until after."

"What are you talking about?" Colin asks, his arms full of thick branches. He feeds the fire, but doesn't take his eyes off of either of us.

"He's Fèni-Ogun. Iron-blood. He can't be healed in the same way other Oluso can. He requires too much spirit energy."

"Iron-bloods died out a long time ago. Dèmi, are you sure you didn't hit your head too hard?"

"I'm not crazy. He's one of us. I saw his magic myself. He—"

I put my fingers to my lips when I realize what this means. I see Mummy again as she laid her hands on Jonas nine years ago, the way she slumped after, and the weariness in her eyes. The way she moved my hands away when I tried to heal Jonas myself.

"She knew," I say, tears spilling onto my face now. "She knew healing you would kill her."

Hearing the tremors in my voice, Jonas lowers his eyes and tries to pull his hand from mine, but I bend over those fingers, rocking them near my heart and sob, letting sorrow wash over me. I cry like I'm in the market square again, watching Mummy be cut down in front of my eyes all over again. I cry like I did under that cot alone until Jonas came back then and held me. I cry for Elu and Cree and Etera and all the other nameless faces that have perished without anyone to mourn them. I cry harder when I feel Jonas's other hand curl over my back and feel tears drip into my hair, and for the first time in nine years, I don't feel so alone.

Later, after bundling Jonas up, mashing some of Etera's bean porridge with bitter leaf and feeding it to him, we sit in silence by the fire. His face has more color now, but I know that it will take time for him to fully recover.

"When did you know?" I ask.

"What? That I was born with magic to magicless parents, or that I doomed your mother to an early death?" he says bitterly.

"Mummy wouldn't have healed you if she didn't want to. It was her choice."

Colin opens his mouth as though to say something, but instead goes back to feeding sticks to the fire. I appreciate it.

"I found out when I was about five or six," Jonas says. "My uncle did, really. My mother's brother—you know who my father's brother is." He lets out a bitter laugh that turns into a cough. I give him some water. "Thank you. Anyway," he continues, face pale from coughing, "Uncle Fred dropped a fork, but I stopped it from falling. We use so much iron for everyday things in Eingard because we went through the purges early. So many Eingardian Oluso had died or fled, and no one thought to sacrifice the convenience of a metal fork just in case some might be lingering around. Anyway, my uncle saw what I did and started looking for a tutor for me, someone who knew the old ways."

I nod, remembering the story he told me in Ikolé. "But the king's guard found out and killed him. Why didn't they kill you too?"

"They didn't know. Uncle Fred took care of that. He confessed interest in witchcraft and wouldn't speak when they asked him if he knew anything else."

"He saved you."

"Yes."

"You had magic then, in Ikolé. That's why you were asking me all those questions."

He nods. "I thought I could learn from you. And I did. You showed me that I wasn't a monster. That even though I came from a place where we used chained Oluso as practice dummies in military school, that I wasn't part of either—that I had a choice. You were my first friend. My first everything."

He says the last word softly, and I lick my lips, savoring the warm feeling it gives me. I'm still not sure I can fully trust him, but I don't know if those feelings are mutually exclusive at this point. "So what happened? Why did you betray me?"

He sighs, his eyelashes kissing his cheeks. "I didn't."

"Don't lie—"

"I'm not—I swear! I asked to go to Ikolé, to see the flowers my mother loved growing up. My uncle allowed me, but he sent Mari with me. I didn't know that they'd tracked your mother down, or that Edith was part of any plan. I think Edith would have injured herself or something if I didn't take a tumble into the okonkwo bushes that day. It was only later, after Mari killed your mother, that I realized what I'd done. You offered me your friendship, and I brought calamity into your home. I was trying to help you escape, to redirect Mari—again, I swear I was—but understandably, you panicked once you realized who I was and that there were things I hadn't told you."

A calmness seeps into my bones as I think about the anger I've carried like a wound for the last nine years. It was so real, so visceral, and now . . . it is gone. The knot that always hardened in my chest when I thought of Jonas no longer lives inside of me, a quick thrum in its place, making my pulse dance beneath my fingers.

"Why didn't you tell me who you were in the first place?"

He sighs again. "I've asked myself that question so many times over the years. I think at first it was because I didn't want to frighten you. Growing up as the king's successor doesn't leave you with many friends. Everyone wants to prove they're better than you or get close so they can make an alliance marriage in the future. Everyone has a motive for everything. That didn't happen with you. You just . . . were. I liked that."

Colin snorts. "Yeah, poor you, growing up as scion of the king with everything at your disposal. You've really had a hard life. Your fellow Oluso have been fighting to exist while you've been frolicking with maidens and getting your portrait made under the king's nose—and with all the king's luxuries."

Jonas clenches his jaw. "You have no idea what it's been like living with my uncle, hearing the things he says every day about those people—my people. Knowing that one day he expects me to take over and massacre other Oluso in the name of 'safety.' I wake up every day afraid. Afraid that he'll find out what I am."

"That must be terrible, to live in fear of potential hate. Well guess what," Colin says, "that's the life Dèmi and I and all our friends and family have lived in the open *every day.*"

"I . . . I know. And like you, I do what I can to protect those I love. Like my mother. My uncle would hurt her if he knew I had this power."

"Why would he hurt her?"

"Because that's the only way I could have any magic."

Colin narrows his eyes. "I thought you said your parents had no magic."

"They don't. My uncle's family hasn't had Oluso in it for generations. But it won't matter to him that my mother has no Oluso blood either. He believes what he wants, and what he believes is simple: mixed blood is the enemy; the Oyo queen allowed open borders and preached equality; she created the evil that corrupted the kingdom; he liberated it."

"He massacred the entire royal family," I snap. A voice in my head mocks me, whispering, *And your father helped him.*

"Yes, and how do you think he'd react knowing what I am?" Jonas says. "He'd burn the kingdom down and every Oluso in it before allowing his successor to be one. He already thinks I'm soft-hearted for treating the maids with care and refusing to stay in the room when he hosts his disgusting bacchanals. He laughs when I tell him to stop calling the rest of the kingdom savages or bush people and punished me for granting a pardon to a Berréan woman and a Goma man who married."

"Did he tie you to an iron pole?" Colin asks.

"No—"

"Then whatever punishments you've faced are *nothing* compared to what *real* Oluso go through."

Jonas looks away at that, ashamed. I feel for him—his couldn't have been an easy life, living in secret, but I also understand the truth in Colin's words. Because that's been *my* life too . . . and Jonas still has his mother. And after what we've seen today, with Cree, and Elu, and all the other frightened Oluso, I don't know if I can extend him any more grace.

I don't want to discuss that, though. What I want is an actual answer. I drag my fingers through my hair. "Why didn't you tell me the truth when we met again? Why did it take so long—for me to almost get myself killed—to learn this?"

"I wanted to tell you everything, including my magic. I wanted a second chance, but I figured I had to earn it with you."

"You wanted to earn my trust by continuing to lie to me?"

Colin snorts at this, and Jonas flushes.

"It's stupid, I know. But there was a lot going on. I was so surprised to see you in my room, and then I didn't think you'd listen while you were trying to kidnap me. And once we got to the forest, there was one thing after another." He gives a strangled laugh. "It sounds twisted, doesn't it? That the king's successor is the very thing he hates." I don't smile—he gets no sympathy from me on that. He winces, clutching at his chest, and I think it's more than his wound causing that reaction. Finally, he says, "I needed time to tell you what I wanted to say, and I needed to show that you could trust me."

Colin jumps up, shoving his hands in his pockets. "And I need to take a walk. Food's sitting too heavy in my stomach. Too tired to talk anymore anyway."

"Don't wander too far," I call after him as he stalks off. He waves a hand in a jaunty salute and slips into the darkness.

"He's angry," I tell Jonas. "To be fair, we all are—me included. Colin—he doesn't talk much about his background, but I think he was kicked out for being born Oluso. Will, my guardian, caught him trying to pick his pockets several years ago, and he's stayed with us since. He goes home to Berréa every few months, but he comes back angrier."

"He must hate me. I must sound like such a spoiled brat to him."

"To me too," I say, but smile to show I'm joking—mostly.

He smiles back, then stops as if remembering something. "So how did you end up with Will?"

"He found me. I knew my mother had friends in Benin, but I didn't know where. The Aziza cared for me in the forest and sent me on my way again, and before I knew it, I was in the city. I was wondering how I would get to my mother's friends when Will came up to me. He said I looked just liked her. But I think it was more than that.

"I think the Aziza sent him to me."

We are silent again, then he says, "I'm sorry, but would you mind helping me lie down? I'm exhausted. You're probably tired, too, seeing as I nearly killed you."

"Yeah—try not to do that again."

He chuckles, but it's weak. "I'm sorry."

I bundle the remains of my extra clothing into a makeshift pillow and put it down, then ease him over it. "I'm fine. You took a lot out of me, but not enough to kill me. I'll be all right again in another day or two. I have a lot of stamina."

As I tuck his blanket over him, he takes my hand. "Can I show you something?"

I swallow. "Sure."

He pushes his blankets aside and begins to unbutton his shirt, fumbling on the first button. I pull his hands aside and do it myself, ignoring the way my heart dances in my chest as my fingers brush his skin. There is a nasty wound, like a pressed wax flower under his right nipple. When I skim my fingers over the wound, he catches them up and caresses them. "It'll get better in a few days. Leave it, please. I don't want it to draw more magic out of you."

He moves my hand instead to the left of his chest, over his heart, and I tremble as I feel his heart fluttering beneath my fingers. "My Oluso mark is right here. No one has ever seen it, except me. I want you to be the first."

I lick my lips and trail my fingers down. At first, there is nothing, just mottled red and white skin, then a faint blue mark appears, a crescent with a flower in full bloom. I press my fingers gently on that mark, as though those petals will wither if I am not careful. And when he pulls my hand to his lips and kisses my fingers, heat drips from my belly into a lower part that stirs, a seed sprouting leaves for the first time.

We stay like this, watching each other, until Jonas tugs me closer, and asks, "What are you?"

"That's what I'd like to ask you," I answer with a giggle. "Who ever heard of an Oluso with no Oluso forebears? It's impossible."

He sighs and kisses my fingers again, and I shiver when they tingle. "I like you," he says, his face going red. "I don't know if you'll let me, but I like you all the same."

I pull back, even though my heart is singing. Even though I'm pretty sure I like him too. Maybe it's the madness of what we witnessed tonight, or the feeling that my life could end tomorrow. Maybe I'm selfish, and I want Colin, but there's something here that makes it hard for me to look away. So I whisper, "Why?"

He smiles. "You're brave in ways I don't think I could ever be. And you're strong, and warm, and you help people, and try to see the best in them, even when they don't deserve it. I still remember, you know, how you treated me in Ikolé. I insulted you, and you still explained everything to me as best as you could. I've seen you jump into a river to save a child even though you couldn't swim, and what you did for those prisoners—"

"Enough," I say, sighing. "Thank you. But you don't really know me. I'm not brave or nice all the time. I'm something else."

He smiles. "I know. Something more." He kisses my palm, caressing the callused skin with his lips, and my breath catches in my throat.

"I'm sorry. I should have asked first. I was jealous earlier when you kissed Colin, and I was imagining what it would be like to kiss you."

"Are you sure you want to find out?" I ask softly.

He pulls my fingers in response, and I bend down. My lips hover just above his when a twig snaps, and I jerk back just in time to see Colin sauntering out of the woods. His eyes are heavy, and he looks lost in thought.

"Welcome back," I say, clearing my throat, but he doesn't seem to hear me. When I repeat the words, he flashes me a smile and pulls out his own blanket, twisting his arms behind his head. "Think I'll go to bed early. 'Night. Feel free to crawl under my blanket if you're cold," he says with a grin. I smile at him, knowing he's trying to comfort me in his own way, but he turns away and closes his eyes. Within moments, his chest is rocking with the rhythm of sleep. I get ready to make my own bed.

Jonas tugs at my fingers again, and he inches over. "I'm a little cold, would you mind?"

I raise an eyebrow, and he shivers. "Please, just for a little while. I just want to talk. I've waited nine years to talk to you again."

Sighing, I pull my blanket from the bag and curl up next to him, lying on my arm. "What are we going to do now?" I ask, thinking of Lord Ekwensi's plan. How could we deliver Jonas back to the king who would kill him if he found out the truth?

Which makes me realize that I am now the one holding the biggest secret.

Jonas closes his eyes. "Sleep. We're tired, so let's sleep."

"No, I mean—"

He touches my face. "Dèmi, do you know any songs? When I was little, and I got really sick, sometimes Edith would sing. I liked her songs. But they're gone now." He sighs, and I touch his forehead,

Okàn àwon ènìyan sòrò	*The people's hearts speak*
Nígbà tí wón pè é	*When they call on Him*
Bàbá ní wón n wí	*Baba, they say*
Fún mi ní okun sí i	*Give me more strength*
Láti bá àwon òtá mi jà	*To fight my enemies*
Fún mi ní orò sí i	*Give me more wealth*
Kémi má ba à salàìní	*So I am never wanting*
Fún mi ní ìyè sí i	*Give me more life*
Kémi má ba à bèrù ikú	*So I don't fear death*
Sùgbón nígbà tí Bàbá bi mí pé	*But when Baba asks me*
Kí ni èdùn okàn re	*Of what I desire*
Gbogbo ohun tí mo wí ni pé	*All I can say is,*
Fún omo mi ní okun	*Give my child strength*
Kó lè máa dìde ní ojó gbogbo	*To rise up each day*
Fún un ní orò ogbón	*Give her the wealth of wisdom*
Láti mo ònà rè	*To know her way*
Fún un ní ìgboyà láti gbe aye	*Give her the courage to live*
Láàrin èrù àti ikú	*In the face of fear and death*
Rànmí lówó láti fé e kí n sì tó o	*Help me to love her*
Títí tí n ó fi mí ìmí ìkehìn.	*Until my last breath.*

startled at the warmth that meets my fingers. Brushing his skin, I call on the wind spirits, and watch as little white flecks coat his brow like snow. Then I sing the words Mummy used to sing when I was just a baby on her knee, words that soothed my fearful heart many times over the years.

By the time I finish, Jonas's fingers are tangled with mine, and he is breathing lightly, fast asleep. Closing my eyes, I push aside the storm in my heart and let my dreams carry me far away.

BURIAL

The rain wakes me, slapping noisy kisses against my skin like a dog licking its master's face. I sputter under its cold embrace, scrambling to my feet. The fire is out, and Colin is nowhere to be seen.

"Jonas," I call softly, shaking his shoulder. Saying his name brings heat into my cheeks and my heart flutters as though the word is something unspeakable. He stirs, rolling toward me, but his eyes stay shut. Cradling a hand under his head, I pull him up and press his back against the boulder. He squints at me, then closes his eyes and groans.

"Come on. We need to get out of the rain." I look up at the angry sky as a flash of lightning cuts through it. "We don't want to get caught up in a storm."

He coughs weakly. "I feel like I've been trampled by a horse."

"Or like you've been shot with an arrow. Now, get up. It'll get worse if you sit there any longer. We need to find Colin."

Colin's voice comes from behind me. "No need. I'm right here." He is standing at the edge of the trees, and although the rain is coming faster now, like stones in the sky's hands pelting us for our misdeeds, it bounces off the air around Colin. As he shifts closer, the blue aura hugging his skin like a cloak widens, and the rain in his path falls away. He grabs Jonas's shoulder and hauls him up.

"Come on. The water spirits say the rains will be on for days. Luckily, we're close to the meeting place. There's a natural shelter there."

"We're in Old Maiduguri?"

He nods. "I recovered more stamina than I thought. We're three miles outside the city. There's a sign up by the road, and a stable nearby."

I scurry under Jonas's shoulder as Colin moves under the other one. Together, we hobble to the copse of trees nearby and take shelter under wide palm leaves. "We can't walk three miles with him like this," I say, watching Jonas's labored breathing.

"Don't worry about me. I'll be okay. I've suffered an injury like this before."

"You've taken an arrow to the chest?"

"A sword. My uncle was dissatisfied with my graduation review from military school. He felt the fights were too easy for me. He wanted to see what I'd learned."

I think back to the knotted thread of flesh I glimpsed last night curving down from beneath Jonas's navel to a path I dared not trace and stare at the ground, hoping no one will notice the heat in my face.

"It's hard sometimes. You can't please them even when you do everything they ask. I know the feeling," Colin says. He shares a glance with Jonas, and they grin at each other as though sharing a secret.

I jerk as thunder rumbles out, echoing through the trees. Then the sound grows louder, alternating clapping beats like a set of batá drums deep in conversation, frenzied as they announce the birth of war.

"Horses," I whisper before digging into the raffia bag. Shaking the coins from my ogbene, I wrap it around the tree before me and climb, hitching my toes on the hardened spines the way I saw the village palm-wine tapper do many times growing up in Ikolé. At the top, I lean back, tethering myself with one hand. There is a parade of purple and gold swimming down the road, and horses, decked out in similarly colored livery, bearing their charges through the curtain of rain swallowing everything. Some of the soldiers are holding the long metal poles I have learned to fear, brandishing them like flags. If we're fortunate, the lightning will destroy some of the poles before it has a chance to kill one of us.

I shudder as the voice in my head adds, *It would devour some of these soldiers too. Wouldn't that be nice?*

Scurrying down, I practice keeping panic from making my fingers unsteady. "There are soldiers. Hundreds of them. We need to get out of here."

"What about Ekwensi?" Colin asks.

"I don't know, but something's wrong. There weren't supposed to be soldiers blocking our way into the city," I snap, throwing my hands on my head. "What if they know? What if Ekwensi called them here?"

"To catch two Oluso he employed? He wouldn't. The king would kill him if he knew he was behind this. It doesn't matter—we don't actually have to go into the city, just to the graveyard near it, remember? I'll get us around the soldiers."

Jonas looks between us. "What is going on? What does Lord Ekwensi have to do with this?"

Colin runs his fingers through his hair, glancing at me. I shake my head. "It's fine. He needs to know anyway."

"Know what?"

"We're sending you back to your uncle. Ekwensi is here to re-trieve you."

He is silent a moment, then says, "Why? Why would you take me just to send me back?"

"There is a provincial election at the end of the winter festi-val—" I start.

"And you need to make sure Lord Ekwensi wins it. That's it, isn't it? He's trying to curry favor with my uncle using me."

I look away, and he pulls himself up, using the tree for support. "Okay. But I'll ask again: Why? What's at stake for you?" he asks, looking pointedly at me.

"The Oyo Oluso are dying. There are new raids each year, and the okri trade is getting bigger. People are afraid to have children because they don't want them to end up enslaved or killed. Even local Ajes who might have patronized an Oluso family before have stopped helping. You were there in Ikolé with me. You saw what happened to my mother. She healed so many of the villagers, but none of them could look her in the face or even tried to defend her when the guards came. Nine years, and nothing's changed. I don't want what happened to Cree and Elu to happen to anyone else."

"If Lord Ekwensi was in charge of the province, that would change things, wouldn't it? He would at least protect some of the Oluso here, is that it?" Jonas says the words as though he under-stands, but his face is thunder, eyes wide with anger, nostrils flared.

I swallow. "Before I agreed to do this, I rescued two children. The boy is barely five years old, and the girl can't be more than seven or eight. They had injuries all over, but they were being put up for sale. I asked the trader how much he wanted for them, and he said I could have the boy for five lira. The girl cost twenty times more." I spit, as though I can push out the poison in those words.

"Children are being bought and sold while people watch, all because of what they are. Do you think I could just stand by and let that happen?"

His shoulders droop, and he looks away, but not before I see the tears glistening in his eyes. Pushing away from the tree, he drags a hand across his face. "Right. So what's the plan, where do we meet Lord Ekwensi?"

To his credit, he doesn't argue more. He knows as well as we do that this is a viable choice. I hate that we have to do this, but as much as I'm starting to see him as my friend again, I can't give way. If he wants to prove himself to me—to all Oluso—he has to help.

Colin, though, doesn't seem as convinced. He watches with a frosty look until Jonas claps him on the shoulder. "Don't worry, I won't betray you. I'm one of you, remember? And I have a debt to pay. I cost Dèmi her mother—I won't sit by and watch other children lose theirs."

"I didn't ask—"

He shakes his head. "I have one more question, but I'll ask it when we get to where we're going. Can I do at least that?"

Colin shrugs. "If you'll help us, then sure. We need to go."

Jonas picks up my bag, wincing as the weight settles onto his shoulders. With a breath, he nods. "Lead on."

When I reach to take the bag from him, he walks away, trudging after Colin. I roll my eyes and follow. Nana always says that "the ass is stubborn no matter what you say to it." I have a feeling the same goes for Jonas.

Unravelling my ogbene, I pull the cloth over my hair and follow. We walk for several minutes, the silence broken only by the squelches our feet make as they push into the dirt and soft Maiduguri soil. The orange-red clay swallows my skin up to my ankles, and as the rains get heavier and the ground begins to swell toward us, I shudder. It is as though we are being pulled into a pool of blood.

After what feels like an eternity, Colin stops, holding a finger to his lips. We are standing below an outcropping, at the edge of an iron gate, and beyond, stone slabs rise from the ground like watchful shadows. Looking around first, Colin scrambles onto the ledge and gets his footing before motioning to me and mouthing, *The gate*. Jonas is faster, leaping onto the ledge and tapping the gate with a finger. It swings open with ease and he steps through the threshold as I take Colin's hand and climb up. As I pull the gate closed, ignoring the sting it produces in my fingers, I catch sight of the glimmering dome and the white towers that mark Old Maiduguri's regional palace. I have heard stories of that place, know the tale of an Oyo-born Ifé queen three generations ago who built it to serve as a sanctuary during times of war. But I know the tale from last Harmattan too. Of the Ngio people who marched for several days from southeast Oyo to meet the Maiduguri regional lord and a visiting Alistair Sorenson. Of the way they were slaughtered, Oluso and Aje alike, for questioning the king's policies. Of how they screamed, claiming sanctuary in the palace, as the guards ripped them from their loved ones and dragged them to their deaths.

Curling my fingers into my palm, I run to the cave sitting atop the cemetery hill, dodging in between the gravestones, not stopping even when I slip and knock down a loose one. At least whoever was buried there *has* a marker. The people who died that day—the victims of Alistair's Betrayal—were denied a final resting place. Instead they were poured into a single pit of this blood-awful clay, consumed by the earth that birthed them, nameless and forgotten. I won't let that happen to anyone else. Not if I can stop it.

Shivering with cold, I stumble into the cave and suck in a breath, letting the warm air fill my lungs. Jonas breaks in behind me, breathing hard, and I take the bag from him then, tossing him a blanket soon after. Colin beckons to us. "Come. The trail goes a ways in, but he's here. I sense it."

Summoning a wind spirit for light, I follow him into the darkness. The sound of water dripping intensifies as we move farther in, and there are squeaky noises interrupted only by bouts of screeching that echo through the cave and make my heart jump. Stone grooves dance over every inch of the cave's walls, forming an intricate pattern punctuated only by wet moss that tickles my fingers and makes my nose itch. Soon, we come upon pools hollowed into the ground and push ourselves against the walls, hugging each other as we inch past. And then the noises become louder, shouts congealing into audible human voices as we chase a swath of light that appears nearby.

". . . told you it was unwise to trust a girl to do a man's job. The king came earlier than expected, and now we need an excuse to check this cave every day."

"I know you're angry about losing two hundred and fifty lira to me, Vermillion, but there is no need to be so testy. You always were an awful gambler."

"What do you reckon Alistair will think about this latest gamble? I doubt he would put faith in your bush methods, Ekwensi. Once a savage, always a savage."

"I wouldn't hurl insults if I were you, Vermillion. I seem to recall that your estate has been having trouble of late. Is it the money? Perhaps I should forgive you your debt . . . or call it in?"

Ekwensi's voice retains its smooth nature, but there is an edge to his words and the air in the cave is tense. Shielding my eyes, I step into the light. A stocky, red-faced man is holding Ekwensi by his collar, a knife pressed to his throat. Ekwensi flashes his toothy smile, and I shudder as I remember the Ishan proverb Baba always spoke during training: *Oduma noi mo akon uhameh gbole a.*

It is only the toothless lion that cannot eat its prey.

"Welcome, young ones," Ekwensi says without taking his eyes off the other man. "I trust your journey was smooth. You're here a lot *earlier* than expected."

A soft glint draws my eyes to the tongued blade he is holding against the man's heart, and after grunting, the other noble pulls his smaller knife away from Ekwensi's throat and slips it into the sheath at his belt, but not before I catch the slight trembling in his fingers.

Ekwensi taps his left shoulder with his right hand twice, greeting us. "Nabi's Day shines up you. Make you wake free."

Colin taps his shoulder in answer and finishes the greeting. "We stand as free as the sky and wind."

Ekwensi nods at the other man. "This is my associate, Lord Vermillion." Catching sight of Jonas, he bows. "Your Highness. I apologize for any trouble you have suffered up until now. I trust my associates have taken care of you?"

"They have treated me fairly, Lord Ekwensi. I am unharmed," Jonas says. "At first, I thought they were assassins, but once I realized they were protecting me from a coup, I felt at ease. It's been a long journey."

Ekwensi's gaze flicks to mine and I shrug. I can keep secrets too. Let him think Jonas ignorant. It's better that way.

Jonas stands erect, shoulders back, as though he were presiding over court, even though he must be in agony from his wound. Moving to the other noble, he says, "Lord Vermillion, interesting to see you here. I understood you were protesting my succession rights to the throne, in favor of Cousin Albert. How is your dear son these days? Did Auntie Callia send you to help rescue me?"

Vermillion blusters. "Your Highness, I only arrived today. Lord Ekwensi spoke of sending agents out to rescue you once we received news of your kidnapping, and I came out to see that you could return home safely."

Jonas returns a placid smile. When he speaks, his words are sharper, his High-Ceorn more distinct. It's frightening how quickly he's transformed into someone else. "How kind of you. Send Auntie Callia my regards. I miss her plum pastries."

"She misses making them," Vermillion adds immediately. "She makes those pastries especially for you, Your Highness."

"Really?" Jonas continues, brow lifted in what I now know is mock surprise. "The next time I'm invited to the lower palace, I'll bring some wildblossom tea. I didn't like that dry root tea she gave me last time. Made my throat burn."

"Of course," Vermillion coughs. "Well then, Ekwensi, let's get on with this, shall we?"

Ekwensi raises his blade like a village chief conducting the start of a festival. "Please, Your Highness"—he points to a raised slab of rock—"rest here. You've traveled a long way. Fortunately, your uncle is nearby. I'll deliver the good news, and we should be on our way to Eingard soon.

"As for you, young lady, thank you. I am forever in your debt." He offers his hand, and I reach out gingerly to take it. He swallows my fingers in his, and pulls my hand to his mouth, his kiss on my knuckles like candle wax burning me. I snatch my hand away as Colin comes to my side. He may have saved Colin at Lokoja, but I haven't forgotten that he wanted me to leave all those trapped Oluso, that there's something he's not telling me.

Ekwensi sighs. "You may go. I'm sure our paths will cross again. You have my word that things will change. Believe it." He turns on his heel.

"Wait," I whisper. "You said you'd tell me about my father. You promised."

He stops. "Did I?"

Vermillion throws an annoyed look our way. "Just pay them, Ekwensi. Don't be too cheap."

Ekwensi chuckles. "You go report to His Highness. Don't forget to steal all the credit while you're away." He pauses, then adds with a smile, "Please do refrain from asking His Highness to spare you money. I'll let you off what you owe me."

Vermillion sniffs. "I'll stay. Make sure the prince is safe. You go."

Ekwensi shrugs. "Very well. But in a moment, yes? Unless you want to pay my soldiers?"

With a snort, Vermillion stalks several feet away, engaging Jonas in small talk. Ekwensi turns back to me and Colin.

"I promised *nothing*, but I will tell you this—Osezele is not the monster he's made out to be."

"He murdered fifty thousand people," I hiss.

"And he saved four hundred thousand. Those who perished sacrificed themselves for a greater cause. They wished for their loved ones to survive. Osezele made sure of that."

"How? His actions made it easy for Sorenson to take over Ifé."

Colin speaks up, "I heard he made some kind of bargain. A blood price."

Ekwensi wrinkles his nose in distaste. "You could call it that, yes. The Oluso in the capital were in danger. Sorenson's forces were slaughtering only Oluso as they invaded. Osezele asked the spirits for help, but the only way to save all those people was an exchange. It was commendable, really. Saving the other Oluso after they'd betrayed the iron-bloods. I couldn't have done it."

I furrow my brow. "I don't understand."

To my surprise, Ekwensi looks to Colin. An unreadable look

passes between them. Colin gives a half smile, but it doesn't reach his eyes. "Magic in exchange for Aje status. The capital Oluso had their spirit bonds broken."

"They all became Aje?" I ask, confused. "But that's madness. Losing your magic is like dying. It's dishonorable to break spirit bonds."

Ekwensi speaks with steel in his voice now. It is clear I've overstepped. "They survived. There was no way to escape the purge. They were surrounded. Alistair's puppy, Mari, let him into the city. With the blood sacrifice they were able to live long enough to pass on their bloodlines to their children."

"The Oluso did not all die," I mutter to myself. "They were transformed."

"Sometimes you must be willing to do the heinous to protect the ones you love. Power only understands power." He stops, directing his last words at Colin. "And only power can cover your failures."

I bristle at this. "Colin is no failure."

Ekwensi puts his palms up in mock surrender. "I did not mean to imply so." He looks back at Vermillion and Jonas. "Time is short. I must go to the king. We can revisit history another time."

I catch his shoulder and he stiffens, looking down at my hand as if it were bird droppings. "Just one question," I say. "If power is so important, why are you bargaining with the king?"

He rubs his temple. "I thought you were wise, like your dear mother."

I clench my fists. "You knew my mother?"

"Remember this, Dèmi. Power can only take you so far. Sacrifice even further. Your mother protected you with everything. I only seek to do the same for our people."

"Ekwensi!" Vermillion shouts. "Are you going or should I report you for insubordination?"

Ekwensi bows, suddenly the formal courtier, but his words are tight, dripping with venom. "I am finished, Vermillion. I will return shortly with your dear brother-in-law."

With a sweep of his cape, he leaves. Lord Vermillion stalks over to us. "You heard him. Get going."

My head is full of questions. Finding out about my father did nothing to quench my thirst for more. But now I think of the complicated lines of succession the village chief in Ikolé had to adhere to because of his many children, and the scandals that erupted because of it. I think of teas that are likely to make your throat burn, and ones that can kill, and make a list in my head. Then I lock eyes with Jonas, who is sitting alone, body upright, every inch the princeling, and ask a question with my eyes. After a moment he shakes his head and I have my answer. Taking a breath, I turn to leave when Jonas shouts, "Wait. Remember, I had one more question."

He comes to me and holds me close, pulling me into a hug while his uncle stands there gawking. He whispers in my ear, "Will I ever see you again?"

Pressing my nose into his chest, I savor the warmth of his arms around me and the soft, earthy smell that radiates off his skin. Then I push him back and clap his shoulder. "Of course. Royal parades happen every few years, you know. We'll come pay our respects as subjects." I smile, letting some of the weight in my chest drip into my eyes, and turn away, rushing headlong back into the darkness before the light can catch my tears. Colin follows me without a word, and as we move farther away from that open cavern, Jonas calls out after us, "Our promise ends here. But I'll be here—when you need me."

I don't stop, though the words make my heart twist even more. I tell myself it's the residue of the blood vow stripping away. Then as we venture into the welcoming darkness, Vermillion's voice drowns Jonas out.

"Your cousin told me something rather interesting, and I'm hoping it's true. He says you request wooden utensils for a special reason. That you like the feel of them."

I let those words become empty echoes, focusing instead on the path ahead of me. By delivering Jonas I have cleared a path for other Oluso to survive. It may end up being a temporary solution, a quiet before the storm of war and heartbreak, but it is something. Ekwensi can create the hope that Ifé's Oluso need, and that is enough. So I walk on, burying the embers that awoke in my heart just the day before.

Mourning is a luxury only the living possess.

BEATEN

We are nearly to the other side of the cavern when Colin asks, "What did he say to you?"

"Nothing. He wanted to know if we would come see him when he becomes king."

"You mean he wanted to know if *you* would go see him."

"We need to start making our way home."

"Dèmi—"

I speed up my pace, but he easily catches up, grabbing my shoulder. "I don't want to talk about this!" I plead, but he slaps a hand over my mouth.

"*Listen.*"

Nothing. I'm contemplating biting his hand when a dull roar reaches my ears.

Jonas.

I take off, rushing toward the path I had just abandoned. Colin is faster, leaping over a puddle in front of us as he edges past me. We burst in as Jonas pushes Lord Vermillion off him, staggering to his feet. He presses his fingers to a bloody patch on his shirt as blood drips from a gash on his leg.

Lord Vermillion rushes forward, but I catch him then, kicking him in the side and using his momentary shock to elbow him in the chest. He staggers but recovers, breathing hard. "You witch! You think you're going to save him, don't you?" He spits, blood mingled with saliva landing at my feet. "I'll kill you first then."

He swings at me and I dodge, pivoting as the blade comes down, and Colin slams into his back, knocking him on his knees. He stands and laughs again. "I've only been bested in combat once, by the prince's father, and even then he fought unfairly, attacking me when I was still adjusting my armor. Do you really think you pests are match enough for me?" He twirls his sword, the sound like a whip cracking the air.

Colin grins. "It's old bastards like you who get to talking when you know you can't win a fight. Trying to scare us, are you?"

"Uncle, stop this madness. The king will execute you for this, even if you survive. Cousin Albert and Auntie Callia will be cast out."

"Who would know? Who will stand as witness to my crimes?"

"We—" I start, then fall silent. Testifying in the royal court would mean going to the palace and meeting Alistair Sorenson. It would mean meeting the king's guard. And maybe some of them would remember the girl who disappeared into the forest after striking a royal guard's captain. The one the captain died chasing. There's no way Mari survived Cree's explosion.

Vermillion cocks his head at me and laughs. "You see? I knew Ekwensi had secrets. You can't walk up and request an audience with the king, can you? But don't worry. I have my story straight." His voice becomes high, mocking, "'My liege, my only crime was trusting that Ekwensi's agents were actually there to help. But they nearly killed me and murdered the prince before I could stop them.'"

"Once I'm done beating you into the dust, I'll drag you in front of the king myself," Colin says.

Springing off his heel, he runs at Lord Vermillion. The other man smiles before whipping his sword out in a wide arc, but Colin is a blur, throwing himself to the ground and rolling out of harm's way. Lord Vermillion tries again, stabbing at the ground, but I bring up the rear, jumping onto his back and slamming my elbow in his neck. He gurgles and drops his sword as I press my dagger to his back.

"Never turn your back on an opponent. Didn't you learn that in military school?"

He chokes, blood dripping down his chin. "You will pay for this."

"I doubt it."

The blare of a horn nearly makes me drop my dagger. The resounding clap of boots reminds me of stampedes I used to watch out in the grasslands when Baba would take Colin and me out for training. From the corner of my eye, I catch flashes of purple and gold, and my chest tightens all at once.

"On your knees. His Royal Highness, Ruler of Ifé, Warden of the Four Regions, King and Conqueror Alistair Sorenson is before you," a voice commands.

I don't move, wishing instead that I could fold myself into the air and disappear like Colin so often does. The command comes again. "On your knees, unless you no longer wish to live."

To my surprise, Colin obeys, collapsing like the airy Berréan sweetcake I made for his last name day. Gone is the sullen and defiant boy who stood before the Aziza queen. Jonas, even with his injuries, hazards a low bow, but my limbs are frozen, my fingers tightening further around the dagger at Lord Vermillion's back.

"My king, I would pay you the honor of a bow, but I am currently not at liberty to do so," Vermillion gasps out.

A voice sounds out, its rich melody flooding the cave. "I see your situation quite clearly, Alain. No need to stand on ceremony."

From the corner of my eye, I study the man who has just stepped into view. He is tall, though a hand shorter than Jonas, with thick red-gold hair settled around his face and cut neatly around his ears and neck. Golden armor covers every part of his body save his face, and a long, purple overcloak flows from his shoulders. He holds up a hand, and one of the soldiers at his back rushes forward with a bow and a quiver of arrows.

Vermillion begins to speak, the words tumbling out like rocks being flushed out by a waterfall. "My king, I was lured here by Ekwensi. He spoke of using agents to recover the prince. But the moment he left, his agents attacked. I attempted to defend the prince, and things went awry, as you can see."

I growl, digging the dagger into his back. "Liar. You attacked us and tried to kill the prince."

"Come, come. No need for such argument," the king says. He smiles, crinkles forming in the corner of his eyes. I notice then that his eyes are the same startling blue as Jonas's, but there is something else in them, sparkling and bright, like light dancing on a pool of water. There is also something missing—any semblance of warmth. He beckons, and two soldiers help Jonas up, bringing him to the king. The king puts a hand on his shoulder.

My stomach twists and I lick my lips. Something is wrong. The Alistair Sorenson who has haunted my dreams most of my life has been little more than a specter—an ugly, iron-toothed monster whose lips are stained with the blood of the innocent and whose eyes are colder, and darker, than any Eloko's. But when the king speaks again, and his warm voice washes over me like a welcome coat in the bitter cold, I begin to tremble and shake.

"Ekwensi," he says, and I see him step forward. "I won't bother asking you what is going on. I know you're not so foolish as to attempt to kill my nephew in front of me, so that leaves me with only one conclusion. My dear brother-in-law has been a bit testy of late, and a little too inclined to complain. So, why don't we just resolve this problem straight away? I'll leave it to my nephew's judgment."

Jonas winces, and I catch the flash of movement then, his uncle's gloved knuckles pressed into his shoulder. I shove Lord Vermillion aside and take a step forward, but the king shifts in an instant, nocking an arrow into his bow, the iron shaft aimed at me.

"Tell me, Jonas, who speaks truth? If your uncle is to be believed, then my most faithful dog needs to be disposed of along with these two miscreants. But if your uncle is lying, he and his entire household will be put to death for attempting a coup."

Lord Vermillion gets on his knees. "My king, I have done nothing to undermine your authority."

"You did not bow in my presence, for starters. I can hardly excuse that."

"You said you understood."

"But I did not say there were no consequences." He looks at Jonas. "I have always told you that, Jonas, haven't I? There are consequences to every action. As the future ruler of this kingdom, you need to accept that. You cannot excuse one transgression when it may birth future insurrection. So, tell me, who will you choose? Do I kill the girl, or your uncle?"

"Uncle Alistair, please," Jonas begs, his eyes swollen with fear.

"What have I told you about that?"

Jonas shrinks back. "My king, I am sorry."

"Don't be sorry, choose. I'm getting tired holding this thing. I might just let an arrow fly and allow fate to choose for me."

I swallow, trying to settle the fear twisting in my belly. There are twenty guards at the very least, blocking our way out. Colin seems to have moved while I wasn't looking, and is at the back, pressed to the opening from which we came. I need to think of something, and fast, but my mind is blank, my muscles aching with the need to move.

"I will choose," Jonas says, sighing. Then he steps in front of the king's arrow, blocking me from sight. "I choose myself."

The king merely chuckles. "Why?"

"Because I know what you really want, and I have never seen you offer an enemy a swift death at the hands of an arrow."

The king presses his face closer to Jonas's, but his words echo throughout the cave, dripping with undisguised pleasure. "And what do I really want, my dear nephew?"

"Certainty. Loyalty. You want me to prove my allegiance to you, and you want to test both Uncle Alain's and Lord Ekwensi's."

The king begins to clap, the sound of his gauntlets striking the wood of the bow like the scream of iron on bone. The guards follow suit, as though they are watching a masquerade rather than contemplating murder. "I'm impressed. Looks like all my investment in you has not been wasted, boy. In that case, you know what to do." Tossing the bow and arrow quiver back to a guard, he pulls out his sword and hands it to Jonas. "I've chosen. Kill both of them."

Lord Ekwensi speaks up now. "My lord, might I ask that you stay your hand and spare the girl?"

"And why would I do that? She failed to bow, too, you know. Despite whatever orders you might have given her, she should still show some respect."

"My lord, I fully agree. If it is your wish that she be disposed of, then I will comply."

I suck in a breath, meeting Lord Ekwensi's empty gaze. Is he really going to leave me to die? Colin inches up behind me, slipping his hand into mine. Jonas stares at us, panic heavy on his face, then almost immediately the king raises a hand. "So be it—stop! You two, come forward. I will spare your lives today."

Colin's shoulders drop a little, and the hum of magic that flowed between our fingers a moment before dies out. Jonas remains frozen, horror etched onto his face, fingers gripping the king's sword. I will my body to move then, shifting a foot forward as I wait for the fight to start. But the king merely steps forward himself, peering at us. He raises both eyebrows when he catches sight of Colin, while Colin lowers his head, eyes glued to the ground. When the king looks at me, though, his eyes grow wide, and he breaks into a wide smile. "How lovely. Ekwensi, where did you find such a lovely girl?"

Ekwensi coughs, and the king reaches for my face. I take a step back, dagger tight in my hand, but just as I am about to bring my blade up, he stills his hand in midair and nods. "Fate smiles on me today." He turns to a guard. "Take them. And send a hawk to Lord Kairen. Tell him I found something he's been looking for. I want the usual prepared for him—food and wine—but leave the rest of the entertainment to me. He's always had a taste for exotic women."

The fear in my belly burns into something more, but when I turn to flee, Colin traps me in his arms. "I'm sorry," he whispers as the guards surround us. *Sorry . . . ?*

No—I won't be betrayed again. I stomp on his foot and push away, trying to break past him, but a guard catches me by the hair and yanks me back before I can scream. Colin takes the dagger from my hands as more guards grab my arms. "Don't hurt her, please. She's just scared," he shouts. "Get away from her." The guards look to the king, and after he gives a small nod, they back away.

"Don't be an olodo. Trust me. We'll get out of this," Colin hisses in my ear. "This is the only way. If we make any more trouble, they might decide to kill us, and who knows what will happen to Nana and the others then?

"I'm Colin—you know me. *Trust me.*"

I still. Trust has been a precious commodity for me for too long. But I'm not sure I have a choice—I'll go along with what Colin is saying. Because one thing I can trust is that Lord Ekwensi could easily lead soldiers to Benin. This mess is no one else's but mine, and I will not have my loved ones murdered over it.

The king tsks. "There's no need to be so glum. We merely want to offer you a reward for recovering my nephew. Ekwensi speaks highly of both of you. Besides, I want you to be able to enjoy the show we're about to watch."

I lift my head at that. A guard hands Lord Vermillion a sword along with a small pouch. I watch as he pulls a handful of koko from the pouch and sucks it in between his teeth, grinning all the while. It is rumored that with a large enough dosage of koko, the user ceases to feel anything, but after a few minutes, even lifting a spoon can be excruciatingly painful and the crippling sensation requires even more koko to overcome. It is part of why the drug is so popular with soldiers—the power to become invincible, to sow death, blood, and terror for their enemies, and to reap the short harvest of glory is too much to pass up.

As the guards steer us to the corner of the cave, I keep my eyes trained on Jonas. His back is tense with waiting, his neck taut and fingers rigid, bracing himself for the coming storm. I say a silent prayer then: *Olorun bíku bá sunmo ítosì ki é bámi yé òjò íku.*

If death is near, please help it not to see us.

Lord Vermillion's eyes bulge, and the veins in his forehead swell in size as saliva starts dripping from his mouth. The king pushes Jonas forward. "You should be more than able to defeat Alain, even with his enhancements. If you fail, you will be in charge of putting every single member of his household to the sword, personally, in exchange for my intervening to help you. If you win, then you will have proven yourself to me, and I will spare Alain's house. Is that clear?"

"Yes." Jonas's voice is strangled and resigned all at once. He is being forced into the worst situation an Oluso can find themselves in: if he kills Lord Vermillion, he risks losing his magic and going mad; if he refuses, he will be forced to spill innocent blood, and madness is certain. I bite my lip, wishing I could do something. The king is only a few paces away. If I could get behind him and get in one good blow, I could kill him and end these horrors now, end the terror that has plagued Ifé since the day he came to power. As though he can read my mind, Jonas looks at me. The tender caress of that gaze makes my insides knot, and I miss it immediately when he turns to parry the heavy blow Lord Vermillion brings down on him.

He pushes Lord Vermillion back, but the other strikes again, taking a large swipe at the younger man's belly. He barely jumps back in time when Lord Vermillion rushes him again. They fight like this for several moments, Lord Vermillion attacking, bearing down, while Jonas blocks and dodges, arms getting slower with each parry. It reminds me of the winter festival courtship dances—the Benin girls who dance with multiple suitors because their parents are desperate they marry well. The suitors keep coming until the girls, tired of holding out for the best, let a fortunate suitor carry them off like a festival prize, knowing full well that they will never be the same again.

Except I doubt any of those girls had been recently shot through the chest.

Even as Jonas blocks the latest cut and Lord Vermillion catches him in the stomach with his boot, the king and the guards do not move, watching transfixed, like ooni with their heads barely visible above water, scouting their prey before they hustle their giant, scaled bodies out of the water and devour everything in sight. If I don't do something, Jonas will be swallowed up.

Jonas scrambles off the floor just as Vermillion's sword comes down again, and he strikes his uncle in the side. Vermillion roars and weaves back, bringing his sword down in a wide swath. Jonas twists out of the way and knocks his uncle in the face with the pommel of his sword, kicking his knee in when Vermillion clutches his eye. The two stand at odds, breathing hard. Then before Vermillion can lift his sword again, a bewildered look washes over his face. He begins to choke and spit up blood, dropping his sword as he puts his hands to his neck. Throwing his sword down, Jonas goes to him, but Vermillion is staggering now, crumpling to the floor in a heap.

Pressing his fingers to Vermillion's neck, Jonas looks back at the king. "My king, he's dying."

Alistair Sorenson yawns. "How pitiful. He couldn't even kill you with the extra strength he gained. Oh well." He turns, flinging his cloak. "Ready the carriages for Eingard. I have a gala to host tomorrow."

"But my king, he'll—"

"Jonas, you know I don't like repeating myself," Sorenson snaps.

Jonas lowers his head immediately. "I understand."

The king tosses his gauntlets to a waiting servant. "Alain was overdue punishment considering he's been plotting against me for months. Fate handed you the victory today. Take it, and let's be on our way."

Lord Vermillion cries out in anguish, blood and saliva spilling from his mouth, but the king is already walking away, the guards following in his wake. Lord Ekwensi and our own guard escort are all that's left as Lord Vermillion's cries turn to childlike whimpers. Jonas stands over him, sword in his hand, and I know immediately what he's considering. The mercy the king will not give may be the sword that ends up taking Jonas's life and setting him on the path to madness.

"Don't," I say. "He's dying anyway."

He hesitates, sword shaking in his hand. Then Ekwensi is there, plunging a blade into Vermillion's shaking body. The body trembles a few times, then slows to stillness. Ekwensi closes Vermillion's eyes. "It is done. Now, before the king thinks twice about why you're not following, we must go.

"*All* of us," he says, looking at me.

BLISS

We are stuffed into gilded carriages like palm fruit in a sieve press before it is crushed to make tombo. Lord Ekwensi rides with Colin in the carriage ahead of us—which Colin was none too pleased about—leaving me with Jonas, two guards, and the king's medicine man.

"You, girl, help me," the medicine man says, attempting to pull Jonas's shirt over his head. Steadying myself against the wooden paneling behind my bench, I inch over, trying to hold back the roiling in my belly. I felt the kiss of iron as I was shoved up the carriage step moments before, and the nausea that sprang up since then confirms that this carriage is nothing more than a moving cage.

Doing my best to hide all that from the Eingardians, I spread my legs wide, keeping my feet braced against the parallel bench bottoms. One of the guards across snickers as my skirt rides up, revealing the backs of my knees, but I ignore him, focusing on Jonas's bruised face instead. When I'm finished wrestling his shirt off, I kneel, reaching for the clasp on his trousers. He places his hands over my fingers, his face taking on a crimson hue. Nodding toward the wound spanning his lower belly, I brush his fingers away.

"You don't have time to be modest now. You need help."

The medicine man puts his hand on my arm, squeezing. "Your Highness."

"What?"

"You must address the prince by his title."

I grit my teeth. "Of course, excuse me, Your Highness."

The medicine man shakes his head. "I don't know where Ekwensi finds such people sometimes. I understand you were in charge of protecting the prince, and yet you let this happen to him."

"It's not her fault, Jarvis. She *was* protecting me. Take your hands off of her."

Jarvis shoots me a disdainful look. "Of course, Your Highness. As you wish."

I work Jonas's trousers down to his knees, moving gingerly. His left leg is covered in dried blood, and there's an ugly cut etched into the flesh above his knee. Jarvis reaches into his satchel and produces two bottles filled with greenish-blue liquid.

"Your Highness, this is an acid we've been developing for three seasons. I will use it to close your injuries. Rest assured. We have tried this method with the kingdom's soldiers, and it has not failed us since."

I have heard of methods like this, methods that became more popular once the kingdom began to purge Oluso. There are few Ariabhe Oluso like me who can perform healings, so the people have turned to different methods. Burning wounds closed is only the latest craze, and the reports of sickness, pain, and infection that claim the lives of some who go through this are shouted down and dismissed as unfortunate accidents.

But we've heard them all the same.

"Are you sure you want to risk burning it closed? Without even cleaning the wound?" I ask, horror overriding the nausea gripping me.

Jarvis purses his lips. "We don't have the tools to do any clean-ing. We need to close His Highness's wounds before he loses too much blood."

"Yes, but—"

The carriage jumps as we knock into something, throwing me onto Jonas's legs. I spring right up, and though he is grinning at me, I see the slight twitching in his mouth that speaks of pain. "Car-riage rides are always like this. It's better to sit down so you don't get thrown around."

Grabbing the raffia bag, I dig through it until I find the remains of my medicine packet. "Here. I have some bitter leaf and yarrow. It should be enough to seal the wounds for now. Thankfully the belly wound is shallow. We can start with his leg wound first."

"You may do things that way in whatever back hovel you come from, girl, but as a royal medicine officer schooled in the capital, I actually know what I'm doing. I will not be questioned by an inso-lent upstart. Are we clear? Now, move aside. The king entrusted *me* with his nephew's care."

As he uncorks one of the bottles, the carriage jerks again, splashing some of the liquid. It falls on the gleaming copper broach on his cloak, and smoke rises in the air as coppery red morphs to gray ash in an instant, crumbling until it is no more. Thrusting the bottle at me, Jarvis throws off his cloak, bundling it up.

"Right," he says, no longer so confident. "It may be too risky to close your wounds this way, Your Highness. The roads are too un-even. This part of the kingdom is unfortunately notorious for such things."

Slapping the stopper back into the bottle, I shove it back into Jarvis's hands. "This part of the kingdom was once notorious for having excellent medical care."

He sneers. "Oh you mean those juju masters you see in hopes of healing people?"

"Jarvis, enough," Jonas says, breathing hard. "I'm not going to sit here bleeding while you argue. Listen to what she has to say."

Jarvis lowers his head, glaring at me. "Yes, Your Highness."

"We need to sew up the leg wound. I can do it, but I'll need your help." I pull the curved bone needle and the spool of cat silk thread from my packet. "We'll have to do this on the floor. He might fall off the bench if we try there."

I wait, counting breaths as Jarvis eyes me suspiciously. Jonas doesn't hesitate, though, beckoning to the guards, and they shift him gently onto the carriage floor. Still I wait. After what feels like an eternity, Jarvis moves to the carriage floor also. He coughs, looking at Jonas, and says, "I am happy to help, Your Highness. Please remember that if this experimental treatment fails to work, I did offer another." He tosses his satchel on the floor next to me.

One you immediately abandoned because it was lunacy, I think but don't say.

Splitting the bitter leaf and yarrow into thirds, I wrap one in a strip of linen and hand it to Jarvis. "When I tell you, spread this over his belly." I stretch my hand to the guard behind me. "Your skein." He glances wistfully at the swollen leather bag before handing it to me. I dip another strip of linen into the mouth of the skein, pouring water onto it. Then I face the guards once more. "You'll need to hold him down."

Jonas gives them a silent nod, and they take their places, one holding his feet and the other at his shoulder. I smile down at Jonas. "This will hurt, but it's the best I can do right now . . . Your Highness."

He smiles as though I am the only person around. "Your best is more than enough for me."

Pulling his head up, I shove bits of the bitter-leaf mixture into his mouth. "This will hurt, so bite down."

I pour water on his wounds, hands shaking as he screams between gritted teeth. After wiping his belly, I help Jarvis smear the poultice onto the wound and bind it after. We move to his leg. The bleeding has stopped, red and yellow threads of flesh showing through cracks of pale skin. I suck in air, letting the sting of blood and the sharp bitterness of the poultice wash over me before bending over the wound. My belly pulses, threatening to unravel and spill the food Etera had given us only the day before, but I suck it down.

I don't know when I first push the needle into his flesh, guided only by the weak light beaming through the carriage window and Jarvis's unsteady hands. But as I pull the needle through again and a tiny stream of blood leaks from the other end of the cut, I nearly stop. The muscles in Jonas's leg stiffen and his other leg trembles, foot knocking against the guard's hand. Biting my lip, I loop the thread through and keep going, not stopping even as Jonas's cries grow louder and my eyes fill with tears. Once or twice, the carriage bounces, and I wait, hardly daring to breathe, before starting up again. Soon, it is over, purple flesh on the edges of the crisscross stitch as though Jonas's skin is merely a patch of cloth. After applying the last of the poultice to the linen, I tie it over Jonas's leg myself.

"That was . . . better than I expected. You'll have to show me how to do that," Jarvis says quietly as the guards help Jonas back onto the bench.

"I thought you were against juju medicine."

He wipes his hands with a handkerchief. "I have only heard negative things about it until now. But your treatment seemed to work well. Perhaps there are one or two good things about it after all."

"Perhaps," I say with a sardonic twist on my lips. The guards get Jonas back onto the bench and I take my seat beside him once more; he squeezes my hand. His fingers are cold, his face red as though he's been out in the sun too long.

"Thank you," he says. I nod and he drops his head onto my shoulder.

"Your Highness, are you all right?" Jarvis asks.

"I am well, Jarvis. I just need rest." Jonas lifts his head slightly. "Would you mind?"

Jarvis stands, uncomprehending, then light dawns in his eyes. "Of course." He squeezes in between the two guards, angling his knobby elbows while Jonas pushes against me, sliding until his head is in my lap. I wipe hair from his face, enjoying the feel of the silky strands, when one of the guards snickers again, looking pointedly at where Jonas's face is buried in the swells of my hips. Swallowing, I pull the sheepskin blanket that lay over Jonas's lap closer until it is snug up to his chin and partly covers my legs. Then I lean my head against the carriage window and watch the world pass.

Swaths of green, jutting mounds of stacked-stone towers, punctuated only by blue streams and small, orange pools. I catch the shadow of a dome, faint lines like the beginning of a sketch, and white towers with arched windows one more time, before it is gone, the Maiduguri Palace swallowed into distance and clouds. There is nothing for a while, just cracked earth and empty fields, then barren trees sprout like ancestral totems, waving gleefully as we race by. The air is pregnant now with cold. Twisted palm trees give way to stark birches and staunch elms. Green leaves become red, and the earth takes on a white sheen. Peat houses speckled with brown-and-white tufts rise up under a darkening sky. Small children with red faces and dripping noses run after the carriage, yelling. The horses neigh as white balls sail into the air, pelting the sides of the carriage and hitting my window with a loud thump. As the powdery remnants drip away, I see smoke rising from every house, and that some of the children have faces like mine, Colin's, and Nana's.

When I try to sit up to get a better look, Jonas stirs, wrapping his hand in mine before turning over. So I lie there, watching, as the peat houses fall away and stone buildings take their places, many with colorful square signs hanging from their eaves like children competing for attention. Wyldewood Inn, one boasts, with an image of a pig with fruit in its mouth. Another, Maud's Tavern, and a swollen skein. The biggest merely displays a buxom shadow whose painted curves make me bite my lip and look away.

"I like things simple and spelled out, don't you?"

The guard from earlier is watching me, tracing his tongue along his bottom lip. His fair face is ghostly in the darkness, and the lock of brown hair hanging over his left eye makes him look more boyish than the gleam in his eyes suggests. He nods in the direction of the disappearing brothel.

"Haven't been to that place yet, but I've heard good things. Want to know what I've heard?"

"No, thank you."

"You don't have to be afraid. I heard Lord Kairen is really nice to his girls, gives them gifts of all kinds. I'm sure you'll be settled in his rooms in no time, bathing in rose water and sucking on honey cakes while the rest of us have to fork over our hard-earned coin to take one of you darkies on a straw bed and have done with that. Doesn't seem fair, does it?"

I tighten my fingers in my skirt, summoning every ounce of venom I can into my words. "Is it fair to bed a woman who has no desire to take you in? I will cut my own throat before I allow Lord Kairen or any olodo like you to touch me without my say-so."

He smiles, giving me a once-over, before saying, "Do you think the prince will protect you? Did you offer some to him first, is that it?"

I am about to leap to my feet when the guard across from me opens his eyes and hisses, "Brom, shut your mouth before I rip your tongue out."

Brom twists his mouth, offering the second guard a sullen glare. Jarvis sleeps between them, none the wiser. The guard across takes a swig from his skein, then holds it out to me.

"No, thank you," I say.

"It's tombo. Since we were down in Oyo for a bit, the captain let us get some. It's cold out. It'll warm you up a bit."

I hesitate. The palm wine could help calm the humming that has pulsed through me since the moment I entered this carriage, the reminder that somewhere in these walls, there is iron slowly devouring me. I sniff, letting the sweet smell enter my nostrils, then shake my head. "It's all right. I'm all right."

He shrugs and takes another swig before wiping his bearded chin. "Suit yourself."

"Where are we?"

"Wyldewood. Two hours from Nordgren. I'm from these parts."

I raise an eyebrow. "I thought lowborn men couldn't become part of the king's personal guard."

"Wyldewood is one of the holdovers from the last kingdom, more jumbled up than the rest of the northern cities. Not many high-born families to be found around here. Not any with money anyway."

"So what happened?"

"Lord Ekwensi happened. He argued that I should be given a fair trial when I tried to enroll at Nordgren's military school. He said he would vouch for me, and pay my way if need be. The king agreed so long as I passed my battle trial, and I did."

"You owe him a debt then."

"More than I can repay." He smiles, offering me a hand. "I'm Mikhail by the way. That shit over there is Brom, as I'm sure you heard. He's not half bad most of the time, but he has some ugly habits. He's from Ellaria. It comes with the territory."

"Ah."

Ellaria is one of the northernmost cities in all of Ifé, and one of the oldest. Its wealth comes mainly from the production of wool for the kingdom, but it is also known for having some interesting characteristics. My dark skin and sugary eyes would do more than make me stand out there—it would also get me killed.

I smile coyly at Brom. "With all the Ellarian talk of pure blood, you can't go to a brothel there, can you? You'd probably recognize some of your cousins if you did."

He lunges at me, but Mikhail catches him, throwing him back into the bench. "Sit down. I won't repeat myself again. If you move for the rest of this journey, I will have you discharged. Are we clear?"

Brom nods, curling into his seat. Mikhail grabs the pole running across the carriage roof. "You may sleep if you wish. I'll stand guard. Need to stretch my legs anyway."

"Thank you."

Leaning back, I take small breaths, waiting until my raging heart settles into its faint rhythm once more. Strangely, even with Brom leering at me and the hum of iron singing through the air, there is warmth spreading through me like fire, drawing from where my fingers lay entwined with Jonas's. I think I know why, and even though it's an impossibility, I smile and close my eyes. It occurs to me now that I have not settled in like this since before Colin and I left Benin—no, since before I saw Amara at the market that day. I have been drawn tight like the threads that danced on my mother's fingers, waiting to be plunged into patterns and pulled into life. Even now, a part of me is waiting, trying to scry the realms of possibility for what lies beyond this carriage. Another part is merely being. There is a joy in this, in lying between sleep and wakefulness, in feeling hope flutter in this blue half-darkness, in holding warmth in the chill of the carriage. So I let that joy fill me.

All too soon, the carriage stops, catching for a moment before jerking to a halt. When I open my eyes, I am alone in the darkness, a sliver of light beaming in from the open carriage door. As I step out, Jonas is there, helping me down. I am about to speak when I see it. The castle looms before us, curved stone buildings illuminated by the rows of lanterns littering the path before us, capped turrets like jagged teeth biting into the sky. Guards lined in rows shout in unison as Alistair Sorenson descends his carriage.

"The king returns. Long live the king."

They chant as he walks between their torches, the echoes of it caught up on the harsh wind that threatens to blow me over. Jonas pulls his blanket over my shoulders as our guards bring up the rear, waiting for us to go forward. The castle gates are open, but I can see nothing beyond them, just a still darkness.

"Come on," Jonas says. "Let's get you out of the cold. You don't want to be out in Eingard during winter nights."

The calm that swaddled me in the carriage is gone, replaced by a chill that eats its way up my spine that has nothing to do with the weather. Jonas squeezes my hand before letting go, leading the way. "Welcome to Château Nordgren, my home."

TRIUMPH

A host of attendants bow and curtsy as we enter the main hall. The room, large enough to contain Will and Nana's house and more, is lit by a hanging wheel with horns like a kudu stretching from it. Lanterns of various sizes dangle from the horns, illuminating the shadowy purple of the attendants' uniforms—identical buttoned coats with high collars and straight trousers for the men, and high-necked, starched dresses cut off at the knees for the women, supplemented by large aprons. Beyond them, twin marble staircases twist like mating snakes onto an upper landing, with one large door visible beyond.

As I take in the unmoving suits of armor standing nearby and the threads of gold filigree etched in intricate patterns over the walls, a stiff man with peppered gray hair and spectacles sidles up to Jonas. "Welcome home, my lord. The king requests that you and your companions join him in the battle room." He bows, waving a hand toward the dimly lit corridor on the right.

The attendants step back, heads down. But a few of the women steal glances at me, faces bobbing away when I look back at them, like naughty children feigning disinterest in the treats others are being given. There are flashes of surprise hidden by well-placed hands, and traces of confusion revealed in wrinkled foreheads and swelling cheeks. It is the last glimpse of a young woman, not much older than me, with leathery skin, that scares me though—the wide-eyed fear, the trembling lip that is uncontrolled even as the woman next to her shakes her. Before the corridor walls meet us, I glance back at her once more, but someone else steps in front of her then, and she is gone. Erased. Just like I'll be if I don't play my part and figure out how to escape this place.

The corridor is wide enough to fit ten people standing abreast, but Jonas and I walk huddled together, following the gray-haired attendant. Guards line the walls on either side, like the suits of armor in the main hall, hands resting on their swords, eyes staring in front of them, still as wood. Not even the flare of the attendant's torch, pushing light onto their shadowed faces, seems enough to startle them. One by one, they bow as Jonas walks by, and I keep my head low, hoping the shadows will embrace enough of me. I clutch at my necklace, trying not to let my anxiety consume me. The corridor stretches into another long hallway, with several rooms only a few feet apart. The attendant speaks to the guards in front of the second door, and we are let in.

The king is seated at the head of a long table. "Good of you to finally get here," he says. "Come. Your food is on its way in."

Ekwensi, at his right hand, leans over, pouring wine from a metal jug. Colin, seated to his left, locks eyes on me, then looks away as two attendants rush up, pulling out a chair to the king's right and one next to it. I know he asked me to trust him, but I still don't know what to make of my best friend working for the man who has terrorized our kind even before we were born.

To my surprise, Ekwensi picks up the king's full goblet, taking a few sips before setting it down. There is something unsettling about watching this proud man act like a servant in front of the king. The king watches him, and after a few moments, drinks from the goblet as well.

"Nothing like mulled wine after a long journey," Alistair says, smiling. Attendants place full cups before us. The king raises his goblet to Jonas. "To your safe return." They drink.

"I know you must be tired after such a long journey, but we have a few things to discuss," the king says. "Jarvis tells me your medical treatment went well. He didn't care to treat your injuries in a moving carriage, but as you know—"

"The king must be able to do three things: bear wounds for his people without complaint, be a man of his word, and plan well for the future in order to build a great kingdom," Jonas intones, the words even and clear, like a speech rehearsed one too many times. "You had to be here to plan for the succession gala tomorrow, so you were merely keeping your word. As your successor, it was my duty to withstand the pain of my injuries while protecting your honor."

The king nudges Ekwensi. "You see, Tobias? The boy understands what's being asked of him. All your fussing was for nothing."

"You were right, as always."

I stifle an incredulous laugh at this strange song and dance, the pathetic way Ekwensi hangs on the king like a lapdog. I am grateful when another flurry of attendants make their way in, carrying platters of food. Roasted chicken, fat pies, tarts topped with a thick layer of custard, and honey cake covered in syrup. The savory smell of cooked meat tinged with the sweet aroma of the desserts makes my stomach growl.

The king stabs the chicken with a dagger, splashing its juices all over the table. He holds an impaled drumstick out to Jonas. "You did well today."

"Thank you, my king."

Ekwensi takes over, carving the meat, and the king looks from me to Colin. "Please, eat. I prefer not to talk with an empty belly. It's likely to make me angry."

I want to laugh again. My sides are tingling, my eyes prickling with unshed tears. Alistair Sorenson wants *me* to eat with *him*. The man who took my family from me, whose very existence threatens my kind, is asking me to dine with him as if I'm an honored guest.

"Eat." The word comes again, and now I realize my mistake. There was no asking.

I stare at Colin, willing him to look up, but he keeps his gaze fastened to his cup. So I shift my attention to the iron fork by my plate and wait, watching as Colin reaches for a tart with his bare hands and starts eating. After a moment, I follow suit. The king's jaw stiffens, but he eats quietly, stopping only to exchange words with Lord Ekwensi. There are weapons fastened to the walls: axes, swords, spears, shields. I am too busy counting them to notice that the piece of custard tart in my hand is still hot. A moment later, I wrestle scalding, too-sweet custard down my throat as it tangles in my teeth and clings to my tongue. Jonas hands me some wine and I choke it back gratefully. Colin does not even look up from his plate.

The door creaks open, and a man in full blue robes steps in, his long black hair tamed by the golden circlet pressed against his fore-head. The guard that follows him is decked in armor and crowned with a horned helmet, black strands of hair peeking out just beneath. I drop my tart in surprise—it seems that Mari survived.

How?

The man strides over to Colin and strikes him across the face. I shift in my chair, but Colin's expression freezes me in place. He is smiling his signature grin, but his hazel eyes are heavy with rage and something I've only seen him show a few times—remorse.

The king stands. "Lord Kairen, I trust your journey was swift and safe. Would you care to join us for dinner?"

Lord Kairen bows over one hand, Berréan-style, and the jeweled rings on his fingers glitter. "Your Highness, forgive me. I should have greeted you before disciplining my wayward son. Thank you for the safe escort here, and yes, if you can forgive my ill manners, I will join you. I am forever in your debt."

Ekwensi lifts a hand and an attendant comes forward, carrying a bowl. Lord Kairen dips his fingers, sprinkling the water lightly over his rings. He sits, wiping his fingers before tossing the cloth to Colin. "You should clean your face. It's not good to leave blood at the dining table."

Colin presses the cloth to the open gash in his cheek. "Welcome, Father. I missed you too."

Now I see the hazel eyes in the man's weathered face, the strong nose and jaw. This man is undoubtedly Colin's father, the man Alistair Sorenson wants to gift me to.

"Colin is your son?" Jonas asks. "Excuse me, Lord Kairen. I thought you didn't bring your son to any of the royal meets because he was much younger."

"Nicolás is his proper name, Your Highness. He is only a year younger than you. But yes, I have another son, Matéo, who is six years of age. Nicolás's mother, my first wife, sent him to a year-round regional school, so I have been unable to bring him to royal meets. I hoped to visit him at his school after assisting you at Benin Palace, but then you were kidnapped."

A memory echoes in my mind. The lord at Jonas's door in Benin Palace waiting to check on the prince—the one who ran up to my wind wall. I look at Colin now, remembering the frantic energy he'd exuded when he met me in Jonas's rooms, the way he showed up long before he had to be there. Then there's the way his eyes would shift anytime I asked about his family, the refusal to heed authority, the way he understood when Jonas explained why he hadn't revealed his powers.

Lord Kairen speaks, but I hear Colin's voice—the same high accent, certain sounds dancing on his tongue as though he is tasting them. "I still don't understand how my son was involved with rescuing the prince, but I'm grateful he could be of service to you, Your Highness."

"Oh, undoubtedly, he has been of service to me in more ways than you can imagine." The king turns to the guard. "Mari, do be sociable and take that thing off. My invitation for dinner naturally included you as well."

Mari saunters into the room smiling, the scar running across her face rippling like a shadow over water. There is a new mark, an ugly purple-red burn spread over one ear. She sits next to me, an arm's breadth away. "Thank you, Your Highness. But now without the shield of a helmet, I cannot admire Kairen's son without being accused of plotting to poach him for my battalion."

I meet Jonas's frozen gaze. We're caught. Mari is merely toying with us, every inch the cat rejoicing at having cornered its long-hunted prey. No doubt the king already knows what happened in Lokoja. It's only a matter of time before Mari attacks.

The king rubs his chin. "A fine idea."

"I'm not so sure about that, Your Highness. My son can be erratic and headstrong. Those are not good qualities in a soldier."

Mari raises her glass. "They're perfect qualities. You need to be stubborn and a bit impulsive to be able to carry out His Highness's vision. Those are the very qualities he chose me for."

"A good leader is made great by those he chooses to support him. Wouldn't you agree, Tobias?"

Ekwensi bows. "It is as you say."

"So what would you say, Tobias, if I say you have chosen well? That the agents you chose for this rescue mission are so interesting I want them for myself?"

I still, not daring to breathe. The king's words coil around my chest and throat, choking the life out of me. Ekwensi, too, is silent. Mari's eyes are on me, hungry wolves on a wintry night, watching the still underbrush for any hint of movement. I just want this to be over, to fight and be done once and for all. Then Lord Kairen laughs, a rich, booming sound that swallows the room.

"You jest, Your Highness. I am grateful for the compliment you pay my son, but as you are aware, he is my heir. If you take him for your army, I will have no heir until my younger son is of age." Colin looks up at this, the mention of him being Kairen's heir clearly news to him.

The king raises a red gold brow. "Did my words sound funny to you? I'm sorry, Kairen. I know Berréan humor is a little different, so I'll say it in terms you can understand. I am giving you the honor of appointing your son to my army."

Lord Kairen's eyes grow dark, but he is otherwise outwardly calm. In his most reasonable voice he says, "Your Highness, my younger son is six years old. I cannot make him heir, not without risk. If you appoint Nicolás to your army, by the time I travel home, even if I were to travel without rest for four days, I am sure I would find Matéo dead. There are many eyeing my estates, and even more who would kill to have a place in your council."

"So you would refuse the honor I would bestow on you?"

Mari's gaze shifts to Lord Kairen, and I take a breath. Lord Kairen lowers his head. "Of course not, Your Highness. Whatever you will, I will do it."

The king turns to Colin. "And what of you? I heard you survived several assassination attempts as a child, and now I find too that

Tobias trusted your abilities so much that he sent you to rescue my nephew. You must be a remarkable fighter. If you join my army, you will grow even stronger. If you serve me well, I might even allow you to inherit your father's estates."

Colin stands abruptly and bows. "Your Highness, thank you for considering me for such an honor. It is as my father says, however. I have much to learn. I do not desire to fail you." His back is stiff, his posture perfect, a marionette dancing for its master.

"A wise answer." The king turns to Lord Ekwensi. "Tell me, Tobias. How did you end up bringing me both Kairen's hidden son and my lost daughter?"

The words linger in the silence, and I try to make sense of them. Jonas makes a sound, half choking, half gasping, and Colin looks at me for the first time since we left Old Maiduguri. I open my mouth, but my words will not come, the air in my lungs pulling away from me. My fingers steal up to my throat, brushing against my father's ring. It sits heavy on my chest, its iron song growing louder as I rub its weary, battered body. The etchings on the inside of the ring are as familiar to me as the back of my hand, even after years of missing it. This ring was the last thing my father left my mother before she ran away, pregnant and alone. The trembling in my heart gives way to a consuming anger and I can no longer contain myself.

"You're not my father!" I roar, jumping to my feet.

Mari yanks me back, armored fingers digging into my clavicle. "Sit. The king is speaking."

"Mari." The king's voice is low and even, as though speaking to a small child.

"Alistair, she—"

He puts a finger to his lips, but she shakes her head.

"You *promised*. You promised to choose me instead. I helped you back then."

"And I *did* choose you. Open your eyes, Mari. Yetundé is dead. You killed her yourself."

"I tore out my own heart," Mari seethes, rising to her feet. "And I have yet to see you make good on your promises."

The king settles back, drumming his fingers against the table. "What would you have me do?"

"After, we rule together. Jointly. Equally. Let me handle the lords."

He considers a moment, then shrugs. "Done. And now? What do you want so badly right now that you're willing to bite me like this?"

She grins and taps the burn on her ear. "You've already promised me the child. Don't go back on your word."

She pulls me closer, and I see myself reflected in the dim pools of her eyes, misshapen and lumpy. She exhales and tosses me back as if suddenly holding something rancid. The arm of the chair slams into me, and I nearly sprawl onto the floor, catching myself just in time. She smiles. "I owe you that and more, little girl."

"She's the image of her mother, isn't she? Fire and strength," the king says.

"But this one is brutal in a way Yetu could never be. I'll train her. With time, she'll be the perfect child."

Ekwensi clears his throat. "This is my mistake, my lord. I made contact with her and Lord Kairen's son through an old friend. He takes a few students with special aptitude each year and trains them. When I told him your nephew was in danger, he sent me those two. I had no idea, my lord, that they would be of such importance."

The king grabs Ekwensi by the neck and slams his head on the table. "Is that all you have to say?"

Ekwensi chokes, blood running down his forehead, one eye half closed. "Yes, my lord. Of course! Please believe me."

The king lets go and Ekwensi stumbles, hand over his quickly swelling eye.

Jonas speaks up then, "My king, am I to believe that Dè—that this girl is your daughter?"

Mari laughs, and the king glares at her. "She is not—not truly. Her mother was to be my bride."

"But she loved another," Mari adds triumphantly.

"What does that mean, then?" Jonas asks.

"That she's an orphan in need of guidance," Mari purrs. "I will adopt her as my successor. Raise her with our ethics. In time she will see truth."

"I'll kill you first," I say through gritted teeth.

"My king, although this girl's mother betrayed you, she saved my life," Jonas says quickly. "Should she not be given a reward? You can't give her to Captain Mari without her consent."

"Ah yes, I promised her a reward." The king waves a hand and guards charge into the room, carrying two long metal poles. I take several steps back, looking at Colin, pleading. His eyes flicker to me, then back to his father, but he does nothing.

"Brom tells me that you and this girl have become quite close. So let me give you something, a present in honor of your succession tomorrow. This girl's father is one of your oldest friends, someone, in fact, that your parents knew quite well. He stayed in your home eighteen years ago. He was last seen going for a walk with you and your mother."

Jonas goes white, and his hands start to shake. "Uncle—"

"Iron Blood Osezele, the man who crippled your mother."

I find my voice. "You're lying. Stop lying."

"What reason would I have to lie? These are well-known facts. Your father was my tutor and a friend, yet he betrayed me. I don't want you to go another day without knowing the truth."

I slap my temples, but the words will not leave my mind. They come again and again like a nursery rhyme. My father. Jonas's mother. My father hurt Jonas's mother. The blood sacrifice, all those Oluso, I could begin to understand. Perhaps it was an impossible situation. Life for life, blood for blood. But Jonas looks at me, anguish in his eyes, mouth wide as he chokes on air, and I am lost. "It's not true," I repeat over and over, as though the words are a spell that will set things right again. I reach for him. "Jonas, please."

"What do you think, dear nephew? I took up arms to protect our kingdom. Tens of thousands lost their lives so we could tear down the system that allowed unchecked power like that to run free. Those men and women died because of *her* father's actions. Your mother was merely the first casualty, and had I not been there in time, she might have died too."

Jonas's eyes go hard, and he straightens, looking at me as though I've grown two heads. "No, Uncle. You're right."

My legs give out under me and I fall, gasping as pain spreads in my chest.

Colin, to his credit, speaks up, a hint of defiance in his voice. "Weren't you two allies? Osezele helped you take the capital for revenge, right?"

The king clucks his tongue. "Kairen, you haven't educated your son properly."

Lord Kairen cuts Colin an angry look. "No, my liege. I will correct that shortly."

"No matter," the king says, getting to his feet. "I'll set him right." Grabbing Colin's jaw, he squeezes, and Colin tenses under the pressure.

"I would never ally with scum. I found that man attacking the capital while on a march to liberate the kingdom. He may have taught me the power of iron, but his own pride, his foolishness in thinking the magicless weak, was his downfall. You know, I was the one who put a knife in his heart."

It is those last words that push me over the edge. With a scream, I lunge at the king, driving my fist into his jaw. He reels, but battles back, knocking me to the wall with a sweeping kick. The guards advance, swords boxing me in like thorns in a thicket. The smell of iron is thick in the air, blood after a hunt, that metallic scent lingering over me. Sweat drips down my back even as a cold wind seizes into the room through the open door where more guards are lined up.

"What will it be, little girl?" a guard says. "Come quietly, or have us take you by force?"

"Force."

Flexing my fingers, I pull the wind in, letting it glide against my skin. The guards' swords begin to shake, and the plates on the table rattle. Mari jumps back, and Lord Kairen stands as my skirt blows around me and my feet slip off the ground. Magic blossoms in me, spreading through my fingers and my toes until every inch of me is on fire. It feels so good to give in, to let it envelop me until the power is all I feel, and the darkness inside melts into nothing. I will not let them take me.

I am not a scared little girl anymore.

"Dèmi." Jonas's voice is low, hardly above a whisper, but the wind pushes his voice into my ear. "Dèmi, don't. For me, please. Or if not for me, for her."

For her? Who . . . ?

It doesn't matter, because I fall then, crumpling onto the stones, the will in me drained away. Pain explodes in my head, and my arms and legs twist under me. I try to move, but my body will not obey. I can't understand what is happening to me, but I know this: my magic is gone.

Colin rushes for me, but his father pulls him back. I am power-less as Mari brings the pole and shackles. I feel the cold knife of iron slip into me as they tie me on, strapping my arms on either side of my body, shackling my legs above the pole, until I am hang-ing between air and metal, held aloft only by my screaming wrists and ankles.

"Secure her properly," Jonas says, his voice wobbly. A guard puts his weight beneath my body, supporting my back and holding up my head. Mikhail.

"Sorry about this," he whispers.

I close my eyes. My whole body aches, but the pain in my head is worse, sharp and twisting, like a pick digging into my skull. Every-thing is dark, but I can see Mummy, still wearing that desperate, hopeful look she gave me as she died. I remember Ayaba's words. She was right: Jonas has brought me death, and Colin despair. I wonder now if the choice she offered me had been a cruel joke, a mistake made long before I stepped foot in this castle. I open my eyes, and the world is blurred now, nothing but too-bright colors and sounds.

". . . in the east wing. I'll deal with her later. Double the perim-eter guards. I don't want anything interrupting the succession gala tomorrow," the king says. "Kairen, can you explain what special ap-titude your son has that requires he train with a known magic user? I hope you're not hiding anything from me . . ."

I should be glad to hear those words, to let them soothe the rage that has swelled inside me ever since I found out that Colin held more secrets than I knew. Instead my heart is twisting, fresh agony swimming up at the thought that they might hurt Colin too. I want to thrash and scream, drag my magic back, and unleash my fury, push out all my hatred and anger, even if it means destroying everything in the process. Instead, I close my eyes again. Soon I am rocking, bouncing, like a boat left out during a storm, at the mercy of perilous waves. My stomach rumbles in protest, and I puff out shallow breaths, trying to hold the nausea at bay and keep the bits of tart that made it to my stomach in there. Somehow, I do, and before long it is over and I am lowered onto cold stones, breathing in a lungful of musty earth and dry wort. I lie there, alone in the darkness, as the whispers swim over me, wondering which "her" Jonas spoke of, my mother or his. As hot tears crawl down my face and the darkness creeps over me, I know the answer then is the same as it was when he first said it to me—it doesn't matter.

I have failed both of them.

BLINDNESS

I wake to a small hand running over my face, tickling my nose and eyelids. A chubby-faced baby stares back at me, slapping silky fingers against my cheeks. There is a whistle, like steam rising from a boiling pot, and the child rises, stumbling to the woman sitting with her back pressed to the bars and tugging at her blouse. Scooping the girl into her lap, the woman pulls down her blouse and suckles her.

"You must have done something truly spectacular for Mari to come down here with you," a voice says. Another woman sits a few feet from my head, tracing the stone floor patterns with a stick. My arms and legs are still shackled, but the pole is nowhere in sight. She points the stick toward me, her dirt-stained face accusing. "They didn't bring food this morning. What did you do, hm?"

Pushing off my side, I sit up with difficulty. The light from the tiny window at the top of the cell is a faint red, a closing of the day. The pain in my head is a dull ache now, and even with the hum of iron ringing in my ears and the throbbing in my bound wrists and ankles, my magic is bubbling inside me, itching to escape. I sigh in relief, but my heart races, remembering the way my magic burned through me. Then all at once, it was gone, snuffed out like a candle in the wind. Even with the whisper of it now against my skin, I can't help but feel afraid.

"Where am I?" I croak. "What day is it?"

The woman scrunches her face in annoyance, but she responds. "The East Wing. Gura's Day. You've been stinking up our room for a day, shivering like a cat in the cold." She shakes her stick again. "Why'd you have to anger Mari, hm? We were supposed to have yam porridge for breakfast. Do you know how long I've waited for that, hm?"

I blink. A whole day has gone by. And I have no idea what's going on, where Colin is.

"Leave her alone, Adaeze. Mari does whatever she wants. If she wants to starve us, she will." A third woman swings up from the cot in the corner, the chain on her ankle rattling as she stands. She perches next to me, one hand at her back bracing as she lowers her swollen belly, her face bright and pink. "I'm Ga Eun," she says. The Oluso mark behind her ear glows before she tucks her curtain of dark hair over it. She nods to the angry woman, whose Oluso mark glows on her tan, bony shoulder. "That's Adaeze. Don't mind her. She's not angry with you, she's afraid for her baby."

Adaeze stomps over to the abandoned cot, settling in with her back to us, but I have already seen the slim rounding of her stomach. Ga Eun waves at the mother and child by the bars. "Samira and Malala." Samira waves a tired hand before pulling Malala away and closing her blouse. Malala rests her head against the curve of her mother's belly. They resemble popular dolls the Goma merchants brought to the market this year—dark-brown hair and pale faces, the smaller doll nestled in the arms of the larger one, dressed in the same fabric.

"You three . . ." I start, the words like dirt in my mouth, difficult to spit out.

"We're all pregnant, yes. I'm due in two moons. Adaeze's baby will probably come in the rainy season, and Samira will have her second right before that."

Malala toddles over, and Ga Eun catches her, tickling the air around her. Malala giggles, collapsing onto chubby legs and wriggling so much that her brown hair winds up in tufts around her face. A pink Oluso mark glows atop her foot as she kicks both feet in the air, trying to roll away from Ga Eun's fingers. I'm confused and delighted by this sight, but then footsteps echo down the corridor, and Malala scrunches her face, whimpering. Ga Eun doesn't seem to mind, though, and instead slaps her hands over her face, then opens them again, peeking down at Malala, and the girl settles, watching her with interest. They play this game, even as the iron bars give way with a reedy whine, and a guard with sandy hair and freckled cheeks enters, carrying a basket and a large pail.

"Ga Eun," he says. But she ignores him, continuing the game with Malala. He sighs, then goes to Samira, passing her a hunk of bread and a covered bowl. After shaking Adaeze awake and giving her some food, he leaves another bowl, bigger than the rest, at Ga Eun's feet. "You should eat a lot today. The baby will be here before you know it."

Ga Eun presses her face to Malala's belly, laughing as the little girl erupts into giggles. He pulls an apple from his pocket and places it on top of the bowl. "Finish that at least."

As soon as the gate swings closed, Ga Eun tosses the apple to Adaeze. "Here. You need to put on a little more, for the baby."

Adaeze smiles her thanks before biting in. Ga Eun pushes her bowl toward me. "Looks like they don't want to feed you. What did you do to make Mari so angry?"

"I exist." She nods, knowingly, then points to her food again. I shake my head. "I won't take your food."

She dips her hands into the pail. "At least drink something," she says, holding a cup of water out to me. I drink, tipping my head back as she pours water into my parched and burning throat until my mouth is no longer dry.

"Thank you."

"Of course. Now, tell us your secrets! Did you spit in Mari's drink? Insult her to her face?"

"I bet she insulted the king," Adaeze calls out. "Mari can't forgive that. You can insult her but not her precious Alistair."

They laugh, and Samira looks up, confused. Ga Eun makes a series of quick hand signs to her, and finally, she smiles. Malala pulls a hunk of bread out of Ga Eun's basket and sucks on it.

I don't understand why, but the truth rises to my lips. "I kidnapped the prince."

I freeze, shoulders tensed, surprised at the ease, the speed with which the words jumped out of my mouth like water wriggling through the cracks of a dam, desperate and yearning. Then I let it all out in a sigh. It doesn't matter anyway; nothing does. The chances that I'll escape, that I'll ever see outside of these walls again, are slim to none. Now I just have to hope that Colin has the decency to protect Will and Nana from scrutiny and that Ekwensi keeps his silence. Nothing matters anymore.

Adaeze's apple falls half-eaten onto the cot. Ga Eun stops tearing off bread chunks for Malala to eat. "If you did that, you'd be dead, not here." She signs to Samira and the other woman makes a flurry of hand signs back.

"Samira wants to know why you would even want to do such a thing."

I lean back against the wall, taking a moment to pull together my scattered thoughts.

"Because I thought it would save us," I say with a shrug.

Ga Eun raises an eyebrow, and I have to look away from her penetrative gaze. Malala toddles up to me and grabs a fistful of my blouse hem, plopping down next to me. I smile and scoot closer to her. She offers a gap-toothed grin and wriggles even closer. Almost immediately, the fog in my mind clears and my words tumble out in a rush belying my still, steady voice.

"I've been afraid my entire life." I swallow, take a moment to let those words live, then start again. "When other children would watch the soldiers come on raids in our village, I would hide with my mother, thinking they were coming for us next, waiting for our turn. I got tired of waiting to die. Why not take the prince and make the king pay for what he's done to us? What he's still doing to us?" I say, and realize I have nothing else to add. I ask, "Why are you all here?"

Adaeze answers me. "We were taken. Spoils of war. I've been here since I was four years old. There were more women before, but many died. Samira came two years ago, and—"

"I joined the ranks this year," Ga Eun interrupts. "Border dispute. The Eingardians asked our chief for the smartest girl in exchange for not collecting extra taxes. Lucky for the chief, I'm also an orphan. No Gomae warriors to fight on my behalf. They handed me over in half a day. I did try to run—fly—but I haven't mastered my bird form. Didn't get far."

"You've been living in this dungeon for years?" I ask, horror twisting my stomach anew.

"Birthing center," Adaeze says. She points to a wall covered in ordered scratches. "Celebrated sixteen name days here." She points to the smaller pile of marks next to the first. "My son lived forty-seven days in here too. He—" She splutters, and starts to cry. Ga Eun is at her side in an instant, rubbing her back. Malala joins in, wailing until Samira plucks her up and holds her to her breast.

Bile rises to my throat as a memory unfolds. Still, small bodies, grasping empty limbs. The babies born to the Benin city asewós with empty eyes like dolls. "Your son . . ." I start.

"He died. This was too much for him," Ga Eun says shortly. "Malala is the first baby who has survived this long. She is strong, aren't you, little weed?" She takes Malala from her mother, plopping her in Adaeze's lap. "We celebrated her name day three moons ago."

"I don't understand. Why do they keep you? Why not kill you like they do the rest of us?" I ask in a shaky voice. I think of the guard, and the way his eyes lingered on Ga Eun, as though she were a ripened fruit waiting to be consumed. "The king doesn't know about this, does he? He would kill you and your babies if he knew."

They share a look, then Ga Eun purses her lips. "He more than knows—it's his idea. It's why we are kept alive. He wants to see if"— she stops and takes a breath—"if any of us can produce children who can survive this."

"Children born of iron," I mutter.

The bars rattle, and Ga Eun falls silent, hand on her heart. Edith, Jonas's nanny, is standing outside our cell, her pale face ghostly in the dim light. I jerk, throwing myself off balance and landing on my back. I clench my fist, but there is no answering whisper, no magical warmth lingering in my fingertips. I am powerless.

Then the figure next to Edith pulls off their cloak, stepping up to the faint light fanning us.

Adaeze springs to her feet. "Nwanne Nna," she says, switching to an eastern Oyo language I've only heard in the marketplace, "what happened to your eye?"

"Do not worry yourself about it," says Ekwensi as he enters our cell, his left eye swollen closed. "Forgive your tardy uncle," he says, accepting Adaeze's embrace before hugging Ga Eun and Samira as well. He kisses Malala on the cheek and holds her tight, whispering, "My precious girl. Baba will be back soon. I promise."

Baba? I catch the quiet smile on Samira's face as she watches the two together. The proud Ekwensi has something to lose after all. But his child is Oluso although he is onyoshi. How is that possible?

He rushes to me, pulling me from my thoughts. "There isn't much time, so listen closely. There is a panel in the wall in the cell on the next block. Knock on that panel three times and the person waiting will take you away from here. Thank you for your help. May the spirits bless you."

He unlocks my shackles and helps me to my feet. I stumble, but Edith catches me, holding me until the world is no longer spinning. I flinch away from her, rubbing my wrists and my ankles. To my surprise, she takes my place on the ground, silent as Ekwensi shackles her feet and hands before pulling a cloak over her. Why is she helping us?

"They won't check until the morning. The king has too much to do with this gala. If they ask, tell them that someone broke in and helped the girl while Edith came to bring your dinner. Nothing more, nothing less. All right?"

The women nod, and Ekwensi smiles like a father looking over his children. He flashes some hand signs to Edith, and she responds in turn. "It won't be too long now," he says, pulling me out and locking the cell behind us.

"We know our duty," Ga Eun responds. "We won't let you down, Uncle."

Malala sidles up to the bars, bouncing excitedly, and when she reaches out a hand to Ekwensi, he takes it, squeezing her little fingers in his. Just then a purple Oluso mark appears on her forehead, and I blink, disbelieving. I was sure I'd seen a pink one on her foot.

"Omo mi, Nwa Nwanyi, what will you do for Baba?" he whispers.

"My daughter," he called her. There is no doubt in my mind now—Malala is Ekwensi's.

"Safe," Malala chirps. Her voice is light, airy, brimming with all the fearlessness of a young child.

"That's right. Stay safe. Baba will return soon."

He squeezes her fingers once more, then turns and pulls me away.

To say I'm confused is an understatement, and yet I dare not delay to ask such questions. But the thoughts race through me even as we cut through the darkness: Why do they call him Uncle? Why is Edith helping him—especially after she helped Mari kill my mother? Why is he helping me now?

Where is my magic?

Ekwensi hurries me down the corridor, stopping only when we see a shadow in the distance. A rat scurries by and Ekwensi looks around before pushing me on.

"I thought you betrayed me," I whisper.

"It's in my best interest not to."

"That woman, the one you made take my place? Can you be sure of her loyalty?"

"She's a hungry dog cast aside like you. She made the mistake of choosing the wrong allegiance in the past and paid handsomely. Alistair ripped out her tongue. I put her back together. She will not fail me."

A few questions answered, at least. But I still don't know what's going on, and that has not served me well this last week. I make to ask more, but he cuts me off with a sharp gesture as we reach a crossroads, another row of cells running by us, and beyond that, a host of lanterns and a narrow passageway where two guards sit at a table. He pinches my arm and whispers in my ear, "Third cell on the right. Go, I'll cover for you."

He steps away from me, and in an instant his brown eyes give way to white fathomless pools. A purple Oluso mark glows on his forehead and his face stretches and curves until it is the face of a stranger, light-skinned and grinning.

I swallow as images pull together in my mind, taking shape and life. The purple mark on Malala's forehead is the same as Ekwensi had back in Lokoja and now. Malala is the Basaari Oluso, the skin-walker whose power Ekwensi has borrowed.

My mouth is dry, my mind stuttering as I try to make sense of what I just saw. "The skin-walking—your child, she—"

Ekwensi cocks his head and smiles. I shudder as a chill creeps up my spine. "Olorun answers prayers after all," he says nonchalantly. "My daughter is gifted."

"How many times have you done this?" I whisper, horrified. "She'll die if you keep using her magic."

"She's young," Ekwensi says, his jaw tightening. "Her life still stretches before her. And I only need it for a short while. Enough time to make her safe."

I shake my head, disbelieving. "What kind of father are you?"

He grabs my shoulder, squeezing until I gasp in pain and I claw at his arm. "One who has to sacrifice months of his child's life for the good of his people. One is who hoping his baby girl survives long enough to live outside a cage." He shakes me off and leans forward until we are eye to eye. His voice is heavy with steel and fury, and I know I've crossed a line. "One," he continues, "who is risking everything to keep his word and get your pathetic, indecisive self out of this prison so you never have to suffer the same fate my sister and those women are suffering. Does that answer your question?"

I swallow and lower my gaze. "I'm sorry," I mumble.

"Keep your apologies. Every advancement requires sacrifice. The sooner you learn *that,* the better. Your father understood that. I was hoping you would too."

I look up at the mention of my father, but the guards' voices erupt into a fresh round of quarrels and Ekwensi taps my shoulder. "Go now. You still have a job to finish."

"I don't know—" I start.

He jerks me forcefully around and points down the corridor. "You don't need to know anything. Just run. Live. Make this sacrifice worth it." Then he flings me away and saunters toward the guards. I take off running. I don't know exactly what Ekwensi is planning, but I know I can't stay here and die. Not after seeing what is really happening in this castle. I wriggle the cell door open just as I hear Ekwensi's voice echo down the corridor.

"Gentlemen. Fine night for gambling, especially with the castle all a-rumble. Mind if I join you for a hand? I have some wine that needs sharing."

Pulling the cell door closed, I press against the wall, feeling my way in the darkness. From one cage to another isn't much of an improvement, and it all depends on trusting this man I'm not sure I have any reason to trust. There's a way to find out, though, and I ignore the sound of approaching footsteps as I touch a part of the wall that moves slightly against my hand. As the steps grow nearer, I knock three times, and the wall gives way with a loud screech.

"Who's there?" a voice shouts, and the footsteps come faster. Just then, the panel opens fully and a hand yanks me into the darkness—it is all I can do not to call out. The panel screeches as it slips closed behind me, but I am already looking ahead, following the shrouded figure guiding me up a winding, narrow staircase. I know now is not the time for questions, and we twist and turn, fingers scraping against the walls, ascending into the chasm with the sounds of our ragged breathing filling the silence. Once, I stumble on a step and nearly fall, but the stranger is there, spinning, catching me, helping me up to the next level. Then the stranger stops, and I knock into a muscled back as another panel opens and light hits me in the face. The stranger pushes me through and pulls the panel closed.

I put my hand above my eyes and blink, waiting as things come into focus. A large bed lies a few feet away from me, covered on all sides with lacy white curtains, but through those long sheets I glimpse a slim face. "My mother." The voice is rich, with a gravelly note that sets my heart racing. I know without turning whose hand is on my back.

Jonas pulls off his hood. "I'm sorry. I had to make my uncle believe you were my enemy. I realized trying to convince him other-wise might get you killed."

I grab his collar, then let go, folding my hands at my sides. "Why did you save me? You have every right to hate me."

He pulls my chin up. "How could I let you die before bringing you to meet my mother? We made a promise nine years ago, remem-ber? Now we can fulfill it."

"So it's . . ." I swallow, dropping my gaze as my heart twists in pain. "You're right. I still owe you a debt. I will heal your mother."

His fingers tighten on my face and I worry he's going to strike me, but then he embraces me, burying his face in the crook of my neck. Confusion courses through me when he says, "Do you think I want you only for that?" His breath tickles my ear, and he pulls me closer, tangling his fingers in my hair. "Dèmi, no matter who your father is, I know who you are. Don't forget that." He kisses my forehead and lowers his face to me, his lips only a breath away from mine. "You came here to set things right, to free our people—that's who you are. Tonight, I will take the throne and join you in that fight."

I swallow, then pull back. "Do you even know what the fight is you're joining? Do you know what your uncle is doing? There were Oluso where I came from. Women. And they're all pregnant."

His jaw stiffens. "I know. Ekwensi took me there when we

couldn't find you in the East Wing. It seems there are a lot of things my uncle has kept me in the dark about."

"We have to do something. I doubt those women came here pregnant. One has been here since she was four and—"

"Dèmi," he says quietly, "I know. We *will* do something. In a few hours, I'll officially be appointed my uncle's heir and then I'll have the power I need. If we try to rescue them now, though, we risk attracting my uncle's attention. We need to wait. By the night's end, I will be heir, and everything will change."

"How? Heir is not king, Jonas. He still has all the power."

"I'll reveal my magic to the court. With an Oluso prince, the council will have no choice but to change the law. My cousin Albert is in disgrace because of his father's attempt on my life. My uncle has no other heirs."

"But he'll still be king. Do you think he'll just let you change the law and do nothing? There are ways to make more heirs—the women in the dungeon are proof of that. Open your eyes, Jonas. It's not going to be that simple."

"Nothing is ever simple with my uncle, but this is the best chance we have. We need to take it."

I want to believe him, to trust his words the same way I do the magic humming in my veins. But that magic deserted me when I needed it most, and the pain of that is fresh, an open wound bleeding me dry.

Trust is even harder for me to come by these days.

There is a knock on the door. "Your Highness, may I come in?" I look around, searching for a place to hide, but Jonas slings an arm around my waist. "Yes, Edwina."

An elderly woman walks in, her face slim and full like a coco yam. Catching sight of me, she drops the basket in her hands and rushes forward. "Yéyé? Oh, my baby." She hugs me, the smell of cinnamon and roses emanating from her papery skin. She touches my face and rubs my arms, tears brimming in her eyes. "Wait—I'm sorry. You're not my Yéyé, are you? You look just like her."

"Auntie Edwina, this is Dèmi. Yetundé's daughter."

She sniffles and wipes her face. "She left here carrying you two. I was so angry with her then. I wanted her to make up with Master Alistair. I didn't know I'd never see her again."

"Two?" I ask.

She wrinkles her brow. "You have no twin? Did the other baby pass on?"

I swallow at this, tears burning my throat. "There were two of us?"

She pats my back. "Nothing to fret over now. What's done is done. I'm sure Yéyé kept it from you to keep you from melting as you are now."

And I am melting. I can hardly take it all in, so I settle on a path that I think might lead somewhere, if only to my own sanity. I take her hands in mine. "You knew my mother?"

"Knew her? I raised her. Her first steps, words, courses—I was there for them all. The Queen Mother was busy with many things, and Yetundé was a curious child, always trying to find things out. She was the brightest and most adventurous of all her sisters." She touches the beads at her throat, fingers trailing over seven cowry shells. "And now they're dead. All my babies are dead."

Jonas reaches out to her, giving her arm a reassuring squeeze. "Uncle will kill Dèmi, too, if we don't protect her."

Edwina raises her chin and squares her shoulders, like Mummy always did. "He will have to kill me first." She opens the door and five attendants walk in, women of varying heights and coloring, dressed in soft blue dresses tailored to fit their frames. "We're ready when you are," she calls to Jonas. "Alistair will regret the day he spared my life."

I turn to Jonas. "What's going on?"

"Lord Ekwensi and I agreed that this was the best way to keep you safe. Come to the gala with me. If everything goes well, you will be free. If it goes badly, you will have a chance to escape before anyone knows you've gone missing."

"I'm not fond of everyone deciding what's best for me. Especially those I don't exactly trust."

Especially when Ekwensi seems to have other plans and is fine using forbidden rituals to borrow his child's magic. But I don't say this part out loud—can't. I want to trust Jonas, to share everything with him, but there's a part of me that's afraid; a part that thinks he might reconsider revealing he's one of us; a part that believes Colin was right and Jonas doesn't know what it means to be Oluso after all. But I push those thoughts away and tell myself I need to escape first, get my bearings. Find Colin.

"Were you fond of the dungeon?" Jonas asks, but there's a joke in his tone, and it's clear he isn't trying to make this a choice between one or the other. "There's no way we could leave you there. But you're right, it's not fair of you to simply trust us. This party, though—it's the perfect opportunity to make sure you're safe."

"Why can't you just sneak me out now?"

"There's no time. With the party, there are more guards than usual, and if you didn't know, you stand out."

"Because of my skin?"

"Because you're beautiful."

I flush at that, but then look down at myself. I have never felt less pretty in my entire life. "Jonas, I can't just walk into the gala like this," I say, pointing at my filthy state. "Your uncle would have me arrested. Mari might even think twice about adopting me."

He grins. "You're not going in like that."

He nods, and before I can do anything, the attendants surround me, pulling me into the other room, not even pausing to tug at my clothes and hair. "Wait—" I say, but they cluck at me as they strip me of clothing. They push me into a full bath that stinks of rose water and honey and work all at once, scrubbing my back, arms, and feet. One even scrubs beneath my breasts, and I cover them with both hands while another plucks at my hair, pulling it tight to my head. After a few minutes, they drag me out and stand me naked before a large mirror. Mirrors are luxuries most people in Ifé cannot afford, so this is the first time I have caught myself in front of one. I stare at my body. Full hips, large breasts, a long, curved neck, and broad shoulders. My arms are muscled, my legs short and thick. My hair is braided up the sides to a ridge of coily puffs crowning my head.

Am I—I think—as beautiful as Jonas sees me?

Taking a bowl of white paint from beside the bath, Edwina spreads it over one side of my face, then the other. I close my eyes, feeling the brush of those fingers as they speak knowledge into my skin. When I open my eyes again, half my face is covered, diagonal marks sloping one way, circular lines meeting them and flowing out in branches, stretching out to my neck. On the left side of my face, there are simple marks, seven dots beneath my eye and three on my forehead. These markings hold the history of our people, and more—the blessings of the spirits. She weaves strings of coral beads through my hair, like the queens of old would wear when they graced the court. Finally, she hands me the mask Ayaba gave me and fastens her necklace to my neck. Among the cowry shells now is the curved bone Ayaba graced me with.

"It's Gura's Day. The Day of the Beautiful. The spirits told me today that someone was coming. I waited, watching until the sun came to rest. Then Jonas called and asked me to dress the woman he would bring to his official appointment. I knew when I saw your face, and the things stored in your bag, that Ayaba sent you to me. May your journey be fruitful."

Right then, I decide. I won't allow my fear to keep me from fighting. I wrap my fingers around the bone. Even if my magic fails, and everything falls apart, I will end this madness once and for all. "Thank you, Auntie."

And thank you, Ayaba.

She fastens the mask to my face as the attendants draw me into the dress I am to wear. I gasp when I see it. The dress is black gold, with ornate patterns carved throughout. Its sleeves bloom like chrysanthemums crowning my shoulders but leave my arms uncovered. The high neck opens out in front, dipping just to my breasts. It curves to my body, hugging my breasts, waist, and hips, but halfway down my hips, it fans out like a waterfall, the silky fabric running along the ground.

"I made this dress for your mother to wear at her betrothal. She never got to wear it, but it seems that saving it was not a waste." Edwina turns to the doorway. "Your Highness, your lady awaits."

Jonas stands in the doorway, wearing a dark shirt with embroidered gold epaulets, and matching trousers that make him seem even taller. His mouth is open, his face alive with excitement. He bows over my hand, then draws my palm in, kissing it. "It is my honor to fight at your side," he says, invoking the tradition of the warrior chiefs who were once tasked with protecting the kingdom.

I take a breath, letting the flutter in my belly spread through me, and utter the customary response. "It is my honor to walk at your side."

Hand in hand, we step out into the corridor, attendants following in our wake. We are both beautiful, we are both powerful. And, come what may, we are both together.

It is time for war.

TRAITS

The guards bow as they draw open the doors at the head of the marble staircase. The silence gives way to a chorus of noise. Jonas tucks my arm in the crook of his elbow as we come to the top of the landing. "Are you ready?"

Can anyone be ready for this sort of spectacle?

Purple-and-gold linens hang from the ceiling and walls. Acrobats hang from these, their bodies bent at impossible angles, limbs flailing and tangled, baby birds taking flight. Lanterns behind them, twisted in cloth and hanging from horned chandeliers, cast a golden glow on everything. Colors swirl and twist as people come together and apart, gliding fish in a pond—flashes of reds, yellows, greens, and blues lingering as they streak by. People dance in ordered rows, a caterpillar of bodies wriggling together as a woman's voice screams through the room, each note of her song drowning the air.

"Dèmi?"

I nod.

As we reach the last step, the attendant blows his horn before announcing, "His Royal Highness, Prince Jonas Aurelius Sorenson, and his companion." The gojes cease crying, the harps and orutus following suit. The shekeres alone shiver, cowry shells clanking against their gourd prisons, accompanying the songstress's final high note. Horses, wolves, pigs, and dogs stare back at us, masks arranged carefully over pale, watchful faces. For a moment, all I can hear is the dying rattle of the shekeres, then the king's voice fills the room.

"Lords and ladies, please join me in welcoming my nephew."

He claps, and soon the whole room erupts in claps and cheers, thunder echoing in the air. The king settles back onto the throne at the head of the room, and Jonas bows, pulling me with him. A gaggle of women in fluffy dresses surround us like puppies waiting to be fed. They curtsy almost in unison.

"My lord." "My lord." "My lord" is the rallying cry. It sounds to me like the squawking of chickens.

Jonas smiles, his blue eyes twinkling. "Ladies, before I dance with any one of you—and trust me, I will make time to do so—I need to take care of my companion. Please, excuse us."

We sweep past, dodging attendants carrying platters of food and ladies with powdered cheeks giggling behind fans. The songstress begins another song, and this time dancers pop up beside her, mimicking the intensity of her song with their bodies. Men bow and watch me curiously, some tugging at Jonas and trying to draw him into conversation. Some complain about the cost of spices for the year, others talk loudly about the close of the hunting season with winter. Then there is the chatter lobbed at us like stones, snatches of conversation about dresses, whose mask is the best, when the next royal event will be, if the king will order special entertainment. Women gasp in excitement when they lay eyes on Jonas, only to sour immediately when I come into view. By the time we burst through the wall of bodies, I am grateful for the swell of cool air that settles between my breasts.

"I thought the goal was for me to blend in," I say, looking around the room. Most of the women fluttering about have skin that glows soft peach under the lanterns. Most of the attendants, dancers, and acrobats radiate blues, reds, and greens, darker pebbles easily traced in a sea of light colors.

"My uncle invited the governor of Benin along. Lord Ekwensi told him I would be bringing his daughter. The precious daughter of the kingdom's head tradesman is an important guest."

"You should have told me that before. What will I do when people try and talk to me? I don't know about much besides cloth and jewelry trading. More, I don't know anyone here. Don't you think the daughter of Benin's governor would have met people here?"

"She hasn't been invited before, which is the exact reason why my uncle won't mind me sticking to you all night. He wants to make a good impression. Marriage alliances are powerful tools he respects."

I splutter. "Marriage—"

"Lord Sewell looks as though he is raring for a talk. Stay here, I'll be back in a moment. If he catches both of us, he won't stop asking questions until he figures out who you are," Jonas says, nodding at the red-faced man with a lizard mask charging toward us.

"I don't have to answer his questions."

"Yes, but I need to try. His voice is louder than an elephant's bleat, and we don't want to draw my uncle's attention. Your name is Bunmi, by the way."

He strides away before I can answer, and a group of women sidle over, hair swept up in similar styles, dresses puffed out like oversized cakes. One in a coral dress and a bird mask steps up. "And who might you be? My father said only council families and special dignitaries were being invited. Whose do you belong to?"

"She must be a castoff of Lord Kairen's. Look how dark she is," a girl in a mouse mask answers.

"I'm nobody's castoff," I say, trying to keep the edge from my words. "The prince invited me."

A third girl adjusts her fox mask, the reddish orange matching perfectly with her dress. "Girls, there's no need for all the fuss. Auri has always liked a bit of fun. Remember when he stuffed pudding in Lady Heatherwort's bag? He probably wanted to show one of the servants a good time. Leave the poor girl alone."

Mouse puts her hand on my shoulder. "I just hope she understands what her position is. It's nice to have a bit of fun every now and then, but one should know when to stop."

I throw her arm off. "Touch me again and I'll show you what fun is."

She jumps back, hissing. "You think because Auri brought you here that you're untouchable, don't you? When this is over, I'll ask Uncle Alistair if I can have you as one of my handmaidens. I doubt you'll be so bold then."

"What's going on here?"

A woman in white walks over, tiger mask accentuating her sleek cheekbones and her slim, rouged lips. The other girls crowd her, hanging on to her arms like children fighting for their mother's attention.

"Elodie, we were defending your honor," Bird says. "This girl claims to be Auri's personal guest."

Elodie? *Where have I heard that name before?*

"I don't think she's one of us. We should tell Uncle Alistair," Mouse adds.

Tiger looks at Fox, who shrugs. "Don't ask me. Phenalia and Asthenia were the ones talking. But it's true that we don't know who she is. I think Auri might have brought in one of the servants."

"Don't say things like that, Brigitte. It's insulting to both Auri and this girl. I won't have it."

Mouse smirks. "I don't think she knows who you are, Elodie. If she did, she wouldn't be hanging on to your intended."

The word "intended" penetrates the annoyance building inside me at the same time as someone takes my arm. A deep voice says, "She's Lady Bunmi Odaro, daughter of Louis Odaro, governor of Benin. I think if you ladies want to continue receiving silks for your gowns you should be careful when speaking to her."

Colin smiles at me, a leopard mask hanging low on his neck. "Sorry I'm late. I was having a look around." There is so much in that gaze, so much I need to ask. I want to knock him to the ground and punch him until he tells me what is going on. Or better yet, cut him with my words and give him a taste of the anger filling me. Instead, I squeeze his hand gratefully.

"Thank you for coming."

Mouse and Bird cast nervous looks at me while Tiger curtsies before us. "Excuse me. I haven't introduced myself. I'm Elodie, Prince Jonas's fiancée." She offers her hand to Colin. "I believe you must be Nicolás, Lord Kairen's firstborn." He kisses her gloved fingers, and she smiles graciously before taking my hands in hers. "Welcome, Lady Bunmi. Please excuse my friends' foolishness. It is an honor to have you here."

Now everything clicks in place. Elodie, the one who sketched Jonas so well. His fiancée.

I offer her a smile, but my chest is tight, my stomach quivering. I can still feel the warmth of Jonas's skin when we slept side by side in Maiduguri, the longing in his gaze when we held each other in his mother's rooms. Just another thing he's kept from me. I seethe even as I curtsy, hiding my fists in the folds of my dress. All this time, I have been a fool.

A fool who keeps believing in foolish things.

I swallow. "Thank you, Lady Elodie. The pleasure is all mine."

"You must be starved, having traveled such a long way. Refreshments? Our personal cook handles the palace's parties. Come, let's

find you a fresh custard." She pauses and taps her chin. "Or perhaps some curry if Ahad thought to make any? I don't know what
you're used to."

Colin bows slightly. "A custard will work well, Lady Elodie. The
Benin folk are up to date on Eingardian customs. Lady Bunmi *is*
from a loyalist family."

She flushes a soft pink, her cheeks blending in with the ornate
pink-orange mask she still wears. "Yes, I didn't think on that. Now
that our kingdoms share a—um—now that our kingdoms are so . . .
well aligned, it makes sense that you would be familiar with our
cuisine." She sweeps forward briskly. "Follow me."

Colin tucks my arm in his elbow and pulls me along. "Sorry
about that," he whispers.

"What?" I return harshly. "You insinuating that I'm one of those
oloté who would sell their own kin to become Eingardian or the
fact that you failed to mention your mysterious father was a council
member?"

He tugs me closer as we pass a gaggle of staring young men.
"Both. My mother is . . . *was* Eyani Al'hia. You might know her as—"

"The Scourge of T'Lapis," I mutter, staring at Colin in disbelief.

Elodie looks back over her shoulder and Colin flashes her a
smile before increasing our pace.

"The woman famous for razing whole villages in a matter of
hours, the general whom all the regions plied with concubines so
they could win her favor—that woman is—"

"My mother, yes. But my father wasn't a gifted concubine.
Mother wanted to visit Y'cayanogo, the volcano out to the west, to
strengthen her magic. She needed a desert guide. My father is from
Ismar'yana, the only desert city left."

"Hold on," I say, coming to an abrupt stop. "She what? Where?
I'm so confused."

He points at the long table Elodie has stopped at, laden with so many dishes, all in polished iron platters and pots. "Don't eat any of those green tubers floating in that pot. Jonas says they take perfectly good vegetables and leave them in saltwater for months. Disgusting."

Elodie rejoins us. "Please, eat whatever you'd like. I'm going to see if I can't get Ahad to bring some periwinkle stew. I hear Benin people love sea snails."

My mouth drifts open at the mention of one of my favorite childhood dishes, then I remember who I'm standing in front of and quickly cover it. "Thank you," I respond with a low bow.

Elodie looks as though she has more to say, but glancing at the hand Colin now has around my waist, she steps back. "I'll return shortly."

Colin springs into action, swiping a handful of doughy fritters from a pile while deftly avoiding the iron plate. "Eat quickly. I don't know how long it'll take him to finish up." He nods at Jonas, who is listening intently to a group of well-decorated soldiers. "And I doubt they fed you in the East Wing."

"Then talk," I growl, taking a few fritters. I bite into the puffy akara flesh and welcome the sweet and sharp taste of honey mixed with ground prawns. Despite thinking themselves superior to us, Eingardians always seem to like our food. I wouldn't have thought to add honey though.

He brushes a crumb from my cheek before continuing. "It's a simple story. Mother fell for Father during her pilgrimage to Y'cayanogo. She made him a concubine of the first rank. Mother had mostly wives in her court, and they resented that Father could give her a child and they could not. Soon after, I was born, and they tried to murder me. So, Father poisoned them one by one and took over Mother's court."

I choke on a piece of dough, and Colin knocks a fist in between my shoulders. When I shoot him a dirty look, he grimaces. "Iron cups. No choice. Maybe on our way out, we can get you a drink of water in the kitchens?"

I brush him off. "What happened then? Didn't Eyani—I mean, your mother, didn't she make your father her heir? Why would she do that if he killed her other concubines?"

Colin smiles a sharp, wistful smile, and I have to tamp down the urge to end the conversation here. His face says it all—there is pain and love here, too, inextricably linked, too much to let go of. When he speaks again, his voice is deeper, stony. "Mother respected only the strong. Those who could carve out a home for themselves. Father survived the desert, then he adapted to rule her court. She was proud. She didn't even mind that he was poisoning her too. She considered it her fault for underestimating him."

"Your father killed your mother?"

Colin nods. "Official records said she died of an incurable stomach illness. Her innards were lined with discolored ridges, and her liver was swollen—probably from all the drinking over the years. Father used to have me put red powder in my mother's drinks. To help her sleep. She died when I was eight."

I gape, at a loss for words. Now I understand the anger Colin wears like a second skin. Lord Kairen used him as the weapon that ended his mother's life.

"My father married an influential lord's daughter and took over T'Lapis. She's Matéo's mother," he says, peeling back my clenched fingers and placing an almond biscuit in them this time. "When I was nine, and started manifesting Mother's gifts, he sent the first set of his assassins after me. I used what Mother taught me and survived. After a few more tries, he gave up and decided to make a better weapon out of me."

"Stop right there. Your father tried to kill you?" Anger and horror war within me as I take in his words and remember the first time we met, the mistrust and defiance that he projected after he got caught stealing in the marketplace. Was he running from his father's assassins then?

"Unfortunately, no periwinkle stew," Elodie says, sighing as she glides over to us. Colin takes a step back from me and the moment is lost. I want to hurl insults in her face, but the anger I feel is not her fault, even if a little part of me wants it to be hers.

A drummer launches into a short drum dance, flinging his drumsticks this way and that and spinning for the captive audience. He pounds out ten lingering beats, announcing that Fox Hour is half spent.

"Elodie." Jonas walks up, a soft smile on his lips. "Good to see you two have already met."

She touches his arm with the ease of familiarity. "Of course. It's my duty to make everyone feel welcome."

"You are known for nothing if not doing your duty." He nods to Colin before taking my arm again. "Elodie, I leave you in the capable hands of my friend Nicolás."

Colin scowls but offers his arm. "Lady Elodie."

I frown, feeling suddenly possessive. Colin and I weren't done talking. There's so much I still need to hear from him.

Jonas responds to Elodie's questioning look. "I want to dance with Lady Odaro before she gets too tired. She's traveled a long way."

"I'd prefer to rest," I protest, annoyed at the easy camaraderie between them, but Jonas draws me away before I have a chance to finish. I glance back and catch Elodie watching with an amused, intent expression.

She mouths something, but I don't catch it because soon we are in the center of the room, walled in by a shield of bodies. "Do you know how to pair dance?" Jonas asks as the musicians pull their horsehair bows along their orutus.

"What makes you think I want to dance with you?"

He's taken aback, but recovers quickly. "What do you mean?"

"I don't think your fiancée likes this," I say pointedly.

"Dèmi, I'll explain—"

"Don't bother." I look around and realize all eyes are on us. I hate that this charade is required of me, but I'm the one who is in danger, not Jonas. So, taking his hand, I turn halfway, and take a step back, mirroring his steps. "You forget we were expected to learn Eingardian customs in school. We were punished for trying to dance makosa or azonto."

He pushes me under the arch of his arm and catches me on the other side. I stiffen as his fingers press into my back. "Dèmi, I'm sorry. I wish I could make you believe that."

"Sorry for what? Your secret fiancée or the injustices that come with being Oyo-born? It's no worry, though—let us do this dance."

"You look like you want to hit something," he says, a bit softer. "You look like you want to hit *me*."

"I'm all right. I just don't like this place. We should be making plans to save those women in the dungeons instead of parading ourselves like okin."

He sighs, twisting me until I am wrapped in his arms. "We are trying to save them. What do you prefer we do, attack the people here?"

"I prefer that we be out doing something instead of playing these social games. People are dying while we're messing around. It may be normal to you to listen to people complain about spices and masks while trying to get your attention, but it's not for me. After you show the court your magic, what happens? You'll marry

Elodie and continue preparing to be king while I go back to Benin and do the hard work, and that's if I make it out alive. Then, even if the council changes the law, will that stop people from selling Oluso children? Will it stop them from hunting us?"

Will it keep fathers from trying to kill their children?

I keep this last thought to myself. Colin's story wasn't lightly shared, and even if he were all right with me sharing it with Jonas, it's not my story to tell.

"They will stop," he answers. "I'll make them stop. Killing our people will be a crime and an insult to the Crown. I'll make them see that, so please, trust me a little."

"You use that word a bit too much."

"Which word?"

"Trust. You want me to trust you with life and death when you're too busy eyeing me to tell me you have a fiancée."

"It's a marriage alliance, and it's not official yet. Elodie and I are friends. We don't care for each other. Not in that way. She hates it as much as I do."

"You don't know anything, do you?" I shake my head, rattling the beads in my hair.

"What do you mean?"

"You're the only one who believes that," I say, and then go silent, focusing on the dance.

The next song starts up, the songstress launching into Orchean, one of the languages spoken in Goma. The tinkling notes of a mbira echo through the room, leading the charge before the gojes, harps, and orutus rush to its aid.

"I know what I want," Jonas says before grabbing my shoulders and kissing me. I do not want him to kiss me with his lying mouth . . . and yet there's nothing I want more once it happens. His mouth is warm on mine, and I part my lips as his tongue slips against them.

His fingers tighten on my waist as I pull him into me, tasting the softness of his lips, his scent flooding into my nostrils. My body hums and my heart screams in delight even as my mind tries to tell me that I can't trust him.

I tell my mind to shut up.

Then he lets go, and I open my eyes. All the dancers around us have stopped, standing there with open mouths, watching us.

Smiling, he pulls me in again, moving to the rhythm of the song. I am aware of everyone watching us and I finally give in to the social war we are weaving. Our display possibly ruined an alliance for his uncle, and I delight in that as much as I delight in the danger of it all. Right here, under the king's nose, we flout everything Alistair Sorenson believes in. It's not rebellion, not in the way I hope, but it's something. And it's with Jonas—handsome, duplicitous, earnest, complicated Jonas.

I wouldn't trade this for anything.

We dance, arms parallel, his hand on my waist, and mine on his shoulder, whirling as the music twinkles on. To the court, we are scandal, our mere presence eating away at the bubbles of laughter coating the air, the sparkles of the swinging chandeliers. But as I turn in toward Jonas, and he melds into me like gear pieces grooving together, I know that we are fire. The tingles in my fingertips extend all the way down to the tips of my toes, and the furnace in my belly pushes lower into my loins. I spin with him until I cannot remember where he begins and I end, until the heat from our bodies makes my head dizzy and my lips part from thirst. The music dies, and there in the silence, I am breathing, snatching at puffs of air for all they are worth, but the world is a hazy mess of shadow and light, and his icy blue eyes are all I see as he leans into me and presses his lips to mine. His kiss tastes of blood and honey, and nothing has ever been sweeter.

THUNDER

"How long have you known?" I ask when we are still again, an island in the storm of raging waves. The flurry of excitement and bravado that swallowed me a moment ago is swelling into a mix of disbelief and certainty—Jonas and I are mates.

He stares at me, eyes wide, as though seeing me for the first time. "I don't know. I'm not sure exactly, but I've known for a long time. Ever since—" He stops, eyes clouding with sorrow. "Ever since that day, I've known."

I step back before I can stop myself, but he reaches for me all the same. I pull at the collar of my dress as though it would be enough to let the air in, to birth the breath that will remind my lungs to move. "So when we made that promise in Benin, and after, when you showed me your mark in Maiduguri, you knew then?"

"I didn't understand it myself when I came back from Ikolé. I was worried for you, wondering if you'd survived. I started feeling ill, like the world had lost its color. Many thought it was a lingering effect of the poison, or some dark residual magic your mother left on me. But Edwina knew. She told me that something must have gone wrong with my mate. She was one of the few who knew about my being Oluso."

"I was recovering with the Aziza then." I touch his neck, startled at the tingle that grows in my fingers. My Oluso mark flashes on my hand. "All this time, how did I not know that we were mates?"

"I—"

"Ladies and gentlemen, your attention, please," the king calls out. "Every year, we hold this winter festival to celebrate the history of our kingdom, to reflect on the mistakes of the past and to look toward the future. This year's winter festival is special because I have that honor."

An attendant appears before us. "The king wishes to see you, Your Highness."

Jonas takes a breath and presses a quick kiss to my lips. "I'll be back," he says, following the man.

"And so, I wish to make some appointments." The king waits as Lord Ekwensi steps onto the dais, a cloth tied around part of his head, sealing his swollen eye from sight. "For his commitment to helping me create a stable kingdom, I appoint Tobias Ekwensi, formerly regional lord of Ogun and Ikwara, as the provincial head of the Oyo region."

Raising his sword, the king taps one of Lord Ekwensi's shoulders, then the other. "Rise, noble servant. You have done well this day."

The now Regional Lord Ekwensi bows, and a few people clap, though I see many with pursed lips and tightness around their eyes at the news. Then Jonas steps up and the king turns back to the crowd, golden robes sparkling in the light. "I also wish to appoint my brother's son, Prince Jonas Aurelius Sorenson, as my heir. As you know, in the interest of the kingdom's affairs, since liberation from the former queen's tyranny, I have been unable to take enough time to father a child. Many years ago, my brother suggested I raise his child as my own, and I accepted. Unlike the past kingdom, I believe that greatness is not determined by blood but by the courage to face the difficult things we must contend with. This week, I'm sure you all heard the rumors of the prince's abduction, an ill-fated plot perpetuated by my sister's husband, Lord Vermillion. Despite having to fight meascan assassins, my nephew was able to return to us as we see him today, unscathed and prepared to accept the crown. What greater sign of courage do we need than that?"

"None!" a voice shouts. Many heads nod in agreement.

Jonas kneels as the king lifts his sword. "Let it be known henceforth that Prince Jonas Aurelius Sorenson is heir to the kingdom of Ifé. May his days be long and his reign great." The king brings down the sharp edge of the sword, stopping only a breath from Jonas's shoulder. "And may his shadow stretch over all the land." He brings the blade down again, edge kissing the top of Jonas's shirt.

I release the air trapped in my throat when he hands his sword off and places an iron circlet on Jonas's head. "Long live the prince," he shouts.

"Long live the prince!" This time there is no hesitation. The room echoes with chants, cheers, and claps.

Jonas moves to the edge of the dais as his uncle sits back on the throne. As he opens his mouth to speak, the king raises a hand. The room falls silent as the king speaks. "I'm sure my nephew would like to say a few words of thanks, but before that, I have prepared a surprise to honor the appointments today. I know my nephew is anxious to get back to entertaining Governor Odaro's daughter, so we will have his appreciation speech later. Please welcome Lady Odaro when you have the opportunity, and excuse her strange habits. As you all know, Oyo customs are particular, and this is her first time at court."

Roars of laughter overtake the room. So many people are now watching me and whispering to their companions as though I am a wild animal brought in for their amusement. The desire to call the wind is only mitigated by knowing how disastrous that would be . . .

and fear that the wind won't actually come. I don't know what to do, then, so it's a relief when Jonas steps in front of me, shielding me from their gazes as the attendants open two large doors on either side of the dais.

"Ladies and gentlemen, this way, please," an attendant says. "The king has prepared a show for your entertainment."

The hairs on my arms and the back of my neck prickle. Jonas takes my hand and I clutch his with all the strength I can muster as we are ushered through the doors. Wet grass slaps against my feet as we wander down the outside path, well-trimmed hedges hemming us in on either side. Lilies wave as we walk by glasslike ponds toward a sandy building with shadowy arches flanked by silent guards. We follow the attendants through an arch, climbing up into a sloping stadium with stone benches rising up like gravestones. I stare, a knot forming in my belly as an attendant directs me and Jonas onto an open, flat platform with a raised dais and a throne sitting atop it, guiding us into seats at the edge of it.

Lord Ekwensi joins us a moment later, followed by Mari and a sandy-haired man whose high forehead and arched brows resemble Jonas entirely. Colin and Lord Kairen bring up the rear with Elodie as the king takes his place on the throne, a horn in his hands. When everyone is seated, bright flowers lying against those gravestones, the king lifts the horn to his lips, talking into it.

His voice amplified by the horn, Alistair says, "Loyal subjects, today I spoke of correcting mistakes of the past. The former queen championed one such mistake. She allowed meascans—magic users with fearsome, uncontrollable magic—to live freely amongst the people."

He pauses and a few people stand and jeer, urging him to continue.

"When my father, our late king-consort, Mattias Jonas Sorenson, cautioned her against it, she ignored his advice. In fact, it was not until her actions produced a casualty that anything was done."

He nods at the man who bears a striking resemblance to Jonas before speaking on. "My brother Markham's wife, the Lady Arianne, was damaged by one of these monsters, a man called Iron Blood Osezele. Under the guise of a peaceful walk with my sister-in-law and nephew, he attempted to murder them using his accursed magic. He was caught, and swiftly brought to trial, but Queen Folakè, in her folly, refused to execute him. That day, I took up arms on behalf of our people, to rid us of this scourge."

The ground rumbles as the crowd stomp their feet and shout. I put my fingers to my necklace, clutching the bone blade Ayaba gave me. Gone are the assessing, haughty nobility. The arena atmosphere is thick with energy and wine-fueled bravado.

The king lifts a hand, the iron bars etched into the high walls of the arena open, and people trickle out like ants, filling the circular middle, staring up at us. I rise to my feet. Children clutch onto their mothers; men and women look about, shackled hands above their heads as though the light from the lanterns hanging on the walls is too much for them. The king comes to the edge of the platform.

"Meascans," he says, addressing the chained gathering, "a few days ago some of your kind set fire to the fields of Lokoja, burning down a year's worth of crops. The soldiers tried to stop them and contain the flames, but to no avail. It was a magical fire unlike anything they'd ever seen. My guard captain was nearly killed. The next day, the city was buried in sand—a sandstorm no doubt caused by the evil you meascans wrought."

Sheer terror grips me, and my hands begin to shake as I see Cree on fire once more. I remember now Elu's warnings, that a Harmattan storm was coming for Lokoja. That the people would die if they didn't run. She died for the crime of protecting innocent lives.

Ekwensi springs to his feet. "The captain reported that only a small portion of the field, close to the wildlands, was damaged. The fire couldn't have done that much damage." Mari is there, though, and with a firm hand, pushes Ekwensi back down in his seat, wincing at what can only be a brutal grip.

If the king notices, he doesn't show it. He keeps going. "The survivors of Lokoja are destitute, crying out for the kingdom's aid and justice. And I, your king, have decided to give it to them. So, I'll offer you an opportunity to prove your worth as citizens of this kingdom, to prove you are not scum like the vagabonds who burned an entire city's crops without remorse. There are three hundred of you. I will take only three—three who will be hailed as heroes, whose non-meascan relatives will be given an opportunity to live here in Nordgren and be well cared for. Three who will be made onyoshi after their honorable deeds and given a place in my service. Three who will be worthy."

He pauses and I rock back on my heels, dread filling my belly. When he speaks again, I know without a doubt that I cannot run. I have to find a way to stop him here and now.

The king continues, "When I give the word, the guards will release you from your chains. You are welcome to use whatever tools are at your disposal to dispatch your fellow meascans. I advise killing the children first if you have any mercy left in your dark hearts."

The arena is silent, then slowly murmurs rise through the air like offerings to the spirits, loud and bountiful. The people in the middle of the arena stand in stunned silence, then some begin to cry, falling to their knees, chains rattling. Children wail as mothers press them close to their breasts, trying to silence them.

The man who looks like Jonas touches the king's shoulder. "Brother, this is madness. You cannot make execution into a sport. These people are already in our custody. Must we kill them like this?"

Mari stands, hand on her sword hilt. "Are you questioning the king, Markham? If not, I'd advise you to watch your words."

Markham squares his jaw. "This isn't right. Surely the people will not stand by this."

The king merely lifts an eyebrow. "Let's ask them." He brings the horn to his lips again. "All those in support of my decree, please rise. I want to hear your voices, and your thoughts. As your king, I have always pledged to listen to your concerns. I will do so in this too. All who believe my ruling is just, stand."

A few people jump to their feet, then a few more. Some sit, looking at one another, then, one by one, they get to their feet. In mere seconds, only a few people in the arena are sitting. I crash into my seat, my legs rubbery under me. Jonas, too, remains seated. To my surprise, Lord Kairen remains seated next to Colin, as does Elodie.

Markham shakes his head. "This isn't right, brother. As one of the captains of your guard, I've supported you in many things, but not this. This will bring defiance from the people. Those who fear us will now despise us."

The king pats his shoulder. "The people have spoken."

The standing audience stomps and cheers, the storm of their movements like claps of thunder. I scan their faces, wishing this were all a horrible dream, but their noise is like wildfire, spreading and consuming everything in its path—hungry for destruction.

The king goes to the platform. "Meascans, prepare yourselves. If you refuse to obey, guards will be sent in, and the ground bathed in your blood. Not a single one of you will live.

"I should warn you, too—if any of you attempt to use your foul magic against the gathered crowd, iron"—he gestures to the walls around the courtyard, where archers are poised with their metal arrows nocked—"awaits you."

He nods to Mari, and she drags Ekwensi from his seat, pushing him half over the platform next to the king. "In the spirit of correcting mistakes, I hereby strip Sir Tobias Ekwensi of his titles and land. As you all saw just now, he sought to go against the will of the people in defense of his fellow meascans. It has also been brought to my attention that he has been involved in treasonous practices against me, and I will not stand for those from him or anyone. Now, please be seated. We will give our meascan friends a moment to prepare."

Mari pushes Ekwensi onto his knees and the king presses his sword against his neck. "I knew when you brought that girl here that you were up to something. You were either foolish enough to trust meascans to save my nephew or you were in league with them. Either way, it will not stand. Kairen insists that his son has nothing to do with magic, so I had to make a choice—his son or you. You're not as young as you used to be, and the boy is teachable, so I'm afraid it's you, old friend. Whether you were a victim of Vermillion's plot or the instigator, I don't care. You die here."

"How long have you known?" I whisper to Jonas who sits, watching this unfold with glassy eyes.

He looks at me, his face ashen, the muscles in his neck twitching. I feel it then, the anger and disbelief roiling in his heart, the fear and terror. He didn't know. And in that moment, I trust him. I know without him saying a word what he is thinking and give a brief nod.

In a flash, he is on his feet, hand outstretched. Mari screams as her sword glows red and curls back on itself. Pulling the bone blade from my neck, I stab it into my skirt and drag it through, freeing my legs from swaths of fabric. As the king watches Jonas, eyes wide with shock and something else—excitement?—I move, running at him with full force, brandishing my blade.

No more hiding.

BREATH

The guards leap in front of me, and I have just enough time to steal a spear from a flustered guard and parry the one who charges me. Shoving him back, I whip around, kicking the guard closest to him. One grabs me by the collar of my dress while another rips the mask from my face. The beads in my hair break, rolling onto the floor in waves. Then someone screams and the pressure on my neck is gone. I turn to see Colin with his foot on a guard's back. Throwing down her damaged sword, Mari rips one from the hands of a guard and rushes toward me. Jonas waves a hand and she stops, frozen in place. She shakes, and a shrill sound cuts into my ears as her armor peels itself away from her body, unravelling into a pile on the floor like fish scales. She trembles in an under-jerkin and tight trousers, her scarred arm an angry red against her pale skin. Eyes wild, she turns to the king. "Alistair!" The king lifts a hand, and more guards march onto the platform. Some run into the arena, surrounding the trapped Oluso like dogs herding sheep.

"Drop your weapons and stay where you are," the king commands. "Archers, prepare!"

The archers step up, arrows nocked in their bows.

"If any of you move, we will slaughter every last one of these meascans, and their blood will be on your heads. If you try to attack me, the guards have their orders. They will kill everyone in that arena, even if it means dying in the process. None of you will escape alive, unless I want you to."

"Uncle, don't do this," Jonas cries.

The king shifts his hand slightly and the guards move in, closing in on the Oluso who scramble back in fear, chains dragging on the few still chained. Throwing my head back, I scream, letting the anger that has slept in my body for years out into the world. The audience begins to shriek, some jumping from their seats and running, others shaking in their seats and clutching their heads. Elodie faints, and when Lord Kairen collapses onto the platform, blood seeping from his ears, Colin rushes to his side. Markham is on his knees, hands over his ears.

Jonas shoves his hand against my mouth, and I stop, breathing hard. "Don't. If you do it again, more people will die." The audience members settle like bees on a flower, fanning themselves and talking to one another, watching the platform as though this is the entertainment they were promised. Some tend to the fallen, helping them to their feet.

What do I care about that, though? These people were going to watch my brethren kill one another for sport. If my shout will end this, then so be it. Except I see, then, that one person remains standing, unaffected by my shout.

The only person who matters.

The king laughs, chuckling as though he is watching a masquerade. Mari joins in, too, dry laughs that resemble a dog's barking. The king shakes his head. "Poor, foolish child. I grew up with your mother. I've always worn beeswax.

"What did you think you could do? Wound me?" He clucks. "Do you think others haven't tried that? I thought you might be as intelligent as Yetu. I hoped to build something from the misfortune of your birth. I suppose I was wrong."

"You mean using her to create new Oluso, right? Those women you kept below—you intended to make her one of them," Jonas shouts.

The king wags a finger at Lord Ekwensi. "Now Tobias, why show the boy things he wasn't prepared for?" He sighs. "No matter. This is as good a time as any to see what he's made of.

"It's amazing, dear nephew, that you've managed to keep this"—he waves a hand toward the pile of Mari's armor—"from me. Granted, we only spent a necessary amount of time together, and you were raised mostly in the keep. But still, after all those times when I forced you to fight with disadvantages, it turns out your greatest advantage was at your fingertips after all." His voice rises, trembling with excitement. "Good. After all these years, Fate is still on my side."

He holds his arms out, a father welcoming his child home. "You are bone of my bone and blood of my blood. For years, I've searched for a way to bring iron-bloods back, to have the greatest power that accursed magic can give, and all this time you've had it. How? Your mother's family was also non-magical, extensively checked before she married my brother." He shakes his head, talking more to himself now. "It doesn't matter. None of that matters." His mouth trembles as he speaks. "You are the child I wanted. And now you can take your rightful place and help our people."

"What are you talking about?" Jonas asks.

Ekwensi laughs, a harsh, bitter sound. "Yes, Alistair, tell them what you really want."

To my surprise, the king takes a few steps toward me. "I loved your mother, better than I loved even myself." Mari bristles but the king doesn't notice. "Yetundé was always the one for me. We played together as children, shared our first kiss together. As the youngest daughter of the queen, she had the chance to make her marriage a love match, and although I was the first son of my father, I hoped that if the queen requested I marry her daughter my father would accede. But my father hated magic. He wanted the help of an iron-blood to harvest our failing mines, but he didn't want the dirtiness of magic tainting his bloodline. He opposed the queen the first time she suggested a betrothal between your mother and me. Maybe if he hadn't, things would have been different. I might have been your father."

I bare my teeth at him. "You could never be my father."

He nods. "Maybe if your mother's family had been Eingardian, my father might have reconsidered. But he had other prejudices too. No one without full Eingardian blood was good enough for his family." His eyes go flat, lost in memories of the past. "I thought Yetundé and I could run away together, get married in secret, con-summate the union before my father could say anything. A child. Once a child was born, my father would be honor bound to recog-nize our marriage—an alliance forged by blood. I invited Yetundé to visit me here in Nordgren, thinking we could be together. Instead, I watched as she fell in love with the iron-blood my father hired."

He clenches his jaw. "I tried to get her back, to do something that would send that man far away. All it did was make her hate me. So I turned to other things. After Arianne got hurt, your father came to me, seeking revenge for the Oluso's betrayal, and Yetundé ran away. I fulfilled my father's dream and took the kingdom. Thanks to the ironwork your father taught me, we were able to make the weapons we needed to win. We lost thousands of soldiers, brave women and men who fought till their last in the process. I never wanted any-thing like that to happen again. Thankfully, your father's fit of mad-ness resulted in him killing the old queen's forces for us."

"Then why are you doing this? By murdering these people, you'll stoke the flames of war," Markham says, coming to his feet. "Those who previously sided with us against the Oluso may fear that we will turn on them one day. What then?"

The king shakes his head. "Don't you see, brother? Father was right. He understood that if I married Yetundé, my allegiance would be divided. Our children would be Eingardian, but they would also be Oyo-born—half-castes caught between one world and the next. What I took to be his hatred was love. Yetundé proved it as much herself when she chose that man over me. She chose her blood before mine."

Mari strokes his jaw. "She didn't know what she had when she had it. It's not your fault. She was short-sighted. Even when I told her how much she was hurting you, she refused to listen. She started this. She fought me when I tried to keep her from running away. She betrayed me too."

"Do you hear yourselves? You're mad! Love is not an excuse for murder," I shout. "My mother didn't force you to all this. You chose it yourself."

"I did choose. Your mother taught me that blood matters. Her meascan blood mattered more than anything we'd built together. I thought magic was the problem, but after Yetu left . . ."

He pauses, the soft look in his eyes disappearing. "After the war, I learned even more. Many meascans refused to fight, protecting their precious blood as we struck them down, afraid to do anything that would kill their magic. The ones who fought didn't hold back, striking at anyone they could reach. I saw what terrible power magic brought, and I knew one day there would be more magic being born, more meascans rising up. Magic isn't the problem, but the hearts of men—divided allegiances. People will always fear those with more power, and those with power will always fear that they will lose it."

I shudder as I realize what this means. "You want magic. To control it."

He presses on. "I already have it. Young women with *some* Eingardian blood and strong magic in their families, the ones you met. Fathered by men with families loyal to me. A true honor."

My throat tightens as I choke out the words, "An honor? Rape? Forced subjection? You want children born of iron, children who would survive chains."

I understand now, too, that he doesn't know Ekwensi fathered Malala. I doubt he would gloat if he knew.

He lifts his hands like a spirit priest calling down rain from the sky. Mari watches him with the adoration of a worshiper, eyes focused on one thing. "Children who would have the strongest magic this world has ever seen, and allegiance to the kingdom. Eingardian, born and bred, loyal to their king, incapable of being subdued. My children."

"The moment they kill, the magic in their blood will shrivel and die," I sneer.

"As long as they keep the other meascans in check and ensure the kingdom's peace, I'm sure they would consider it a worthy sacrifice."

"It's evil."

"No more evil than watching meascans destroy the kingdom with their uncontrollable magic, killing other meascans and people alike. It's justice."

"But that's all hearsay, myths. Your armies have murdered far more people than any 'rogue' Oluso might have done. I've seen those reports—I know the lies you spin around them."

"You know *nothing*," the king says. "But you will."

"Uncle—I won't let you do this. Even if it means killing you," Jonas says, his voice broken and angry.

"How will you stop me?" The king claps and more soldiers edge onto the platform.

Colin stands at Jonas's side. "I have no desire to support your disgusting ideas, so count me as your enemy."

"Stand down," Markham calls, and the guards lower their swords, although some waver, unsure who to listen to. "Brother, this is madness. I haven't followed you all these years for this. I thought we were protecting the kingdom. I have no wish for needless bloodshed."

"How can you say it's needless? After what happened to Arianne? You *still* side with these animals?" Mari scoffs. "I will kill you myself if you stand in my way."

"It's about power for you, isn't it? All this is an excuse for you to rule," he says.

Mari smiles. "Power only respects power. Your brother, at least, understands this. He has no illusions whose side I'm on."

The king turns to Jonas. "Son, you have the chance to lead this kingdom into peace. When the court witnesses what you can do, when they see that you are the last iron-blood, they will support my vision. Your children will be the future of Eingard, and the protectors of all Ifé."

Jonas takes my hand, fingers intertwined on the blade I still carry. "As you said, Uncle, blood matters. Dèmi's blood calls to mine, and mine to hers. We're mates. I have no intention of having children with anyone else. Half-caste or not, our children will protect *all* of Ifé and break the chains you have set for our people."

My heart twists at his words and at the choked noise Colin makes, but I keep my eyes trained on the king. He looks down at our linked hands and sighs. "It's unfortunate you have decided to oppose me, but it can't be helped. You will see, too, in time, that I speak the truth." He snaps his fingers and the guards at the bottom of the arena move in, charging the bound Oluso. Arrows fly from the walls, and there are already moans.

Jonas turns immediately, and the shackles binding the Oluso give off red sparks, fireworks commemorating another winter festival. Then with a raucous symphony, the chains fall off, and the guards in the arena stop the charge, backing away like lion tamers watching their quarry for any signs of rebellion.

With another look up to the walls, the arrows in their quivers spark, and shouts of dismay and fear echo as the archers throw off their now-useless weapons.

"Thank you for that," Ekwensi says, the sound of his voice like honeyed water, spreading warmth in my chest. "I knew a long time ago, Alistair, that you were beyond saving. But still I waited. I planned and hoped. I even brought you this girl, thinking that when you saw her, things might change. But I can wait no longer. My father once told me that truth has many faces, mouths that help us see more clearly. But justice has only one face—a sword for those who warrant it, whether they be the victims of yesterday or the victors of today." He rises to his feet. "I trusted you when you took my sister and promised me a new life, even after I killed a few of your soldiers. I thought what I saw in you that day was mercy, that perhaps things wouldn't be so bad after all. Even after my sister died and you took her child for your dungeons, I clung to that. But now, I see the truth." Orange flames spark out of the air, hugging his body like a cloak. "That's what I am after all . . . an igbagbo."

I gape. The Oluso mark on Lord Ekwensi's hand is aflame, alive after all. I remember the way he spoke to me in Benin, the ease with which I shared the hidden truths of my heart. He knew even then what I wanted—that I desperately sought a chance to protect the people I loved, and he used it. Igbagbos, truth-seeker Olusos, were once hailed as advisers and judges, trusted with resolving disputes and passing fair judgments for all of Ifé. Their words caused even the most reluctant to share their deepest desires, and even act upon them if given the opportunity.

"You . . . you . . ." I start, but the words are thick in my mouth, and my breath refuses to rise in my throat. Strong magic is emanating from him in waves—nothing like the whisper of magic I felt when he borrowed Malala's powers.

"I told you the truth that day, Dèmi, because you deserved it. I asked what you were willing to do to break our people's chains, and you've shown me." He nods at Jonas and Colin. "You also have noble hearts. They will serve well in the world we're going to create." He holds a fist up, the air surrounding it crackling with energy, white sparks crackling at his fingers. As he opens his palm, lightning breaks through the clouds, striking an edge of the wall separating the audience from the pit of the arena, and it crumbles, people screaming and scrambling to get away as rocks go flying. The guards in the arena back away, running for the iron gates. There's no mistaking it—Ekwensi's magic is alive and well after all.

Lightning strikes again, tearing down another part of the wall as Ekwensi steps onto the platform railing, his voice thundering through the night air. "Brothers and sisters, do not stand idle. Your chains are broken. You are free! Look at how those who would destroy you now flee. This is the truth you must face. You were given power by the Father of Skies and Spirits to help your brethren, to build a new world together. Those who feared your power lost theirs because their evil hearts came after your own. They killed your ancestors, and still you refused to fight. They bound you in chains, and still you refused to fight. Will you let them paint the streets with your blood and offer your children as sacrifices for sport? Will you refuse to fight when the truth asks that you fight?"

The newly freed Oluso draw closer in, like flowers straining to reach the sun. A woman shouts from their midst, deep voice belying her slim frame. "What would you have us do? We can't fight back. If we kill those who imprison us, we reap the seeds of madness and destruction."

Ekwensi shows off his withered hand, his Oluso mark burning through it. "I believed that once. I believed that if we became the very weapons these people made us out to be, then we deserved the judgment of having our magic stolen from us. Then I learned the truth." He pulls back his sleeve, revealing cuts all the way down his arm. "I have killed men for their crimes. I raised my sword in war. I even committed murder on behalf of this fool you call king. Yet I stand before you with power granted to me by the spirits. And so it was revealed to me: If you fight in the name of justice, if you lift your swords in the service of truth, the spirits will hear you. Your magic will not leave you. Fear not. Raise your voices, lift your hands, and take the freedom that has been denied you!"

Whether it's the quality of his words or the compulsion of Ekwensi's power, it is not long before the Oluso decide. The slim woman is the first to move. She presses her hands against the rubble of the damaged wall and purple flames consume the stones. The arena walls crumble like sand castles in the grasping fingers of the sea. The king backs away from the platform, for the first time genuine wariness in his eyes as the Oluso climb the wall's remains, hoisting themselves onto the arena seats. Audience members pile into the medians, shoving and kicking at one another, jettisoning masks as they rush for the exit arches. Pieces of torn clothing sail like lanterns caught in the wind. A child riding on someone's shoulders is cast off as the escaping nobility knock down his companion, bouncing off the wall of bodies until an Oluso mother, her daughter strapped to her back, catches him in her arms. She stares at the child as he begins to cry, then calmly places a hand on its head. The child stops crying at once, and she looks back, staring at Lord Ekwensi. The other Oluso stop, watching.

"The king would advise you kill the children first if you have any mercy," he says.

"No!"

Catching the wind, I leap into the air. Maybe if I'm quick enough, I can reach the child and end this madness. But I know I won't make it.

Colin moves even quicker, though, fading into the air just as the woman lifts the child like an offering. He materializes in front of her, reaching for it. But she hands the boy to another woman and bends, undoing the knot of her wrapper. She straps the boy to her daughter and ties the knots together. Then she follows the other Oluso, climbing once more.

Lord Ekwensi turns back to us, smiling gleefully at the king. "Looks like we have more mercy than you thought."

Then a cry comes as the slim woman catches a fleeing woman by the neck and tosses her down the steps. Blood sprinkles the stones like rain. She throws back her head and howls, and I understand then that the call is not a cry of remorse but a rallying cry of wolves hunting on a wintry night—a call to war. In an instant, the Oluso near her join in and howl before charging forward.

TWILIGHT

The sky is iron and blood. Lightning tears through the clouds as an Oluso man drags an Eingardian man from the fleeing crowd. As the Oluso rears back, black flame engulfing his hands, a bubble swallows him, sealing him off from his prey. Blue lights rain around Colin, dancing together to form a wall of water cutting the rest of the Oluso from the crowd. The slim woman smashes her fist into a seat and the stone morphs into a pillar, crashing into Colin's makeshift wall like a battering ram.

"Dèmi," he screams.

Angling my body down, I kick off, shooting at him like an arrow. I reach him just as the second pillar cracks his wall, sending water gushing down the steps. Whipping my staff above my head, I rush at the woman, but as I close the distance between us another stone pillar lunges toward me. Pivoting around, I aim for her again, but the ground reaches out, growing around my feet, sinking me up to my waist.

"I don't want to fight you," she says.

"Then stop what you're doing."

She shakes her head in disbelief. "Why do you protect them?

You heard what the man said. They brought us here. They want us to kill each other. Why would you fight for them?"

"I don't fight for them. I fight for us. Even if Lord Ekwensi is right and we won't lose our magic after this, what about our hearts? Do you think we can stop ourselves from becoming oppressors if we crush them?"

She pulls up a trouser leg. Purple welts cover her tan skin. "I've had it the easiest out of everyone else because they captured me last. They dragged our entire family from our beds. I was the only one awake enough to fight back before they shackled me. They put me in their cells a day ago, but there are some who have been there for months, waiting to die, being used as entertainment for these animals you protect. Look around you. Look at how weak and ill our people are. Would this place be standing if we were all at full force?"

Oluso hang about, ghosts lingering between this world and the next, faces drawn and dirty. Some are huddled together, stretching their limbs, massaging dying flesh. Others, small children mostly, are sitting, rubbing their arms and legs. Only a few stand with the slim woman, hatred burning in their eyes.

"My family is dead," she says. "My children are dead. You want me to spare the lives of those who wanted them killed? Even after this, do you think they'll stop? They'll keep killing us until we become nothing. Like we were never here."

I swallow. She's not wrong. Moments before, the king stood above us, excitement dripping from his face like saliva from a hungry dog. The audience hid behind their fans and polite laughs, eyes sparkling as they waited for the show to begin. Even now, Mari is on the platform, eyes fixed on the king, not caring that she took my mother from me and destroyed my life. The king has the gall to blame my mother for all this—for the wicked choices he made. My heart races as my magic swells in me. Why shouldn't we give these people what they deserve? Why shouldn't they pay in blood and tears the way they have made us do for years?

"Dèmi," Jonas calls out to me, half-bent over the railing. Even from here, I can see the fear in his face, and something else— understanding. I hear Mummy's words then. *Dèmi, a leader is the feet of her people. She bleeds, so the legs can swim, the hands can paint, the bellies are full, and the faces look on to another day. The cold wind may blow, and the toes dry up in rot, but the feet keep moving so the body may live.*

Hot tears spring to my eyes, but I hold on to the familiar twinge of pain that shoots between my ribs and push the wind around my feet, breaking from the ground into the air. "Listen to me. I am here. We are here. We are here because they told us we had no place in our own kingdom, because they made us ashamed of our skin and the gifts born in us, because they said our blood was tainted. We are here because they told us that our words were no longer important, that our languages meant nothing, that we would always be less-than and we were better off dying in cells or in the bush. They told us to bite our tongues and die of poison, to smother our infants in their cradles, to let our spirits die in our beds. But no more. Our voices will not die. We will not be silent. We will rise like the spirits of our ancestors and do what needs to be done. We will tell our stories and we will fight." She looks at me, her face shining, yet I'm not done.

"But not like this. Not by staining our hands with their blood. But by fighting for peace."

The slim woman rises toward me on a stone pillar. "How are we going to get that peace? Peace doesn't exist without freedom. How do we get our freedom if we don't take it?"

I look at the platform where Lord Ekwensi stands, watching us with a smile. The king is beyond him, his face perfectly still, a snake awaiting its moment to strike. "I will get us our freedom back." Lifting my arms, I call the wind spirits. A hail of white lights falls in the arena like snow. Then, one by one, they drift toward the arches, forming a wall of wind and dust. The crowd backs away in terror as they are snatched into the air, only to drift safely down onto seats moments later. Seated now, they look up to the sky, hands against their faces as the wind bites their hair and clothes.

They look up at me.

"My name is Abidèmi Adenekan. I am the last surviving heir of Princess Yetundé Adenekan, daughter of Queen Folakè, the former queen of Ifé. I hereby challenge *your* king, Alistair Sorenson, to a trial by combat for the kingdom's crown. In the event that your king wins, I will honor tradition and submit myself to be executed as payment for my challenge. If I win, your king no longer has claim to the throne. His life and fate will be in my hands." Pulling Ayaba's blade from the loop at my waist, I slash my palm, watching as my blood drips into the earth. "I swear this in Olorun's name."

Sweat drips down my forehead and I wobble slightly as I glide toward the ground. The windstorm cost a bit of my stamina, but I keep my head high as I toss my blade on the arena floor—an open challenge. In the days of Ifé's birth, the kingdom resolved royal disputes by hosting competitions between recognized heirs. Of those heirs, only those who displayed wisdom, courage, and were supported by the people could compete. If two candidates remained after wisdom tests and trials of courage, the competition was decided in a fight to the death. The victor held the fate of the other candidate's life in their hands. The first queen spared the life of her brother, reasoning that a good ruler must be willing to die for the people and show mercy when needed. It's a beautiful story . . . but this is an ugly day.

There will be no mercy from me.

Mari spits. "Insolent, foolish girl. Think twice. I don't wish to waste you on this useless fight. Alistair won't accept your unlawful challenge."

Alistair Sorenson unsheathes his sword. "I accept," he says, launching it straight at me. It spins several times before landing near my feet. Mari grips his shoulder, shaking him. "You can't. This was not the plan."

He picks up the abandoned horn. "Loyal subjects, I promised you some entertainment, and here it is. These meascans seek to challenge me, to make you afraid. They deny the mercy we would show them. They seek to destroy us. I accept this challenge because I believe that a king must bear ills for his people. I accept it because we need to show them that we are not afraid. We are better and stronger. We need not fear them."

Jonas locks eyes with me, and suddenly I can hear his heartbeat, a step beneath my own, thundering in my chest. His spirit melds with mine, a lingering touch on my skin, a secret whispered against my neck. I reach out, heart swelling with wonder, my body aching with want as I feel him. I am struck by the joy that rises in me, the sweetness of being with my mate. Then his fear tangles with my resolve as his thoughts flow into my head.

"Don't do this. Let me fight my uncle instead. I think he's up to something. I can't risk you."

"Do you think I would risk you?" I shoot back. *"Even if I die, I want to do it knowing that I fought for our people, and that you'll continue fighting even without me."*

"You won't die. I won't let you. We will fight together."

I wasn't sure how honorable that was, but I also didn't think Alistair Sorenson was above such tricks himself.

"Together."

Lord Ekwensi claps his hands, the flames around him gone now, the image of the perfect courtier. "A challenge given and a challenge accepted. Now all we need are witnesses and a few rules."

"As a member of the king's council, I submit myself as witness," Lord Kairen says, getting to his feet.

Markham nods gravely. "As a member of the king's guard, and his military advisor, I submit myself as witness."

Mari steps in front of the king. "I oppose this farce. I refuse to honor this unlawful challenge."

The king shoves her aside. "Don't get in the way, Mari. I fight my own battles."

"Go out there, and I will take everything from you," she whispers harshly. "The nobles are on my side. Do not forget who made you."

He shrugs her off. "You won't do anything, Mari. You love me."

"I loved Yetu," she answers. "I still killed her. I told you—I won't keep you if you become a weakness."

They share a charged look, then he turns away, making his way into the arena. As he steps in, the crowd rises, cheering as he waves to them. The Oluso watch warily, fear heavy in their eyes.

"Conditions?" Lord Ekwensi asks.

"I have none," I answer.

"I have one," the king answers. "Mari, your bracelets."

Mari's frown morphs into a rueful smile as she uncuffs iron bracelets from her wrists and throws them over the railing. Catching them, the king tosses them to me. "Put them on. These are the only way to make this a fair fight. No magic, unless it's iron born. I'm quite partial to iron magic. Makes weapons like this beauty."

"Those will weaken her. That's not fair," Jonas yells.

In response Mari throws some iron anklets over as well.

"Dèmi, do you accept these conditions?" Lord Ekwensi asks.

I pull the bracelets onto my wrists, biting my lip as the sting of iron burns my skin and sets my blood on fire. I can no longer feel Jonas within me, and all thoughts of fighting the king together vanish. It's no matter, though—this was always going to be my fight. Then, after strapping on the anklets, I toss Ekwensi my bone blade and he throws it next to the king's sword, far out of reach. Moving my foot back, I bend my knees and brace myself. "I am ready."

"Dèmi, no—"

"Trust me," I tell Jonas, thinking about all the times he'd asked that of me.

He swallows . . . then nods.

"Dèmi," Colin shouts. When I meet his gaze, he tosses me his ear cuff. I smile and kiss the silver wing before fastening the cuff to my ear. Growing up, there were so many times when Colin disappeared for days to spend time at his father's. Each time I'd give him something of mine. A necklace, a lock of hair. The message is simple—return victorious. Come back to me.

Ekwensi lifts his hand. "On my signal, you will begin." I wait, flexing my fingers and my toes, willing my body to keep up one last time. Then Ekwensi's hand falls like an executioner's ax and I take off, running for my blade as the king sprints toward his sword. We reach our weapons at the same time, then we move back, circling each other. The king moves first, stabbing at the air in front of me as I jump, twisting slightly. He tries again, and I spin just in time as the tip of his blade snags on the belly of my dress, ripping it open. Taking a few steps back, I try to get hold of my breathing. I need to calm down. If I spend too much time trying to avoid his attacks, I will tire myself out. Since his blade is longer than mine, I have to find a way to get in close to strike.

I hear Baba Sylvanus in my head: *A battle is won with more than brute force. You must portion your resources.*

Alistair swipes at me again, slicing open my shoulder. I stagger back, clutching my arm as the crowd roars their support. My magic sings at my fingertips, itching to escape, but I let my arm hang limp. With this much iron, there's no way to get my magic out. Using it is a violation of the rules anyway.

Switching the blade to my other hand, I face him, arms up, ignoring the burning pain in my shoulder. His back leg shifts as he stabs at me again, but this time I am ready. Feinting to the side, I ricochet and kick his exposed belly. He stumbles back, nearly dropping his sword as I edge away from him. My foot feels strange, but I bend my knees, waiting. Both hands on his sword now, he rushes me, cutting across my body. I dance away, but he steps in again, catching my thigh. Pushing off my injured foot, I stab his arm. He grunts, face red with effort, and grabs my blade, yanking it from me and tossing it away.

"Nothing to hide behind now," he says; then he steps in and brings his sword up. As I bend to avoid the blow, he pivots, punching the side of my head. I stumble to the ground, black spots flitting across my vision.

"Never does to rely too much on one weapon," he says. "You could benefit from a course at one of our military schools."

Then he drags me up by the hair and punches me in the belly with quick, decisive jabs. I inhale, trying to snatch air back into my lungs, but the pain is too much.

"Keep your eyes open," he says, slapping me across the face.

I tumble with the force of his blow and hit the ground, tasting dirt.

"Stop!" Colin screams, but Ekwensi grabs him by the neck.

"This is her fight. Don't dishonor us by doing whatever is in your head," he commands.

Colin tenses, muscles flexed and straining. "Honor means nothing if she dies."

"You think her weak?" Ekwensi asks.

Colin moves back at that, swallowing hard. Ekwensi claps him on the shoulder. "Good boy. Let's await her good news."

My belly is on fire, and my cheek is swollen, but I get to my feet and put my arms up. The king claps, smiling as though he's watching his horse perform a new trick.

"I commend you, really. Most people would've given up by now."

I lunge at him, sliding as he slashes at me and swiping at his legs. He stumbles then recovers, but I am faster, yanking the bottom of his mail armor and smashing my head into his. Pain explodes in my skull and I let go, the ground rising up to meet me, and I can only hope he feels the same, if not worse. I lie there, blood slithering across my face, staring at the sky.

"Move!" Jonas's scream is loud, making my ears ring, and I obey, rolling to my feet as a spear sails into the ground, impaling the spot where I lay moments before. Mari looks down at me, hand raised above her head, face red with anger.

"That's against the rules," Jonas shouts. Markham barks a command and two guards grab Mari's arms. I don't doubt she struggles, but I also don't have time to see how that plays out.

I wipe the blood from my brow and stand, blinking dark spots from my vision. The king gets to his feet, clutching his sword with one hand and I understand his gamble now. If Mari's spear had hit, I would be dead, but even if it failed—if Jonas had stopped it with his magic or I used mine to save myself—the fight would be declared invalid. Either way, the king would not bear the blame for what Mari had done.

I swipe at my bleeding mouth with the back of my hand. "That was a dirty trick."

He smirks. "This is war, little girl. You kill or be killed."

He throws himself at me and I step back, but not before he slices my side open. I scream, but he's on me again, kicking my stomach and, when I fall, stomping on my ankle.

I writhe, pain and shock coursing through me. I'm going to lose, and it's my fault. I'm no killer. Sorenson is a career soldier. This is more than I can take.

Jonas stands at the edge of the platform. "Get up, Dèmi. Please."

I strain for the bone blade inches away, but the king brings his foot down on my hand this time, and I don't even have the breath to scream as my bones shatter. All I know is fire burning me alive. I collapse, spent.

"This was a waste of time," the king says. Then bending, he yanks my father's ring from my neck and inspects it. "Your mother carried this around a lot. This will work as a trophy."

Fury rises in me like a wave. "Give that back," I sputter. "Give it, give it, give it."

The king turns his back on me, waving at the crowd. I push my battered body, curling into myself. My mind is a broken mess, filling with images—of Mummy, of Cree and Elu, of chaos and fear and blood everywhere.

"Fight's over," Colin says, rushing toward me.

"It's a fight to the death," the king says. The guards cross their spears at the arena entrance, barring Colin.

"I will fight you in her place," Jonas shouts. "You can kill me. Leave her!"

Ekwensi regards me with something akin to pity. "This is how you fight?"

I struggle to my knees, using my good hand to hold myself together. "Give. It. Back!" I scream at the king. A man's voice comes alive in my mind: *Are you ready to bear the weight of this power? Even it if might mean your death?*

"What power?" I whisper, looking around. There is no one immediately nearby, save for the spectators watching gleefully. In the distance, Colin pushes past the guards, and Jonas jumps down to meet him, but as they run toward me, Ekwensi waves a hand and they go flying, slamming into the arena walls.

"Finish the fight! Win our freedom!" Ekwensi commands as I take a faltering step toward the boys. I'm sweating, but my lips are so dry, my skin so cold.

The voice keeps speaking: *Iron is loving but demanding. Once you submit to it, you must sharpen it and let it sharpen you.*

"Who are you?" I ask, louder now.

The king starts laughing. "I beat her so badly she's losing her mind!"

Then the ring dangling from his fingers glows orange and he drops it with a hiss. The ring flies into my waiting hand and suddenly a man is standing before me. He is tall, with thick white dreads, a thick muscled chest, and skin the color of garri, the smoked golden cassava porridge I loved eating as a child.

He holds out a fearsome, jagged iron spear. It is weirdly curved, sloping to one side as though it's been cut in half. "This is yours, Abidèmi. Crafted from the deepest reaches of the earth. Ogun-blessed."

I take the spear with a trembling hand. It doesn't burn. "Are you—"

He shakes his head. "I have no right to be called your father. Not until I redeem the debt I owe. When you finish here, find me."

"Where will you be? Where have you been?" I ask incredulously. How can my dead father be standing in front of me?

"Between the river and the path. See you soon."

He fades into dust as he speaks and the spear disappears from my hands as well. I look up in time to see the king running full speed at me, but magic is roaring through my body, tearing at my skin, forcing me upright. The iron bracelets and anklets sing in unison, welcoming me. I spin on my uninjured foot, catching the force of his blade with my bracelets. The force pushes me back, but I let it, pirouetting around as he thrusts his sword at me again. This time, I don't avoid the blow, and I see the king's eyes widen in surprise as his sword impales me, pushing through my belly.

"Fought . . . wrong way," I gasp.

All this time, I thought I could win, that the spirits would judge between me and the king and grant me victory. I wanted so badly to defeat Sorenson once and for all and bring him to justice. I wanted to believe so desperately in the world, the one Mummy dreamed of, where Oluso and Aje were good and kind, and reconciliation—hope—was possible. But I know better now. The Aje will never let us go, not when they can subjugate us. Ekwensi is right. I entered this fight with the wrong attitude from the start. It's as Baba said: sometimes you take a blow to deal a death blow.

I grip the king's shoulder with my good hand. Then I let the magic loose, willing the iron in my belly to grow. It wails as it extends through the hilt, stabbing into the king's hand. He screams and tries to move back, but it's too late. The sword keeps extending until it is the length of a spear, slicing into his chest and connecting us.

"Let's die together," I whisper. Then I touch the blade and it shoots out of me. The king stands, dazed, his sword now a lance through him. I touch the bracelets and they become knives rushing toward him. As I watch, they whiz past his arms and legs in a dance, ripping at his armor and skin. He falls, and I creep closer, dragging my foot. My body is heavy, my arms trembling, but I don't stop until I'm standing over him, watching as he writhes in anguish.

"Do you yield?" I ask.

He rears back and spits. I wipe the spittle from my face and touch an anklet to his leg. The anklet morphs into a spike, impaling his knee. He bellows in agony. His mail armor peels away, transforming into more spikes that dance around his head like hornets threating to embed their poison.

"Dirty witch!" he coughs. A spike nails his hand to the dirt. He screeches, face contorted with rage. "She caused this . . . she hurt me . . . then she let me live."

I kneel at this, yanking up his slumping head. "What do you mean?"

He sneers through the blood and bile spilling out of his mouth. "I hurt Arianne. I framed Osezele. Yetu knew . . . but she ran away . . . let me free. Her fault . . . I only loved her. Her fault."

I grab his hair and slam his face against the ground, raising my blade. Even after all of this, he still has the mouth to blame my mother. I want to do it now—plunge my blade into his neck, tear his face until there is nothing but bone and dust. I want to watch as his blood runs into the earth, bathing it the way he promised the Oluso that theirs would. I want to end this nightmare that began the day they took my mother from me.

But then rain begins to fall, dripping onto my face and hair, pitter-pat sounds like whispers tickling my ear.

Mummy loved the rain. Even after a long day at the market and blistered fingers worn from days of weaving, when it rained, she would bring me out to watch the sky. Suddenly I am young again, holding my mother's hand.

"Look, Dèmi," she says with a laugh, whirling me around, "Olorun is crying."

"Why would Olorun cry?"

"When Olorun made the world, and his children began to fight, the rains would come. Giant floods. The rains would cleanse the blood from the fields and bring the forest creatures out of hiding. It grew the flowers and made the water spirits dance."

"Did that stop the fighting?" I ask, wriggling as cold water sluices down my back.

"Not always. But I think it reminded our ancestors there was something beyond bloodshed. That there was something still worth protecting, and if they kept fighting, there would be nothing left to live for." She kisses my forehead. "Like you. It was raining the night you were born, you know. You came out with your eyes wide open, screaming at the world, and Mama Aladé and I washed you in that rain."

I come to myself now, wounded, bloody, tears mingling with the rain slapping at my cheeks. "My mother let you live because she didn't believe she had the right to take life. Perhaps she believed you'd take another path. I don't know. But I know that everyone has a choice—Aje and Oluso. She showed you mercy, and you took that gift and used it to commit murder. That was *your* choice. No one made it for you."

I nod, my choice made then. "But that ends today."

I flick a finger and the spikes dart toward his head. He covers his head with his working hand and screams, then the spikes pause, just inches from driving into his skull.

"You're not even worth it," I say, sobbing. "I won't lose my magic over a nothing like you."

Turning to the platform, I throw my blade down. "That's it," I croak. "I've won."

The crowd is silent, save a few Oluso whooping with excitement. Markham stares at me, unmoving. Jonas, Colin, and the guards stop fighting. Only Mari glares at me before tossing her horned helmet into the arena. Then without a word, she turns on her heel and sweeps out of the arena.

I watch her go, unsure of what to do. The bloodlust is still fresh in my mind, urging me on, *Kill her, kill her*, the iron chants. But I let her go. I'll deal with her soon. I have power now.

Jonas lifts his hands. "The challenger has emerged victorious. All hail the new queen."

He kneels, and after a moment, Elodie and Lord Kairen follow suit. Colin, wearing a fierce expression, gets on his knees. Markham purses his lips, stretching his jaw as though he wants to say something, then he sinks down, his eyes trained on his brother's bleeding form. The guards look at one another, and some kneel. Others stay watching, including Ekwensi. The crowd rumbles, buzzing with noise. A few people get onto their knees, but most remain where they are, defiant children daring me to punish them.

"Why do you not kneel?" Jonas asks.

"Because the fight is not yet over," Ekwensi says. He looks at me. "Dispatch the former king."

I shake my head. "The king can no longer fight. We end with this. I grant him mercy as his queen. I want him arrested immediately."

"You spoke of freedom, of getting peace for our people," he says, giving me a cool look.

"Peace starts now. Sorenson will be allowed to live his days in agony. The worst punishment is for him to see us thrive. Let's give him that," I argue.

Ekwensi grits his teeth. "By allowing that man to live, you undermine our cause. You defeated him today. Fine. Do you think his people won't come for you tomorrow? Look how the people defy you." He points at the mostly standing crowd. "While their king is alive, they have hope. You need to crush that hope once and for all."

I droop, suddenly exhausted. "Ekwensi, I'm no murderer. I fought for our people. I stand here bleeding for them, even now. I will fight however many times I need to for our people. But I won't kill. You know what it means to us to kill."

"I told you, if you kill in the name of justice, the Spirits will hear you. There will be no punishment," he insists.

I shake my head weakly. I can't trust what he says. Not when he's been keeping secrets all along.

"I don't know how you kept your magic," I say finally, "or what you've been up to all this while, but I refuse to start my reign with bloodshed."

He leaps off the platform, landing near me. "As you wish. You will not start your reign with bloodshed. Your hands will be clean."

He brushes past me, stopping only to pick up the king's fallen sword. I stagger after him as he kicks the king over and presses his foot against his throat.

"No!"

He brings the sword down, but it stops in midair, glowing red. Jonas is behind me, his hand shaking as he struggles to control the sword. The sword wriggles, twisting away from Lord Ekwensi and flying back into the rubble. Guards rush into the arena, with Markham leading the charge.

Lord Ekwensi turns to the Oluso. "You *see*? This is the girl who wishes to be queen, a child who claims to want freedom for our people. Yet she protects the man who murdered your family, your friends, and your children. The kingdom declared war on us long ago when they began hunting us in the streets. Now we have a chance to rise up, to defend ourselves, and this girl will not act. Is this a queen you want to follow?"

The Oluso look at one another. Many of them are stricken, faces twisted with anger and disbelief. A few shout "No!"

Ekwensi reaches out a hand. "Or will you walk with me? Take back what has been stolen from you? Fight for your freedom? This child may not understand, but I know you do. Freedom has a price. Are you willing to pay it?"

His words are a spell, and the Oluso fall willingly to it. They climb back into the arena, standing behind Lord Ekwensi. Only a handful—the mother with the two children strapped to her back, and a few others—stay behind. He smiles at me. "I hoped that you and I would be on the same side, but it seems that is not possible right now. In time you will see the wisdom of my words. I'll leave you a gift, something to help you on your journey. We'll certainly meet again, but for now I take my leave. Farewell, my queen." He bows before stepping back, lifting a hand to the sky. Lightning crashes into the arena, sending dust and smoke into the air.

I fly back, slamming my head into the wall, and lie in the mud, choking as smoke grips my nostrils. Soon after, Jonas is shaking me, trying to pull me up, but my lungs are burning, my limbs hanging like dead wood. Screams ring out like bells as flames spark into life. Guards lay strewn across the mud, piled like dominoes, silvery armor glinting in the rain. The king's body is now a blackened lump in the dirt, scraps of gold clinging to his still form. The smell of roasted meat rides the air, and I watch as Lord Ekwensi turns around, the Oluso trailing after him, disappearing into fog.

I blink, opening my eyes as Jonas scoops me in his arms and a warmth fills my chest. "Don't die," he whispers, his tears dropping onto my face like rain. Beyond his face, I glimpse a line of blue in the angry sky, night welcoming the dawn of a new day. I heave a sigh and the world melts into color and dust.

BIRTH

When I awake the world is dark, the lantern in the corner of the room flickering like a firefly dancing in night. Jonas is at my side, body pressed against the edge of the bed, long eyelashes kissing his cheeks, fingers spread over mine. Slipping my hand from his, I ease up carefully, stopping as pain cuts through the flesh beneath my right breast.

"Don't. Not yet," Nana says, pushing gently against my shoulders. "You broke so many ribs and we need to make sure they heal properly. It will be difficult for a little while longer."

I collapse into the softness of the bed, but my back is tense, like an animal on the verge of death, knotted and trembling with pain. My head throbs with a dull ache. "Nana? What happened? Where are we?"

"You're still at the northern palace. Colin came to us, and Will and I traveled here immediately. Baba is with the kids—they're fine," she says before I can ask. "As to everything that happened, I was waiting for you to tell me. Colin tried to explain, but he didn't do the best job."

I smile. "He's not the best with stories." My voice is hoarse, my throat dry and itchy. "How long have I been out?"

"Ten days. We were starting to get worried, but he"—she nods at Jonas—"told us you would be alright. That it would only be a little while longer." She settles back into the chair on the other side of the bed. "So . . . the prince is your mate."

Jonas stirs, the skin between his brows puckering, and my heart quivers. All I want to do is reach out and smooth the crease there, to linger with the whisper of his skin against my fingertips. "Yes."

"He has no Oluso forbears. Will checked his family history. Barring illegitimacy, we can't figure out how he could be Oluso."

"He looks just like his father."

"And his mother's handmaiden attests to being there when he was born, so there are some missing parts in this puzzle. I sent word to my father. If anyone can figure this out, he can. The prince is an iron-blood, though, that's certain. Just like your father."

I suck in a breath, wincing as the pain beneath my breast claws at me. "The king said something before he died. That he framed my father for hurting Jonas's mother. That my mother knew. Is that true?"

Nana picks up a sugarcane stalk from the basket at her feet and sets her knife to it, blade whirring like wind cutting through leaves. "Baba told us what happened, yes—or at least what Yetundé told him. There was nothing your mother could do. When she found out she was having you, she had to choose: go back and risk you being hurt while trying to clear your father's name, or leave and protect you. She chose you."

"If she had gone back, there wouldn't have been a war. Things would be different."

Her blade stills. "You can't know that. What have I taught you? Even with my Cloren blood, I can't see everything, just bits and pieces of a future that might change."

"Shards of broken mirrors," I say quietly.

"Exactly. Your father was teaching the Sorenson family iron-work. They could have still used that knowledge to make weapons and started a war, even if your father was proven innocent. There's no way to know."

"You're right. It doesn't matter. Either way, my father betrayed us."

Even though my father showed up to help during that fight with Sorenson, he disappeared without leaving me more than a cryptic message. In a way his secrecy, his choice to teach Sorenson iron-work, harmed us all.

Nana sighs. "It may not have been as simple as that."

"It seems that simple. Because of him, so many Oluso have died."

"And because of you, many are living and will live free." She puts a sugarcane strip in my mouth. The tangy sweetness explodes on my tongue and pushes sugary wetness down my throat. "Speaking of which . . ."

I look to her, confused.

"Amina and Rollo are doing well. The Lokoja Oluso are settling in a house near Baba. With the king gone, things will change. You challenged him and won."

"Some victory. I couldn't even convince the Oluso who witnessed it all. Lord Ekwensi is out there, already sowing discord. Did Colin tell you about that?"

"He didn't have to. I had a vision the night before he came. I saw Lord Ekwensi eaten up by flames, and there were—"

There is a knock at the door, and Nana jumps to her feet. Jonas sits up, rubbing his eyes as an old retainer enters the room flanked by two guards. "My lord, if you please, your father and the council members are waiting in the throne room."

Jonas takes my hand. "How are you feeling? Are you well enough to attend?" He runs his fingers along my cheek, each touch a stolen kiss, pouring warmth into my belly.

"Your Highness, they spoke only of you. Not . . . er . . . not the lady."

Jonas whips around, and I shift onto my elbows, the ghost of his touch still fresh on my face. "The lady is your queen. I doubt my father and the other lords would be so foolish as to forget that."

The attendant coughs—this is entirely above his paygrade—and Jonas rubs his forehead in acknowledgment. "We will be there shortly."

"Excellent, Your Highness. Thank you."

Jonas turns back to me. Heavy shadows lace his eyes and a patch of dark hair covers his chin. "I'm sorry. It'll take them a while to get used to things, but they will learn."

"I suspect they haven't had time to adjust to things quite so quickly since you've been in here for the last few days," Nana says with a smile.

He flushes, pale skin blooming like a night flower. "I couldn't leave her."

I reach out a hand and he comes then, tangling my fingers with his, leaning me against his arm as he pulls me up. I let out a hiss, clutching my ribs as the fire there burns anew, making it hard to breathe. He pulls me into him, his face cool against mine. "I'm sorry. I couldn't do more. I was trying to save you, but I couldn't do more than this."

Nana lifts her head at this. "What are you talking about?"

He spreads his palm, and my heart begins to pound, my magic singing in my veins as a green flame springs up in his palm. I gasp, and all at once, the hum in my body quiets to a whisper, slipping away like water between my fingers. The flame flickers and dies.

"My magic . . . you took my magic."

He shakes his head. "I tried to borrow it, and even pulled it out somehow, when I thought you would die. You started healing, but suddenly it stopped so you didn't heal fully."

"A pair bond." Nana's eyes are wide, her mouth half open. "The two of you—" She shakes her head, eyes glassy as she mutters, "It can't be. A pair bond can only be formed between two iron-bloods. This shouldn't be happening. This can't be happening."

"What do you mean?" My heart is drumming now, my stomach fluttering with excitement and fear.

She puts her hand to her mouth. "Nothing. It's rare, that's all. Mated iron-bloods were once able to tap into each other's magic and use it. It was a gift other Oluso did not have, and there were some who feared what that could bring." She smiles, but her eyes are watchful, twin stars drawing the light in. "The prince was able to access your magic as your mate. I assume he tried to heal you, but you ran out of stamina soon after."

"Please, call me Jonas."

"Jonas then. Tell me, Jonas, when you tried to help Dèmi, what did it feel like? Did you feel tired or strange?"

He twists his mouth, the hairs on his chin tickling my face. "It felt like a hand closing over my heart. And when I pushed against that hand and tried to breathe, things just happened."

"Interesting."

I lick my lips. "The last time you said that, you dropped me into a river."

She rolls her eyes. "I had to see if you would figure out how to swim on your own. My father did that with me, you know."

"It happened before, when we were with my uncle," Jonas said. "The guards came for Dèmi, and I didn't know how to save her."

I turn toward him. "It was you in the battle room, then—when my magic failed."

He presses his face against mine. "I didn't mean to do that. I just wanted you to be safe and was hoping you'd stop fighting."

"Hope is a powerful thing, I guess," I say.

Nana clears her throat, and I pull away, the air around my face suddenly hot. "It's not something the two of you should be worrying about right now. I don't know much about the pair bond myself, but I'll ask Baba when I get a chance. The two of you should keep it a secret for now."

"So many things we don't know," I say.

There is another knock at the door, and the attendant calls out, "My lord?"

I bristle at this. "Your queen is preparing. Tell those nobles to wait or get out of my castle."

The attendant mumbles a "Yes, my lady."

Jonas sighs, his breath cool on my neck. "The nobles are more powerful than you think. We actually need them to accept you before you're officially known as queen."

I frown. "What do you mean?"

He runs a hand through his hair. "I mean I don't want to take you in there, not while you're still recovering, but it's important that we send the right message. The council won't respect your authority unless you make them. The moment I walk in without you, they will take it as confirmation that things haven't changed. I also don't know what they have planned. There might be others waiting to kill you as soon as I leave this room."

It is said that the first queen was crowned on the battlefield, the blood from her wounds coating her body like ancestral paint. I wouldn't dishonor her by lying here, doing nothing. Scooting to the edge of the bed, I swing my legs over, pushing onto my feet even as my body screams in anger and the cold gnaws at my bare feet. "I didn't win against your uncle so I could die in my bed. Let's go."

My head grows heavy, and my legs are shaking by the next step, then Jonas is there, his hand on my waist, shoulders bent toward me. Nana rushes over, brushing at the simple ankara dress I'm wearing, but I wave her away. We go together, fused flesh on bone, inching until we reach the door, caught in a dance only we can hear the music for. The attendant shoots us a wary glance before moving ahead, his lantern guiding us through the shadows. I pick up speed as we go, the stabs of pain lending rhythm to my steps, hopeful beats accompanied by sharp inhales of breath. There are cracks in the corridor walls, and stone pieces litter the ground like pebbles in a stream. We step carefully around suits of armor strewn across the floor and fallen paintings facedown as though weary of being displayed. The main hall is in shambles, crushed marble forming a mountainous heap where the twin stairs once were, jagged pieces sticking out like bones. Beyond, the wall is gone, and most of the ballroom with it. Scraps of cloth hang from the ceiling, tattered banners of a celebration long dead. The stage where the Goma singer pushed her songs into the world is now a pile of wood, kindling for a fire waiting to be born. The chandelier lies on the dais, kudu horns crowning a broken throne. The floor is marked with black patches, gaping wounds that seem to bleed endlessly.

"This isn't the worst of it. Lord Ekwensi destroyed at least half the castle. The guards are still digging out entire wings and putting out fires. As of this morning, almost everyone was accounted for," Jonas whispers, his voice carrying in the stillness of the hall.

"The East Wing?" I ask, my heart in my throat.

"Empty."

I swallow. "At least they weren't hurt. He wouldn't have let anything happen to them."

Jonas squeezes my shoulder, and I sink into the warmth of that touch. There is something strange in knowing that he can feel the lull in my breath and taste the words hiding on my tongue, that he knows without my telling him who "they" are.

"My lord, my lady, this way," the attendant says. His face is shrouded in shadow, the gnarled fingers hanging from the lantern bent and ancient. He glides on without another word, and we follow in his wake, sailing through the sea of broken things until we reach a door with light swimming under its eaves. We are ushered into a room with six chairs on either side and a throne at the end of a rolled carpet. Thirteen pairs of eyes latch onto us like leeches searching for open wounds. Lord Kairen is on the left, two women to the right of him and three men to his left. Markham stands in the center by the throne, six men to his right.

Markham steps forward, brows raised. "Jonas? I thought the lady would still be resting."

Pulling away from Jonas, I steady myself. "I've rested enough for ten days. I am ready to assume my duties."

The council members exchange glances, some leaning over to whisper in others' ears. Heavily ringed fingers sparkle like fireworks, and silky, well-woven robes catch the light, gleaming like jewels.

Lord Kairen gets to his feet, and I spy Colin behind his chair now, a reluctant shadow. "My son told me a great deal of your strength. And while we all admire that and everything you did to bring the prince home safe—"

"We do not speak with those unworthy of our notice, much less foreign upstarts who walk in thinking they can take over the kingdom overnight." The woman to his left adjusts the necklace adorning her long neck as she speaks. "You are fortunate we do not have you killed where you stand, and if you are wise, you will leave the palace before we remedy that."

Colin opens his mouth, but Jonas is faster. "Lady Ayn, this is your queen you speak to. What you just said borders on treason. I suggest you reconsider your words."

She scoffs. "Queen? I haven't agreed to any queen. I recall your uncle crowning *you* his successor. Unless there is something you have to reveal to us, there will be no queen."

"I wasn't aware you got to decide who was queen, Lady Ayn," Jonas said coolly. "If you remember, we had a trial by combat. Dèmi won. You were all witnesses. My father and Lord Kairen were official witnesses." He locks eyes with Markham. "You knelt at her feet."

Markham holds up a hand. "In the days since that trial, there has been chaos. There are reports of villages, northern villages, being attacked. Several prisons have been broken into and the meascans there released. A Geifenwellian came in two nights ago claiming that meascans led by a man matching Lord Ekwensi's description massacred his fellow guards. I sent an entourage along with him." He tosses a pouch and I catch it, nearly stumbling as I do. "This is all that's left of Balman Keep."

The pouch is full but light, and when I yank the string drawing it tight, a cloud explodes in my face, coating my skin with glittering dust while the remnants run through my fingers like sand, scattering about the room. Throwing the pouch down, I scrape at my skin, but grains of dust crawl into my blouse while I rub some out of my eyes.

"Bodies, stone, and land, Lord Ekwensi burnt them all."

Jonas helps me, brushing the dust from my face and blouse. "What does that have to do with this?"

Markham puts a hand on his shoulder, pulling him back. "Son, you can't tell me you don't understand what this means. Lord Ekwensi declared war on the kingdom, and the meascans are crawling out of their holes to join him. They are killing without fear or remorse and their power is only growing. But you want to put one of them on the throne? One related to the last queen? After what happened to your mother? If you can't at least think of her, think of the people. Their king is dead. War is stirring up. They need stability. They need *you*."

"Father, Mari already confessed. You know that Uncle hurt mother, not Dèmi's father." Markham clenches his jaw, but Jonas continues. "This is even more reason why we need Dèmi as queen. All Ekwensi wants is to be assured that the Oluso will no longer be hunted. What better way to stop him than to give the people an Oluso queen? One with a rightful claim—one who probably should have been its queen if Grandfather and Uncle hadn't usurped the throne long ago. With things the way they are now, Ekwensi will grow in strength and many who want their freedom will join him. We must prevent that, yes, but me being king is the worst possible way to do that."

Lady Ayn springs to her feet, her purple robes fanning out behind her. "Alistair made some questionable decisions, but while he ruled, there was peace. He was prone to certain weaknesses of character . . ." She stops, nodding at Markham. "Of course, what happened to Arianne was probably an unfortunate accident, my apologies."

I spit dirt and blood, the wad of saliva landing by Lady Ayn's feet. She recoils and I edge forward, baring my teeth. "You call Alistair's rule one of peace? When Oluso were being murdered just for existing? Further, you used my father's actions as justification to start a war. Now it was merely a mistake?" I curl my hands into fists, pressing until my nails bite into my skin. "A mistake doesn't cost the lives of thousands."

She swats the air as though killing a pesky fly and clears her throat, the gold feathers waving from the iron circle on her head. "As I was saying, while Alistair made some mistakes, he always did what was best for the kingdom. When he chose you, Prince Jonas, there were some of us who had our reservations. But we came to see in time that he was right. We must respect tradition and give the kingdom the heir it has been waiting for. Even considering the unfortunate accident of your blood, it is best after all that you lead us. You understand the kingdom's needs. You understand your duty to your people. This girl is an outsider, unprepared for these responsibilities. What will happen to Eingard if she is allowed to rule? To all the kingdom?"

Jonas takes a step back. "So now that is all it is? My magic, and the fact that my uncle viciously attacked my mother, those are all just accidents?"

She smiles, rouged lips almost black on her pale face. "*Unfortunate* accidents. Alistair was wrong in many ways, but he did the right thing in choosing you." She spreads her hands, a painter bringing a creation to life. "You may have their magic, but you are not like them. You were born to be king. It is what Alistair wanted. It is what we all want. Do not fail your people when they need you most."

"You talk of stability and tradition, but you won't honor Dèmi's right. She nearly died fighting the king, but you would ignore all that for your own ends?" Colin's words are strangled and short, but there is an edge to them, an anger radiating like steam seeping out of a boiling pot.

Lady Ayn shifts her gaze to Lord Kairen. "Ferdinand, control your dog before I do it for you."

Lord Kairen shoots Colin a look and Colin charges out of the room, slamming the door after him. Lord Kairen turns back to Lady Ayn. "Respectfully—if you call my son a dog again, we will have much different words between us."

She shrugs off the threat, obviously secure enough in the belief in her own power to not feel intimidated. "You'd really defend your bastard?"

"Maybe," he says, and I realize that this has nothing to do with being offended for Colin's sake. "I won't listen to *you* say such things about my bastard."

I clench my fist, furious now. I'm sick of their little power plays. Colin doesn't deserve to be treated like an abandoned pet. Lady Ayn and her casual bigotry is more foolishness that I can tolerate, and I need to set an example for my court. I lift a finger to summon the wind when Jonas places a hand on my arm.

Jonas turns to Markham. "Father." Markham lowers his head. Jonas looks around the room, and the council members stare back, unflinching. The throne glows behind him, iron and gold wrought together in a twisting spire that rounds out the wide back and long seat, layered gold cloth hanging off the edge of the footstool. Finally, he turns to me, his face drawn, eyes wary like an animal caught in a trap, arms wrapped around his body like a traveler in the cold, searching for warmth alone.

I reach a hand out, swaying as the knot of anger in my chest unravels, pulled apart by those icy blue eyes. My jaw is set and my fingers tremble with the urge to call up a storm and rage until this room is no more than the dust on the ground, until these cold faces with iron crowns, scorpions waving their tails as they prepare to eat their young, fall over like chess pieces. But the sugary scent of dust still hangs on my skin, and I think of the people beyond this room—of Amina and Rollo, Haru, Will, and Nana, and even Colin—

pebbles whose lives hang at the mercy of this stormy river, whose worlds will be ground into dust at the hint of a mistake.

Jonas links his fingers with mine as I say, "You're right. The kingdom needs peace, and Jonas is the right person to give it. I don't know anything about governing, and it would take a while to learn. We don't have that time. Lord Ekwensi is out there and growing stronger by the day. I didn't come here to become queen. I came to help my people." I squeeze his hand. "Our people."

"Are you sure," he asks me, his eyes wide. "It's yours—"

"Do you think I *want* to be queen? Besides, we're doing this together anyway, right?"

He smiles even as Lady Ayn curls her lip in a snarl, chafing at even being a part of this conversation.

"Together? Please. Your *kind* caused this mess. If we had wiped out you meascans when we had the chance, this wouldn't be happening."

"And if you hadn't vilified them in the first place and ruled this kingdom—which we *are* a part of—with hate and bigotry, the Oluso wouldn't be fighting back."

"How *dare* you speak to me—"

"Lady Ayn, I would ask that *you* check how you speak to Dèmi. She may not be your queen, but *I* am your prince, and I'm saying that such intolerance gets us nowhere." She looks like she wants to retort, but Jonas grits his teeth and says, "And the correct term is Oluso, and lest you forget, *I* am one of those you seek to kill."

She purses her lips. "Of course, Your Highness." She sniffs, her expression so oily now that I'm surprised she doesn't simply glide out of the room. "I was not referring to *you*. I was trying to express that we have a mea—an Oluso problem right now. Namely, how do we encourage others to keep from joining Ekwensi's ranks?"

"We start by treating them like human beings and not monsters," he says pointedly. "And that begins with this decree, my first action if I'm to be king: Oluso can no longer be hunted or sold. Those who have been bought by others or forced into servitude must be freed. Immediately. Those who attempt to capture or kill any innocent Oluso will be considered enemies of the Crown."

Her mouth falls open. "But our economy, Your Highness—"

"I'm not done," he says, firm. "I have another condition. If I accept your wish that I become king, then I will choose my own queen. Lady Ayn, I am dissolving my engagement to your daughter. I will marry this girl instead." He lifts our entwined fingers. "Since you will not honor her right to the throne, I will do so in my own way."

Lady Ayn splutters, eyes bulging out of her head. "Your Highness, this cannot be . . . this is unlawful. The traders who have made their livelihoods . . . the families who have taken in meascan servants . . . and poor Elodie . . . you would have half-caste children over my Elodie—"

"Lords and ladies," Jonas calls out, "I have made my position clear. If you trust that I will be a good king, then you must agree. If not, then you'll have to find a new king and deal with this mess yourselves. Know, however, that I am Oluso and so is my mate. We will work to bring peace to this country one way or another. I hope, for all our sakes, you will help us in that goal."

The council members protest, squawking like geese sold at a market, talking over one another. Lady Ayn staggers to her seat clutching a hand to her heart while Lord Kairen smirks at her comeuppance. Markham stands alone, silent. Jonas strokes my fingers, and we wait, listening to the swell of voices rising like a tide. The voices go on and on, echoing each other, surging into crests, then ebbing into quiet murmurs and disbelieving stares.

Markham's voice stills the room into silence. "And if we refuse? You would walk away from your people?"

"Never from the people, but from this institution you all hold so dear that doesn't seem to care about what's going on outside the walls of your keeps. As Jonas said, we will fight for the kingdom, but not with you," I answer. "We will fight for all, not just those whose lives you deem worthy."

Markham nods, and I am unable to read him. He holds so much sway, it is clear, and without his support, I know we're on our own.

With a determined look he says, "I accept. Any objections? We can keep arguing about this, or we can agree to the prince's conditions and work out the details later."

Council members stare at one another, but no one speaks. Markham takes a seat in the small chair next to the throne. "Good. We have much to discuss."

"Then I will leave you to it." Keeping my head high, I walk slowly to the door with my back straight and gaze steady as Mummy once said a queen should. Jonas catches up to me, offering his arm, which I gladly take while trying not to show how weak I am. When Jonas and I are safely through and several yards away, I crumble then and shake, hands on my knees, head against the wall. "You have to go back in there. You can't leave them to their own—"

"I know. And I will. But first I'll make sure you're okay."

"I'm—"

Not okay.

I let the tears that hung in my throat break free. I cry, for Mummy and the hope she birthed me with, for her warm fingers and the twinkling bell of her voice, echoes of her I carry in my chest. I cry, for the father who was once a faceless ghost, a sand etching whose story has been erased and redrawn by the sea's uncaring waves, over and over until its lines fade into sand. Murderer or not, I feel his weight against my throat, the cold kiss of the ring he gave my mother before disappearing. The burn of the spear he placed in my hands. I cry, for the hope that swelled in my breast the moment I stood above the king knowing I'd won, and for the way my heart trembled, tightening like a flower bud when the council denied my claim. I hadn't lied—I had no desire to actually be queen. But I thought that they'd actually respect their own laws.

How foolish of me.

But most of all, I cry, for Will, Nana, and Haru; Rollo and Amina; and Baba. And Colin. And Elu and Cree. And all the Oluso I have seen over the years, faces worn with age and worry, eyes dim with fear, mouths tight and twitchy yet singing songs of hope and longing, holding on to dregs of joy in a life cursed by being, dancing to the call of the blood warming their hearts and teaching their lungs to breathe.

My chest burns and my lungs scream, but I sob until my belly feels empty and my throat is dry. Jonas is there, his arms around me, his body quaking with mine, and when I finally look up, my face cold and lips cracked, he kisses me, small little kisses like a pup licking its mother's wounds, and rubs his face on mine, warming me. We stay like this, children swept out to sea clinging desperately to each other as the salty waters beat at our skin and hair and the wind pulls us farther away from land. Then a shadow falls over us, and I look up to meet Colin's angry gaze.

I jerk, nearly slamming my head against the wall, but Jonas steadies me, keeping a hand behind my head. He kisses my knuckles, then stands, nodding at Colin. "I'll give you two a few moments."

"How gracious of you," Colin spits. "To what do I owe this kindness, Your Highness?"

Jonas ignores the acidity and shifts back to me. "I'll be in the solar, at the end of the hall. When you're ready. There's something I want to show you before I go back in."

I smile and he waits a moment, eyeing Colin before turning

away. The steady beat of his footsteps echoes down the corridor as Colin collapses onto the empty spot next to me, his hands resting on his knees, gaze trained at the wall opposite. "So, the prince is your mate. Congratulations."

I lift an eyebrow—Colin is my best friend, but he's also a child sometimes—and he shrugs, but the motion is too quick, awkward like a newborn fawn easing onto its legs. "It was obvious even before he said anything, you know." He smiles, but his hazel eyes are dark, molten gold turned dull and stagnant. "I saw the two of you at the king's ball, but even before that . . . you, you always looked like you were drowning. And nothing I did, not the jokes I made or the stories I told you, could take that look from your eyes." His hands tighten into fists. "But I saw it when we were at Benin Palace, the two of you looking at each other, like you could finally breathe."

He swallows, and I dig my nails into my palms as he turns to me, forcing myself to keep looking, even as a lump of dread swells in my throat. He grins now, but his lip trembles, the slight dimple in his cheek quivering like melting wax. "Does it have to be him?"

I want to close my eyes, to make the gnawing in my heart settle into nothing, to reach out and press my head against his and clasp his shoulders like I am twelve again and we are wrestling for dominance, aware of Baba's watching our every move, but drunk on the air between our faces and the bursts of laughter that tickle our sides, and the solid feeling of our bodies as we tangle together like tiger cubs fighting, glorying in the joy of having a friend. Instead I say, "That's not what you really want to ask."

He's right though. I'm not sure even now that Jonas is the right choice. Jonas may be my mate, but Colin knows me in a way no one ever has. Perhaps in a way no one ever will.

His mouth curls, and his tongue darts between his lips. He squints at me like a little boy caught in a lie, afraid that the sky will rain down on his head. "You're going to make me say it, aren't you?" He shakes his head. "Amara was right. I should have done this years ago." He springs forward, face inches from mine. "Why can't it be me?"

I say nothing, but his gaze roams to my lips and lingers there. He leans in, brushing a hand against my cheek, but I stare unmoving. Eyes sparkling now, he licks his lips before closing the gap between us, but right as he brings his lips to mine, I stiffen and he pulls away, jaw tight. "It's not all good, you know. It's a choice, just like anything else. Mates aren't necessarily the right choice. Your mother chose your father, and look where that got her."

Fury rises in my chest like smoke, and before I can think, I shove him to the ground, my fist cocked above his face. "That's different," I say between gritted teeth. "It's not the same and you know it."

"Isn't it? Ekwensi was right after all. You defeated the king, and you won the right to the crown fairly, but do these people acknowledge that? Do they even care? You think they won't hesitate to find a way to get rid of you? You think *he* would fight at your side if there was something at stake for him? Do you know why I ended up in Benin? Why I'm not my father's chosen heir? My own father didn't want his magical bastard to affect his political power, so he tossed me and my mother aside, only bringing me back here when he thought it could add to his advantage. Think of how he'll try to use you, as queen."

I remember then that he had stormed out and didn't know.

"I'm not queen. Or, rather, I will be, but to Jonas's king."

"He took it from you!"

"No," I say. "Of course not! I gave it up. Willingly. But we will still make decisions together—I made him promise me."

He scoffs. "And you truly believe that? You think he won't drop you the moment you pose a threat to him? You say you gave it to him, fine. But did you really think about what that means, what you're giving up . . . to one of *them*? When they know how you could always challenge the next king? They're afraid of you, and he's—" He shakes his head, frustrated. "How many times do I have to say this? He's one of them!"

"But I won't challenge him," I say, confused. I sink back then, dropping my hands to my sides. "And you can say it all day, but you're wrong—Jonas is one of *us*. He wouldn't betray us. Not like that."

"You may be his mate, but you've only known him for, what, a couple of days? Magic connects you, yes, but not loyalty. Not *love*. Not anything but the gods. I meant what I said: being someone's mate is not always a good thing." He eases up, though, dusting off his shirt. "Dèmi, I know you're not a fool, so all I'm asking of you is to think. He's *one* of them, and he will always be. Lord Ekwensi was right. Unless we take things by force, nothing will change. The council will continue to do what they want—right now that's exactly what's happening in that room because you aren't in there, on the throne, telling them what to do. They'll frame innocents for crimes they didn't commit and start wars to protect what little power they have—we know that because we've seen it before. They'll kill not only when it's necessary but when they feel like it. They'll discard whoever they have to. Just like my father did me."

Shaking my head, I take his hands. "We won't let them. Your father was an idiot to treat you the way he did, but things will change. You left before you could hear it, but there's a new decree—one *from* Jonas. Any person who trades or kills innocent Oluso are criminals by law. All Oluso who have been enslaved must be released. They can't hunt us anymore. We can heal the bonds that have been broken, rebuild the communities that were destroyed. The people we love will be safe, and more."

"Dèmi, if you believe that, then I was wrong. You *are* a bloody fool."

I leap to my feet, wincing at the stab of pain that radiates from the wound singing beneath my breast. "And you're the wise one wanting to join with an Oluso who has broken our spirit bonds. Lord Ekwensi is killing people. You want to join him and go mad too?"

"You heard what he said. There's a way to get around that. He has killed only those who would destroy him and he still has his magic."

"And does that make any sense? That he's suddenly found this loophole that goes against everything we've ever known about our magic?"

"We've seen what he can do. Isn't that proof enough?"

"Or maybe it's just another form of madness that you're too blind to see."

"Please. He isn't some Baba, wandering around the village insane. Ekwensi has all his faculties and power. More, he has the will to use it."

"To kill! To do something that goes against all that Oluso believe!"

"Liberty has a price," is all Colin says.

I gasp, the pain more acute than my broken ribs. "And so does our friendship apparently. You're right—I am a fool for wanting things to get better without spilling more blood, so why listen to me? Do what you want. You always do." The words burst out like poisoned darts, sharp and biting, and when I see the strained look on his face, I know they have hit their mark.

He throws his arms around me, surprising me into stillness, but I leave my hands at my sides, ears still stinging from the insult he gave. "I'm sorry," he whispers, cool breath tickling my ear, "I just wanted to . . . I wanted to make things right. But you're right. I said too much. I should have just said what I came to say."

"Which is?"

"That I love you. I have since that first day in the market, and I always will."

"I—"

The air vibrates with energy, and suddenly Colin's arms are melting. I step back as he falls toward me, copper skin melding into mist and dust, and water splashes against my cheek as his face reaches mine. Chill rises up my back once more, and I catch the dancing smile in his eyes, still bright with mischief but marked with shadow as his lips touch mine. My mouth fills with the taste of salt and wind as wet droplets wriggle down my skin. Then the air is still, and Colin is gone.

TWINING

I walk down the corridor on shaky legs, like an omioja shifting onto land from the sea, back bent, body heavy and eyes searching. When I reach the slim door Jonas had gone through, illuminated by the lone lantern hanging on the corner of the wall, I push it open and step into a small room with a vaulted ceiling and long chaises. Before I can let go of the brass handle, Jonas sweeps me up in his arms, cradling my back and legs, ferrying me to a hearth with a furry rug and a mountain of pillows. He lays me against the pillows and pulls a blanket gently around me before thrusting a mug of steaming liquid that smells of ginger, swilled grain, and cinnamon under my nose. A sliver of yellow fruit swims in the golden-brown nectar.

"It's soba tea with biwa," he says, mouthing the words as though trying to taste the shapes. "Nana left a pot. She says it'll help with the healing. You're to drink it all before breakfast or she'll make you drink agba?" He cocks his head. "No, that's not quite right, it was—"

"Agbo. Bitter-leaf tea." I smile, remembering Nana brewing the dark-green tea at my bedside once when I took with a fever that would not break. Then Nana fades and Mummy is there, and I am even smaller, little hands playing with the ring on the necklace hanging from her throat, squirming as she tries to get me to sip the hot tea. "Nana used to make it for me when I got ill. It was one of my mother's recipes. And she learnt it from Baba Sylvanus."

"Baba Sylvanus?"

"You haven't met him yet. But you will."

He nods. "Colin?"

I stroke the cuff still hanging from my ear and sigh, the breath echoing loudly in my ears. "He's gone. He says the council can't be trusted. That you can't be trusted."

"And what do you think?" He watches me like a groom facing an arranged marriage, lifting the veil on his bride's face for the first time. I sense him then, a soft presence lingering at the edge of my mind, touching me like fingers stroking the strings of a harp.

Reaching out, I run my finger along the body of the mug, then onto his skin, tracing a path. "Would I be here if I agreed with him?" As I say the words, I draw him into my mind, folding his presence into me.

His chest swells out and he places the mug by the teapot on the hearth before coming back to me, twining his fingers with mine. I know, because of our bond, that he could already see the scenes that play in my thoughts, the jarring reflections of the moments before when Colin left me behind. I know that even if I did not speak but merely bounced the words inside my head and sang them in my heart, that he would understand my answer. He knew the moment I walked into this room that I'd made my choice. I know now, as he brushes his lips against mine, and the heat of his body seeps into me, what the deep ache between my legs and the heaviness in my heart means. So, I lie back, letting the weight of his body sink mine, pulling him into me until my hips strain up, rocking with hunger and want.

"You . . . you need to get back."

"Just want to make sure you're okay," he says again, with a grin.

Then his fingers knot in my hair, and he kisses me until my mouth is hot and my body aches from bending. The blanket writhes between us, chafing my legs, and he moans against my mouth, drowning out the voice twisting in my ears, trying to calm the inferno in my chest. Then his elbow knocks into the wound at my side and I cry out. He rolls off me then, eyes wide with fear, face flushed. "I'm sorry. I should have been more careful. I—" He gulps in a breath and closes his eyes. "I didn't mean to lose control. I won't . . . we won't do anything. Not until you're healed, and not until you want me to."

I nod, sobered by the pounding in my head that began the moment he touched my wound. Colin's words echo along with that pain. *Nothing will ever be the same. Freedom comes with a price.* Even now, with Jonas, I cannot enjoy a moment of peace. Jonas wraps an arm around me and pulls me up. "Come. I have something to show you."

He leads me past the hearth to the curtained alcove on the left, and we pass through, stepping into the early morning air, with blue and orange starbursts swallowing the sky. The sun is gliding up, golden rays ripe like fresh biwa fruit, and even the slight touch of cold that permeates the air and turns my breath to a frosty cloud is not enough to wash its kiss from my skin. Jonas pulls me farther onto the wide balcony, and there in the corner, in a wooden box packed with dirt, are blue flowers with golden centers, waving gaily in the morning breeze, flowers I haven't seen in years.

I rush to the box, breathing in the strong, earthy scent that rises up to meet me. "Where did you get these?"

"From that flower I found in Ikolé. I held on to it and did my best to help it grow. For a while, I thought it would die, but when

I showed it to Edwina, she knew what to do. We've tended to it all these years, and some more sprouted. We lost a few along the way, but they are doing well."

"How? Violets can't be kept too cold. They shiver and die."

He uncovers a metal-backed, glass tray that hangs above the flower pot. "It's a light catcher. My teacher made it. It's got a filter that traps light from the sun, so when the sun is out, the violets get enough light. And when it's not, there's enough light left over for them. Since they mostly like the dark, I just put a wool cloth on the catcher and let them rest after a bit."

I smile, touching the smallest violet lightly. It wiggles away from me as though it is shy. "Violets were my mother's favorite flower."

"And mine." He puts his hands on my shoulders. "But like many beautiful things, they're hard to cultivate, and even more difficult to protect."

He spins me to the balcony's edge. The city stretches out beyond the castle's hedges and walls, snow-covered houses lit with shadow from the dying night and smoke curling into the waking clouds. "This is only a small piece of our kingdom. There are people in those houses, and rich or poor, pure-blooded Eingardians or not, you are their queen-to-be. I'm sure that even here, there are Oluso like you and me, hiding, afraid, waiting for the soldiers' bells to ring and to hear the iron poles scraping down the cobbled paths to their homes. Can you see it?"

He points to a patch of burnt earth, the hedges around it singed into different shapes and sizes, then beyond to the gap in the stone castle wall. "Lord Ekwensi is out there, and all the Oluso who chose to go with him. They left because they feared for their lives and their freedom. We owe it to them, and to all the Oluso throughout the kingdom, to make them feel like they never have to make that choice—to let them know they have a choice. It won't be easy, not with the council, and kingdom politics, and people who have made their living off the suffering of others, but we will find a way to keep our people safe, Oluso and Aje."

I turn to look at him. "Colin was right though—it won't be simple. The council has their own agenda, and every day, Ekwensi is gaining followers. You heard what your father said. Balman Keep is one of the legendary prisons. It's not easy to destroy a prison like that with a handful of injured Oluso."

He shakes his head. "Nothing worth fighting for is ever simple." He grins. "Did you storm into Benin Palace thinking that kidnapping the crown prince would be a simple affair?"

I flash him a small smile. "I didn't think too much about it, to be honest. I did what I had to do to protect the people I loved."

"Good. Then that's what we need to do. We need to do everything to protect our kingdom so that everyone, Oluso and Aje, Berréan and Gomae, can be treated fairly and equally. Even if that means destroying every tradition that has been built in the last eighteen years and burning the rest of this castle down. Even if it means stripping the regional lords who hold Oluso as slaves of their power. We've already started by changing the law. There's so much more we can do. With you and me as the kingdom's rulers, things will only improve. We won't make the mistakes of our predecessors. We won't turn a blind eye to injustice."

His cheeks are flushed, his eyes bright with excitement, and all at once the weight in my chest falls away like a cocoon. Hope rises in its place, fluttering like a butterfly slipping between a child's hands, desperate to live a full life. Taking a breath, I look out again, catching the blue-gray promise of the sea to the west, and craggy lumps with snow-streaked tears, mountains that the sun is climbing now. The world is caught in half-light, and shadows still dog the bright streaks weaving across the sky, but beyond those, a few stars glitter and sparkle like wind spirits catching their first taste of morning air, and for the first time, I can see a future.

Linking his fingers with mine, I settle our bound hands over my heart. "I doubt the Eingardian nobles want an Oyo queen, but they'll have one anyway. Let's do it."

His arms tighten around me, and he squeezes my fingers. I lean against him, marveling at how well we fit, like tree roots nestling into the earth, wrapped up in one another.

"With pleasure, my queen."

We both smile, and Jonas says, "You know, we should probably go back to the council."

"I've been saying—"

He stops me with a kiss, something at once tender and enough to make me need his arms to hold me upright. He pulls away, touching my face with everything I'd ever wanted in a touch, before taking my arm.

We walk back to the council, ready to change the world. And with Jonas at my side, I am no longer alone. The people I love are safe. It is enough.

For now.

DRAMATIS PERSONAE

PEOPLE

ADAEZE: A pregnant prisoner at Nordgren. Secretly in league with Ekwensi. An Igbagbo Oluso.

ALAIN VERMILLION: A feudal lord, uncle to Jonas, father to Albert, and brother-in-law to the king.

ALBERT: A cousin to Jonas and next in line of succession.

ALISTAIR SORENSON: The Eingardian king who hates magic and the Oluso. Conquered most of the kingdom during a war known as Alistair's Betrayal. Was in love with Yetundé when they were teens but didn't have his affections reciprocated. Has always held a grudge toward Iron Blood Osezele, Yetundé's mate.

AMARA: A former okri who is a merchant and Dèmi's friend. Age fourteen.

AMINA: An okri girl who can freeze water. Rollo's sister.

ARIANNE: Jonas's mother, injured when Jonas was a young child. In a frozen state.

BABA SEYI: The local madman. Once a merchant, he lost his magic and sanity after setting a rival's house on fire and accidentally killing the merchant's child.

BABA SYLVANUS: An old man in Benin who helps Will train Dèmi. A telekinetic Cloren Oluso.

BAYO: The head boy in Dèmi's class.

BIOLA: Mama Aladé's youngest daughter.

BROM: A king's security guard who hails from Ellaria. Holds severe prejudice toward other regions and believes people should be of pure blood.

BUNMI ODARO: Governor Odaro's daughter.

CALLIA: Aunt to Jonas and mother to Albert.

CAPTAIN IYANNA: Leader of the king's guard. A half-Oyo, half-Berréan woman who is loyal to Alistair because he plucked her out of obscurity.

CHIEF DARBY: Mari's lieutenant who is with her in Oyo.

COLIN: Full name is Nicolás Al'Eyani. Dèmi's best friend and confidant, as well as a Masden Oluso with strong but unstable magic. He's two years older than Dèmi and the son of Lord Kairen of Berréa and the Scourge of T'Lapis, Eyani Al'hia. Age nineteen.

CREE NATAKI: Elu's younger sister. An Angma Oluso who has been in hiding in Lokoja for most of her life.

DÈMI: Full name is Abidèmi Adenekan. She is Fèni-Ogun and Ariabhe Oluso and the daughter of Iron Blood Osezele and Princess Yetundé Adenekan. Dèmi grew up in hiding with her mother before being taken in by Nana and Will. She turns eighteen the night she kidnaps Jonas.

DEWAN: An Oyo-born guard in Benin.

EDITH: An Eingardian woman who is Jonas's nanny when he is a boy. She holds strong prejudices against other regions until Alistair cuts out her tongue as punishment. Once she realizes the Oyo-born and Gomae are the only ones who help her, she allies herself to Ekwensi.

EDWINA: An old Oyo-born woman who was once Yetundé's nanny. She alone knew Yetundé was pregnant when she escaped the palace.

ELODIE: Jonas's fiancée, a beautiful painter who is Lady Ayn's daughter. She is graceful and well versed in politics. She is very curious about other regions. Age twenty.

ELU OYERA: Prisoner woman in Lokoja. She is a rare Angma and Cloren Oluso. Wife to Haroun and mother to young Haroun.

ETERA: Friend of Ekwensi in Lokoja. An executioner Aje who is in love with Sanaa. A Basaari Oluso.

EYANI AL'HIA: Colin's mother, also known as the Scourge of T'Lapis. A feared warlord who boasted a harem of seventy concubines, including Lord Kairen. She valued only strength and taught Colin how to fight.

GA EUN: A pregnant Gomae-born prisoner at Nordgren, allied with Ekwensi. A Cloren-Igbagbo Oluso who has resonance with both objects and earth.

GIDEON: A teenage shipper whom Amara fancies.

HAROUN: Elu's husband; a coward.

HARU: Will and Nana's six-month-old daughter. Magical gifts are unknown.

ISADORA: Lord Kairen's second wife. Mother to Matéo, and an influential Berréan lord's daughter.

JARVIS: The king's medicine man. He's pretty arrogant but not above apologizing.

JONAS: Full name is Jonas Aurelius Sorenson. An Eingardian boy from the Maven Keep who is Alistair Sorenson's nephew and the crown prince. He is in love with Dèmi and knows of some of the atrocities his uncle has committed against the Oluso and other regions.

LADY AYN: An Eingardian courtier on the royal council and Elodie's mother. She values profit and respectability above everything else. She is prejudiced against the Oluso and other regions.

LORD FERDINAND KAIREN: A Berréan politician and honorary Commandant of the king's guard. He is also Colin and Mateo's father and was once a concubine of Eyani Al'hia, the Scourge of T'Lapis. He has complicated feelings about his son and has considered both murdering him and using him to cement his legacy. He is from the secretive desert tribe of Ismar'yana, who were tasked with caring for Mount Y'cayonogo.

LORD TOBIAS EKWENSI: A regional lord over the Ikwara and Ogun areas and Alistair's trusted retainer. In truth, he is an Igbagbo Oluso who is critical of the king and is a revolutionary.

LOUIS ODARO: The governor of Benin.

MALALA: A toddler and Samira's daughter, who is a prisoner at Nordgren. She is actually a very strong Basaari Oluso and is also Ekwensi's secret child.

MAMA ALADÉ: Dèmi's mother's best friend and Biola's mother, who is a Cloren Oluso. Also mother to Tolu and Wunmi.

MAMA ENAHO: A sweet-shop owner.

MARI: Yetundé's best friend and former lover who betrayed her to become Alistair's second in command and romantic partner. She is obsessed with power, having come from a low-status family. She would rather kill her loved ones than let them become her weakness.

MARKHAM: Jonas's father and Arianne's husband. He is also a member of the royal council.

MASTER SHEP: A child-slaver and okri dealer.

MATÉO: Colin's six-year-old half-brother.

MATTIAS JONAS SORENSON: The king's late father who envied and feared the Oluso. He also had prejudices and anger toward other regions. He rose to power despite being the youngest in a family of twelve.

MIKHAIL: A king's security guard from Wyldewood. He grew up poor, and Ekwensi was the first person to give him an opportunity to succeed. Holds no prejudice toward other regions or Oluso.

NANA: A Cloren Oluso and Will's mate. She is also Haru's mother and masquerades as an unassuming jewelry and glass art artisan. She has strong visions and is proficient with weaponry. Age twenty-seven.

NNANDI: A guard who helps Dèmi in Lokoja.

NNEKA: A palace servant who just wants to gets her job done so she can go home.

OSEZELE (ALSO KNOWN AS IRON BLOOD OSEZELE): Dèmi's biological father and Yetundé's mate who is believed to be the key to Alistair's victory during the war. He is believed to have murdered fifty thousand Oluso, including Yetundé's family.

QUEEN FOLAKÈ: The ruler prior to Sorenson. Yetundé's mother.

ROLLO: An okri boy and Amina's younger brother. He has the rarer Igbagbo ability and can shapeshift.

SAMIRA: A deaf Oluso prisoner at Nordgren who is Malala's mother and Ekwensi's mate.

SANAA: Etera's pregnant Oluso fiancée.

SISTER AISLINN: An Eingardian missionary who runs the village school.

WILLARD (ALSO KNOWN AS WILL): An Eingardian-Oyo Oluso and Nana's mate. He has strong Masden abilities and masquerades as an instrument maker. He is also Haru's father and Dèmi's guardian. He is tall and grew up in Eingard, passing as full Eingardian from time to time. He has heterochromia and is twenty-nine.

YETUNDÉ: Dèmi's mother, an Ariabhe Oluso, and the former princess of Ifé. She grew up with Alistair and Mari. Though she and Mari were very involved, she gave her up once court politics made Mari a target. She later fell in love with Iron Blood Osezele and ran away while she was pregnant to protect her children.

ZARA: A woman with whom Colin had a tryst. A palace servant.

SPIRITS | CREATURES

ADALINE: A green-haired omioja whose baby was nearly stolen by a mami wata. She ends up speaking for Eofa.

ADÉ AND OBI: Tree spirits. Chi Chi's mother and father, respectively.

ANASAZI: The elephant matriarch who left behind the bone blade. She protected her herd and the forest lands during the war.

AUNTIE ANOZIÉ: An elder gwylfin. Ogié and Osemalu's mother.

AYABA: The Aziza queen. Gave up her unborn child to harness enough power to save Dèmi's life.

EOFA: An omioja from the Stugarrt region who was turned into a mami wata. She lost her baby, Luna, to overzealous fishermen.

ÌYÁ: The mother spirit who watches over the forest.

NAYA: An omioja baby who was kidnapped by the mami wata.

OGECHI (ALSO KNOWN AS CHI CHI): A young tree spirit seeker who has strong affinity with creatures and can change her speech to communicate with them.

OGIÉ: A gwylfin. Chi Chi's best friend.

OLADELE: A male omioja who desperately want to be recognized by the leaders of his clan.

OLORUN: The Father of Spirits and Skies. Also known as Y'l-shad, the All Seeking Mother. The premier spirit who rules the Spirit Realm and holds balance for the world.

OSEMALU: A gwylfin. Ogié's twin brother.

XIAOQING: An omioja elder who once became mami wata but now presides over the rituals for all omioja.

YAWARA (ALSO KNOWN AS AUNTIE YA): A tree spirit friend of Dèmi's.

ACKNOWLEDGMENTS

I believe a life lived with gratitude is the sweetest life of all, and no story graces the world without so many lives, people, and champions urging it on, welcoming it graciously as it is born.

So thank you to the one who knows my name and purpose, and made me all I am and more.

Thank you to Mummy, who took me to the library as many times as I wanted and talked to the headmistress on my behalf so I could write stories and poems after finishing my work. To Daddy, who named me, taught me the power of story to shape and shift history, and never let me be ashamed of who I was and all those who had come before me. Also, for always remembering and holding on to every last piece of our history and customs, and reminding us that that was the real magic. And for every painful sacrifice you both made so we could be more.

To my three munchkins, my A., O., and E., who grew too big with me, gamed with me, skinned their elbows and knees jostling for footballs, chasing wall geckos, and embarking on adventures, I am so grateful to be your sibling—I could not be who I am and love my weirdness if not for you three. Maman, nous avons gagné!

To my cousins, spread out across four continents, I love you all so much. Let's show them all what it means to be fourth-culture kids.

To those who came before me, who wept in silence, fled their homes, climbed rubber trees, beat scorched earth, and made cakes of blossoms so I could live, thank you.

To Kiana Nguyen, my fearless agent, who has the absolute best taste in shows and reminds me continually to stand tall, speak up, and take chances, thank you for working with me and never letting me shy away from the work. You are one in a million.

To David Pomerico, my editor, who speaks softly but with conviction and saw what this book and world could be, thank you for drilling down and pushing me until we did justice to each character (and to fire-making!!!). Also, thank you for your patience, and for pulling me off the making-characters-nasty-jerks cliff.

To Nicky, Desirée, Rebecca, and Suyi—you are the writing community I dreamt of but never thought I'd have. But even more important, you are the friends who remember that I love a good bergamot scone, I'll eat hobak juk any day of the week, and I'll always tell you I love you with food. You are heroes beyond measure, and I am eternally grateful to call you friends and read the beautiful work you make.

To Auntie Naae and my darling Haena, who read my first manuscript and cried, thank you for believing in me, and for making me take care of myself. Also thank you for saving me all the kimbap ends. I'm still hungry.

To my Froomies—Judy, Cynthia, Alexia, and Daisy (shoutout to Will and Mike too), I love you all so much. Thank you, thank you for encouraging me always, cheering me on, showing up to all the things, and being a phone call or just a door away. I can't imagine going through life without all of you, and I'm glad I won't have to. Thank you for loving me well and telling that scared girl she could jump off that cliff, catch the wind, and soar! We are so overdue for a together trip!

To Lucas, Anthia, Amy, Brittany, and Courtney, thank you for being my first readers and champions. Book club had nothing on us. We were always golden!

To Lillie, who I love more than I can even say, who taught me to love myself and stop taking my ideas for granted, this book is for you! Thank you, also, Papa and Mama Noe!

To Cynthia Leitich-Smith, who was my childhood idol and who became my mentor and friend, I cannot thank you enough. I will always remember that everyone deserves to be a hero in a story and I will always love you for being one of mine.

To Charlotte G., who supported me, introduced me to the fam, and cried at my reading, and Ann, who bought me maple ice cream and championed my work, thank you both over and over again.

To Daniela, Eric, and Lucy, who've cheered me on since day one, I can't thank you enough. Let's see if we can beat that irrelevant lady's record.

To my BDay Squad, this section specifically exists so I can enshrine "badger muffin" in a book. But seriously though, here's to more years of being each other's community.

To Sam Clark, Jason June, Korinne-Salas Young, and the rest of my SCBWI fam, thank you for your guidance and kindness. Here's to more Jane Austen seed cakes.

To my squad of sisters and cousins—Tanisha, Jumoké, Misa, Rachel, and Ekata, I cannot finish saying how grateful I am for all of you. You are unbelievably bright lights in this chaotic world, and I thank you all for the encouragement, love, compassion, and care you've gifted me.

To Connor, Kyle, Angie, and Rachel, my sweet and lovely friends who make such beautiful art and never give up on me and one another, thank you.

To Sean, my father in another life, I will always be grateful for you. PS: Sasha Knight still makes me cry and you were the first one to say you could see my books in a library. We're here now!

To Mia, who taught me to tie a baby sling, and Tempest, who taught me to speak up; Marshall, who is the warmest, most supportive friend; J. Elle, who is everything you can ever ask for in a champion and friend; and Ayana Gray, who is kind and lovely: thank you.

To Tiffany and Monica, my partners in crime and plotting literary and community takeovers in the name of justice, I can't wait to give you both hugs, drink some Summer Moon, and play board games with you. You were both right—it's finally happening. Please grab Ethan and Greg and let's launch our nationwide storytelling tour.

To Auntie Yang Soon, Uncle Won Suk, Jun Woo, and our dear lovely Joshua that we still miss, thank you for everything. You all are wonderful beyond compare, and I hope you never forget that. I'll try to remind you as much as possible!

To Landon and Kristin, my other Mom and Dad (see, I didn't Britishize this time), thank you for the prayers, tears, and many, many rounds of Five Die. Thank you for loving me so completely and giving me the best gift I could ever have. Thank you for being my family.

To Kendall, I love you, I love you, I love you. Thank you for walking with me, believing in me, and being my live-in American English consultant. Thank you for reading every word, pushing back on every plot point, and telling me my names were beautiful. Thank you for so much more than I can say in words and deeds. Thank you also for being our Bean's other favorite person.

To my Beanie, my lovely little K, my Professor and Wriggletron Extraordinaire, I will always love you. And no, you cannot put those pens in your mouth.

Please turn the page for a FairyLoot exclusive chapter. This is an alternate scene in Lokoja, set after Dèmi, Jonas, and Colin emerge from the Benin Forest. Here they attend a local wedding and find that not every Oluso marries a mate. They sometimes choose another. . .

TRUTH

I blink, waiting for my eyes to adjust to the dark stillness of the room. The air is hot, sweat crawling in between my breasts and sticking to the underside of my armpits. There is a soft hiss, and I jump as clammy fingers brush my outstretched hand. A sweet and musty stench, like sugar left burning in a pot, chokes the air, and when I huff and breathe through my mouth, something grainy and soft dances on my tongue. I spit as the bitter taste of ash and soot fills my mouth, and stumble a few steps. Everything in me is screaming, begging to be let out. And suddenly, I am young again, waiting for Mummy to fetch me from the village school, hoping she will find me in the pit the other children have thrown me in.

"*We're going to bury you alive,*" they sing, high voices bandying the words about.

Then there is a quick spark, a match hissing flame into being, and the bright orange of a kerosene lamp pulls Nikau into the light again. He thrusts the lamp in my face, and I take it, steeling my shaking hands. Those childhood ghosts melt away like smoke running from flame.

"Who are you? And what do you want with us?" My voice sounds cracked, and my throat feels drier than before, but the words come out flat and even.

He moves around the room, lighting candles that sit on the thin, wooden ledges affixed to the corners of the walls. Now there is a table in full view, and a large pair of metal tongs lying on it. A broken plate sit next to the tongs, its jagged edges catching the light. A thick apron hangs off a lone chair, and once Nikau moves away from the wall across, I see the giant, black rectangle in the wall, bulging out like a bag of sweets hidden in a child's too small pocket—a simple forge, a living to many of Ife's inhabitants. But to me and my kind, a grave.

It is said that when Olorun wove the physical realm, and set Ìyá to watch over the forests, he left Ogun, the iron spirit, in charge of the skeins that broke the earth, the mineral wefts that curled in the darkness of caves, and ran like molten blood on swamp floors. When the first Oluso set about building Ife, they relied on their silver fingered brothers and sisters, the Oluso whose iron blood could call up minerals from the earth and carve them into shapes with a simple touch. Then war broke out, and the iron bloods were the first to be destroyed. The magic they once held became poison that ate the life blood of their brothers and sisters, a curse of remembrance.

I pull at my blouse, and fan it back and forth, as though those quick, bursts of motion could calm my mind and drown out the heated air that is smothering my lungs. "I thought you were making things up when you spoke to the guard, but you're really an alagbede."

He stops, crouching over the table, fingers inches from the tongs. "I don't lie. Not about things that matter anyway." He picks up the tongs, and stands there caressing the pincered edges.

Alagbede. The word used to carry the honor of uniqueness, the prestige of being a blacksmith, a rare commodity to be sought out by whole villages. But since Alistair Sorenson learnt the hidden arts of metal work from a lone iron blood, and used that knowledge to take over all of Ife, iron masters have popped up everywhere. Enslaved people from Oyo, Goma and Berréa mine the very mineral that is used as a sword against their people. And Ajes from all over the kingdom, afraid of the power the Oluso might wield, use metal work to strike us down before we can even begin to be.

What was it that Mummy liked to say? *The weeds choke out the flowers of the field so that they might survive, not thinking that once all the petals fall, the bees will cease to come. With the bees away, no new seeds will come, and without new life, the weeds must either eat themselves or die.*

I used to think those words were so sad, that if only the weeds would grow along with the flowers, there would be enough room for everyone. But now I know better. No weed helps a flower along when it can feed on the nutrients in its roots. I don't know what Nikau is just yet, but I refuse to be eaten alive and buried in this field.

"If you're so truthful, tell me this, why did you help us?"

He scowls, scooping up the broken plate. "Because I was asked to."

Colin narrows his eyes. "Who asked you to? Was it Lo—"

I pinch his arm, and he yelps, the question dying on his lips.

Nikau studies us in silence, and after a moment he nods. "I will answer your question if you can answer one of mine."

I cast a glance towards the metal bar across the door. There's no way we'll be able to leave this room as easily as we came in, not without a fight anyway. I lick my cracking lips. "Go ahead. Ask away."

"I know how you came here. The gwylfins that attacked the guards, they carried you here. Is there any way to get them to come back?"

I drop my shoulders, caught off guard. "Why?"

His forehead creases. "Can you or can't you?"

Jonas holds a hand out, as though Nikau is a horse in need of reassurance. "If we can, what does that mean to you?"

Nikau grins, light dancing in his eyes. "Everything." He stalks towards me, tongs in one hand and the broken plate in the other. I round on my left heel, poised to strike, but just as quickly, he brushes past me, a rush of cool air exploding in his wake. He tosses the plate and tongs on a rubbish pile and rubs his hands together.

"So, where do we begin? How do you call them back?"

I cross my arms. "Why? What do you want with them?"

He twists his mouth, and a muscle twitches in his jaw. "Can we just agree to make an exchange? I helped you three out there, so help me out. I won't ask any questions like where you came from, or why you were attacking him," he nods to Jonas, "in the street. Just help me with this, please."

Jonas shakes his head. "They weren't attacking me. We just had a small disagreement."

Nikau runs his hands through his thick, dark hair, and I notice now that his fingers are trembling. "Whatever. Seeing as you snuck into the city, you clearly didn't want to talk to the guards. I helped you out, so I'd appreciate it if you returned the favor. Please."

Colin and Jonas look at me, but I don't know what to say. Finally, I mutter, "And if we don't? Why should we trust you? For all we know, you could be working with the guards and as soon as we called the gwylfins back, you'd have us arrested for consorting with demons."

Ever since Alistair Sorenson came to power and began to openly hunt Oluso, there have also been a wave of false accusations. A merchant whose neighbor is outselling him calls the guards to report "suspicious activity" or "consorting with demons", and the suspected neighbor is tied to metal poles and hung by their wrists and ankles for a day. Even if the neighbor dies, with broken and dislocated limbs, as long as there are no burns on the skin, no signs of magical poisoning, then they are declared innocent at their death. The merchant is commended for "promoting social harmony", and has to pay his neighbors death fees and taxes, but beyond that, there are no repercussions.

Nikau rubs his neck. "Please. I know it's wrong of me to demand something from you. But please go along with it and help me just this once. Do you want money? I can pay you."

"I don't want your money."

He runs his hands through his hair again, leaving his fingers tangled in so his hair stands up. "But you refuse to help me?"

I look at Jonas, and he meets my gaze, sadness in his eyes. If he did not understand before, perhaps he does now. This is what his betrayal cost me. Trust and hope, the flares of goodness that my mother worked to keep alive in me, are little more than ash on a long extinguished flame. Even if I want to help Nikau, I find words scraping my head like an unwieldy comb. *What if you're wrong? What if you trust, and because of it, you die?*

Nikau sighs, and moves to the door, unbolting it. "Then please leave. If you can't help me, it's better you aren't here anyway. The guards visit my shop without warning sometimes."

Perhaps it is the weary sigh he gave, like a dam giving way under the onslaught of water, or the way his dark brown eyes have dimmed, but I find myself saying, "We'll help you. But first you have to tell us something."

He shuts the door. "What do you want to know? I'll tell you anything."

"Why are you so willing to trust us? For all you know we could be bandits."

He purses his lips, considering. Then finally he says, "There's someone I want to protect, and I would rather gamble on the off chance that you'll be able to help us rather than take the chances we have now."

"Even if you might die?"

He tucks up one side of his mouth into a half smile. "If that is what it takes, then yes. I know she would do the same to protect me."

I nod. "Okay. We'll help you. But you still haven't explained why you need the gwylfins."

The air beside him starts to swell, taking shape, and I blink furiously, trying to clear my vision. A cloak appears, followed by a dress and leather boots, then a rounded face, crimson brown like the esoo meka sold in local markets, framed by beaded, thick braids. Once her hands materialize, the young woman reaches out to take one of mine while I stare dumbly. Pressing my fingers to her belly, she smiles. A firm roundness, solid like a polished stone yet soft, meets my fingers, and just then something pushes against my hand, sending tingles up my spine.

"We're due in a few months. Twins. We thought we'd have more time to get away from here, maybe go to back to the Hinche islands, where my parents are from, but there isn't enough time. Nikau is the only village smith, and they would look for him if we disappeared."

Her belly vibrates again, and I pull my hand away. "You're Oluso."

She nods, an Oluso mark flashing green on her left cheek. "I saw the three of you come down with the gwylfins while I was out with my sister. I knew I had to create a chance to talk to you." The words tumble all out in a rush, and suddenly, she weaves, eyes fluttering wildly. Nikau is there, catching her up in his arms.

"It's not good for you to be in here too long. What if it hurts the babies?" he says tenderly.

She presses a hand against her back and rubs. "It'll be alright,

Nik. I used too much magic today. I just need to eat and I'll get all my energy back, you'll see."

I shake my head. "No, he's right. Too much iron exposure isn't good for babies. Trust me. I've seen children come out too small, and others who . . . who didn't make it." I look at Nikau. "Do you have another room?"

I don't mention that those children were born to a small portion of the asewós who live in the Benin public houses—the ones whose chains keep them from moving more than a few paces from the beds where they are subjugated and used all day. Their fellow asewós may go home when they please, counting their pay out, putting in enough money to remedy for the crimes of debt and theft that landed them at the public house, but those women who live in chains are kept there until the moon sings itself to sleep, and the sun chases the waning moon into another day. All for the crime of tainted blood.

Nikau ushers the woman gently past the door just beyond the table, a cozy room with a large cot, and a cooking stove in the corner. He eases her down on the bed, pulls off her cloak and hands her the wide fan lying on the small table nearby. She breathes her thanks and fans herself while he pours out a cup of dark liquid from a calabash hanging near the stove.

She accepts the cup, and turns to me, but she keeps her eyes flat to the ground. "Forgive me for not greeting you properly, my sister. I drink this cup to you." She takes a large swig and drinks heartily before passing Nikau the cup. He sets it down on the table, then pours more of the calabash's contents into three more cups.

Leaving his head slightly bowed, he passes us the cups. Colin sniffs at his while Jonas looks to me. I rub my fingers against the smooth, cold body of the cup, and am reminded of going to the river to catch fish with Mummy, giggling as the fish rub their sleek bodies against my wrinkled fingers. The woman watches me quietly, but the faint crease in her forehead, and the way she twists her fingers together in her lap tell another story. Making my decision then, I toss the drink back, letting the sweet, syrupy taste of blackcurrant explode on my tongue and soothe my itching throat. Jonas follows suit.

"We would offer you tombo, but we don't have any right now. The governor ordered all the fresh palm wine delivered to the soldier's barracks every night, so raibee will have to do." She bows her head slightly. "Again, please excuse us."

I set my cup down. "Okay. So we have accepted your hospitality. Will you now tell us what this is all about?"

Colin grunts, full cup dangling from his fingertips. "Speak for yourself. I won't be drinking anything until you explain what one of these iron dogs," he jerks his chin towards Nikau, "is doing with *you*. Last I checked, iron dogs and Oluso don't mix, seeing as they make a living off of destroying us."

The woman presses her back to the wall, sucking in her lip. She looks at me with heavy eyes, but I shake my head. "No. Let's start there. Answer his question."

She and Nikau exchange a look, then she turns her back and he starts unbuttoning the back of her dress. Colin flushes, raising his free hand, "Woah. I have no interest in bedding you. I'm not one of those bastards who can be bought off by sex. I like it consensual, thank you. I just want answers."

Nikau steps back. There is a web of angry, pocked marks stretched across the woman's back like planted rows in a field. I open my mouth, but air is caught in my lungs, and the words I want to say weighed beneath that air.

The woman speaks, her voice hushed and low, like a mother telling her child a bedtime story. "My name is Widelene. My parents were born on the Hinche Islands, so when the war broke out, we were the last ones it got to. By the time the soldiers came to our island, Mama and Baba had ferried us off. We came here, to stay with an old auntie of mine and her husband. They didn't have any children, so when Mama died giving birth to Stéphanie, and Baba was carried off by the soldiers, they kept us. My uncle was good to us. He was the one who taught us how to use our gifts, control it. But auntie was afraid. She'd seen her brother be taken off by soldiers, and she was afraid they'd come for her next, so she marked me every time I made a mistake. Sometimes part of my body would go invisible, other times I'd flash out and reappear after half a day. She didn't like that. She said she had to mark me like the tree I was named for so I would remember not to make any more mistakes."

My stomach clenches just hearing her tale. "Oluso are not

supposed to commit violence, let alone scarring a child. Excuse me, but your auntie was a disgrace to our kind."

"She isn't Oluso. Neither was my uncle. Our magic comes from Mama's side of the family. Omohuyi blood. Mama would turn into a hawk and watch for soldiers coming, and once, when we were on the road here from Hinche and soldiers were nearby, she morphed into a lion and scared them off. I took after my grandmother's Bashir lineage with my invisibility power."

"Then how did your uncle teach you?"

"He went to people in the village he could trust. Elders who knew a bit about the old ways."

"Hm." I murmur in understanding. "Your uncle risked a lot. He could have sold you to make profit or given you up to the soldiers, but he didn't. That's why."

"Why what?" Colin asks, looking between us.

"Why she could fall in love with an Aje. She experienced kindness from one."

Wideline smiles. "My own father was Aje, but he loved my mother. They were mates. My uncle treated me like his own daughter. My auntie wasn't cruel because she was Aje, but because she chose to be. If I had grown up somewhere else, or maybe if I'd been born after the war, I could understand an Oluso's distrust for Ajes."

"But that's not your story," I say quietly.

She smiles wider, but tears are streaming from her eyes. "I grew up with Nikau. He lived in the hut next door to my uncle's. He was the one with me the first time my arm disappeared. We were swimming and I felt this sharp pain. We thought something had bitten it off."

She sobs, and Nikau pulls her to his chest, kissing her forehead and rubbing her back. He scowls at us. "I was there after every time her auntie beat her, plastering her wounds, getting herbs from the local medicine woman. Her uncle died when we were in our teens, and we feared her auntie might try to sell her, so when I heard the guards were looking for someone to train as a smith, and that that person would be given permission to marry anyone they wished, I took the post. I didn't ask questions. I wanted to save Widelene, and I would do it over again if I had the choice."

"If she's your wife, then why run? You could have your children here. No one would question it."

His scowl fades into weary look. "That's the problem. She's not. And she can never be, if the local governor gets his way. I went up to Eingard to train with those bloody *neckers* for an entire year, and during that time . . . " He stops, mouth tightening with anger, but when he tries to speak again, his shoulders draw down and his eyes are heavy. Widelene puts a hand on his arm and they stare at each other. I look away, ignoring the tightness growing in my chest, tracking other things in the room instead—the threadbare blanket on the cot, the sparse furnishing of two chairs, a spider weaving an extensive web at the corner of the cot. Alistair Sorenson's iron masters are handsomely paid, why then does the rug have several threads running loose at its ends?

"You've been planning to escape for a while, haven't you?"

Widelene turns to me. "Yes. How did you know? Are you—"

"I'm no Cloren, but I have eyes. This place is in disrepair. You haven't been spending money."

"We were saving it for the marriage decree, but we started putting it all aside for our escape and the children."

"You realize that I may not be the only one who's noticed that you haven't been making purchases?"

She gasps, bringing her fingers to her mouth. "Do you think that the guards . . . that they—"

Swiveling on my heel, I grab the wooden chair lying in the corner of the room and drag it closer. As I pass by the stove, the smell of minced meat catches my nostrils and my stomach twists and tightens in protest. Before sitting down, I turn to Colin. "Drink."

He frowns. "We still don't know the whole story."

I raise an eyebrow, and he purses his lips before tossing back the cup's contents. "Now," I say, meeting Nikau and Widelene's grateful looks, "Why aren't you married?"

"My auntie made a betrothal for me while Nikau was gone. When I refused, she threatened to accuse me of witchcraft and abandon me and my sister to the city officials. I am to marry the local governor's son."

"And you want us to help you escape before it becomes obvious that you're not having the governor's grandchild?" Jonas finishes.

"Yes." Widelene squares her shoulders, but her fingers are still trembling. "I want to start over somewhere else, and be able to marry Nikau and have our children in safety. I want my sister to be free of my auntie. I know this is asking a lot, but I need your help. So if you can give any, we would greatly appreciate it." Nikau covers her hand with his and squeezes tightly. "We can pay you," he says again. "I've got twenty lira saved. I can offer you fifteen, but we'll need five to set up in a new place."

Colin laughs, a twinkle in his eye. "Fifteen lira to stick our necks out for you? That's a shoddy price to bet our lives on isn't it? What say we make it eighteen?"

I know he's joking, but I throw him a dirty look all the same. I still remember the glee on that trader's face when he attempted to sell me Rollo for five. The life of an Oluso means nothing. "We don't need your money. We don't want it. We'll help you, but in return you have to forget you ever met us. No one must know we were here."

Nikau offers his arm, and I see now that it is covered with a series of black spirals, tattoos spread over his golden skin like grooves on the bark of a tree. I've seen similar tattoos on Nana's back, but nothing like this. "As a son of the Ohaca tribe, I make you this solemn promise. If I fail to keep my word, let me by haunted by the spirits of my ancestors and taken to an early grave."

Widelene nods. "I too, make you this solemn promise."

"We need to come up with a plan then. What about your sister?"

Bending slightly, Widelene brushes against the cobweb at the bottom of the cot. The spider scurries onto her arm, and drops into her lap. Before I can swat it away, it begins to grow, legs snaking out, beady eyes swelling in size. Black becomes brown, and whiskered pincers turn into a long snout. Gone are the legs, a scaly, bronze back replacing them, and a fairly large pangolin lies where a tiny spider was. Jonas gasps, but Colin merely rubs his cheek, looking on as though nothing happened.

Widelene ruffles the hair between its piqued ears and wrinkles her nose apologetically. "Sorry, my sister likes to listen in on things, and it's easier than explaining everything to her later. She always wants to know what's going on. Who, what, when, why, you know. My uncle used to call her *I too know*."

I laugh. "I have an uncle like that. He once stood in the rain for several days just to see if that would make him prefer the cold to warm weather."

"Did it work?"

Colin rolls his eyes. "No. But we had to clean his house every day that he was out there and bring him food in the rain."

She giggles. "He sounds like a handful. Just like this one." She shakes the pangolin off her lap, and it bounds over to the corner. Coily black ringlets sprouts between its ears, and when the scaly back becomes a slender human one, I look away, pulling Jonas' arm to ensure he does the same, and pinching Colin when he doesn't.

After a few shuffling sounds, Widelene's sister says, "If we're going to escape tonight, we might as well do it on full stomachs. Widé, what have you got cooking?" She plucks a wooden ladle from the wall and pokes at the contents of the pot on the stove.

"Stéphanie, at least introduce yourself to our guests."

Stéphanie looks up, her slim face a near copy of her sister's. The patterned blue dress she is now wearing looks too small for her tall frame. "Why? They want us to forget them anyway. Why introduce myself to people who will leave my live shortly?" Her voice carries the same jaunting rhythm as her sister's, words bouncing from her lips like alternating drum beats.

"At least leave enough ewa oloyin for them to eat. You always eat so much after transformations. Let them have some first."

Stéphanie sulks, but she replaces the pot lid, and goes to a wooden trunk at the back wall. "You're not going to give them meat pies too, are you?" She fishes out a half moon shaped pie and takes a bite. The smell of curried mince meat and carrots seeps into the air. "You should at least let me have most of these since you're giving them all the beans porridge."

Widelene shakes her head slowly. "I made fourty of those thing morning. If we're missing more than one or two, I'm not feeding you for the rest of the night."

Stéphanie peers into the trunk. "I only count twenty three. Are you sure pregnancy isn't making you crazy?"

Widelene scrambles up so quickly that I barely have time to move my legs out of the way before she barrels across the room to the trunk. "You ate that many? Stéph, are you trying to make me crazy?" She tries to swat Stéphanie but the girl dances out of reach.

"You're not having that many people over anyway. What's the harm if I eat a few meat pies?"

"You ate seventeen!"

Stéphanie wrinkles her nose. "No, I only had twelve. Nik took the rest."

Nikau lowers his head, suddenly fascinated by something on the floor as Widelene rounds on him. She slaps the back of her head a few times. "I don't know what to do with the two of you. Even if we escape, I'm sure they'd find us just by looking for foot shortages in nearby villages."

"That's why we need to get farther away. Somewhere at the edge of Oyo, like Port Harcourt. I hear they make powdered *akara* and have six flavors of custard there." Stéphanie says, smacking her lips.

"Speaking of food, I would prefer some to the money you offered us. We are in fact, quite hungry," Colin says.

I shoot him a look, and he shrugs. "What? Are we going to pretend our mouths aren't watering? My stomach hurts so much that it's hard to think."

"Seeing as your manners have also disappeared, I'm inclined to believe that."

Even if we are starving, it is impolite to demand food of someone whose hospitality you've accepted. Maybe Colin doesn't understand because he is not Oyo born, but food rituals are sacred. By accepting the drink Widelene gave us, we pledged her our trust. We will have to eat the food she offers, whether of fine quality or poor taste. Even if it is a paltry meal of akamu, we are to eat heartily to show our gratitude and in doing so, honor Widelene for caring for us. I lick my lips, recalling the taste of the corn porridge Mummy used to make and the heavy sweetness of the honey she poured on top when I complained of the sharp taste. Paltry or not, I would eat akamu if it were placed in front of me.

Widelene touches my arm. "Forgive me for offering so late, but all we have is some ewa oloyin and meat pie. Will that be enough for you?"

"That's more than enough, thank you."

Nikau springs up, kicking off his heavy boots. When Widelene turns back from the stove to look at him, he retrieves them and arranges them neatly by the side of the cot. "I'll go fetch a few chairs. I doubt any of you like eating standing up."

"I don't mind it," Stéphanie says in between bites of another meat pie.

"No one asked you," Widelene says, frowning. "Look at you, eating in front of hungry guests. You'd better fetch all the extra firewood tonight and help me make another batch. And just so you know, you're making the dough. It's a wonder we had enough filling for these ones the way you kept pinching from the pot."

"That's not fair!"

"You're right. It's not fair. It's dark." Widelene says, giggling at her own joke. "Maybe if you were born fairer, you could have passed for Eingardian and gotten the guards to give you some extra meat for free. Or better yet, you could be adopted by an Eingardian family who would have the money to feed you and your *longer throat*."

Stéphanie scowls and stuffs the rest of the meat pie into her mouth. Stalking past us, she passes out of the room and slams the door. Widelene clucks at the still vibrating door. "Excuse her. She's still growing up. Our uncle could never raise a hand to her when she needed it, and she's turned wild because of it. Doesn't know how to respect her elders."

"It's fine. Is there anything we can do to help you? Are you making more meat pies for the journey out of here?"

Widelene holds out a bowl of beans porridge with meat pie, offering it like a worshiper begging favor of the spirits. I wait, but she gestures for me to eat, so I take a bite. The sweet and peppery taste of the porridge hits my mouth, and fills me with warmth.

"How is it?"

"Delicious."

She passes out bowls to Jonas and Colin, watching too as they take their first bites of food. Jonas' face brightens like a child eating a sweet for the first time, and Colin bends to his bowl, shoveling food in his mouth. Nikau comes in with our chairs, and we arrange ourselves by the stove.

Widelene sits next to Nikau and rests her hand in his. "We're going to get married. Tonight. We invited a few friends, and a priestess. The food is for that."

I stop my spoon halfway to my mouth. "You're inviting people here? Tonight? When were you going to tell us?"

"It's just a few people. I told the garrison captain I was having a few friends over. He already gave his permission. Our friends are bringing supplies for us, and once the priestess marries us, we will be ready to leave," Nikau says.

"So you want to leave tonight?"

He nods. "If possible. The longer we stay here, the longer we risk getting caught."

I look at Colin, but he is busy chasing the last beans in his bowl. Jonas meets my eyes, and flashes me a brief smile. My heart catches in my chest, and I hate that the fear swimming in my belly fades in an instant.

"We weren't planning on leaving Lokoja so quickly. We thought we'd stay one or two days," I say finally. "But if you really want to go tonight, I suppose it can't be helped. We'll need a few things from you though, blankets and food for the road. We're on a journey ourselves."

Widelene breathes a sigh of relief, and Nikau smiles. "We can help you with those things. Thank you. From the bottom of my heart, thank you."

I nod and go back to eating, but there are a few things dancing about in my mind. How are we going to get out of here, and once we do, what if I can't call the gwylfins back? Then there are the people coming tonight, potential witnesses who will see our faces, and act as marks against us if we are caught. What if one of them recognizes Jonas? What then? Can I be certain Nikau and Widelene have told me the entire truth?

Mummy used to say that the truth was like a coco yam, born with its roots deep in the earth, and its leaves reaching towards the sky. It sleeps undisturbed, until it is called into question, and everything depends on how it is cared for after it's harvested. A well sunned coco yam will make the most delicious fufu, filling and light, rewarding the farmer who reared and protected it well. A coco yam that sits too long in the dark grows bitter in taste, and once the rot sets in, there is no way to save it. It hardens and bloodies the white flesh, until the coco yam is no more. As I hold the meat pie, and savor the warmth of its soft flesh against my fingers, I wonder what seeds have already been sown here, and whether a sweet and hearty taste awaits me, or the bitter sting of dust and ash. Smiling at Widelene, I take a bite.